Praise for *The Mayfair Bookshop*

"*The Mayfair Bookshop* is a moving, touching tale of a Bright Young Thing turned bookseller/author and her quest to find fulfillment, inspiration, and love in the chaos of the World War II home front. Eliza Knight brings Nancy Mitford to life as an appealing and uncertain young heroine in the days before she is burnished by fame and success—you cannot help but cheer her toward her destiny!"

—Kate Quinn, *New York Times* bestselling author of *The Rose Code*

"Nancy's razor-sharp wit and hidden heartaches both make for riveting reading!"

—Stephanie Marie Thornton, *USA Today* bestselling author of *A Most Clever Girl*

"*The Mayfair Bookshop* reminds us that women and books have the power to shape the world, and we all have the power to forge our own destinies—even in times of extreme adversity."

—Sophie Perinot, award-winning author of *Médicis Daughter*

"Hits all the right notes: intrigue, great heart, and hope. Not to be missed!"

—Heather Webb, *USA Today* bestselling author of *The Next Ship Home*

"Eliza Knight's sympathetic and utterly believable portrayal of Nancy Mitford is the icing on this fabulous cake of a novel where present-day romance, a literary mystery, and the lives of England's most controversial sisters keep the pages turning."

—Janie Chang, author of *The Library of Legends*

"Taking readers from country houses to the London Blitz, *The Mayfair Bookshop* is an homage to Nancy's timeless truth: that the pursuit of love, in all its forms, is worth fighting for."

—Bryn Turnbull, author of *The Woman Before Wallis*

"Woven with an intriguing modern timeline, this story brims with complicated relationships, infamous characters, heartbreak, and, ultimately, triumph. Moving and compelling, this is a must-read!"

—Kristin Beck, author of *Courage, My Love*

"A wonderful depiction of the legendary Nancy Mitford and her sisters in their element—both united as Bright Young Things and torn apart by love and war. Along with its added touch of mystery, *The Mayfair Bookshop* will keep you curled up and turning the pages."

—Kaia Alderson, author of *Sisters in Arms*

"Fans of Nancy Mitford and Amazon's *The Pursuit of Love* series will love this emotional look into the life of an author who hid personal tragedy behind a brave facade and turned her story into a timeless tale."

—Georgie Blalock, author of *The Other Windsor Girl*
and *The Last Debutantes*

"Take one fascinating family, add in a legendary bookshop and a few Bright Young Things, and you have the bookish equivalent of chocolate cake: a delightful treat. Nancy Mitford had an extraordinary life, and Eliza Knight skillfully manages research, legend, fact, and fiction to bring us a truly absorbing novel."

—Natasha Lester, author of *The Riviera House*

"*The Mayfair Bookshop* gives us not one but two engaging heroines to truly root for. Knight has created a captivating look at life's pursuit of love, literature, and dreams both realized and dashed set against a devastating war that divides sisters along the lines of political ideologies. Told with the wit and spunk of Nancy Mitford herself, Eliza Knight's immense talent shines on every page."

—Renée Rosen, author of *The Social Graces*

"A fascinating view of a pivotal moment in history told from the perspective of an extraordinary woman at the heart of it all. Filled with intrigue, heartbreak, passion, and daring, Eliza Knight beautifully celebrates the life and influence of Nancy Mitford. Vivid and unforgettable!"

—Chanel Cleeton, *New York Times* and *USA Today* bestselling author of *The Most Beautiful Girl in Cuba*

"A romantic and moving love letter to bibliophiles everywhere, *The Mayfair Bookshop* offers a testament to the magic and power of books and bookstores to shine light on our darkest hours. Beautifully written and featuring a colorful cast of characters and delightful cameos, this historical novel is not to be missed."

—Laura Kamoie, *New York Times* bestselling author of *My Dear Hamilton* and *America's First Daughter*

THE

Mayfair

BOOKSHOP

Also by Eliza Knight

TALES FROM THE TUDOR COURT SERIES
My Lady Viper
Prisoner of the Queen

ANTHOLOGIES
Ribbons of Scarlet
A Year of Ravens
A Day of Fire

May 2022
The Book is "meh"

THE

Mayfair

BOOKSHOP

A NOVEL OF NANCY MITFORD AND
THE PURSUIT OF HAPPINESS

ELIZA KNIGHT

wm

WILLIAM MORROW

An Imprint of HarperCollins*Publishers*

P.S.™ is a trademark of HarperCollins Publishers.

THE MAYFAIR BOOKSHOP. Copyright © 2022 by Eliza Knight. All rights reserved. Printed in the United States of America. No part of this book may be used or reproduced in any manner whatsoever without written permission except in the case of brief quotations embodied in critical articles and reviews. For information, address HarperCollins Publishers, 195 Broadway, New York, NY 10007.

HarperCollins books may be purchased for educational, business, or sales promotional use. For information, please email the Special Markets Department at SPsales@harpercollins.com.

FIRST EDITION

Designed by Diahann Sturge

Title page photo © David Bleeker - London / Alamy Stock Photo

Library of Congress Cataloging-in-Publication Data has been applied for.

ISBN 978-0-06-307058-5 (paperback)
ISBN 978-0-06-322616-6 (international edition)

22 23 24 25 26 LSC 10 9 8 7 6 5 4 3 2 1

*To my dad, who instilled in me a love of reading
at an early age and never said no to a trip to the
most magical of places—a bookshop*

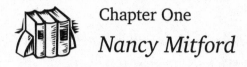

Chapter One
Nancy Mitford

Mid-March 1931

Darling Evelyn,

There is no place more perfect to wear a divine coral tiara than one's own fabulously orchestrated book launch party. Especially when the evening crush is hosted by my own famous younger sister, Diana, Lady Guinness.

Though I would have been happy to drink from a bottle running through the street dressed as a character in my book, my sister—you know how she is—has insisted on throwing a soiree, and will no doubt outdo herself. A sentiment felt deep in my heart since my parents have always looked down their noses at my prose. But not you, my darling friend, not you.
Until then . . .

Love from,
Nancy

IN THE HOUSE ON Buckingham Street, a stone's throw from the royal palace, golden light dripped from every crystal chandelier. Gardenias, roses and lilies overflowed from dozens of Waterford vases. An eight-piece jazz ensemble played a mixture of the latest hits and older, less jazzy, favorites sure to get even the elder generation dancing.

The posh four-story brick manse was elbow-to-elbow with amusing people, grasping crystal coupe glasses from the champagne tower. Half the guests were clever; the other half hoped to be photographed. All of them were here for the free champagne and delicate canapés being passed by footmen outfitted in Guinness livery—how patrician.

Upon first entry to the famed house, there were stacks of hardback copies of *Highland Fling* with my name in bold across the jacket. Each invitee would take home their copy of my first novel, my neat autograph scrawled inside and a caption I'd brilliantly coined myself: *For the illusionists in us all, with love,* Nancy Mitford.

Amongst the one hundred or so acquaintances in attendance, there were only a slight few who would understand the meaning behind the words. And oh, how they grinned like mischievous fiends.

While the guests and entertainment attested to my sister and her husband's *joie de vivre*, the house's furnishings were stiff—and so were at least a dozen old biddies—and dripped of *my mother-in-law decorated*. How very miserable for my sister.

One piece leapt out—the abstract art from the hoax the lot of us had played on society two years ago—where it hung prominently in the drawing room. We still laughed about the creation of the anonymous and talented artist "Bruno Hat" and subsequent bogus exhibition that had scores of our friends bidding on a unique and quite hideous corkboard and rope-framed piece.

There was only one thing missing from the celebration—my

love, Hamish St. Clair-Erskine. My sometimes fiancé and sometimes not. Right now, we were not. Still, I longed for his return. Longed to laugh again as he made me laugh. But after his latest debacle at uni, his parents had sent him off to New York City. Oh, bother, why did they seek to destroy a perfectly extraordinary man?

With the last of the books autographed, I smiled at those guests hovering near the marble table I'd used to sign. I stretched my fingers, in dire need of a champagne coupe, or maybe something a little stronger: a cocktail with a dash of cherry.

Squeezing through the horde of bodies, I made my way to the tower of bubbly only to be intercepted by one of my dear friends.

"Why, if it isn't the brilliant Evelyn Waugh," I gushed, tugging him into my arms. Looking dapper and tan from his recent trek across the globe, he seemed in good spirits after the not-so-unfortunate demise of his marriage to that horrible cow who'd so sorely abused him.

"And if it isn't my equal in clever articulation as well as good looks, Nancy Mitford."

I laughed, the first true one of the evening. We'd kept in touch over the months through letters, and thank goodness for that. Evelyn encouraged my pursuit from writing columns in *The Lady* to becoming a novelist.

"Have you thrown us all aside yet for a life of luxury and success?" he teased.

"Never! It's a silly book. Really, darling, I only wrote it because I wanted one hundred pounds." I laughed and tapped him on the hand clasped in mine, as the sound of another champagne bottle being popped sent out exuberant cries from the occupants.

"I daresay you will see a lot more than one hundred, and we

will all be insanely jealous," Evelyn teased as our friend Nina Siefield joined us, swirling an olive in her martini glass.

"As long as it keeps me dressing better, what more could I care for?" I flashed a playful smile. I spoke the truth, but also not the truth. Writing *Highland Fling* had been uproarious fun, and while I wanted to have the same success as Evelyn for his novel *Vile Bodies*, I truly gloried in finally having some extra funds.

Being from upper-class stock didn't always bode well for pin money. While Diana now lived a life of divine luxury with her new, wealthy husband—heir to the Guinness fortune—our parents had always kept a tight rein on what meager means their noble titles afforded them. We were cash poor always, to the point where our mother sold eggs from the family hens.

"Indeed," Nina mused. "You will be a literary star, darling. Incomparable. Now, Evelyn, come dance with me, for I'm growing bored as sin."

"I'm next, Evelyn, darling. I want to hear all about your exploits in Africa," I called after them.

Evelyn took Nina's nearly empty martini and guzzled the last dregs.

Nina flashed me a wink and dragged our friend toward the dance floor, where the band struck up a rousing song full of trumpets and saxes blowing, drums beating. The entire room was a veritable who's who of Bright Young Things, as the grouchy old set liked to call us. We were the prominent youths born to aristocrats and socialites. That coveted set of young persons who cared not a whit for being followed and photographed.

The grouches thought us wicked, an absolute disgrace to all the rules of the older generation. We threw extravagant parties to excess, laughed a little too vulgarly, traipsed about London in costume on elaborate treasure hunts, drank an unhealthy amount of champagne and showed entirely too much ankle and leg. In short, the Great War was over, and we were determined to enjoy ourselves.

In need of air, I searched for an exit, my gaze scanning over another of my good friends, who happened to be the cover illustrator for *Highland Fling*. Mark Ogilvie-Grant waved me toward the floor, where the rest of our friends tapped their feet and swung their arms in time to the music.

I turned away as if I'd not seen him at all. I couldn't face his knowing look of sympathy. Mark alone was privy to me putting my head in a comrade's oven last month, prepared to let the anesthetic sensation of the gas take me away from a world that made me miserable. I'd not even had the courage to share it with Evelyn.

Tears struck the backs of my eyes, but I downed my champagne, reaching for another with the dazzling smile I'd been able to perfect since birth.

"Darling Nancy!" a thick male voice said from behind. "Dance with me, you gorgeous creature."

With a smile I didn't feel, I whirled into the outstretched arms of the ruggedly handsome, and utterly dull, Hugh Smiley. Charming and rich. Everything a woman should want in a husband. I almost said yes when he'd asked me. But I could never marry another when I pictured myself with Hamish. I had this vision of me penning passages in my latest novel, while he regaled our growing family with stories of the hunt.

"Only because you look so dashing in your new dinner jacket." I tossed back all of my champagne and then gave him my hand.

"You are the very vision of glamour." Hugh kissed my hand and placed it on his muscled shoulder—larger, I suspected, from his time as a grenadier—our bodies rocked into the glee of a Charleston that Adele Astaire had taught us one night out on the town a few years back.

"Glamour is but a dizzying illusion, darling." I winked. "Don't you read the papers?"

Hugh laughed, though his eyes widened with the slightest hint of befuddlement—witty chatter always did bog down the slow-grinding gears of his brain. "Do you mean to say waking with a headache and blisters on your feet is not the picture of opulence?"

"It is much more fun to imagine us all playing bridge until we're sliding under tables, too drunk to keep our seats. Or running amok through the streets of Piccadilly dressed in royal costume."

"Or gambling away our fortunes," he followed with a toothy grin.

I laughed because I had no fortune to lose, and because Hugh was at least smart enough not to do as he suggested. Poor lamb worked so hard to prove he wasn't a dullard. A big blond oaf with gobs of money. If I married him, I could go about town in the latest fashions, ride in fancy cars and dine nightly at the Ritz, but I'd much rather have my mind tingle in delight of someone with a modicum of intelligence than a bursting purse.

"May I cut in?" Mark's intelligent blue eyes sparkled, a touch on the wicked side, with his blond hair a bit disheveled.

If only he had asked me to wed him, I might have been persuaded to let Hamish slip away. Rakish and clever, he was a friend

I could always count on when I wanted to have a rollicking good time, or an ear to divulge my darkest secrets.

Hugh flashed an irritated smile. "We're not—" he started to argue, but I took my hand from his shoulder and passed it to Mark.

"Now, darlings, there's plenty of Nancy to go around." A lie, a bitter lie, for there was barely enough of me for myself.

"I've saved you from that half-wit," Mark said in a conspiratorial whisper.

"We are but a lot of beautiful butterflies."

Mark looked about him suddenly, then turned back with a wicked grin. "Apologies, for a moment I thought your father had walked into the room."

"Oh, Mark, you are one of Farve's favorites, not like the other puppies."

"Now a question for the witty author. Tell me, dear, who is this hero in *Highland Fling* based on?" Mark's eyes skipped about the lively room, coming back to me. "Or is he not in attendance?"

Was it so obvious? Hamish could always draw a crowd—ever the hero. Flamboyant, loud and charming. He was as likely to down five brandies and call for a game of charades as he was to announce they were all going shooting at his family's castle in Scotland.

Oh, how I missed him.

"Why would you think I'd based him on anyone?" I asked with a coy lift to my shoulder. "My characters are all so unique, don't you see? There's not one amongst our friends so ostentatious of style or mischievous of humor."

Mark laughed, the music quieting for a moment before a

slower song came on and he tugged me away from the dancers to find us fresh glasses of Dom Perignon.

"This is why I shall always love you, my dear Lady," he said using my nickname. "You are just as truthful as you are not."

Dearest Mark,

My latest novel, Christmas Pudding, *is a riotous jumble of words that can barely form a cohesive sentence let alone elicit the humor and frivolity of my first novel which brought about zero of the acclaim I'd hoped these six months since its release.*

I bit my lip, pressing the point of the pen to the paper. A blot of ink bubbled on the surface.

With a huff, I crumpled the letter and tossed it onto the banked fire, where it lit into vibrant and desperately hungry flames with the other five starts to the same letter.

Setting down the pen, I rubbed at my temples.

It was too hard to be funny and clever with this second book due to my publisher when all I wanted was to curl up under my desk and never come out again. I was deliriously miserable in my loneliness and thought often of that night I'd put my head into the oven, wishing I'd seen it through.

I am so often surrounded by hordes of people, and yet none of them make me happy. And here I'd inflicted yet another dreary letter upon Mark, who seemed to be the only friend in the world who understood exactly how I felt.

Beautiful Nancy Mitford, though not quite as beautiful and clever as her sister Diana.

Not quite as happy.

Not quite as married.

Not *quite*.

Oh, how I loved and despised her at the same time. She had everything I wanted in life, and yet how could I begrudge her happiness?

At the sharp ring of the telephone, I hurried to the front hall of Rutland Gate, our family home overlooking Hyde Park, to answer. "Mitford residence."

"A call for the Honorable Nancy Mitford."

"Speaking."

There was some static and a muffled "I'm putting you through, sir."

"Darling." Hamish's voice came through the earpiece, endearing and sending a wash of relief through my body that made my hands tremble.

"Hamish, is that you?" Feeling faint, I perched on the end of one of the Victorian oak chairs that flanked the sides of the console table.

"The one and only."

"Come back to London; it's positively dreary without you."

"Ah, but you see, sweet lady, I have returned."

My heart skipped a beat, and I gripped the earpiece harder. "How?"

"New York City was vile. London is the only city for me."

I couldn't help but smile. "Never leave again."

"As long as I shall live." We both knew that was a lie, for as soon as his father was fed up with him, off he'd be sent again to

America or Canada. "London seems drearier than when I left less than a year ago."

I frowned down at my feet, the threadbare woven tapestry older than the Rutland Gate house itself as he continued.

Hamish drawled, "Anyway, New York was a downright bore, and not a drop of spirits in the place, unless you know the right people. Can you imagine it? Being arrested for drinking a brandy!"

"Which of course you did."

"Of course. Well, the brandy, not the arrest. So, tell me, darling, where is everyone? I expected half a dozen invites the moment I walked through the door."

And when was that?

"The Ritz. The Café de Paris. The ballet. We are everywhere, Ham—private parties are all the fashion. All one has to do is bring their favorite bottle." Of which I'd been imbibing steadily, out until two or three in the morning, every day this week. Survival was paramount.

"Let's go to the Café de Paris for lunch. I'll pick you up. Shall I invite the usual?"

The usual meant the lot of the Bright Young Things were about to converge upon the café and suck down large amounts of champagne and brandy. We'd all have no care for any economic concerns, myself included. Hamish had returned, and I desperately wanted to see him.

"Marvelous. They'll all be glad to see you."

"Not as glad as you," he said.

The tone was teasing, and it struck me in a way nothing he'd ever said before had. Almost irritating in its arrogance. Unaware

I'd rejected all suitors in favor of him. Why did it feel sometimes like I loved him too much?

I swallowed around my doubts and pushed out a laugh. "Not nearly," I admitted.

When the doorbell buzzed, I waited impatiently upstairs for our butler to answer. I'd spent the entire last hour trying on one outfit after another, curling my hair with tongs, and putting on fresh lipstick—scarlet red. My nails were newly varnished in the same shade, partly because I thought it pretty and partly because Farve hated it. Powder hid the dark circles beneath my eyes, and a swash of blush on my cheeks kept me looking healthy. Gold rings in my ears, bangles to match on my wrist and a pearl necklace with a gold *N* charm dangling from the center that Hamish had given to me the Christmas before.

His voice boomed in the entry hall. "Darling, Nancy! Come down from your perch!"

I rounded the corner, waiting at the top of the stairs until he noticed me. Dark hair styled to perfection, he stood straight in flannel trousers, a blue shirt and black sweater. Casual and elegant all at once.

"There you are." His eyes filled with merriment, a curl to his lips as he scanned my dark blue crepe dress. "Brilliant. I have missed you so. You have no idea what it's like to be across the ocean from everything you love."

He loves me. My heart fluttered, and I somehow managed to keep my face stoic as I glided down the stairs on surprisingly steady legs. At the bottom, however, I dropped all pretenses and threw myself into his arms, breathing in his scent of sandalwood, spice and a touch of lavender that reminded me of France.

"You smell delicious," I said.

He wiggled his brows. "I knew you'd love it—it's French. A Krigler." He pressed a chaste kiss to my lips, which we'd never have done had my parents been about.

Chaste as it was, it made me tingle all over. How I loved him. *"Le parfum est céleste tout comme votre retour."*

"*Oui, ma chérie*, I am in heaven being back on British soil. And I've a gift for you." He reached into his pocket, pulling out a small white box tied with a light blue ribbon.

My stomach leapt into my throat. Was he about to propose again? I could barely speak, and my hands shook as I reached for the white box, our fingers brushing. I tugged on the ribbon.

His mother's ring? Or had he chosen one for me that would speak to my uniqueness, the very Nancy qualities he adored?

I grinned up at him when the ribbon fell to the floor, waiting for him to join the blue slip there on bended knee, but he continued to stand, mischievous dark eyes beneath slanting brows concentrated on me.

I opened the lid, realizing as I did that it wasn't a ring box, and feeling utterly foolish. Oh, how disappointing that he'd not come back from America missing me so much and with the desperate need to make me his forever.

Instead, inside I found a copper figurine of Lady Liberty, the symbol of freedom, set on white tissue.

A tight smile crossed my lips for the impersonal gift given with such a message from France to America as it was to myself. Was he setting me free? Telling me with no words at all that he wished to break ties for good?

The pearls around my neck tightened.

"Well, isn't that . . . divine?" I set the figurine on the table beside the telephone and picked up my clutch, slipped on my mackintosh, taking the offered elbow Hamish held out to me.

"I'm glad you like it."

I hated it. "So kind of you to think of me."

Hamish filled the conversation from my house in Knightsbridge to Piccadilly with incessant chatter about the underground jazz clubs he'd managed to infiltrate in New York City, and the night he'd run from police after the whisky den had been exposed.

"That's when I decided to leave the wretched place. How can it be illegal to have a drink? Ridiculous."

"Indeed," I managed. Did Hamish not recall that his penchant for drink was what had got him sent across the pond? Not that I held any place to school him on his imbibing habit. I already planned to get properly sozzled at the café if only to erase from my mind the humiliating excitement of the pre-unveiling of Lady Liberty. "I should think I never want to go there."

Hamish swung his car into place in front of the Café de Paris, causing a screech from a passing mother pushing a pram. I mouthed *sorry* to the glowering woman, while Hamish slid across the hood on his rear to open my door. I stepped out onto the slick and shiny street, rainwater dotting the tips of my shoes.

I raised my brows at him, which made him grin. "Learned that in America."

"You're lucky not to have ripped your trousers." I pressed my hand into his and allowed him to help me out of the car into the dreary grayness of London. "And they are very likely wet now."

"Try not to be so dismaying, Lady, else you'll wrinkle that fine brow of yours."

Taken aback, I readied a response, but he pressed a quick kiss to my lips, and then dragged me inside before I could reply. We were instantly overwhelmed by our friends. Any semblance of conversation was quickly overtaken by the music and the shouts of those admiring the roller skaters performing on the low stage. Two men dressed in black trousers and white button-downs, and a female dancer in white satin and lace.

"Sit, sit," said Mary, Hamish's sister, patting the chair beside herself.

I took the offered seat with Hamish on my other side. With the round tables pushed together, we were joined by the usual crowd. All cheers and questions for Hamish, who presided over his audience with tales of illegal gambling and drinking in underground clubs he guessed were run by the American mob. Either proper rubbish or another terribly convincing argument as to why I should never venture there.

"Anyone catch the eye of the infamous Hamish?" a friend asked with a wiggle of his brows.

I took a long sip of champagne trying to find humor in that idiotic line of questioning. Was it hard to imagine that Hamish might have pined for me?

Hamish put his arm around my shoulders and pulled me close, his French cologne making me dizzy. "Nancy is the only woman I'll ever hold dear."

Though I didn't want to admit it to myself, there might have been literal truth to his words. Both my brother and Evelyn had been adamant that Hamish was more inclined to the masculine sex, and I was loath to believe them. That couldn't be the reason we'd not yet wed.

One of the male skaters veered off from stage and approached our table. He pointed at me, and I shook my head, but Mary waved her hands enthusiastically.

"Me, pick me!"

The skater beamed. "You, miss."

"Divine!" Mary scrabbled over our laps amongst laughs until she freed herself.

Another round of champagne was poured, our glasses raised in Mary's direction. The band struck up a rousing song as she appeared onstage, skates on her feet, and imitating the Charleston of the skating performers, nearly losing her balance more than once.

Hamish ordered a brandy, and I wondered if he had the pounds to pay for it or if he would ask me to spot him as he usually did.

A squeal from the stage caught all our attention as Mary was flung high. A wrist was clamped in one of the performer's hands and her ankle in the other as he swung her so high above his head and in so quick a fashion, I could barely make out which end of her was what.

"Extraordinary," murmured those at the table, while Hamish looked increasingly worried, and a beau of Mary's exclaimed, "Dear Lord!"

At first Mary appeared to be quite enjoying the belly-roiling act, but her squeals of laughter turned quickly sour, and both Hamish and her beau leapt over the table to run for the stage in hopes of saving her.

Longer in the leg, her beau reached her before her brother, and good thing, because the skater lost his balance and sent poor Mary flying through the air. Amidst screams and shouts, a table tipped when the partygoers lurched forward to be of help. The gallant suitor leapt toward Mary, catching her in his arms before she could be decapitated by a nearby flying table.

I let out the breath I'd not realized I held. Every last drop of Dom Perignon I'd drunk threatened to come up.

"Dear Heavens, that was mad," Nina sighed beside me, clutching her neck.

"Dreadful," I muttered, letting go of the table I'd been clasping hard between my fingers. "Never trust a skater who's likely had more spirits than all of us combined."

A few friends joined Hamish at the front, holding him back from giving the skater a beating, not that it might have hurt all that much given Hamish's slighter build. And since when had he started roughing up the entertainment? America had not done him good.

Across the table from me, Peter Rodd rolled his eyes. "Should have embarrassed himself as he did at Eton when he tried the same on me."

I pursed my lips. "Were you swinging around his sister?"

Peter snorted. "No."

"Intent on harming some other female?"

Peter shook his head, a knowing curl to his lips that I didn't quite understand. "Not my place to share why he got the beating of his life; suffice it to say we are not the closest of friends."

I raised a challenging brow. "Shame."

Peter was rarely serious, and a bit of a know-it-all. I found his arrogance cast a shadow on his handsome face. Mary sobbed as her beau escorted her outside for air, his arm protectively around her shoulders.

"I do not find it to be a shame at all," Peter said, "save for whenever I want to ask you to dance, he is right there."

I folded my arms over my chest and then flashed him a wide grin. "Hamish has not been in town for many months, Peter. Find another way to flatter me than your pretty and insipid lies."

"You're stunning," he said. "Even with that blistering tongue."

Heat rose to my cheeks as I took note of his wicked handsomeness. No dullard like Hugh, and he lacked Hamish's immaturity. Yet he was also a bit too arrogant.

"What do you think of America?" I asked.

"Loathe it."

"Fascinating. We might yet be friends."

"I thought we already were."

Hamish slid into the chair beside me, glowering in Peter's direction.

Peter smirked and turned his attention back to the stage, where the next set of skaters had assembled. Hamish ordered a sidecar and offered one to me. Suddenly sensing the need for air myself, I shook my head.

"I'm going to go check on Mary."

Walking away, I felt several pairs of eyes on me but didn't turn around to see who watched my exit—fearful that none of those eyes would belong to Hamish. I kept my back straight and my hips swinging gently. I might be nearing thirty and getting close to spinsterhood, as my mother liked to say, but I still drew the eyes of everyone I passed. Cecil Beaton continually asked me to sit for his photographs. Plenty of people took notice.

Just not the one who mattered.

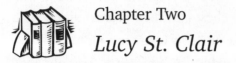

Chapter Two
Lucy St. Clair

London, Present Day

LUCY HAD EVERY INTENTION of ordering the vegetable breakfast roll and a cappuccino, but what came out of her mouth was, "Bacon roll and a white chocolate mocha, please."

The Caffè Nero, down Curzon Street, was teeming, and the scents of coffee, bacon and sweet confections were just too tempting.

She'd arrived in London yesterday after accepting a special collaboration project from her boss, Mr. Sloan, at Emerald Books in DC, working with the marvelous Mayfair bookshop Heywood Hill. She loved her job as a special library curator. The chance to prove herself with a prestigious client—Miranda Masters—was going to open so many doors for her future career, including a possible promotion.

It was a dream come true every day to help shape the home libraries of private collectors, picking out amazing books that some clients would appreciate, covet even, while visitors to their homes might only gaze admiringly at the spines and wonder what they cost. Rare books to a curator or collector were a gem, but to an outsider, they were a status symbol of the elite.

This morning was her first day at Heywood Hill, one of the

oldest bookshops in London, having opened in the 1930s. What really drew Lucy was *who* had worked there—famed author Nancy Mitford.

Nancy's book *The Pursuit of Love* was Lucy's all-time favorite, and that of her mother—the pain of whose recent loss still caused Lucy's heart to seize. The opportunity to stand in Nancy's footsteps was one she couldn't refuse. Years ago, Lucy had cut out an article about the bookshop and glued it to her vision board. It was still on her bucket list of amazing bookshops to visit. And there was a mystery her mother had pondered over the years regarding Nancy Mitford that Lucy herself had been dying to solve. This trip to London might provide the answers.

Not to mention learning a little more about her family history. Originally from England, someone emigrated to the US in the mid-1950s. Lucy had heard plenty of stories of the Bright Young Things—the champagne-drinking bohemian aristocrats and literary darlings of the age—from her mother, especially when Lucy had been in college and partied a little too hard. Nancy Mitford had been a part of that set—going from one house party to the next, traipsing around London dressed in costume and treasure hunting. They were the talk of the town, their pictures and exploits splashed in the tabloids. Oh, what fun that must have been.

The two weeks in London Lucy had to curate the special library project would also provide her with plenty of time to delve into the mystery her mother had been tracing—the identity of Iris. While she waited for her breakfast order, Lucy pulled out the well-loved copy of *The Pursuit of Love* by Nancy Mitford, and read the scrawled handwriting on the inside flap.

My dearest Iris,

Without you, my path might have followed a less elegant tra-jectory than Anna Karenina. I will be forever grateful not only for your lack of pity, but for your friendship. For pulling me back from the tracks and setting me on a path that pushed me to pursue love, happiness. To leave the darkness behind and really live. No truer friend could have ever been found.

With much love,
Nancy

In all the texts, letters, biographies, those named Iris didn't match up with someone who'd been close to Nancy, nor had they revealed how she saved Nancy's life. Together Lucy and her mother had pondered what answers about the mysterious Iris might be revealed in London. Now Lucy had the chance to find out.

"Order for Lucy."

Lucy put the book back into her oversized purse beside another curious package. She'd found it in her mother's safety deposit box, just before taking off for London—letters from Nancy to various people. There was no receipt or note with the package to let Lucy know how her mother had come across them, but she hoped they might provide her with additional clues, and bring her closer to the mother she missed so much. She planned to read one each night after work.

Breakfast in hand, Lucy skirted morning commuters on Curzon Street, her eyes over their heads, tracing the perfectly polished bronze number 10 on the bookshop's black door. A door that was literally going to open up opportunities for her. Then a blue circular plaque caught her eye.

ENGLISH HERITAGE
NANCY MITFORD
1904–1973
Writer
Worked Here
1942–1945

Lucy's heartbeat leapt up a notch, and for a moment she saw her mother, smiling down at a younger Lucy with another Nancy Mitford tale.

Beneath it was a second plaque: the British royal crest. Heywood Hill Ltd was a bookseller by appointment to Her Majesty the Queen.

Lucy took a deep breath. She was about to step into a place that held so much history. If anyone had asked her last week if she'd be stepping into the queen's favorite bookshop today, or a shop frequented or run by famous writers, she would have said, *In my dreams.*

"Today is the first day of the rest of my life." She gripped the cold metal door handle and pushed.

Announced by the tinkle of a bell over the door, she froze a moment, taking in the euphoria that was Heywood Hill.

A calm quiet permeated the shop. Lucy smelled paper and glue, doubtless the result of thousands of volumes on polished wooden shelves and stacked on tables—familiar scents backed by a faint hint of something herbal. Crystal chandeliers illuminated the shop's treasures, and over soft, background music, Lucy could hear the subtle sound of pages being turned. What a satisfying euphony. Anyone who said a bookshop wasn't heaven was just crazy.

Lucy stepped farther into the long and narrow shop, the sounds of her shoes muffled by the blue carpet. The first room opened into a second, framed by two elegantly polished marbled-wood columns with gold scrollwork at the top. Mounted above an empty fireplace in the left corner was a gilded frame that bespoke of London 1920s. Lucy thought she caught a trace of the comforting wood smoke from decades before. Rich history hung like magic in the London air and whispered to her like faint conversations from the past, redolent of chic perfume and pipe smoke.

Beyond, there was one more room, boasting bright red polished wood shelves. Apparitions of literary figures floated between them in her mind's eye—Ernest Hemingway and Evelyn Waugh. Daphne du Maurier and the mysterious Nancy Mitford. She gave a deep sigh—it felt like home. Two weeks wouldn't be enough. She could stay forever.

"Can I help you?"

The voice came from the room just behind her—where a desk was cleverly tucked from view by a midrise bookshelf. Turning, she saw a man she'd walked right past without even noticing.

"I'm Lucy St. Clair."

He unfolded his lanky body from a chair that seemed too short for him. His cropped salt-and-pepper hair was in disarray, as though he spent a lot of time tugging on the ends. Round spectacles slid down his nose, but he made no move to push them back into place. "Ah yes, we've been expecting you. I'm Oliver. We spoke on the phone. I presume you have settled in, and your room above stairs is satisfactory?"

"It's lovely." The one-bedroom flat over the bookshop was incredibly cozy, with a perfect view of the street.

"Brilliant." Oliver smiled widely, showing off a gap between his two front teeth. "Curating offices are downstairs. I'll show you the way."

They descended a narrow flight of stairs into the offices, past several people wrapping books carefully in paper—finishing off the packages with blue-and-white Heywood Hill ribbons and stickers. In addition to these workers sat a blonde woman reading what looked like a special edition of *The Iliad*, with two others behind computers.

"Your desk." Oliver indicated her workstation. "Everyone, this is Lucy St. Clair, from Emerald Books in DC. She's on loan to us for a couple of weeks. Or rather, we are on loan to her."

Lucy shook hands before setting down her coffee and purse and offering a smile to the woman positioned beside her.

"I'm Ash," the blonde said. "I run the subscription service."

"Fun." Lucy knew the satisfaction of receiving an email from a client saying a book suggested on their behalf had been a hit.

"Barbara and Louisa work with the subscription service too." Ash gestured. "The pair packing the books are Mabel and Harry. Best get to it and not let your coffee get cold. If you have any questions, just ask."

Lucy offered Ash another smile, then settled into her desk, taking the list of first-edition books she wanted to locate for the Masters' library from her purse.

The primary place to look was in the shop's database. She

was fortunate to immediately locate signed first editions of *The Wonderful Wizard of Oz* by L. Frank Baum, *Dracula* by Bram Stoker, *Rebecca* by Daphne du Maurier and *To the Lighthouse* by Virginia Woolf held in the rare-books section.

Lucy paused mid–triumphant stride as she scanned the shelves, her gaze falling on a display of books by Nancy Mitford—as well as several written by other members of the Mitford family. *Hons and Rebels* by Jessica Mitford was another of her mother's favorites, and in fact Lucy had been named for Jessica, whose middle name was Lucy.

She pulled out *Highland Fling*, one she and her mother had read together half a dozen times.

She cracked open the familiar volume, reading the first few lines of Albert's rather humorous journey of self-discovery.

"I see you've got a Mitford novel," Oliver said, approaching.

Lucy stared down at the canvas cover, threadbare in the corners, the pages yellowed. "She's one of my favorites."

"Were you aware that the owner of Heywood Hill is Ms. Mitford's nephew?"

Lucy nodded. "I love the family tie."

"Agree. The Duke of Devonshire is a bibliophile to be sure, whose father was married to Nancy's sister Deborah."

"But they weren't the original owners, right?"

Oliver shook his head. "No, but the late duke and duchess had a great fondness for it. In the early nineties they endeavored to become part of its legacy. The original store was actually down the street at number seventeen. They moved a few years after opening."

Lucy stared at the Mitford display again, her eyes this time alighting on a black-and-white picture of two young women outside of the shop. Was it too much to hope that the girl beside Nancy was Iris? "Who's that with Nancy?"

"Anne Hill, the wife of Heywood. Nancy helped Anne during the war, when Heywood was shipped overseas. A lot of literary greats have filled the shop."

Lucy's skin prickled. To be sitting in the very place that a famous writer might have plotted out their books, or discussed a particular scene, was exhilarating.

"If you're interested in Nancy and her family, perhaps I could arrange for you to visit Chatsworth House and have a look at more books and letters?"

Lucy flashed Oliver a grateful smile. This was too good to be true; the answers to the questions she and her mother had pondered for years might be within reach. "I'd love that."

"Of course, it will have to be when the house is open to the public. We wouldn't want to disturb them."

"That would be amazing. And not just because of the Mitford connection. What bibliophile wouldn't want to see one of the grandest personal libraries in the world?"

"I'll make the arrangements." Oliver walked away, leaving Lucy in a state of shock.

Day one on the job in London, and she felt incredibly productive. If only her mother were still alive to help her uncover the truth of Nancy's past, her mysterious friend and the letters.

Later that night, curled up in a chair with a glass of wine, she untied the twine that wrapped around Nancy's letters. Rather than have to decide which one to open, she simply picked the one on top, smoothing her thumb over the scrawl on the front of the envelope addressed to acclaimed author Evelyn Waugh.

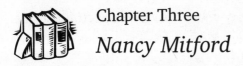

Chapter Three
Nancy Mitford

August 1933

Darling Evelyn,

Do you recall this past May, when Hitler's followers hurled thousands of books into bonfires while giving the Nazi salute? Burning ideas that were deemed "un-German." Such great authors and brilliant minds as Albert Einstein, Helen Keller, H. G. Wells, Jack London.

London's book White Fang *was the only novel my father claims to have ever read, having loved it so much he never need read another again—absurd, no? I can't decide if I believe him, but I honestly can't recall having ever seen him pick up a book to read.*

Burning books with ideas that don't align with the Nazi regime is only the beginning of a dangerous censorship, don't you agree?

For that matter, burning any book for any reason. Well, unless it's one of mine. I'm fairly certain there are a number of people who want to toss my prose upon the flames.

Speaking of books, I am dying for a new bookshop. If

only I had the money to set one up. I'd be an amazing book-
seller.

Love from,
Nancy

DIANA STUDIED ME WITH her sapphire eyes over the gold rim
of her yellow-primrose-painted teacup. Our sister Unity perched
across from me on the slope-backed settee beside Diana.

We sat in the drawing room of the tiny cottage on Eaton
Square she'd recently let—the Eatonry, we'd named it. The walls
were painted a soft butter yellow, and the furniture was equally
muted and elegant, with pops of color on the fringed pillows,
and flowers that adorned the mahogany side tables.

Diana, beautiful and cigarette thin, had seemingly lost her
mind at some point in the last year. She'd left her handsome, rich
husband and taken up as a lover of Oswald Mosley—the leader
of the British Union of Fascists. Why Diana had left the privileged life of being married to Bryan to become a mistress who
waited for her Fascist paramour to sneak over boggled the mind.

I'd never understand why Diana disrupted her whole family
instead of having a quiet *affaire d'amore* behind her husband's
back like any other respectable lady in society.

To help Diana stave off a modicum of social gossip, and keep
myself from living at Swinbrook—or *Swine*brook as I liked to
call it—I'd rented a room from her. There was an air of nostalgia about us being under the same roof. Though I suppose we'd
never been complete bosom buddies in our lives. As Mitford
sisters go, we would fiercely protect one another from outside

sources of pain, but behind the safety of our walls, we might be the one employing a well-placed smack.

From somewhere within the dwelling came the screech of two little boys, and the muffled call of their nanny.

"We're going to Germany. Should you like to join us?" Diana asked.

"We?" I raised a brow and poured milk into my tea.

"Bobo and I," she said referring to Unity's nickname.

"Oh, the kindness of you." I took a dainty sip and put on a good shop front.

Unity was lucky to be here with us at all. Muv forbade Jessica and Deborah from visiting this vulgar house of iniquity—or at least that was how our mother viewed Diana's new residence, sans husband, but frequented by a paramour. Funny enough, our sister Pamela, clever hen, moved to a cottage in Biddesden, where she managed Diana's ex-husband's farm.

I think Muv would have forbidden everyone from visiting Diana if she could, considering her beautiful daughter was the center of the scandal of 1932. Salacious affairs and divorce would do that to a gal. C'est la vie. She was in love.

Being the elder, wiser sister, I warned Diana that her social standing would be nil if she went on about getting in wrong with the world, but that I would always be on her side. As would anyone who cared about her. Muv would come around, along with the rest of society.

"Oh, come now, Naunce." Diana's lip curled sweetly. "I know you prefer travel to boring, old, dirty London."

Unity bit into a blueberry scone and then chimed in, "We're leaving in a few weeks. I'm going to meet Adolf Hitler."

I tried not to show my horror at such a statement. The man

was a monster, yet posters of Hitler lined Unity's walls, whereas normal girls her age might have gummed up fashion prints or at the very least a profile of a picture star like Laurence Olivier or Cary Grant. The idea of Hitler being her crush was absolutely batty. How exactly did she plan to see her desire come to fruition?

I opened my mouth to ask Unity what she was thinking, but Diana cut in.

"One could be so lucky," Diana quipped. "We're merely going for distraction."

Lucky? The madness . . . Poor Diana. Mosley didn't seem bent on monogamy and had gone off to Paris with his *other* mistress. A distraction was most definitely what she needed.

Diana tapped her teacup with a perfectly manicured nail, hesitating in something she wanted to say.

"What is it, Honks?" I asked Diana, referring to her childhood nickname.

"I received an invitation from Putzi Hanfstaengl, who happened to be at a party I attended, and also happens to be Chancellor Hitler's foreign secretary. He says we should come and see for ourselves the truth of which is mangled in our British papers."

"Indeed, it can't be as bad as all that." Unity gave an exaggerated roll of her eyes.

I tried to keep the horror from my face. I shook my head, having unquestionably no interest in joining my sisters on this particular tour. For it wasn't going to be exploring Neuschwanstein Castle or to stun our parents by a trip to Sylt beach, where sunbathers and sea swimmers did so in the nude.

I loved my sisters with every breath, to the deep marrow of

my bones. However, I also knew Diana was willing to risk everything for Mosley, and her new lover was part of something dark and sinister.

His views on the world, on humanity, aligned with a Germany that seemed from the outset horrifyingly wrong. If Diana could prove to me that this visit would show otherwise, I'd be happiest to hear it. But I didn't doubt for a minute she would make this trip, not for the distraction against her lover's infidelity, but because she hoped to strengthen her ties with Germany as some sort of gift to him.

I sipped my tea, wishing I could add something a little stronger as I pondered my sisters' choices.

Unity had always followed at Diana's heels, lapping up the crumbs she dropped as if they were gold nuggets from the mining camp Farve once owned in Canada. Now in this instance, the tables had turned with Diana suddenly following in Unity's fanatical footsteps. Unity's extremism regarding the British Union of Fascists, and her latest craze about Hitler, appeared to be hitting new excesses, and appealing to Diana for some reason.

So often in our family I felt like the odd woman out. A voice of reason? I'm not so certain, but at the least, a varying voice on absolutes.

My gaze skimmed the pamphlet on the table with the announcement of the annual rally in Nuremberg, Germany, where Adolf Hitler's Nazi Party had seized power, banning all other political parties and destroying democracy in the country. With the Nazis having ultimate rule, Hitler wanted to speak to his people about their victory. A rally my sisters planned to attend.

"Why not go somewhere far more interesting, like Inverness?" I suggested. "We can see if all the hubbub about the Loch Ness monster sighting a few months ago has merit. Maybe convince Nina to have a house party. Muv and Farve can watch your sons. Perhaps teach them the ways of the child hunt."

I laughed softly, remembering Farve's favorite game of sending us out into the Cotswold landscape and how he'd come after us on horseback, hounds baying at discovering our scent. An elaborate, and rather eccentric, game of hide-and-seek.

Diana had lost interest in being a socialite the moment she'd left her husband, and Unity had always been a bit shy around our friends, and they a little unnerved by her considering her penchant for keeping rats as pets. And so I wasn't at all surprised when they shook their heads.

Diana settled her teacup on the tiny matching primrose dish. "We're headed to Bavaria. Munich first and then Nuremberg. The arrangements have been made, but as I said, there is room for one more should you change your mind."

"While the invitation holds some fascination for me, I'm afraid I must decline." I smiled sweetly and picked at a blueberry on my scone, the fruit ready to burst from the womb of baked flour.

"Oh, Lady." Unity gave a slight scowl. "What better have you to do?"

The question stung, but I brushed it off, never showing a sign of weakness, especially with my sisters. "Well, silly, I have a wedding to plan. Some of us have to set our expectations on reality rather than fantasy." It was a low blow, a dig at Unity's imagined meeting with Hitler, of finding her own Fascist lover.

"Is it truly going to happen, do admit?" Unity countered, a brow raised in challenge. "Already your arrangements have shifted from October to November."

I waved away her comment with a flit of my hand. "Why rush perfection?" In truth, I was rapidly approaching thirty years of age, and whispers of spinsterhood grew to near-shout levels. The worst of them came this year when Muv and Farve suggested I return to *Swine*brook and settle into country life as if I'd already dried up. "I'll be a Mrs. before the year is out. Besides, another book idea has very recently come to me." *In the last few minutes, in fact.*

"Oh, do tell. You know how much I enjoyed reading *Christmas Pudding* aloud to Kit." Diana had been kind enough to share the book widely with her friends, and her lover, Oswald—*Kit*.

My second book, *Christmas Pudding*, had done only slightly better than *Highland Fling*. Though neither were the huge successes I'd hoped for, they both brought with them a minor bump in societal status, along with a few ego-stroking reviews.

Today, a new idea began to stir. A satirical tale I thought my sisters might find flattering, as an opus to their recent conversions to Fascism—which I abhorred. What was sisterly love if we couldn't poke fun? Was that a bridge I was willing to cross?

"You shall have to wait like the rest of the world, for I'm far too busy writing for *The Lady* and *Vogue*, and the wedding, of course."

"Lady is a tease." Diana flashed a mocking smile. "Well, if you change your mind, you know where to find us."

Indeed, I did—at the closest Fascist rally.

"I do adore you," I said. "And thank you ever so much for thinking of me, darling. I hope the both of you have a most marvelous time."

The small drawing room grew quiet, but only for a second before Unity filled the silence with the discussion of a new hairstyle she wanted that would give her the look of a crown of curls, and how she'd acquired a number of black shirts to wear to rallies. Oswald's band of Blackshirts certainly were a bundle of rods, and not in the way they believed.

Diana smiled, nodding, happy to have someone else as consumed with the changing tide.

"Black does bring out the blue of your eyes," Diana said smoothly to Unity.

"I much prefer you in a dull beige," I teased, to which I received two identical tight smiles. "Or perhaps white, or rose. Black is so . . . harsh, do admit."

Unity's chin notched up. "I like black best."

"I look good in anything." Diana's voice was cool, but the hint of a smile gave way to the humor of it, and I laughed.

"Of course, you are *wondair*," I said in the exaggerated accent I'd used when we were girls and I played a doctor preparing to operate.

A laugh elicited from both before Unity ruined the conversation with another round of ovations about Hitler. I pretended to listen while composing a list of books I should like to read, and then pondering just how Oswald had wooed my sister into scandal. What young woman in her early twenties left her wealthy husband, a stable marriage, with two young children in tow, to become the mistress of a notoriously controversial, older politician?

There was something in the way the Poor Old Leader, as we sarcastically called him, wooed Diana. Was it that he supported women's rights, evidenced by the number of suffragettes who'd joined his movement? Or maybe because he positioned himself as the only one who could save Britain from economic ruin. There was some hint of Hitler in him too, believing in a purer race and British superiority. I found all of it repulsive. And he wasn't even good-looking.

I'd attended one of the meetings at Diana's hopeful insistence, a clear intent to gain support from her older sister. While Oswald was a great orator, the men he surrounded himself with were bullies, railing on anyone who coughed or sneezed to keep quiet.

"In other news," I said, taking the August second issue of *Tatler* from beneath my seat. "Do you recognize this Hon on the cover?"

Diana and Unity both squealed, ogling the portrait of me taken in the perfect light by Madame Yevonde. I wore a wide-brimmed white hat with a dark blue bow to match my blue-and-white-checked frock with double-layered capelet sleeves sewn by our longtime family seamstress and maid.

"A beautiful portrait of you."

"The hat is divine." Unity examined the hat closely. "I should like to borrow it."

Diana took the newspaper and read the caption. "'The Honorable Nancy Mitford is not only charming to look at but also extremely intelligent and an entertaining conversationalist.'"

"As we all know." I cocked my shoulder coyly. And yet, surprisingly, I felt oddly at a loss for more words.

A cold wash of apprehension had stilled my tongue. For while I headed for inevitable marital bliss, my sisters were diving headlong into dangerous obsession.

December 4, 1933

~~Hamish,~~

~~I've decided to forgive you for breaking my heart. I am going~~
~~to marry Peter and we are exceedingly happy. The moment~~
~~I say, "I do," I will forget all of the wrongs I suffered at your~~
~~callousness~~

"I *am* a happy bride." I whispered the words to myself, in the
looking glass in the dressing room of St. John's Smith Square
church.

My face appeared pale against the backdrop of my dark curls.
I pinched my cheeks to bring in color, the rouge standing out
even more starkly as put on rather than the natural happy glow
of someone about to wed for love.

My groom would be at the altar, elegantly dressed in a black
tailcoat with a white gardenia pinned to his lapel, waiting for me
to appear in the white chiffon gown with narrow frills and a veil
of lace and gardenias.

A crowd packed into the church like smoked oysters in a can,
ready to watch me glide down the aisle, a happy bride eager for
her perfect future.

For wasn't that what every bride was on their wedding day?

Unhappiness before marriage meant that when the proverbial
vows were exchanged a sudden blessing of joy would radiate
from within, like the sun beaming down after a lifetime of cold
rain.

My groom was that beam of light at the end of a nearly thirty-year period of darkness. Soon I would have my bliss, at least I hoped.

The low rumble of voices mingled with the organ music coming from the other side of the door. To stay and remain in despair, or open the door to a whole new world of uncertainty? Diana had not seemed miserable in her marriage, only dispassionate. Was love a disillusionment?

I gazed toward a small window, gauging how long it would take to climb through.

"I must stay. I must get married today," I muttered to myself.

I'd worked hard over the last few months, if not the last few years, to appear as jovial as a young woman of my circumstances might. I emulated Diana and her beaming expression, the smile that got whatever she wanted. Picking up the pieces of one's broken self was difficult when everyone waited for you to shatter.

"I *am* a happy bride," I repeated, curling my lips into a winning smile.

A knock sounded at the door, and Farve stepped into the small room, resplendent in his black tailcoat. "Your groom awaits, duck."

"We shan't want to keep him." I smoothed my hands down the front of my gown, the silken feel against my damp palms soothing.

Farve grunted and tugged on the end of his mustache. "You look beautiful."

"But do I look happy?"

"Every bit." There was a flash of something in his eyes, as

though he understood the struggle. He held out his arm to me, and I threaded mine through.

Ahead of me eleven pages dressed in white satin Romney tails walked as stoically as their energetic, wiggly little bodies allowed.

The only thing missing on this day was the man I'd professed to marry for five years.

Today, I was not marrying Hamish, as I'd fooled myself into believing would happen.

Instead, the Honorable Peter Rodd, the untitled younger son of Baron Rennell, stood in his place. Gorgeous and wild. He lit up when he saw me, standing there so godlike in his black tail-coat. The smile said he'd been expecting me, would have waited another hour. With the subtle incline of his head, he said I didn't disappoint. The smile promised a lifetime of laughter, of dancing under the stars.

Peter was not rich. He was not titled. And I didn't particularly like his family.

However, a peculiarity whirled in the center of my chest, a thrilling and exotic emotion. I thought it was love. Or at least I hoped. I noticed the way the sun glinted off his golden hair, and how my belly flipped when his warm lips brushed mine. His soft palm sent a shock through me, and when he spoke, I was enthralled.

I fancied myself so in love, so incredibly full of bliss, that I might explode with it. Peter, wild and handsome, had become my world.

There was no one in this room who might think otherwise. Peter had told me the very same thing. Gushed in every letter his adoration and bent over my hand, his lips triumphant as they grazed my knuckles.

We don't speak about his proposal to me at a party when he was deep in his cups and joking, nor that I was the third woman he'd asked that night. We don't mention that I said yes in desperation after Hamish broke things off over the telephone. Or that we both clung to the idea of wedlock as a lifeline.

Our union would change our lives. For the better. A more vigorous and exultant partner I could not have imagined. Our great happiness would be the story poets wrote about. A story *I* could write about.

Genuine heat filled my cheeks now as I stared down the aisle, a tremulous smile on my face. At the end, Peter grinned, chin thrust up, forever confident, a short flutter of fingers beckoning me forward.

How had we not been introduced sooner? Did not anyone realize what joy we might bring to each other?

We couldn't have it any other way.

January 1934

Dearest Evelyn,

I've decided that I hate Rome, and I plan to write all about it in The Lady *unless you stop me. Perhaps my next book will be about a heroine who goes on campaign to boycott the great city with its uneven cobblestones, copious amounts of garlic and tomato.*

What I wouldn't give for one of Muv's simple dishes, and a walk in the Cotswolds in my wellies.

Love from,
Nancy

P.S. Don't tell Peter how much I hate Rome; he is entirely enamored.

"Let me carry you." Peter scrambled from the cab in front of our new house outside London at Strand-on-the-Green just past Kew Bridge. A rush of crisp winter wind flew in, snaking its way down the Astrakhan fur collar of my charcoal wool overcoat.

On the other side he leaned in to take my hand, which held my purse, to pay the driver since Peter had once more conveniently forgotten he should be responsible for such things.

"I can walk," I insisted, shooing away his hand and passing the cabbie the fare. Our honeymoon had officially ended, though I may wager it was over before it began. We'd been bickering most of the trip, and my nerves were at an end.

"Mrs. Rodd," he contended, "isn't this what they do in the storybooks? The handsome groom carries his bride over the threshold?"

I sighed and took his outstretched hand. Peter had a way of smoothing prickles. I could almost pretend there had been nothing sour in Rome.

Also, I was glad not to walk. My ankle still smarted from getting the heel of my shoe caught in a cobble in Italy, and then pretending all was well as Peter dragged me from one major or minor basilica to the next, lecturing all the way. Besides, I was still weak from the stomach upset I'd endured throughout our trip.

Nevertheless, a happy bride was I.

Lifted into his arms, I squealed and clutched my cloche hat.

"Oh, do stop a minute. Our own house." I wrapped my arms around his shoulders, giving a little squeeze.

"Not as grand as someone else might have given you."

Peter was referring, as he had on several occasions throughout our honeymoon when I complained of my pinching shoes, that he was not Hugh Smiley—who had laid his gingerbread house and gobs of money at my feet and I'd rejected thrice. So once more I found myself consoling Peter, who suffered from fits of jealousy.

Oh, the tedium of being a wife!

"This life is all I have ever wanted." I kissed his smooth cheek, then tipped my head to the sky. There weren't as many stars here as in Rome, and there was the scent of snow on the air.

I drew in a deep breath, taking in the view of our cozy cottage. Starting tomorrow I would begin my life as a housewife.

Rose Cottage, our little abode at Strand-on-the-Green in Chiswick, had a panorama facing the infamous river Thames. It was rather modest in size, the pink bricks warm, and the large first- and second-story picture windows faced the river, affording a magnificent view. The cottage was not sizable, nor elegant, but it was ours, and it was so very fine.

A house of my own. No sisters or brother underfoot. No Muv or Farve telling me what to do. I was mistress of this place, and it could have been as diminutive as a hatbox for all I cared.

From the doorstep, the view was spectacular, reminding me so much of the country with its walled garden of roses and the gentle sound of lapping water. Hard to believe that at some point in history it had been a smuggler's cottage, where runners hid from the law with their contraband. The quirkiness in that appealed to me greatly.

A mere eight miles from the center of London's bustling, busy and belching stink. We could go to the city if we wanted, or remain here in relative, peaceful quiet, without the prying eyes of those who wrote about us in the papers. Our eccentricities and the company we kept were so exciting to everyone for some reason.

Here, we'd be alone, save for the few neighbors lining the Thames, who though a smidge too close for comfort were hidden with the walled garden. Standing in the fading sun as we were, Rose Cottage felt much more private than even the Cotswolds in the country. I could almost pretend I was back at Batsford Park, my favorite childhood home. A pity Farve sold it, and so many of our other residences, for economic reasons.

Peter carried me over the threshold in a most dashing manner, and I gasped with happy laughter. In the days he'd waxed on about tollgates or Roman war strategy and other such things that made him too dull for words, I'd forgotten his propensity for romantic gestures.

The reception area of our cottage opened to the dining room and kitchen. Diana's wedding gift to us, an elegant Jacobean mahogany table and matching chairs with gold silk upholstered seats, sat prominently in the dining room. The gold-rimmed porcelain china set we'd received as a wedding present had been laid out with the linen napkins embroidered with our monogram folded neatly in the center on table. The aroma of stewing meat and onions reminded me of how long it had been since I'd eaten last.

Footsteps sounded from the back of the house reminding us we were not alone.

I hastily scrambled for Peter to put me down, smoothing out my cream wool jersey skirt, which had ridden past my knees. Though we'd only a modest income between us—poor by both the standards of our friends and family—with Peter's upcoming job at the bank, my writing, and allowances from our parents, we'd live comfortably. We'd even managed to hire a single servant—and I'd taken a play from my mother's book, hiring an experienced female housekeeper. Gladys Bruce was a sturdy woman with a kind smile and soulful brown eyes that missed nothing. Half Jamaican and half British, she'd been eager to join my household after the death of her father sent her mother back to the island—and Gladys wanted to remain in London. She'd been recommended as not only meticulous, but discreet as well.

She greeted us with two glasses of champagne and a knowing smile.

"Welcome home, Mr. and Mrs. Rodd. Your dinner is nearly ready. Should you like to rest your feet in the drawing room, I've started a fire."

"That sounds delightful, thank you, Gladys." There was nothing so good as champagne bubbles on your tongue.

"*You* are delightful." Peter led me through the house to the drawing room, all charm.

I plunked down on the sofa, longing to kick off my shoes and curl them beneath me, but instead, sat straight, legs crossed, and contemplated what color paint would be perfect for the walls.

The three-hundred-year-old fireplace crackled, emitting the

comforting scent of wood smoke, mingling with a home-cooked meal. Oh, what a perfect place to read. I had a sudden moment's nostalgia for the barn at Asthall Manor Farve, converted into a library.

Peter rested his glass on the chimneypiece and turned to face me, looking rather drawn and serious. After weeks in Rome, I saw now why my father said: *Peter talks like a ferret with his mouth sewn up.* I bit my lip, trying not to laugh. *Poor Peter!* He was blissfully unaware; I hoped to keep it that way.

I grinned back at him over my champagne as a happy wife should, putting aside the nagging ire wishing to break free.

"What is it, darling?" I asked.

"I will begin my position at the bank tomorrow." He slid his fingers over his lapel as if preparing for how he would straighten his jacket when he woke.

"You will be brilliant." I had no real inkling of this. If I were to examine his previous states of employ, I'd be inclined to think it was quite the opposite. In essence, Peter had never been able to hold a job, for reasons I didn't know. But he'd made overtures to Farve that being married changed things.

Certainly, his family made similar arguments, even going so far as to agree on an installment well below what would be necessary to live in consideration of his occupation.

"Indeed." He drained his champagne and walked to the Queen Victoria cellaret that belonged to my grandfather to pour himself a healthy dose of brandy. "Shall I pour you a glass?"

"No, thank you, darling." I lifted my half glass of champagne.

"Suit yourself." Peter turned back to me and took a rather long sip of his brandy. "I should like to invite my boss and his wife to dinner, as a thank-you for hiring me."

"I'll prepare a menu." I immediately began mentally running down the most popular items that Muv used to make when we had guests. Lettuce and pea soup, perhaps a smoked haddock *à la crème*, or maybe celery soup followed by *boeuf braisé*, and instead of pudding we'd have ice cream. French wine and—

"No, no," Peter mused. "I think the Ritz is a better idea."

Oh, how unfair!

A meal there for four would cost a week's wages or more if Peter tossed in a bottle of their finest, which he most assuredly would. I'd hoped his reckless abandon for spending in Rome was merely the excitement of being newly wed, but clearly that wasn't the case.

"Darling." I set down my glass upon the side table, folding my hands in my lap, hoping for demure, as I put my foot down. Not for the first time since exchanging vows. "Do admit, a fine dinner here would be more intimate and welcoming. And perhaps your boss would believe an invitation to your residence more modest of someone in his employ."

Peter scoffed, narrowing his eyes at me as if I'd snatched the last of his pudding. "I plan to make a name for myself at the bank, Nancy. Modesty is the last thing I need to show if I'm to prove myself capable."

Showing off with pretentious overtures one could not afford was not a way to prove oneself capable of success either, but I kept to myself such criticism.

Not that any of it mattered when the following morning, Peter was late for his first day.

I hoped it wasn't indicative of the future of his career and our financial stability, though I had my doubts.

 ## Chapter Four

Lucy

THE THREE-HOUR DRIVE TO Derbyshire country with Oliver was pleasant, especially as the bustle of London gave way to more rural landscapes of patchwork hills and cottages nestled in dales. Along the winding country roads, they passed crumbling ruins, ancient forests and grand estates. They talked mostly of books and which were their favorites. Besides *The Pursuit of Love*, Lucy admitted a deep attachment to both *Frankenstein* and *Pride and Prejudice*. Oliver remarked, with a raised eyebrow, how summarily different they were. But Lucy argued not at all, because both inflicted a deep emotional toll upon their readers.

"What about you, then, Oliver?"

"I'm a fan of Orwell. Particularly, *1984*. Partly, I'll admit, because I'm fascinated at his writing the book on a remote isle in Scotland while sick with tuberculosis, and partly because the book makes him seem a bit of a psychic."

The car approached gilded wrought-iron gates flanked by two gatehouses, and Lucy sat up straighter. Imagining in a flash when men in armor might have protected them. As the car rolled to a stop, a guard stepped out, glanced at Oliver, then pressed a button and the gates swung open.

Oliver rolled down his window to wave *thank you* to the guard as they moved through.

A moment later, Lucy let out a long breath as Chatsworth

came into view. Her pulse sped up, even if a collection of sheep grazing in the grass were utterly unimpressed by the gloriousness behind them.

"And here we are," Oliver said, matter-of-factly, as though they'd arrived at the local Tesco.

To think that people still *lived* in places like this. The stone edifice was beautifully carved with wide columns etched into the face. Long gold-leaf-edged windows stacked across the front, sun glinting off the glass. A show of tremendous wealth from a time when windows were taxed. The outer edges of the roof were lined with grand palisades, topped with sculptures of figures she didn't recognize.

She'd expected to see a number of cars as they parked, given the house sold daily tour tickets, but they were alone.

As if sensing her confusion, Oliver said, "They are closed to the public today, but I got us special permission. Thought it would be more fun for you to see it without a gaggle of tourists."

How thoughtful. Lucy's heart leapt. "Fantastic."

As they climbed out of the Volkswagen, a man in black livery stepped out of the house.

"Mr. Pratt." He gave a slight wave to Oliver.

"Boswell! Good to see you," Oliver called back with an obvious familiarity.

"And Miss St. Clair, I presume." Boswell held the door for them. "Welcome to Chatsworth House."

"Thank you." Lucy was unsure if she should try to shake his hand.

Boswell solved the issue for her by stepping back and beckoning them into the house.

"Mr. Pratt will serve as your guide, Miss," Boswell said, "but should you need my assistance, I am merely a bell away. And of course, the library gallery is open for your perusal."

Oliver leaned in as if telling her a secret. "We get to go where the public does not"—she almost expected him to wink—"and you'll get to climb the secret staircase."

Lucy flashed a brilliant smile. This was the sort of adventure a bibliophile dreamed of, and certainly, given the Mitford materials she hoped to peruse, more than either she or her mother could have imagined when they'd talked of discovering the identity of Iris.

While she was at Chatsworth on her own quest, the tour of the house would not be without benefit to her client. Tucked into her purse was a notebook so she could mark down any books in the family library that might make good parallel additions for her assignment.

"Gorgeous, isn't it?" Oliver spread out his arms in the main entrance hall, which offered a set of red-velvet-covered stairs in the center, thick marble columns and sculpted Roman figures.

The wall to the right of the stairs boasted a granite fireplace with a gilded framed painting of what looked like a goddess in a grove surrounded by nymphs. On the left wall, a matching fireplace was topped with a centuries-old market scene. The ceiling yielded yet another impressive piece of art. The only thing marring the notable space was the ticket desk, topped with plastic holders filled with brochures—a stark reminder that Chatsworth was also a museum.

"Shall we start in the library?" It wasn't really a question, and Oliver's chuckle said he knew as much.

"Yes! And if we see nothing else, I won't mind. I'm afraid I'll not have enough time to see every book as it is."

Oliver motioned for her to follow him. "Given there are over thirty-five thousand in the house, I'm afraid you're right. But there are some you mustn't miss, like Henry VII's prayer book and the Duchess Georgiana's 'The Passage of the Mountain of St Gothard.'"

Lucy took everything around her in as they walked. So much so that she nearly trod on Oliver's heels when he came to a stop.

"The Painted Hall," he said with a gesture.

It was enormous—shining white marble floors beneath, and above . . . Turning in a circle, she took in the upper walls and ceiling, both covered in fantastic and oversized images from the life of Julius Caesar. Busts of Roman figures rested on pedestals, and a dozen feet up on the four corners of the hall were golden balconies. Lucy imagined the Devonshires of the past standing there and peering down at their guests for a fancy-dress ball.

She followed Oliver, climbing the grand staircase flanked by an ornately carved gilded balustrade and passed through the immense stone archway carved with foliage into the Grotto, where Lucy stilled. Perched before her was a sculpture she remembered quite well from the *Pride and Prejudice* movie starring Keira Knightley. Seeing it in person, Lucy found it a little harder to breathe.

The veiled Vestal Virgin. Sitting on her knees with a bowl of fire held in her hands, she looked serene and peaceful. What was most fascinating, however, was that the folds of the veil over her face looked so fine they could have been made from tulle rather than marble. Lucy had to resist the urge to reach out and run her fingers over the smooth white stone.

"Amazing, right? The sculpture is actually created from four separate pieces, though it looks to be seamless," Oliver said.

"It's incredible."

"The late duchess often teased she put the Virgin here as a reminder to have a good and pure heart after being teased so mercilessly by her sisters. Nancy Mitford was the biggest teaser of them all."

As they passed through the house, Oliver pointed out various pieces of art.

"How many brilliant minds have walked in these very halls," she mused.

"Thousands," Oliver replied. "In fact, if we continued down that way, we'd reach the Mary Queen of Scots apartments where she was held prisoner for a time. Though the rooms have since been renovated."

They passed through a gallery of artwork, and again Lucy found herself stopping before a beautiful painting of a woman, white gown fluttering, who looked to be coming down from the sky, like an angel.

"That's Duchess Georgiana." Oliver stood beside her, arms crossed.

"She was beautiful."

"And scandalous," Oliver chuckled. "Rumor has it she and her husband lived with her best friend—as their lover. When she died, he married the woman."

At last they reached the two-story library. There was a glorious wall of floor-to-ceiling windows flanked by books, while the others were books in their entirety, including a gallery level. Ornate sofas and chairs were placed throughout the room, beside tables displaying small sculptures, opened books and manuscripts. There was a grand piano with music set out as if someone had only just left their seat. But the focus of the room was clearly books, and to protect the sacred contents, the lighting was dim, provided by vintage chandeliers harkening to the early days of electricity, with lamps perched on tables and desks. The lingering scents of leather and paper were everywhere.

A woman, perched on a wooden ladder, holding a book and dusting it from the spine out toward the pages, offered Lucy a smile. How many books could she clean a day? With thirty-five thousand volumes in residence, it had to be an endless job—finished in time to start again.

"This is *wondair*." Lucy murmured the Mitford idiom with a smile as she strode to the center of the space, gaze roving from the yawning fireplace, across the myriad of towering bookcases. She'd been in some fantastic libraries in the United States—perks of the job—but never had she been inside one with such a stunning amount of storied history.

"How many of these books do you think the current duke has read?" she asked.

"Over his lifetime? I have no idea," Oliver replied with a half shrug. "If I lived here I'd never leave this room, not even to sleep."

Lucy nodded in bibliophilic agreement, then set her purse down on a cushioned chair. "Can I take pictures?"

Oliver nodded.

She tried to capture it all: a panorama of the entire room, shots of the ceiling, the fireplace and of course the massive shelves.

"Where are the secret stairs?" she asked.

Oliver led her toward a shelf. "Some of these are fake titles," he said, pointing out the volumes. "Like this one."

"*Inigo, On Secret Entrances*," Lucy read with a smile. "Whoever installed this secret door had a wonderful sense of humor."

Some of the other obviously fake titles were equally comedic: Abel N. Willing, *Consenting Adults*; Aygood-Mausser, *Minor Rodents*. Lucy laughed to herself then turned her mind to searching for titles or authors mentioning Iris—she had not forgotten her more personal reason for being in the library. No luck.

"Ready?" Oliver asked.

When Lucy nodded, he twisted an old-looking key that stuck out from between two books, and the whole case swung open, revealing a circular stone staircase. He gestured for Lucy to go first, and she climbed as eagerly as child in a candy shop, emerging onto the gallery overlooking the library. Snapping a few photos, she turned to let her eyes wander over the various leather-bound volumes with gilded titles. Dickens, Austen, Shakespeare, Voltaire—the great and famous were there, but so were the lesser known. There were editions in Latin, French, Italian. The fiction and poetry titles were greatly outnumbered by volumes of political writings, histories, mathematics, botany, science. A veritable university treasure trove of anything a person might choose to read or learn about.

Then there was the Mitford collection . . . at least that was how Lucy thought of it as she stood looking at the shelf. It would seem most of the Mitfords had tried their hand at writing. Nancy's sister Deborah, late Duchess of Devonshire, had penned a book about Chatsworth, as well as a cookbook, and two memoirs. There were books by Jessica and Diana too, and an older volume by their grandfather on their father's side titled *Tales of Japan*. Bound copies of the magazines *The Lady* and *Vanity Fair*, that Nancy's writing appeared in, sat beside original volumes of Nancy's books. Lucy picked up each in turn, looking for written inscriptions, but found none.

The next few hours were all about books. Lucy focused first on compiling ideas for her project, but found herself every so often straying with thoughts of Iris. In the end, she made a deal with herself. Every twenty minutes of work was rewarded with skimming through some of the Mitford collection for clues. So far, she'd discovered that Nancy had an aunt named Iris, but she was fairly certain this was not the same person, for in the inscription Nancy had specifically mentioned a *friend*.

Then Oliver looked up from a large book about birds and said, "Lunch in the café?"

Lucy agreed, and they wandered down to the stable courtyard, where a café occupied a converted carriage house. It smelled delicious, and Lucy opted for a chicken-and-mushroom pie.

As they reentered the library after lunch, Oliver asked, "Would you like to see something special?"

"Yes," Lucy replied eagerly.

Oliver led her to an antechamber off the main library and steered her to a glass-topped display table full of handwritten notes and books.

"Are those original letters?" Lucy peered down in fascination.

Oliver nodded and unlocked the case and the double-doored cabinet supporting the glass top. "And original volumes. There are more underneath."

For the next two hours, Lucy pored over letters passed between the Mitford sisters. She felt twinges of nostalgia for her younger sister and only sibling, Maya, whom she rarely saw, given she lived on the other side of the US. But mostly, she was sucked into the lives and relationships of the Mitford women.

They offered vivid details of their lives, and Lucy began to adjust to their period and personal lingo, except for a few things written in a language of their own making—which reminded her when she and sister used to speak in pig Latin to each other. As the letters moved forward, the women matured, each coming alive in Lucy's mind.

Still no specific mention of anyone named Iris.

Lucy paused in her perusal of the letters, turning to the photo albums. They spanned years, from awkward childhood pictures to confident, glamorous adult poses. The six sisters were incredibly beautiful, and their brother, Tom, dashing. The occasional serious or haughty looks couldn't disguise the often laughing eyes. Lucy got the sense that in some of the more formal shots they were working to conform to what was expected, and barely succeeding in containing the explosive personalities revealed in their letters. Their parents, David and Sydney, made occasional photographic appearances—still striking, if in a more composed and mature way. Leafing through the albums it seemed no wonder the entire family had occupied the society pages, noted for their accomplishments, scandals and beauty.

Nancy, with her dark curls and eyes that were described as green and that seemed to sparkle even in sepia-toned photos, stood out from her lighter-haired siblings.

What would it be like to be standing with them? *To know their secrets?* To be in Nancy's confidence? It was said they'd shocked much of society. But somehow, Lucy thought she'd be on the Mitford side of things. Well, Nancy's, anyway.

Looking back at one of the first letters she'd read, Lucy marveled about the reference to Hamish there . . . Nancy mentioned, with confidence, she expected to be soon engaged to him. Yet

Nancy had married someone entirely different. She paged through another binder of letters scanning for the name again. *Yes!* In a letter to Nancy from her sister Diana. Diana made some rather biting remarks about Nancy's beau—and they appeared to be well-earned. *Hamish St. Clair-Erskine.* Lucy grinned. He was her great-great-uncle. A connection her mother had spoken of a few times as she'd grown up. Seeing it there in writing seemed to make it all the more real.

It was too bad that through all the perusing she'd yet to come upon anything that satisfied her curiosity about Iris.

"I hate to break into your personal time." Oliver startled her from behind, causing her to jump a little.

"It's all right." Lucy's face heated.

"Time to wrap up and head to the inn. Never fear, Boswell will be ready for us bright and early in the morning, for you to return to your perusing, but, alas, we'll have to head back to London after lunch tomorrow."

"Thank you for arranging this; it really has been amazing."

"Always happy to help a fellow book lover."

Lucy carefully replaced the letters, making a note of which volume she was on so in the morning she could pick up where she'd left off.

A few hours later, Lucy fell into the soft bed at the inn, listening to the gentle rain falling. She thought about the Mitford sisters, and how they'd seemed so close even in the face of misunderstandings and downright despising one another's views.

As had become her nightly ritual, she pulled another letter from the package, her thumb rubbing over the script on the front addressed to Nancy's sister Diana. She caught the faintest scent of lilies, and wondered if her mother was there with her, patiently encouraging her to open the letter.

Darling Diana,

Are you ready to meet E.U.G.E.N.I.A.? And better yet, Captain Jack, who you may find yourself falling in love with given the Leaderteases I've conjured. Poor Leader, what's he to do if you leave him for a character in my new book? Enclosed are a few chapters, and I am dying for you to tell me what you think.

Our brother, Tom, is teasing that he might marry Tilly Losch in a double ceremony with the royals if she gets divorced. Can you imagine? Oh, do admit the horror that would be.

Thank you for the lovely present—you are too kind.

Much love, darling,
Nancy

P.S. Do come to Heywood Hill's bookshop Saturday next! I've conjured up quite the guest list for a literary salon.

Chapter Five
Nancy

May 1934

~~Darling Diana,~~

A BUMBLEBEE CRAWLED ON a pink flower petal on the magnolia tree outside my window at Rose Cottage, drunk on nectar, perhaps needing a moment of respite. After a week of rain, there was a break in the clouds, and the sun shone. Blooms burst open in thanks, truly welcoming spring.

I tapped the end of my pencil on the blank piece of paper atop my Sheraton writing desk, a plate of cold scrambled eggs forgotten hours ago on my right, and life passing by outside the great windows of my sitting room. My French bulldogs, Millie and Lottie, lounged lazily on the Aubusson carpet I'd bought secondhand with the help of Mark, waiting for the moment I'd finally take them for a walk.

Beside me, to the left, was a stack of papers and their carbon copies of the first fifteen thousand words of my new book. But this blank, yawning sheet . . . this was to pen a reply to my sister, Diana, in response to her terse correspondence.

Oh, but the bee was infinitely more interesting.

I shuffled Diana's letter into a drawer, not wanting to see the accusation in her words, the desire for me to quit this book. In defiance, I shifted the last paper I'd written on to the center of my desk. Having left off in midscene when the mail arrived, I intended to finish it this afternoon.

A breeze from the Thames blew in from the open window, ruffling the burgundy swaths of curtain. The grass, branches and flowers outside waved, as if beckoning me to abandon my desk. To take a walk. To pretend I wasn't doing what desperately needed doing.

Peter and I were broke.

Which I refused to believe demoted us from the ranks of aristocracy in which we'd both been born. While the notion of us working horrified our friends and family, we needed every pound.

I contemplated having to cut Gladys's hours by half, but feared we'd lose her altogether as her position was the reason she'd stayed in London. So I found a friend in need of a part-time housekeeper, and Gladys had been gracious to split the time between both residences. Now she came in the mornings to clean, wash and press, run errands and then help me to prepare dinner, of which I was a miserable student. By the time I settled in to write at noon, she'd left. Which was all well and good because the bell typically rang then, as if unwanted guests waited until I was alone.

At any moment I expected a knock at the door, another bailiff come to collect on Peter's debts. Would they accept my cup of tea today instead?

We *needed* me to write this book. Yet my family needed me *not* to, afraid of the backlash on themselves. Every day was an effort to write. This book in particular had been a trial on my patience. The words poured from my brain in either manic bursts or as slow and lethargic as Millie rolling onto her back for a belly scratch.

Diana's words came back to me. *You cannot write this book unless you pose to hurt the Leader and myself. This is not the same as "Two Old Ladies from Eaton Square." This is our livelihood and it is not a jest.*

The Leader—or the Ogre, as I preferred—had continued to keep my sister on a string as his mistress. Diana would abandon everything, risk anything, for him. That much was clear. What difference did this book make when she'd laughed at my gentle teasing of Mosley as the Little Leader armed with weapons and chocolate laxatives in the "Two Old Ladies From Eaton Square," an ongoing story I'd penned for the two of us when we were living together the previous year?

What had changed other than the increased passion for Mosley's fanaticism? How had he been able to utterly possess Diana's brilliant mind?

Love was an illusion.

I had learned that plenty in the past decade. Loving first Hamish and then Peter. The romances I'd read in Jane Austen's work, the Brontë sisters and poets past were artifice in words. Even I spun tales that would leave readers with an impression of feelings that were illusory.

The very definition of fiction. A spinning and weaving of conjured events and people. Never mind most of mine were based on those people I knew and experiences I'd had. I was paid to spin those tales, to stir emotion. Indeed, love was a misconception, just as was happiness.

There was something freeing about fiction, about fantasy, that there wasn't when I wrote articles. I quite enjoyed living in the depths of my head. In any case, it was much better than keeping house.

I sat back heavily in my chair, chewing the end of my pencil.

The sound of a motor rumbling to a stop outside the garden wall signified an arrival. The way Lottie leapt from her nap and yapped meant it was Peter. Why had he returned so early?

He banged into the house as I came around the corner in time to see him toss his briefcase to the floor and tear off his tweed jacket. I reached for it as he tossed it, and hung it on the rack, noting the heavy scent of smoke.

"What's happened?" I didn't bother with niceties when he was clearly distraught.

"I was promised a raise; now my boss has insulted my assiduous work ethic and claims never to have agreed. The man is deserving of a slap. I will quit before there are wigs on the green," he sputtered, insinuating there'd be a fight. "Not enough sots in the damn building to pull me off the old goat, and I'd rather not be fined for misconduct."

It was on the tip of my tongue to ask if he'd truly gotten near to brawling with his employer, which would blackball him from any other bank in London, but then he knelt to swipe a steady hand over Lottie's wriggling body, and tapped her nose.

"You're going to have to get another book contract." Peter didn't bother to look in my direction. "I can't possibly keep searching for jobs when they won't pay me what I'm worth. Don't they know who I am?"

I feared that was exactly the issue—they knew all too well.

More stunning was his insistence that I be the one to pick up his slack. In what false world did my husband live that he thought it perfectly fine to shirk his duties, lobbing them at me as he had his tweed? Peter had struggled so far with his first job, and it was a miracle, honestly, that he still held it. Not for the first time I wondered at what role his father played. What power did Lord Rennell have to see that his son maintained his position?

I swallowed away the rising bitterness, just as I'd tucked the letter from Diana into my desk. I wanted to ask Peter the same question he'd posed. Didn't he know who *I* was?

Swallowing away bitterness was a lot harder than hiding accusatory words written on paper. Was a woman's place to smooth over her husband's indolence and lack of economical acumen? Farve had his own set of money troubles, and Muv always made do, even selling eggs and chickens in the village to pay for our governesses. I frowned. In that respect, books were my chickens.

That helped smother my resentment.

At least a little.

Instead of admonishing him, I tried smiling and asked if he'd like me to pour him a drink.

"No. I'm going to the club." He waved me off, and started for the back of the house.

A knock sounded at the door. Peter turned, looked at me accusatorially as if to ask who might be coming round. If there were going to be any straying eyes in Rose Cottage, they belonged to my husband.

"Might be your admirers, the bailiffs," I quipped, gaze steady on my husband who didn't care on any given day for the stack of bills piling up or those demanding payment. Nor for the humiliation I endured when they doffed their caps and stared at me with pity.

How he hoped to pay for another bout of drinking was a good

question. As it was, the only way I'd been able to stave off the bailiffs with their last visit was a quiet slip of a few pounds from Peter's father. Lord Rennell was a lifesaver sometimes, but the man would not live forever, and then his fortune would go to Peter's older brother Francis. Likely Peter's allowance, which barely paid for the gas in the motorcar, let alone the lamps in the house, would end there.

"Being a nag is not very becoming," Peter sniped back.

"Neither is a husband who cannot care for his wife."

I walked past Peter to put the kettle on, giving him the onus of answering the door.

If only it weren't a wife's duty to sweep her husband's nature under a rug and present to the world a prettier portrait.

As water filled the kettle, his earlier words rang back to me. *Wigs on the Green*. A possibly wonderful title for the book I was working on. Boy, wasn't Peter great inspiration for the character Jasper Aspect . . .

Dearest Mark,

I never imagined the expense of running one's own household. I've never had such responsibilities before, and it gives me a renewed respect for Muv, which I'll never tell her, of course.

Peter and I have had to scrimp and save in order to throw a bridge party, of all things. I delight in being a host, and am very much looking forward to the chance to have all of our friends over under our roof—you of course will come, won't you?

I'm looking forward to a night of pleasure and leisure—without the bickering that comes between a husband and wife when going over accounts. I won't bore you with those miserable details.

Instead, let us reminisce on the old days when we used to race through the streets of London on a scavenger hunt, and then loll away the rest of the night at one of our friend's houses. Or take off in the morning in a motorcade bound for the country, where someone's parents would begrudgingly allow us a weeklong house party.

I long for those days now as much as I longed to be a wife back then.

All my love,
Nancy

A rhythmic urgency played from the gramophone, sending a wave of swaying cheer through Rose Cottage, jammed with people. Tables and chairs borrowed from guests had been set up in the reception hall, the sitting room and bedrooms. Glasses clinked, people laughed.

I stood, having presented the highest trump trick at the table, and headed down the stairs to mingle, when Peter cornered me on the landing. He had a look on his face I'd only seen occasionally since we wed. One that promised sinful flirtation. How many glasses of brandy had he sucked down?

He made a pretty picture with his blond hair tousled, blue eyes locked on mine, a lopsided confident grin. I'd not seen a man who could cut a better figure than Peter in trousers and a trellis-patterned pullover. Casual yet elegant.

"I've a jest for you, my darling wife, just told downstairs by one of the chaps."

His fingers danced over my arm, and some of the ice chipped away from my heart. "I love a good joke," I said.

He smiled, and I couldn't help returning a smile, a giddy, girlish excitement curling inside me.

Peter leaned against the wall, one ankle crossed over the other, his fingers still tracing circles near my elbow. "I know, which is why I had to find you straightaway. Are you prepared to laugh?"

I nodded, praying no one came around the corner. I wanted this moment, so fleeting, to last forever. "I should hope I am prepared to laugh at any given moment."

"Then I shall tell you about the man held up by the police."

"Was it you?"

Peter feigned a pout. "Oh, do be sorry for me," he teased, then let out a laugh. "I got it wrong. We'll start over, and this time you say *no*." By now his words were slurring a little, but his mood was light, and I so wanted this to be funny.

I rolled my eyes. "All right."

"Do you know about the man who was held up by the police?" he asked.

"No," I said with mock astonishment, my hand fluttering to my chest. "Do tell me more."

"They told him, anything you say will be held against you." He pressed his finger to my lips before I could reply. "The man asked: 'Anything I say will be held against me?' The police said yes." Peter stepped closer, the laugh gone from his lips, taken over by a look that made my blood hum. "And the man said, 'Right you are, sir,' and then: 'Mrs. Nancy Rodd.'"

The punch line of the joke made me giggle, to think of a man asking for me to be held up against him, but Peter's mouth quieted the sound while he kissed me. I sighed into him, thoughts of illusion fading into reality.

Oh, how I longed for this moment to last. The intimacy of our marriage had come in fits and starts, a bewildering physical affair that oft left me wondering if I'd missed it. There had to be more. Something that his kiss promised, but that Peter failed to deliver, not unlike most things with my husband. He was a constant project starter, but not a finisher. Just once . . .

Footsteps on the stairs pulled us apart. It simply wouldn't do to be seen in such a position, even if he was my husband. We passed friends as we made our way down. In the reception room, a round of applause sounded at our entry.

"Your Peter has cleaned us out," said Mark, standing up from the table.

I shot a look at Peter. "You were playing for money?"

He raised his arms in a noncommittal gesture, and a guilty smile as though I'd caught him with his hand in the till. The same look I'd see when he pulled money from my purse. "High stakes make the game more fun."

Thank goodness he'd won, else we'd have been begging for scraps at Rutland Gate, my parents' house in London.

"Dance with me, for old times' sake," Mark said, when Peter took a seat for another round.

I allowed him to pull me into his arms as another punchy song played over the gramophone. Several other guests joined us, and I fell into the familiar comfort of my dear friend. Mark had helped me decorate Rose Cottage, to give this house a bit of Nancy flair. He also kept me calm when everything around me felt as if it might burst into flames and melt away to ash.

My determination to make this marriage work was exhausting, and yet so very important.

"How are you?" Mark murmured.

"Why, my dear old boy, I have found a promissory note for bliss I intend to cash in if I can find where I put it, and I daresay I'm a fine housewife when our housekeeper is in attendance," I teased.

Mark snickered. "To be sure, my dear old lady, you are the picture of absolute happiness."

"Then I have succeeded."

"Oh, what has Prod gotten up to now?" he teased, using the name my family had given to my husband before we'd wed, a combination of Peter and Rodd. "I cannot wait to read about it." Mark winked, having picked up on the none-too-subtle hints of my discontent.

"Soon you shall."

When the music ended, Diana and Mosley approached with Peter. "Naunce, darling, you and Rodd simply must come to Oswald's rally in Olympia. It is going to be the pinnacle of the BUF movement. We're expecting nearly ten thousand."

It was on the tip of my tongue to decline when Peter spoke up. "Sounds like a jolly old time."

Diana eyed him coolly. Mosley slapped him on the back in the way of old friends and returned him to the tables.

Why had Peter agreed? We'd had conversations about our ideals, and none of them aligned with Fascism.

I supposed it would be good research for *Wigs on the Green* to see Fascism alive and bullying. I'd not been to a rally since the year previous that Peter and I attended, which cemented in us all the more our own political views, which were decidedly not so fanatical and in clear opposition. I had the feeling Mosley hoped to one day be Britain's Hitler, and one was already too much. For a time, it appeared the majority of England felt the same way. Over the months since that rally, there'd been a subtle shift in not only the country, but my family as well.

Unity resided in Germany with several other young ladies, learning the language with aspirations of meeting Hitler, befriending men in his ranks, and Diana was still the lover of Mosley, which had become so widely accepted it wasn't really taboo to have them here together at the party. Even my brother, Tom, was leaning Fascist. Muv too. Farve held out, going so far as to admonish Diana for having taken Unity to Germany the year before for the rally. Furious he'd been at that turn of events, and yet he'd agreed for her to go and live in the dreadful country, which was puzzling.

"I'll buy your black shirts," Diana said as she kissed my cheek that night when they left, referring to the uniform of the BUF members.

The idea of wearing black was ironic, for to me it meant mourning, perhaps grieving the death of my ideals should I ever side with my sister's politics. Not to wear them would make us stand out unnecessarily. "No, please, we can do that ourselves."

"A gift," she said.

I smiled tightly, remembering Diana had a two-thousand-a-year settlement from Bryan, easily four times what we had. "Thank you."

True to her word, the following morning a parcel arrived, holding within it two black shirts and two BUF pins. Placing them on my dressing table, I stared at them for what felt like hours. Peter and I had only spoken briefly after our party about attending, and he thought it a great joke. I suppose I could look at it that way too. The black shirts were hideous, and one could only see them as silly.

When Peter arrived at the cottage from work that evening, I wore my shirt and a teasing smile as I handed him a glass of brandy.

"What do you think?" I asked, spinning in a slow circle. "Do I look as though my morals are corrupt?"

Peter let out a low whistle, and pulled me in for a dance. "You look positively criminal."

"Try yours on. Gladys ironed it."

When he emerged wearing the shirt, I too let out an appreciative whistle. "Why, Mr. Rodd, you look dashing in black. Should I check you for weapons, or perhaps you have a signed portrait of Hitler in your back pocket?"

"Do I look as self-important as the Leader?" he jested.

"More so, for I find you a hundred times handsomer. But I must say I'd rather see you out of it."

"Would you leave your husband for me?" he asked.

"Blessings for me I don't have to make that choice, for I'm the lucky duck who's wed you."

We changed back into our regular clothes, and I eyed his broad back before it disappeared beneath his cotton shirt, wanting to run my fingers over his skin, the way I imagined a lover might. To kiss the center of his spine and breathe in his familiar scent. When Peter lay with me, it was sweet yet perfunctory, and swiftly at an end.

Married half a year, and no results. It was just as well; a baby would only be one more mouth to feed. We couldn't afford a nanny either.

Instead, I turned away, tightening the belt at my waist. "Dinner is ready."

"I'm starved," Peter said enthusiastically, and I wondered how that could be, considering the bill I'd received from his having lunched at his club nearly every day this month.

Reminding myself to be the happy homemaker, I pushed his transgressions from my mind and, with a smile, served the dinner Gladys had helped me to prepare of leek soup and cottage pie.

Peter poured me a glass of wine, and when I sat, he took my hand in his and brought it to his lips, kissing the back. "We're going to be all right," he said, in answer to a question I never asked, but thought nearly every moment of every day.

For, truly, how would we keep getting on like this?

Darling Evelyn,

You asked me to tell you about the rally, and so prepare yourself for the horror of which I am about to fill you . . .

The crowd in Olympia was a bloated mass of humans from all walks of life, most of which wore the same dull black shirt Peter and I had teased each other about relentlessly, finding a common ground in the way fanaticism had somehow brainwashed intelligent people into joining the ranks of absurdity. Do admit, you would have commented on the banal fashion.

Anyways, there was a bit of that fervor in Peter, which gave me a fright. He looked on Mosley with something close to admiration—a stark change. I was tempted to knock him over the head with my purse. He even attempted to join in the Fascist song of "Britain, Awake!" I couldn't decide if it was all for show or if Peter had somehow fallen for Mosley's charm. I daresay, charm *is a word I most certainly would not use in the same sentence with that ogre.*

So, with the trumpeting fanfare and cheers from the crowd, everyone welcomed their Leader. Mesmerized in almost the same way one might slow to watch an accident about to happen, or an argument escalating in the street. Eyes wide, gawking, one cannot look away. Dozens of Blackshirt standard-bearers marched toward the rostrum, Mosley proudly straight-backed behind them, waving to the crowd as though he were the king. If I were Diana I would have been mortified, but she smiled on like he was God's gift to her.

The stadium at Olympia was filled with an incredible number of influential people, along with thousands of boots-on-the-ground members. Diplomats, businessmen, members of the aristocracy, journalists stood side by side with farmers, merchants, laborers.

I tell you, it was the stuff of nightmares. If you don't believe me, try one for yourself—I warn you, though, do not wear red.

Love from,
Nancy

Diana stood beside me, doe-eyed, watching her lover approach the rostrum as though he were a god, his disciples proclaiming their fealty loudly behind him.

When the ballyhoo died down, Mosley started to speak.

From somewhere in the crowd, a man wearing a red shirt

shouted, "Fascism is murder! Down with Fascism! Down with Mosley!"

"Damn Jew Communists have come to crash the party; they'll not get away with it," said the man on the other side of Peter.

I shouldn't have been stunned by his anti-Semitic bias, yet I was. To hear it spat so violently, so close to my ear. I opened my mouth to say something when Peter shook his head. The room exploded with shouts from other BUF members, in reaction to cries of "Down with Mosley." A mass argument in a sea of black and red.

Mosley started again, asking for order, only to be interrupted. Over and over this happened, and each time he paused, eyes on Diana, waiting as a patient father would while his wayward child was dealt with. Blackshirt guards quickly seized upon the protestors, but as soon as they did, others spread throughout the crowd repeated his mantra, causing more disruption—and the signal for more Blackshirt guards to react.

Fisticuffs broke out from all angles, causing the people surrounding us to shuffle, an elbow to be thrust into Peter's ribs, and he shoved back. I feared a riot.

The Blackshirts were swift in their brutal domination. Some of the protestors were dragged limp and bleeding from the stadium, while others fought their way out to the end. My entire body trembled with fear. All the while Mosley stood with an almost gleeful glint in his eyes, as if he'd wanted this to happen. Wanted the protestors to be trampled, to show his might, his power.

I stared at Peter wide-eyed to see such violence at a political rally. My eye was caught too by a shouting Esmond Romilly, my young, naïve Communist cousin, calling Mosley a pig from a row near the front. Diana and Mosley seemed oblivious. As if the brutalization of those who would protest his politics was normalized.

My stomach twisted, and every bit of me longed to flee. However, to get up and leave would not only alienate my sister, but also possibly cause me some harm from the brutes ready with knuckle-dusters.

Discreetly I reached for Peter's hand, clutching it in mine, relieved when he didn't pull away, but held on just as tightly.

Hundreds of protestors were taken out covered in blood. Every single one did not earn a glance from Diana. She'd grown so used to violence, but how could she condone it?

There would be repercussions if I wrote this in my book. What would be the repercussions if I didn't?

The protestors, Communists if our neighboring BUF member could be believed, were against Fascism, and to shout about it was their right, as it was every Fascist's right to shout about socialism. But drawing blood seemed a step too far.

If men were to lower themselves to such base and degrading antics, the House of Lords would be a madhouse, with every man against a bill bloodied. His wig torn off as he was hauled from his green bench. *Wigs on the Green* took on another meaning then, one very political. My mouth went dry.

I feared England would become another Germany. Attending the rally had been a terrible idea.

I shuddered, and Peter squeezed my hand.

"We shall be victorious," Mosley shouted from the podium. "Or at least we shall return upon our shields."

We declined to join Diana and the Leader for victory drinks, claiming I had a headache. When we arrived at our quiet, peaceful cottage, we tore off our black shirts, tossing them in a heap in the corner. I clung to Peter as he made love to me, more tenderly than he had ever before. Desperate to feel his skin on mine, the comfort of closeness. The safety of being human. For the first time in our marriage, I actually felt as though we were one in mind, body and spirit.

Lying in bed, staring up at the ceiling, I turned to face Peter. "I worry for my sister."

"I worry for anyone who goes against her."

"Maybe I should tell Hamilton I can't finish the book."

"You'd have to return the advance, which we do not have."

I nodded. We had no money. Spent the advance, and desperately needed the royalties it would bring.

The next day, in a complete turnabout, the *Daily Mail* put out a scathing editorial of the Olympia rally. A letter ostensibly addressed to Mosley himself, in which Lord Rothermere, founder of the paper, withdrew his support of the BUF and Mosley, stating, "I have made it quite clear in my conversations with you that I could never support any movement with an anti-Semitic bias, any movement which has dictatorship as one of its objectives . . ."

Still shaken by what we'd witnessed, I fled the house, with Lottie and Millie, taking them on a brisk walk along the Thames. They sniffed through grass, snuffled at flowers, while my brain sifted through what I'd seen.

Two of my sisters had fallen for men bent on dictatorship. Two of my sisters had fallen for men who hated members of the human race simply for the ethnicity that ran in their blood.

When I returned to the cottage, I started a letter to Diana, needing to get my thoughts, concerns down on paper. Needing her to listen. To rethink this path she'd chosen. She was in danger. We all were.

Dearling,

I feel compelled to write and tell you of my fears. I fear for you, for your darling kits. The violence at the rally—

I tore the letter into shreds and tossed it in the trash.

Around three o'clock in the afternoon, a courier knocked at the door, and, expecting it to be a letter of debt, I was surprised to see Peter's father, Lord Rennell's, seal.

The letter was addressed to me, and written in a hurried hand. Somehow he'd found out Peter and I attended the rally in Olympia.

Can you not persuade him to stick to the business in hand and not to advertise himself in these Fascist demonstrations? . . . Things are manifestly taking a wrong direction . . .

I swallowed hard, agreeing with everything in the letter. Both of us knowing it already. But who was to tell Peter anything? Peter did what Peter wanted.

Before Peter arrived at the cottage for dinner, I went to our bedroom to freshen up, only to see the black shirts we'd tossed into the corner had been pressed and hung back in the closet by Gladys. I swiftly closed the door against them.

After finishing our haddock and potatoes, I presented Peter with the letter from his father.

The muscle of his jaw ticked with irritation, and he set it down, staring at me.

"I've no intention of going to another rally," he said. "And I don't need my father's permission if I so choose. Nor do I need yours."

"You wouldn't go out of spite," I said.

"No, not even to rile the old goat."

I nodded slowly, relieved. "Gladys pressed our shirts."

"I'll not wear that rubbish again."

Thank God. "Shall we toss them in the Thames?"

"I've a better idea."

We sat on the soft sofa in our sitting room, sipping brandy, watching the shirts burn beneath the ornate chimneypiece.

"You need to finish your book," Peter said.

Immediately I bristled. "Perhaps you should get a better job," I sniped back.

He let out a long-suffering sigh. "Not because of the money, though we do need it, and what's wrong with a wife keeping her husband?"

I ignored his question. "Why, then?"

"Because people need to see the ridiculousness of Fascism. You've a way of penning tales that come off as light. Your sisters cannot take offense if it's satirical."

That showed how much Peter knew about my family. He was wrong in that we took offense at everything. But he was right because my sisters would eventually forgive me.

Three weeks later, in the middle of the night, Hitler ordered his SS men to murder the SA Nazi leaders and hundreds of his opponents, purging the party of anyone who would go against his leadership. Men were dragged from their beds and shot. In the papers, they were calling it *die Nacht der langen Messer*, the Night of the Long Knives.

Unity wrote a long letter about it, detailing her glee at the murder of Ernst Röhm. Apparently, she'd rushed down to Hitler's Brown House to visit her beau, a Brownshirt lad, and get the news. Muv and our sister Jessica were in Germany for a visit during all this. Farve must have been horrified. I couldn't find the words within me, nor the heart to write the next chapter in my book. Not when there was so much violence happening abroad. Not when my sister wanted to be in the center of it all. Instead, my pen found a home in an article for the *Vanguard*, in which I decried Britain's decaying democracy, mocked Mosley and his Fascism and waited for his Blackshirts to come knocking at my door.

Over tea, at Eaton Square, Diana showed me a letter Unity sent her regarding that long, murderous night. How flippantly she wrote about it, calling it exciting, terrific and horrifying all at once. Expressed her concern for Hitler, and that several of the SA men had been rumored to have killed themselves, when in fact they'd been murdered. Oh, the brainwashing of my sister!

Then came Unity's letter to me. At first it was pleasant, wanting me to throw a party for her when she returned to Swinbrook later in the month, and how she needed to get her dress altered. Then it took the turn I'd been dreading.

Now, seriously, about that book . . . I warn you, you can't possibly publish it, so you'd better not waste any more time on it. Because if you did publish it, I couldn't possibly ever speak to you again . . . Followed by her fury at my article in the *Vanguard*. How she had over three hundred postcards of Hitler she must show me, certain of my delight. Delusions. She left off her letter with a

Heil Hitler, and a postscript of how she'd not fumbled with one of Hitler's men in the SS house because he preferred men. Who was this girl?

Did I still have to throw a party for her?

I thought I might vomit.

Compounding all this was Peter . . . Ever since the rally, he came home later each night. Smelling of liquor and perfume. In the cottage, he walked around in a daze, drinking heavily and claiming a flu in the morning to get out of work. Did he not understand a hangover was not the same as a flu?

Did he not understand I could smell her perfume?

I feared for the state of my marriage.

The following month, Hitler horrifyingly claimed total power of Germany, with the vote of his people. And now I feared for the state of Europe.

Chapter Six
Lucy

OLIVER TOOK THE REST of the day off after their long drive from Chatham back to London, but Lucy headed straight to the bookshop, determined to translate her visit to the magnificent house into an action plan for the Masters' library. Given it was only midafternoon, the shop was still bustling with customers.

In the twenty-four hours that she'd been gone, the shop had been transformed for Halloween. The front window housed a large spider in a silken web with a message about stocking up on chilling reads for All Hallows' Eve. Amidst glittering pumpkins and miniature skeletons dining at a gloomy table were several spooky children's books, bestselling thrillers and creepy classics like Mary Shelley's *Frankenstein*, Shirley Jackson's *The Haunting of Hill House*, Edgar Allan Poe's "The Tell-Tale Heart" and Ira Levin's *Rosemary's Baby*.

Lucy loved the atmosphere—boosted by haunting music. Too bad she wouldn't be here on Halloween. A sign on the register desk explained that every child who came into the store in costume would receive a free treat.

Halloween was a favorite holiday for Lucy. Growing up, she and her sister had loved to coordinate their costumes, outfits usually based on literature. They'd been Glinda and Dorothy from *The Wonderful Wizard of Oz* and Coraline and Other Coraline from Neil Gaiman's novel, and as they grew older, handmaids from Atwood's *The Handmaid's Tale*. But Lucy's favorite looks were probably the year they'd dressed up as Pennywise from *It* and one of his victims. Maya had been the clown, chasing Lucy from house to house.

That reminded her of how Nancy in her letters had mentioned how much she loved to dress in costume and parade around London. What Lucy wouldn't give to go back in time and dress up with Nancy.

Pushing her nostalgia aside, Lucy headed downstairs to her desk. She had dozens of book orders to put in based on her Chatsworth list. An hour later, after entering her information into the database and making preliminary phone calls, Lucy leaned back and rubbed at her eyes. She was exhausted. Not only because she hadn't quite gotten used to the time change, but also because she was working her butt off to prove to Mr. Sloan she had what it took to warrant a promotion—a feat she was fairly certain she was accomplishing with flying colors.

"How was Chatsworth?" Ash arrived at the nearby desk and took a seat.

"Amazing. Could have stayed there another week." Lucy made a note on her list to add some classic horror books to the library project.

"Isn't the library to die for?" Ash leaned closer. "What was on display?"

"Three gorgeous leather-bound first editions of Jane Austen's that would've made a perfect edition to my own personal library."

"You wish." Ash chuckled. "As do I . . . Beyond Austen, what did you find most exciting?"

Barbara and Louisa came back into the office, passing everyone cardboard cups of tea.

"Thank you," Lucy said, breathing in the scent of caramel apple. "I adored the secret staircase, but on a personal level, reading letters that related to Nancy Mitford's ex-fiancé, who I'm distantly related to."

"Hamish?" Ash sipped her tea.

Lucy raised her brows. "You've heard of him?"

Ash laughed. "You can't work at Heywood Hill and not know your Mitford history. Besides, I'm an avid Nancy lover."

"As am I." Lucy was reminded again how much she loved working with people in the book business who were as obsessed as she was about all things literature, including the lives of authors. "Speaking of Nancy, do you know anything about a copy of *The Pursuit of Love* that she might have left here for a friend to pick up?"

Ash's brow wrinkled. "I don't think so. Do you mean something that would still be about the place? If so, you could look through the shelves. But I don't think we have any first-edition Mitfords in storage; they're all out on display."

"No, I know where the book is now—my mother bought it probably two decades ago. We've had it in our home ever since. But apparently, originally, Nancy left it here for a friend."

Ash and Louisa shook their heads.

"You might ask Oliver," Barbara pointed out. "If anyone will know about that, it's him. Or he may at least be able to point you in the right direction."

Lucy was halfway out of her chair, but her cell buzzed. Her boss calling for an update on the library account.

"Well done, Ms. St. Clair; you're well on your way," Mr. Sloan remarked as the call wrapped up about an hour later.

Hanging up the phone, Lucy let out a long, satisfied sigh and smiled.

"Some of us are heading to a pub for dinner, want to come?" Louisa asked, glancing up from her desk to ask.

"Absolutely." Lucy swung her bag over her shoulder and followed a handful of her new British bookworm friends into the crisp autumn air.

📖

ARRIVING EARLY THE next morning, Lucy was on the lookout for Oliver. Spotting him hoisting boxes of newly delivered books, she picked one up. "So, Oliver," she said, following him down the narrow steps. "Do you know anything about a copy of *The Pursuit of Love* that Nancy Mitford apparently left here? My mother purchased the volume years ago, and we've always been intrigued by the inscription inside to a woman named Iris."

Oliver wiped the sweat from his brow. "There was a rumor decades ago about a book that Mitford left for someone that was never picked up. But I always assumed it was a reader. What makes you think it was a friend?"

"It's quite an intimate inscription."

"Ah, so blatant." Oliver nodded knowingly, and opened the first box, handing a stack of books to Lucy and then gesturing for her to follow him to the computer to catalogue the titles.

"I haven't heard of Iris, but my understanding is that Nancy left copies of her work for various friends and readers over the years. She was a staple at the shop even before she worked here."

Lucy nodded, not bothering to hide her disappointment. "Well, it's a mystery I mean to solve. So any help you can give would be much appreciated. I've already pored through letters and articles looking for clues. No luck."

"My pleasure. Nancy was and continues to be a bit of a mystery, doesn't she?"

"Yes." Lucy paused. "She offers so many details about herself in her letters and in her public writings, but do you ever get the feeling that it's all a façade? Or at the very least like she's hiding something? Or maybe hiding *from* something. I mean, she had so many friends—I can't even keep all of their names straight—it's as if she never wanted to have a moment alone. She spent as much time as she could with nearly a hundred different acquaintances, but was she really always laughing, bright and carefree—or was she making sure she never experienced a moment of quiet?"

"Quiet can be tough—alone with one's thoughts. I mean, can you blame her?" he asked with a shake of his head, returning to the box for more books. "With family like that, would you want to be alone with your thoughts and disappointments?"

"Good point." After helping Oliver with the rest of the box—and discovering one of the boxes was full of books she'd ordered for the special project—Lucy wandered to her desk, intent on sending her sister an email, or maybe she'd even call her. The more she dug into Nancy's lonely, and yet not alone, past, the more she found herself needing that sisterly connection.

"I found something you might have an interest in." Oliver approached with a stack of threadbare log books. "These were in the back storage room. Logs from the years that Nancy worked here. She kept notes about nearly everything in here, including the salons she hosted. Maybe you'll find something about Iris."

"Incredible! Thank you." Lucy gathered the books from Oliver and set them on her desk, slowly opening the first one.

Nancy's familiar scrawl stared up at her from the pages. There were notes on books that needed to be ordered for certain customers. Records of books and other items sold. Questions Nancy needed to run past Heywood Hill, such as if they could shorten Sunday hours, and if they could increase the number of French books on hand. There were lists of those who attended various salons, which included the names of literary greats. There were notations on which books should be sent to soldiers overseas.

Then Lucy's eye caught on a note near the end of the record. *Need to hire assistant. Iris?*

The note ended there, and the last pages didn't reveal anything else about Iris, nor whether or not she was hired.

Even though it felt like Lucy had made a discovery, only to be turned back around empty-handed, this was one step in the right direction. Iris was real.

Chapter Seven
Nancy

March 1935

~~Dearest Mark,~~

~~Have you ever been so unhappy you thought you might drown from the weight of your own sorrow?~~

SPRING WAS A TIME of rebirth. Time for the earth to awaken itself from a frozen winter and breathe in great gulps of warming air as foliage brightened from brown to green and bulbs unfurled into dazzling petals.

While nature's great awakening was beautiful, mine was only a disappointment.

Prod and I had celebrated our first-year anniversary before Christmas with a tense dinner at the Ritz, joined by Diana and Mosley and several of our friends. The overpriced but oh-so-decadent meal was followed by a bit too much champagne. So I was relieved when the bill was miraculously paid by an anonymous benefactor. We'd spent the night at Rutland Gate so we didn't have to make the trek back to Rose Cottage. I'd woken with a headache that had me quite understanding Prod's insistence on calling it a morning flu.

The difference was I could brush it off with a mixture of my mother's fabulous elixir—raw eggs, Worcestershire sauce and a sprinkle of pepper—whereas Peter was content to wallow in self-pity.

As our fruitless marriage rolled into its second spring, my own awareness blossomed to encompass many things I'd have happily left in winter. Chief amongst them that my husband was not only a disappointment but a philanderer.

Fascinating what a girl would do on the rebound when pushed.

Where might I be, I wondered, had I said yes to Smiling Hugh? Cuddling the baby he'd fathered with my friend Nancy Beaton, whom he'd married instead, no doubt. Certainly not sitting as I was now at one of four bridge tables in my parents' London town house, watching my husband stare lustfully at another woman. A woman I'd considered a friend. Now I stared daggers at her spoon-faced visage, dressed as though she'd come straight from raiding the auction house's castoffs.

Mary Sewell, married to a stockbroker more boring than Prod, had been sleeping with my husband for weeks, if not months.

We'd come to Rutland Gate to host our party instead of dragging everyone out to Rose Cottage. At least, and rather embarrassingly, that's what I said, when the truth was in part because the Sewells lived next door.

Prod wasn't subtle. Not only was the party conveniently close for his mistress, but he'd made certain I was not playing at his table. *The weasel.* He'd forgotten about waking me at four in the morning yesterday by knocking drunk on the door with three friends, demanding scrambled eggs. I'd made them with a smile, not wanting his friends to see me for the sniping, sour castoff

I'd become. But now, when I looked in his direction, he had no smile for me—not even a fake one.

My stomach clenched as Prod's attention went back to his losing hand. Drunk, he shouted loudly about being robbed. The players at his table got up to escape him—save for Mary, who cooed over his bruised ego. Any minute now they would doubtless sneak out to the garden for an assignation.

The only saving grace in my marriage, at least for the moment, was Prod's employment. I'd not had to entertain the bailiffs in weeks, though a reunion was bound to occur between those well-mannered collectors and ourselves soon.

Clearing my throat, I stared down at my own cards. The red and black suits faded into each other as tears welled in my eyes. I pursed my lips, drew in a heavy breath and kept my tears at bay. Everyone waited for me to make a move—both in the game and in life.

"I'll pass." I set my cards down, glancing at Mary's husband, Anthony, who happened to be at my table. "Can I get you another drink?" *Do be sorry for us both.*

Anthony glanced up at me, brow furrowed, appearing ready to decline, but then his gaze shifted to the canoodling pair, and he gave me a hard nod. Poor fellow looked as dejected as I felt.

As much as I tried to act French about it, watching my husband flaunt his mistress was a bit much for even me to take. I wasn't my sister Diana, whose poise in the face of her lover's lovers should have earned her an award of some kind. *How does she do it?*

I stood, smoothing my hand down my flat abdomen as I walked to the cellaret. That level plane of my belly was another endless source of torment. How could life quicken inside me when Prod planted his seed in another garden?

My hand shook as I poured the drinks, but I had enough sangfroid left to purposefully fail to offer my husband a refill. All of my failures tumbled into the glass with the ice I added. *How extra-order.* A little over a year ago, all of my dreams were still naïvely intact. I'd expected to be a mother by now. *Instead of cradling this whisky sour, I should be cradling a baby.*

Instead of flirting with Mary, Prod should be flirting with me. What did she have that I didn't? *Money. A baby. A better-selling book. A fine demeanor.*

Returning to the table, I handed Anthony his drink, which he greedily swallowed. I feigned interest in the game, all while draining my own glass. My gaze kept drifting to Prod. To his lover.

When I could take no more, I stood stiffly. Swaying on my feet, I gripped the table, steadying myself. What would happen if I fainted right now? Would Prod care? Would he shove Mary aside and rush to me? The very idea was ridiculous, childish even, I knew that. But it was no use. I wanted to fall. Wanted Prod to turn his attention to me.

Dragged down by the weight of my heavy heart and inhibitions lowered by one too many whisky sours, I made up my mind. Giving a little gasp, I carefully folded myself onto the Turkish rug in a pretend faint. As I lay on the floor, with Anthony calling to Prod, I could hear my husband's words, brisk and dismissive: "Let's not make a fuss of it; she's only trying to get attention."

He lifted me, carrying me from the drawing room just as he'd lifted me from the cab over a year before to carry me across our cottage threshold. Then he had been attentive, joking, eager. This time he merely deposited me without ceremony onto the bed, and stepped away.

"Don't go, darling." I tried to keep my voice meek, but it came out brittle. I leaned up on one elbow, hoping to look as enticing as a juicy Mary.

Peter narrowed his eyes and took another step backward. "Try not to embarrass yourself—or me—again."

I sat straight up, blinking at him. "*I'm* the embarrassment? I'm not the one cavorting with my lover in front of our friends and all London. You could at least keep your affair behind closed doors like a gentleman. Or is it so hard to hide your true nature?"

Peter scoffed. "Don't pretend you care, Naunce; no one would ever believe the Queen of Ice had an ounce of sentiment in her stony heart."

Except I had, and I'd gotten attached to the idea of being in love with him. I took exception to his referring to me as Stony Heart, a name I'd created and bestowed on my sister Unity, as a result of her Nazi leanings. To have it thrown back at me—and by Prod . . . While I sifted through cruel insults to lob at him rather than a lamp, Prod presented me with his back, and walked to the door.

"You bastard." Angry, hot tears welled in my eyes, hands fisted at my sides. "You would leave me here for her."

Peter turned slowly around. "Give me one good reason to stay."

"You're my husband. I'm your wife. We have a duty to each other."

"That's not enough."

I gritted my teeth, forcing myself not to say the angry words I wanted, but the other ones. The ones I kept locked in the safe. Words that were reserved for no one but me. Words I screamed inside every month when my flux presented itself. "I want a child."

"I'm"—he jabbed at his chest—"not the problem." The way he said it, so arrogantly, gave me cause to wonder how he knew that with such certainty.

"And you're positively no one's idea of a perfect father. Yet I cannot conceive on my own." My voice cracked. I had a ridiculous sensation of shame for presenting him with my raw emotions.

"Lift your skirt, then." He marched forward a few steps, hands as angrily fisted at his sides as mine were.

"What?" I gasped.

"You want a child." His voice was low, angry, as he tugged at the buckle of his belt. "Lift up your bloody skirt."

I shook my head, tucked my legs beneath me, thighs pressed tight. A massive pressure weighed on my chest, as though a boulder landed on top of me. "No, not like this."

"Then not at all." Peter stormed from the room, leaving me crying into my pillow, wishing to rewrite the story of my life.

To run away.

Away from London. Away from Prod. Away from my failures.

Leave it all behind . . . Even my childhood—filled with rivalries, discord and resentment, of always wanting but not having—was a far cry from the hell I found myself in currently.

Dearest Mark,

I long for the summer days of our youth, when we'd all gather at Swinbrook and drive Farve mad. He loved you most, I think, of all our friends, because you would wake up early and hunt. Whenever I lift a lid from a silver dish at breakfast, I can still hear Farve tell you that it's brains for breakfast. Oh, how we shrieked at that!

My siblings and I used to get up to all sorts of collective mischief with Nanny Blor here at Swinbrook. I do miss those times as I walk through the rooms now, and chance a peek into the old cupboard where we held our hen meetings.

Soon I'll be back at Rose Cottage. Pam will return to the country, where she manages Bryan Guinness's farm, though she's considered resigning, which I would have done ages ago. I cannot imagine how awkward it must be to tend his flock with our sister having jilted him.

Jessica's reluctantly preparing to bounce from one deb event to the next, and poor Deborah will be all alone, left to her own devices, unless Muv lets her tag along.

Tom is off doing whatever it is you young men do, a mystery to me, to be sure.

Unity has remained in Germany—is it any surprise? Nothing could tear her away from her beloved Führer. I tell you, Mark, the strangest thing. When she came home for a short visit this past winter, she brought with her his signed portrait, setting it on her bedside table, where she no doubt gave it a kiss each night. I was sorely tempted to steal it and burn it in the hearth.

Diana often visits Unity for company in Germany, rubbing

elbows with those in Hitler's circle in order to gain a lead in for Mosley. I don't know how they stomach it. Unity continues asking me to visit, to meet her mustached, "charming" Fascist. I have to fake my delight for a future visit, while declining and contemplating burning the paper I put such words to. Last week, in the letter I wrote to Unity, I drew a crude scribble of her. Head of bone. Heart of stone. Do you think me harsh? I simply couldn't help myself.

Fortunately for me, Unity is too conceited to think it might mean anything other than a great tease.

Love from,
Nancy

"Do you think Bobo has introduced Hitler to her pet rat?" I teased my sister Jessica about Unity.

I watched a seamstress put pins in fabric while Jessica stood on a stool in her bedroom. Her presentation at court was around the corner, and it was time for her final dress fitting.

Mother was an ocean away in Germany, expected home in time for Jessica to curtsy before the queen and then begin whirling about London as was customary for debs. I was all too happy to keep Jessica company and give the dress an appraising eye, because it kept me away from Prod. We'd barely spoken since bridge night a week before. And yesterday I opened a bill from a little Italian restaurant where he must have wined and dined Mary, for it had not been me imbibing three bottles of Chianti.

"Do you suppose a rat would clamber to meet the Führer?" My sister Pam's words pulled me out of my melancholy line of thinking.

"Muv wouldn't allow that," Jessica piped in.

"But how do you suppose it would go if she did?" I asked. *"Führer, old boy, glad I have run into you on this jolly good day. The Osteria is serving onion soup. Might I make this fine Ratular part of your acquaintance? Go ahead, give his soft head a stroke."*

Jessica doubled over laughing, busting several neat pins in her gown and earning a tutted admonishment from the seamstress.

"Careful, Decca, you'll prick yourself, and you don't truly want Communist red on that pretty gown," I teased.

"Oh, do be sorry for me that it has to be white."

That brought out another round of laughs, which caught the attention of the sweetest of us Mitford girls, my youngest sister, Deborah, who stuck her head round the door frame to see what the fuss was about. She joined us with two of Farve's dogs trotting alongside her. Millie and Lottie perked up their heads where they lay beside me, letting out little warning snuffles as French bulldogs do, reminding me a bit of myself when Prod's gaze followed the swaying hips of some tart.

"Shh," I warned, stroking their heads, then motioned Deborah to the seat beside me. "Soon it will be you on the stool being trussed up for your coming out."

"I'm not far behind." She offered me a cherubic smile. Ah, to be so innocent of all the vile things life would soon bring . . .

"Not at all." I forced a smile, and used it to push away my bitter thoughts. I lifted some of the extra tulle and plopped it on top of my head, standing up to do a pirouette.

"Do I look like our darling Honks?" I batted my lashes and struck an angelic pose, emulating Diana, who'd modeled as Venus for a series of photos by Madame Yevonde a few months ago.

"Oh, Lady, do be kind," Pam said. "Those portraits were absolutely stunning."

"Really stunning," Deborah parroted.

What a hard job to be the youngest of seven, and with five older sisters who were quite opinionated. Poor, sweet Debo. Only our brother, Tom, had the dubious gift of managing to be double-faced—of playing a chameleon as company demanded. Happy to be an obliging Fascist with Diana, while behind her back calling Mosley an Ogre and Hitler a tantruming baby.

In the looking glass, Jessica studied me silently. Meeting her lovely, shining, blue eyes, I hoped her joy wasn't ruined by a man the way mine had been, twice over now, by both Hamish and Prod.

"Darling Decca," I said. "You'll be the belle of the debs when you go to Buckingham. And for certain a *wondair* to every bachelor."

My sisters agreed, Diana's beautiful portraits forgotten, and Jessica smiled wide, looking down at the white satin fabric of her dress, in which she'd greet the queen.

I tossed the tulle aside, thinking of December and the last time the seven Mitford siblings had been together at a ball thrown at Rutland Gate. The guest list had included a parade of the important, including the Churchills—and thankfully *not* the Sewells. Once the evening ended, all of us had gone our separate ways.

Again, I struggled to push my gathering dark thoughts away. Perhaps some air? I rose. "I'm going to take the hounds out for a walk before we're summoned to dinner."

"I'll join you." Pam was always game for a walk despite the fact that one of her legs had never regained full motion from a childhood bout of polio.

"I shall be glad of the company." Though I'd teased her mercilessly since she'd been born, that she'd ruined my only-child life, I was glad for her company. The darkness of my mind was not always a welcomed abyss.

Out in the yard, one of the maids turned over a washtub to dump out the contents.

"Do you remember all those years ago when Unity used to climb atop the washtub and shout orders as though she were the Queen of Swinbrook?" Pam asked, laughing.

"Yes." I laughed too, so hard tears came. Pam couldn't know it yet, but that particular memory had given me a great addition to the speech in the opening chapters of *Wigs on the Green* in which my character Eugenia, the embodiment of Unity in every way, shouted at the injustices of the people, praising the Union Jackshirts and their leader. I'd put Eugenia on the washtub. Oh, the spoof was quite comical, and surely my sisters would find it funny. To be certain they recognized the tease, I could add Eugenia's nanny, tugging on her skirt and demanding she come down, as our Nanny Blor had done when Unity was young.

Darling Evelyn,

The day has come—June twenty-fifth. The pinnacle of my career? I think not. Wigs on the Green *has released to some good reviews, and others not so nice, which I prefer to ignore, given your good advice. Release days are always filled with both trepidation and exhilaration. How do you manage?*

After I lay a finished book at the feet of the reading pub-
lic, having labored months and months on prose that wrung
blood, sweat and tears from my body, rendered blisters on
my fingertips and caused my sleep-deprived eyes to cross, I am
filled with equal parts relief and edgy discomfort. Alas, the
fate of us literary types, no doubt.

Then the questions come. Will it sell? Will it flop? We writers
want each subsequent book to do better than the last. If a novel
doesn't live up to that mark, then one's entire career might be
on the line. Do pity me, old boy, for I'm in quite a state.

With love,
Nancy

The giddy social whirl of the summer provided a wonderful distraction from my failed marriage.

On the day of *Wigs*'s release, I visited bookstores in London, pointing out the cover to customers who didn't recognize me (which were few) and hiding between stacks, dancing on tiptoes as they paid. Would readers like it? Tell their friends to read it? Would I be taken seriously, or would the novel be derided as meaningless, silly drivel? I wanted readers to understand the context, to get the teases, to think more deeply about the state of our affairs, about the rise of Fascism and how it affected all aspects of our communities and our homes. I worried I expected too much. Of course, I was fully aware that not everyone would like *Wigs*. That even those who'd adored *Christmas Pudding* might find it too acerbic.

Despite the tensions between Diana, Unity and myself with regards to the book, I hoped they would be supportive. That they would see *Wigs* for its design—satire, with an underlying message that might resonate.

But Diana wouldn't return my calls. She wouldn't return my letters either. Muv, acting as a go-between, reported that the Ogre was extremely displeased with the book and refused to let Diana have any contact with me. Further proof he was exactly as I'd named him.

I'd signed a copy to My Dear Heart of Stone, for Unity, and given it to Tom to take with him to Munich when he told me he planned to visit her. I prayed she wasn't as angry as Diana, but having misread the less-Fascist sister I had a sinking feeling that the more fervent Unity would be extra incensed.

Several days after my book release, I went to a house party at Lord Beaverbrook's. It was a lark and a distraction but something more as well. His Lordship owned several newspapers, and I hoped attending the party so soon after *Wigs* went on sale might gain me a review in one or more of them. Perhaps a favorable review if I hobnobbed with the baron myself.

Sitting in His Lordship's morning room hours after sunrise, with scones and toast, boiled eggs and bacon on the sideboard, I felt satisfied all had gone well. I'd made a memorable impression. I was surrounded by fellow guests who had also stayed over after the late-night party ended. I lifted my cup of tea, stilling when my eye fell on a copy of our host's *Daily Express*—graciously provided for his guests to read over breakfast—lying under Prod's hand. A familiar face stared out from the front page.

Unity.

I looked closer, reading the headline. *Peer's Daughter Speaks at Nazi Rally in Hesselberg as Guest of Streicher.*

Oh, dear God . . . I shrank into myself and, for a moment, wondered, had Lord Beaverbrook intended the supply of newspapers as a humiliation to me rather than a courtesy to his guests? Because, with this headline, this terrible coverage of my own sister, my satirical Fascist novel, *Wigs on the Green*, was doomed. I was surprised since up to now I thought we'd got on well.

Looking about, I realized there was a newspaper in the hands of a majority of those present. My cheeks grew hot. Everyone at breakfast was reading about my sister standing before a crowd of two hundred thousand, praising Hitler and his Nazis. I looked at the picture again and felt sick. She stood before a podium, her arm outstretched in the Nazi salute. This was no mere infatuation, a girl stalking a boy she had a crush on. This was . . . I couldn't . . .

"Oh, darling, did you not know?" Lady Diana Cooper, Beaverbrook's mistress, and a dear friend of my own sister Diana, must have seen my blush. She shook her head with pity in her eyes. I couldn't tell if she was being sincere or deliberately cruel.

"Of course." I gave a soft, forced laugh and then picked up my toast, hoping to convincingly dismiss the article.

"Have you read her letter to Julius Streicher in *Der Stürmer*?" Lady Cooper asked, looking a bit more stricken than pitying this time.

"I have not." I knew of it, from a letter Jessica had sent to me, but I hadn't been able to bring myself to read it. My sister had given me the gist, however . . . how Unity had claimed to be a Jew hater, and given her full support to the Nazi Party.

Diana Cooper retreated into a polite smile. "Well, do give Unity my best next time you see her."

I nodded, trying not to choke on the dry, flavorless toast.

The ride back to Rose Cottage was quiet, with no sound other than the clunking of our car, which had seen better days. I retreated from society, hiding from the world, not caring what message they took from that. For the next week, started and stopped a letter to Unity so many times. In the end it took me a week to write something I was willing to send. All I could do when the ink finally soaked into the paper was to make a joke of it all.

Then we fled to the continent, where I hoped my holiday with Prod in Amsterdam and Italy would alleviate some of the emotional pain and turmoil I struggled with. But it was not to be.

After lunching under the awning of Prod's father's palazzi with friends, the Adriatic glittering aqua in the background, I was lounging and reading a book when Prod interrupted. "This came for you from your mother." He held out a yellow telegram, his brow wrinkled.

Bad news often came in the form of a telegram. I snatched the paper and read it quickly. *DIANA INJURED AUTO ACCIDENT. AT HOSPITAL. DOING FINE. MUV*

If Diana had been in an automobile accident, badly injured enough to go to the hospital, how was I not to worry?

"Oh God." Much as we'd not been talking, I still worried for my sister. Blood is blood, after all.

"Perhaps we should invite Diana to come to the palazzi while she recovers." Prod said it with an air of largesse that was remarkable given it was not his offer to make but his father's. Still I had to concede there was kindness in it—and a sense of duty to me because Diana wouldn't come alone. After all, she'd been headed to meet Mosley for holiday.

"Perhaps." I folded the telegram and put it in my pocket.

"Do you want to try making a telephone call?"

"No."

Prod passed me the glass of sherry in his hand. "Thought you may want this when I saw the contents of the 'gram." A rare show of affection, particularly coupled as it was with a pat on my shoulder.

I sipped slowly and offered him a grateful smile. After my escape to Swinbrook and subsequent return to the cottage, my husband appeared to be working more. He had spent less time with Mary, or at least less obviously, and eased up on his drinking. We'd even managed to make love a few times, in hopes of creating a child. It almost felt like early days, or at least close enough that I could pretend.

"Life can be so fleeting," Prod mused. I prepared to hear a lengthy lecture laced with theology, religion and the mundane all muddled together—because that aspect of his personality never changed. But for once, he sat down quietly beside me and put his arm around my shoulders.

The heat of his body, the warmth of the sherry, the emotional toll of hearing bad news, had me sinking in. Had me forgetting that back in London his lover waited for his return. Because right now, right here, he was mine.

November 1935

Dearest Mark,

I'm fleeing from home—and Peter—for a few weeks of peace in Paris with Muv, Jessica and Deborah. I plan to spoil myself *with a holiday away from my troubles. What could a wondair like myself have to worry over, you may ask? Well, I shall tell you, with the promise you burn this letter after reading. Remember when I wrote to you of my happiness at the prospect of marriage? I take it back. I've decided happiness must be an illusion.*

On top of that, I'm convinced I am a failure as a novelist. There have been so many critical reviews of Wigs on the Green *that I am thoroughly depressed and wondering if I should quit writing altogether. Should I? Do be honest with me.*

My book sales have plummeted into the abysmal dark of the Thames. Speaking of that river, I have come to an all-new low. Rather than writing, I spent an entire afternoon last week at home in London staring at the Thames waiting for a body to float past so I could call the boatman whose job it was to collect them. Did you know that was a job? I only found out by accident. When at last on Monday, a body finally appeared—facedown and bloated—I waited until it floated to the other side of the river, reasoning that the collector got eleven shillings instead of ten if he had to cross the Thames. This is also true, and I think well worth the extra coin.

In any case, my darling friend, that was the moment I knew I needed to escape to Paris. Though I tell you honestly, I doubt being there will make a difference.

With love,
Nancy

"Are you feeling all right?" Jessica touched my cheek with the backs of her fingers. Her brow furrowed.

"Just the travel." I lied with a smile, pushed her hand away and walked further into the rented Paris flat with its high ceilings and butter-yellow walls. The heels of my shoes clicked on the wood floor. "I need some water." My mouth was suddenly dry. The way it gets right before your stomach decides to let loose.

"Whisky is what you need," Muv said.

I tugged off my jacket and flung it onto a chair before collapsing onto it. The sitting room smelled of fresh flowers, which were in vases everywhere. Gardenias, roses and all manner of pretty things.

"Perhaps a whisky soda, then." I rested my head against the back of the chair and, breathing in slowly, let my eyes close for a minute.

I'd never been one to get travel-sick, and typically, since I'd been a bright-eyed adolescent girl, when I arrived in Paris all of my troubles melted away. But it wasn't the travel that had me feeling ill, and my current state would not simply vanish into thin air.

I felt Jessica's breath as she leaned over me. "Are you going to die, Naunce?" she teased, and I managed a smile.

"Not today."

Muv pressed the whisky soda into my hands. "Have you eaten? The good body needs sustenance to keep itself healthy."

"I have," I lied.

Muv, pursed her lips. "I'll ring for something."

I sipped my whisky and soda, but it soured in my gut. "I can wait until we go down for dinner."

"Some fresh air, then." Muv took my hand and tugged me out of my chair and toward the open window with a gorgeous view of the Pont Neuf. Across the Seine I could see the Louvre and Jardin du Palais Royal. A gentle breeze caressed my skin.

I gulped in the air, pretending it was summer.

"You look like I did before I left Germany a couple of months ago," Jessica mused. "Unity and Diana asked me to stay for the Nuremberg rally, and meet Hitler, at some grand dinner. No, thank you."

Unity's and Diana's faces had been splashed in the paper after that rally. Thank goodness Jessica had avoided that fate, and the rest of the family had been spared the shame of a third Mitford girl associated with Hitler and his band of thugs.

I took another greedy gulp of air. The pain in my abdomen, and my heart, started to ease.

Before arriving in Paris I'd been certain. So *certain* that this time, nearly two years since I'd wed Prod, something had stuck. I'd been wrong. The curse had reared its soul-crushing head a little less than a week ago, a month later than it was supposed to, heavy and painful. I wondered if I'd miscarried.

Knowing there was no baby, I'd hastily agreed to join my sisters and mother in Paris rather than face the anniversary of my wedding to Prod at home. Why should I celebrate a mistake?

Our brief holiday last summer had been fleeting in so many ways. Back in England, Prod had taken back up with Mary and was very public in his misbehavior. Friends who before had been keen to ignore my situation now had difficulty hiding their pity. The letters I got from my dearest friends in the world, Mark in particular . . . oh, how the sympathy that dripped from their pages pained me.

Deborah came through from the adjoining room, exclaiming,

"I'm so glad you came. What a great bore it would have been without you."

"Are you suggesting I'm as dull as the Tollgater?" Jessica asked, in reference to Prod.

I winced inwardly. It was one thing to be aware your husband was a boring fool and another to endure others saying it aloud— or perhaps especially, where the other was a beloved sister.

"God, no, you're not as boorish as that! But if I have to hear you prattle on about the division of labor and wealth one more time, I might just toss you out that window." Deborah joined me at the sill, pulling me into her slender arms, her head tucked beneath my chin.

"Now, girls, ladies do not toss other ladies out windows, nor do they compare themselves to men who wax on about tollgates."

There was the old Fem—something I liked to call Muv when she was in a mood—again, disapproving as ever. She eyed me coolly, no longer asking when Prod and I were going to start a family, and I couldn't decide if that hurt or was a relief. "Clean yourself up now, dearlings."

A relief, I decided. Muv's pity wasn't always kind.

Dearest Mark,

To have returned from Paris at such a time. England is in mourning, and so am I. Not simply for the death of King George (Long live the king!), but for what feels like the beginning of the death of everything.

I think back to that time, it feels like ages ago now, when I put my head in an oven over Hamish. If I'd let the gas take me that day, I wouldn't be going through the pain I am now.

I wonder, will Prod grant me a divorce? I fear not. I think he likes taking money from my purse too much. Besides, old habits are hard to break. Both his and mine.

Everyone knows about Mary <u>Sewer,</u> and every other social climber who's allowed herself to be taken by his charm. Mary remains—which I must say I do not understand. For once the jokes and winks wear off, there is nothing left but a dullard with a blank stare. Perhaps some women like it that way.

Prod's infidelities are so well-known that there would be no need for an elaborately well-played scheme like the one Bryan Guinness created for the divorce from Diana. All he had to do was make certain he was seen with a woman who was not his wife, and the court was content to believe it was he and not my sister who desired a divorce. Perhaps, then, it will be easier for me to get a divorce. Yes, I will remain hopeful, though it will take some convincing on Prod's part, and he is so stubborn.

There was a time not too long ago when I believed marriage was everything. That it was my duty to make it work. Now I know that sometimes there are things broken that cannot be fixed. And I can sense that death knell ringing.

I do apologize, my dear Mark, for ever suggesting you marry. I hope you can forgive me for wishing you ill.

Very best love,
Nancy

P.S. Burn after reading.

August 1936

"MRS. RODD." THE BAILIFF handed me a stack of letters. "We met your postman outside."

I nodded, allowing him and his partner inside. The windows were thrown wide, and a breeze blew in, mostly sweet from the garden, with a hint of something sour doubtless from the Thames. The bailiffs doffed their caps, looking less embarrassed than they had when we'd first started meeting under such circumstances two years ago.

"Have you any of those scones?"

I nodded. "Shall I put the kettle on?" What I wanted to say was they could find Peter either at his club or Mary Sewell's, and would they please go round and arrest him. Haul him away to debtors' prison long enough for me to pay down his debts and start over.

"Indeed, ma'am, indeed."

I left them in the drawing room, and hurried into the kitchen with the letters. After setting the kettle on the stove, I sifted through the stack, when one particular envelope caught my attention, my name scrawled out in pretty script.

I broke the seal and opened the thick folded vellum.

You are cordially invited to the opening night of
G. Heywood Hill Ltd
Presented by Heywood Hill and Anne Gathorne-Hardy
17 Curzon Street, London

They'd done it. I wanted to rush to my desk in the drawing room, where my diary was kept, to mark the date and time, but could not show my excitement for the event in front of the bailiffs. That would have to wait.

Perhaps not all of 1936 would be so bleak. The kettle whistling its ear-piercing cry was a warning not to think it possible, but I refused to believe such forewarnings. To be amongst those in literary society once more would be a dream.

"I'm terribly sorry to be visiting you again, Mrs. Rodd," the bailiff said as I brought the tea service.

I smiled as brightly as I could. "I'm sorry that Mr. Rodd is not here to welcome you."

The reminder that it wasn't my debt I paid always seemed to soften the bailiffs a bit, so I never failed to offer it.

"Sugar?" I asked, pouring out the tea. "So, tell me how your wife is faring with your son. Is he still coloring on the walls?"

The bailiff laughed and took a scone.

Before he left, I gave him as much money as I could spare from my purse. Being a good fellow, he pretended to be satisfied with the meager amount—tucking it away and apologizing for disturbing me.

As soon as I shut the door, I rushed to my desk and marked the day of the Heywood Hill bookshop opening, and then I retreated to my bedroom. I pulled open my wardrobe and began searching for the perfect dress. One that was chic but not too ostentatious. Smart but not stuffy. Nothing satisfied. And I certainly didn't have the money for anything new.

Fortunately, by the evening in question I was gorgeously clad in an Elsa Schiaparelli, on loan from my dear friend, the photographer Cecil Beaton, who'd just done a shoot for the Paris designer. The floor-length dark crepe with bands of gold braid down the front gave me both glamour and confidence as I glided into Heywood Hill Ltd, my arm linked through Prod's, who appeared at least as excited as I about attending.

The bookshop was filled to the brim with a veritable guest list of who's who in the literary world. I received a cordial welcome as if I was one of them. *Maybe I am, or maybe I still can be.*

Prod's reception was a bit cooler, and there were several awkward moments when acquaintances appeared pained to see him. Or more uncomfortably looked as if they might want to shove him out the door. He'd burned so many bridges, my husband. Not only with how he'd disrespected our marriage, but in the way he played and drank and embarrassed everyone at the club or parties.

The shop was narrow, but elegantly appointed, and soft classical music played from a gramophone tucked out of sight.

"The shop is marvelous, darlings." Anne, Heywood's business partner and fiancé, looked gorgeous with her hair styled to perfection, and Hey was dapper in a new tweed jacket. I leaned forward to kiss each on the cheek in turn before accepting a glass of champagne. "Heywood Hill Ltd will be a favorite of literati everywhere," I predicted with a knowing look. "In fact, I think I shall do articles spotlighting you in *The Lady* and in *Tatler*."

My dear friend Mark made his way toward us, with Harold Acton and Evelyn Waugh at either elbow.

"What glory to have us all back together in the same room." Mark brushed a kiss on my cheek.

"Who brought the costumes?" I asked. "I've a feeling we're all in need of tearing up the town."

My friends laughed as we each shared stories of our carefree youth. When Cecil approached with his camera, we posed as if we'd been having the time of our lives. A perfect photo for the articles I'd write. There was nothing wrong with wanting to help myself as I gave Anne and Hey's new business a bit of a boost. No doubt those who'd followed our rollicking a decade ago would drool for a glimpse of us at it again.

Out of the corner of my eye, I caught sight of my brother, Tom, flirting with a younger deb across the room. Dark-haired and dashing, he cut a brilliant figure. When he was done being a ladies' man, he would make someone a good husband. For though he was often called a womanizer, he was exceedingly honorable and intelligent. The best of us seven.

Inside I gave a wistful sigh—wishing my once-a-staple-of-the-social-circuit sister Diana were present. Wishing so many things were different. But her divorce from Bryan and taking up with the Ogre—well, who wanted Nazi sympathizers at the launch of their dream bookshop?

"Evelyn signed his books we have in stock; would you do the same?" Anne asked.

The idea struck me by surprise, but I was also delighted. So often I felt like an imposter in my own skin, and here was a reminder that I was not simply a woman playing at being a writer. I was a writer. A *published* author. Warmth bloomed in my chest, a sense of belonging, of hope.

I was adrift most days, floating from one task to another. Coming here tonight, I'd hoped it would thrust me from the fog threatening to suffocate me, and now I knew it had been for the right reasons.

"Of course." I let go of Prod's arm in favor of Anne's as she led me toward a table in the back room that had a display of *Wigs on the Green* and *Christmas Pudding*.

"You really have done a stunning job with the shop," I said, admiring the floor-to-ceiling shelves, and display tables with their clever advertisements.

Anne waved away my compliments and handed me a pen. "A dream of Hey's, and as I do adore books, it has become a dream of mine too."

I nodded. Anne and Hey were so very much in love.

An exuberant voice boomed from the front of the shop, drowning out the low hum of conversation. *Hamish.*

"I should have mentioned he'd be here."

"Why?" I feigned nonchalance as I continued to sign the remaining books. "There are no ill feelings between us." I tightened my grip on the pen, which had started to tremble, causing me to accidentally make an extra dot over the *i* in *Mitford.*

Prod, having spotted Hamish, moved swiftly to my side. While he might not be jealous, he was territorial. Heaven help me, but I wanted to roll my eyes. He had nothing to worry about where Hamish was concerned.

Several friends trailed Hamish as he drew closer—whether to offer support or hoping for an entertaining interaction between my husband and former fiancé, I couldn't be sure. Cecil had his camera poised in our direction, and I could read the headline now—*Fisticuffs Fly from Mitford Girl's Lovers inside Swanky New Bookshop.*

Though I admitted internally I'd get a kick out of whatever word-weaving a reporter might be able to make from such nonsense, I was not going to provide the drama they sought. Deftly, I maneuvered the conversation into the banality that was summer plans.

"We're going to Brittany," Prod announced.

Since this was the first I'd heard this news, I looked at him sharply, wondering where in heaven he thought the money would come from. But I couldn't articulate that question in front of friends.

My brother, Tom, arrived in time to hear Prod's pronouncement. "Decca told me she fancied a holiday this summer; might she go along?"

I had enjoyed my time with Jessica in Paris. From what she wrote in her recent letters, she was already growing quite tired of her London season. She'd never been one for deb culture.

"Fabulous idea!"

Prod's eyes widened, and I wondered if he'd been bluffing about the whole thing. Well, that would teach him to discuss such things with me first before announcing to the world.

Then Prod nodded enthusiastically, which only made me suspicious. "Ah yes, it would be grand for Jessica to join us."

"What about you, Tom?" I asked.

Tom grinned. "I fear my days are about to become much busier." He wiggled his brows and inclined his head toward the pretty young thing trying to keep up a conversation with Evelyn Waugh, who'd slinked over to check out Tom's new conquest.

I nodded, once more maneuvering the conversation, this time back to more comfortable literary topics, which were unlikely to have Prod involved. How wonderful it felt to be surrounded by books and writers once more. I could for a moment forget about the failures, and dream of my future as a novelist. Whether it was the champagne, the joy of seeing so many of my friends, or just being in the presence of so many bound books, I was invigorated.

The evening ended all too quickly, and as we climbed into a cab, a hole began to open in my chest—an aching for the old days, when we would have stayed out all night getting up to mischief.

Perhaps Prod's impromptu decision for us to holiday in Brittany would offer a carefree interlude reminiscent of the old days. With Jessica there, we'd be sure to laugh.

Except I didn't.

When we arrived, the Sewells were staying in our very same hotel. A handful of other "old friends" were checking in as well.

"What a jolly old good coincidence," Prod said.

But I knew better. I resented my husband's underhanded ruse. If I was smart enough to figure out what was going on, our friends surely would.

It took every ounce of willpower I possessed not to cause a scene right there in the hotel lobby, surrounded by plush velvet chairs and gorgeously kept potted palms, as Mary drifted over to greet us with her suffering husband a few steps behind. Took tremendous self-control, as Prod offered Mary a falsely appropriate peck on the cheek in greeting, not to murder them both where they stood.

Had I been there alone—or with only the set of folks responsible for this travesty—I might well have let myself fly into a rage. But I didn't want to ruin the holiday for Jessica. I didn't want her to realize how deep my mortification ran. To expose myself as a cuckolded woman holidaying with her husband's lover. So I held my tongue and decided to try to make the most of the holiday for Jessica's sake.

By the third night it was evident to everyone, except my sweet sister, what was happening. Prod and Mary *Sewer* were up before everyone else, walking along the beach. I gave up trying to enjoy my evenings, going directly to bed after dinner every night, much to Jessica's chagrin. I felt a twinge of guilt at not making sure my sister was having fun, but the crushing blow to my heart, my ego, as I watched my husband with his paramour and caught the pitying head shakes of others was too much to bear.

Then one dawn as I sat on the balcony overlooking the ocean, watching the sunrise, my blood as cold as the ice in my drink, something snapped. Why should Prod and Sewer be the only ones to enjoy the beach so early?

Donning a summer dress and carrying my sandals, I walked out of the hotel onto the beach. My bare toes felt glorious in the cool of the satiny gold-flecked sand. I wiggled my toes just before the waves swept over my feet. Standing on the beach, staring out at the sea, my hat was lifted off my head by a sudden gust of wind. I should have grabbed for it, but instead I watched as it danced in the air, then fell light and free into the water. It floated on the frothy surface, coming toward me in a tease with the lapping sea, and then flowing back out a little farther each time.

I was achingly envious of that hat. Envious of it being able to float away freely, no ties binding it to my head.

What if I walked into the water right now? Joined the hat?

I took a step forward, and then another, a wave wetting the hem of my sundress, beckoning me onward. The warm ocean stroked my calves, and the pull of the tide rushing round tugged against my dress.

"Naunce!" Jessica's singsong voice reached me, breaking the spell. I snatched my hat off the surface of the water. She ran toward me, cheeks pink. "What are you doing out here all alone?"

Thinking about dying.

I plopped the wet hat onto my head, rivulets running like the tears I longed to shed down my face. Then forced a laugh as Jessica flicked a droplet of seawater away from my nose.

"I was only thinking."

"About your next book? Will it take place by the sea?"

"No, I don't think it will. Something in London. I'm contemplating a bit of mystery this go-round. Something to thrill my readers." Rather than bore them as *Wigs on the Green* had.

"Oh," Jessica gushed. "I just read the most fascinating thriller, *Jamaica Inn*, by Daphne du Maurier."

"Lucky you. I haven't read it yet, but have heard marvelous things." Du Maurier was brilliant, and though we didn't run in the same social circles, we did share a literary agent. I would be delighted if that connection someday led to a tête-à-tête.

Jessica continued to chatter about the novel, which did sound very entertaining, and I did my level best to make amused noises.

As I dusted the sand from my feet and donned my sandals, I spotted Prod and Mary heading toward the hotel. Jessica must have caught sight of them as well, because her gaze sharpened. She opened her mouth to say something, but I stopped her with a question. "Fancy a Bloody Mary, darling?"

Jessica's eyes widened, and she smiled mischievously. "Why, yes. Muv never lets me snag one at her brunch parties."

"Well, I am not Muv, so come on and let's see if you like them." I led her inside, glad to be spared my sister realizing my husband was a rogue for the price of a cocktail.

 Chapter Eight
Lucy

LUCY PICKED UP THE cardboard carrier full of coffees and a bag of scones from Caffè Nero and hurried toward the shop, her mind still reeling from the Nancy letter she'd opened this morning.

On a night after too much champagne, toasting to life the only way we knew how, we peeled the paper in our favorite corner of the shop and signed our names. I wonder a hundred years from now if someone will come along and find it? A jolly surprise or a confused conundrum? Will they know our names or will they wonder what silly ducks had done such a stupid thing?

The weather was gorgeous, and Heywood Hill had its door propped open, a low-sounding beat of music playing out into the street. Had music played like that in the shop when Nancy worked here?

Lucy headed downstairs to her office, passing out the coffees to her grateful coworkers, and then plopped into her chair. She needed to find what Nancy revealed in her letter.

In the few days she'd worked from inside the shop, any initial awkwardness had melted away, and Lucy hoped even when she returned home that she'd remain friends with the Heywood Hill team. But she still thought they might think she'd lost her head if she started peeling back random corners of wallpaper.

Lucy bit into her scone, relishing its divine tang. How was she ever going to eat mundane blueberry muffins after these heavenly scones?

"Oh, a box was delivered while you were out," Ash said.

"Excellent!" Lucy laid down her scone and rose to slit open the box on a table nearby. It contained a selection of books she'd procured for her project. There was a first edition of Georgette Heyer's debut novel, *Regency Buck*, as well as *Vile Bodies* by Evelyn Waugh, and signed original copies of Betty Smith's *A Tree Grows in Brooklyn* and Toni Morrison's *Beloved*. She slid the latest arrivals onto a nearby shelf next to another box containing half a dozen collector's magazines—*Vogue, The Lady, Tatler, Lilliput*—with articles inside written by Nancy Mitford. The magazine covers were destined to be part of the library décor Lucy had planned—each would figure in a shadow box with the corresponding featured articles inside.

"I found something else your client might enjoy." Ash handed Lucy a printout with an item circled. Featured on the page was a collection of twelve special-edition classic fairy tales, leather-bound with gilt pages and satin ribbon markers.

"Gorgeous." Lucy ran her finger over the pamphlet, imagining instead it was the embossed leather.

"They are going on auction at Sotheby's later this week. Do you want me to get you a seat?" Ash offered.

"Yes, thanks." Every day she was grateful a job like hers existed. How else was a bibliomaniac supposed to live than by book after book?

Lucy updated her list for the Masters' library account based on the new arrivals, pleased to see that she'd curated nearly half of what she needed.

She emailed her updated list to her boss. Including an additional design suggestion for the library she'd been pondering since visiting Chatsworth: a secret door with bogus titles leading to a hidden staircase. There was certainly enough space for the feature.

Within a few minutes, Mr. Sloan messaged her back saying he loved the idea, and gave her the go-ahead for the addition.

Mood elevated, she nabbed her scone and walked upstairs to the shop, staring at any exposed wall space that wasn't covered with books. *If I were Nancy Mitford, where would I sign my name?*

She went to the back room, but every inch of the walls was covered in books or wood paneling or paint.

"What's got you puzzled?" Oliver asked as she passed by where he was shelving books.

"Something I read in a letter. Have you seen a place where Nancy Mitford and her friends might have signed the wall?"

Oliver let out a short laugh. "No, I don't think so. We'd have framed that if we did."

Disappointed, Lucy stepped outside for a bit of fresh air. The contents of the letter felt authentic. Maybe she'd read it wrong. But Nancy had written *our favorite corner of the shop.* There was no mistaking that.

What if they'd done so at the original shop? With this in mind, Lucy ambled down the few buildings to 17, which housed a modern-looking bank. Any flavor of the past was long gone. How did Iris figure into this? Would she have been one of the friends signing the wall?

Lucy would probably never find the spot with Nancy's hidden

signature, and that was a bummer. The letter had been to Evelyn Waugh, and filled with merriment and silliness. The next letter she'd read had been one to Hamish wishing him a happy birthday. It had been a restrained Nancy letter, with her usual joviality and jesting greatly curbed. Perhaps it had pained her to write it.

After reading that birthday note last night, Lucy had done more reading on Nancy Mitford's life, mostly her love life and her terrible marriage. Nancy had experienced heartache for years. Why hadn't anyone told Nancy to beg off Peter and Hamish too? The way Hamish strung Nancy along in the prime of her life, and then the harsh way in which he'd broken up with her over the phone with a new fake fiancée had Lucy almost embarrassed they were related. If only he'd been honest and told Nancy that he preferred men, it could have spared her a lot of heartache.

Lucy's phone buzzed. She was pleasantly surprised to see her sister's name flash on the screen. "Maya, I'm so glad you called me back. How are you?"

"Not as good as you being in London—what a dream!" Maya sounded genuinely happy for her.

"You have no idea. I've been more focused than I have in forever. A breath of fresh air, really."

"No doubt." Maya grew quiet.

Lucy could guess she was thinking of their mother's death only a few months ago, which had hit them both hard. "How are you, really?"

"Work keeps me busy, we started a new program at the library"—Maya was a county librarian in California—"Mark is doing well, and just got a promotion."

"Yes, but how are *you* doing?"

Maya was quiet a moment, and then the breath she let out, Lucy could feel an ocean away. "I'm hanging in there. Hard to believe she's gone."

"Yeah . . . Have you talked to Dad?" After their parents' divorce a few years ago, their father had bought a horse ranch in Montana, doing something in his retirement that he'd always dreamed of.

"He's good. Talked a lot about stallions and special oats, all nonsense to me."

Lucy laughed. "Same."

"So, do you think you'll make this a permanent thing?"

Lucy paused a moment, unsure what Maya was asking.

"I mean, London." Her sister filled the void with the clarification. "Do you think you'll stay in London?" Maya said it as if it was a very real and logical possibility.

Lucy whirled in a slow circle, staring at the display of books in the window of Heywood Hill and the charming twilight-lit street around it. Permanent . . . "I hadn't thought about that. I'm not even sure I'll have that opportunity."

"Don't you remember what Mom always said? We make our own opportunities. Even Dad followed that advice. And you've always said you wished you lived in London."

Lucy smiled. "I remember."

The idea of moving across the Atlantic started to percolate in her mind. It seemed crazy. After all, she was here trying to get a big promotion. And she didn't even know how getting a visa would work. Besides, one didn't simply pick up and move to another country, leaving everything behind, just because it sounded like fun.

Back in the shop, Lucy stared at all the walls, imagining peeling away the layers and finding a gaggle of famous monograms. What other pieces of herself did Nancy leave behind?

Just for fun, Lucy spent the next hour examining the corners of the rooms, digging behind books, running her fingers over the wood paneling, but all to no avail. Yet another Nancy mystery she was likely doomed to fail in figuring out.

 Chapter Nine
Nancy

November 1936

Dearest Mark,

I am sending you my change of address. We've left our little Rose Cottage behind for 12 Blomfield Road. It is a beautiful Victorian, though I like to call it a Victoriana on account of its diminutive size. In any case, I hope you'll come by for a visit soon; I could use your direction in decorating. You do have such a good eye for detail.

Best love,
Nancy

CHANGE IS NEVER EASY for anyone. And yet we do not ever remain the same, do we? Every moment, every hour, of every day of our lives is a stumble from one variation of our existence to the next.

Constantly revolving, one can find it hard to adjust. Difficult to put one foot in front of the other without tripping over one's own well-polished shoes.

Deciphering whether the change was good, or better

still, deciding that it *must* be good—or rather *ignoring* the unacceptableness—was a strength I possessed. So I preferred to view our new residence in London as a victory.

There was a quirkiness to the building. Windows so wide they promised to show the soul of the rooms inside to those without and the soul of London to those within. A garret perfect for all the writing I was determined to do. The crumbling shingles on the roof would soon need replacing, and there were a few neighbors of ill repute I would ignore. The door was bright red, as were the shutters. The stone façade was sprinkled with moss, and the gate that opened to the short, cracked stone walkway was rusted. But we were so much closer to the center of London.

Peter wouldn't be carrying me over this threshold. Letting him do so last time was, in retrospect, the beginning of yielding to all of his indulgences and indiscretions. If he wasn't going to change those habits, then I had to stand up to him in some way.

Large trees lined Blomfield Road, a street several of our friends found less than savory for those of our class, but to me London represented freedom. Beyond the busy sounds of London, I could hear the trickling sound of water in the Grand Union Canal, which fed into the Thames, at the rear of the Blomfield house.

Our new neighborhood of Maida Vale was a short walk to Paddington Square, and a brief amble from Regent's Park and Hyde Park. Practically a skip from Heywood Hill bookshop, and the Ritz. With the train at Paddington, we could go anywhere we needed. I'd no longer be stranded in Chiswick with an automobile that barely ran. No longer too far from friends to pop down the street for lunch, or tea. It'd become tiresome, constantly having to carefully plan a trip to Harrods, or decline an invitation because we'd have to make arrangements to stay overnight with either our guests or at Rutland Gate.

I breathed in the London air. Feeling good about this step forward.

A change worth embracing. Peter maintained a steady job for most of the year, and I conceded I likely had to thank the Sewer wench for that. How could he impress his mistress if not with fancy dinners and gifts? Perhaps he'd grown tired of the guilt clogging his veins after *borrowing* from my purse. Or maybe he simply didn't enjoy the company of bailiffs once he'd been faced with it. I'd made sure he was there to greet them, hinting when they'd come round that Prod would be home at a certain time.

Brushing that aside, I determined this move was for *me*, that for once I would make something about *me*.

Living in this little Victoriana on a not-quite-chic street suited me admirably. It was home, and all mine. Well, Prod's too, but never mind him; it wasn't as though he did the decorating, or like he'd be here all that often.

A snuffling snort drew my eyes down to the two furry, scrunched-up bulldog faces at my feet. "Ah yes, we're all done now."

Lottie tugged at the leash. I walked her and Millie up the stone steps to the wood door on which I'd hung a small wreath decorated with dried pink roses from Rose Cottage. A parting gift from our housekeeper, Gladys, who'd set out for Jamaica to care for her ill mother.

Inside was quiet only for a moment before Lottie rushed to

her two little pups at the back of the house who'd not yet been weaned.

I walked through the dining room, which I'd recently wallpapered in shimmering pink moiré with swags of beribboned roses cascading over magnificent urns. Peter balked for only a moment at the feminine design, understanding that allowing my splurging on a little décor was the least he could do given he himself arrived at our new home completely sozzled and smelling of another woman.

"Oh, you sweet darlings." I knelt beside the small blanket where Lottie lay with her two pups, their faces squinched up as they scooted closer to their mother. I'd keep Dollie for myself, and the wee lad, Munch, would be a wedding gift for my sister Pam.

Pam was marrying Derek Jackson, renowned scientist, longtime family friend and an aspiring jockey. The latter of which always made me laugh. Deborah fancied herself quite in love with Derek for a long time, but conceded when Pam showed interest. I gave a small sigh as I picked up a pup and cuddled him to my chest. Most of us Mitford girls seemed prone to being unhappy in love. Perhaps Pam would break the pattern. At least she'd chosen a man who wouldn't embarrass her . . .

I had Prod gallivanting around town half-drunk with a floozy on his arm. Though Diana had yet to marry Mosley, her association as his not-so-secret mistress was bad enough, not to mention his BUF band of thugs whose battle in the East End rivaled the Great War. What a shameful ruckus.

I maintained that Fascism ruined not only our country but all of Europe.

Shuffled footsteps from down the hall alerted me to the approach of our new housekeeper, Sigrid. I snuggled the puppy back with its mother, and stood.

"The tea is ready in the drawing room, my lady."

I missed Gladys, but Sigrid was calm and efficient. She reminded me of Nanny Blor in both demeanor and look, her dark hair pulled back in a responsible bun, but not so severe as to make me think she might be experiencing pinched pain at the temples.

"Excellent. I'll wait there for my guests."

Muv, Jessica, Deborah and Violet Hammersley, who was Muv's dearest friend, arrived shortly after.

"Aunt Vi." I embraced the older woman, offering her the honorific that all Mitford children bestowed on her. I gave her soft, wrinkled cheek a kiss. "It's been an age since we've seen each other."

"Oh, dear, you are trying to add years onto my life—pray take them back."

I giggled, then greeted the others. Once they were settled, I poured the tea. Surrounded by familiar, beloved faces, it almost felt like the days back in Swinbrook when we'd had tea and gossiped. I offered Muv a smile, and when she returned it, some of the strain of life smoothed off her brow.

Since the publication of *Wigs on the Green*, I'd not seen or spoken to Diana or Unity, but Muv, who politically sided with my sisters, continued to make an effort to see me. In a group such as this, the conversation was light, full of jest and gossip, rather than politics.

"What are you writing next, dear?" Aunt Vi asked. She doubtless meant well, but the question made my palms a little sweaty.

I set down my tea, not ready to share what I'd been contemplating for my next project—or the lack of confidence I had of late. "I've not yet thought of anything in regards to another novel," I said airily, hoping she'd drop the topic. "But I am still writing for *The Lady* and *Vogue* and *Tatler*, and an occasional piece in other magazines or newspapers." Fluff pieces mostly, enough to give me some money to pay our bills, and perhaps a new hat.

"Naunce," Muv broached carefully. I wondered if I was about to get a dressing-down. "Have you ever considered perhaps nonfiction?"

"No," I drawled out. I raised the teapot and gave Aunt Vi a smile. She nodded at me. Pouring her a second cup, I watched my mother from the corner of my eye as she tried to figure out the best way to broach a new subject.

"Well, I've been speaking with your cousin Edward, Lord Stanley of Alderley," she said at last. "He asked me if you'd consider a commission from him."

I perked up, setting the teapot down rather than topping off my own cup as I'd intended. "What sort of commission?"

"There's a collection of some ten thousand letters between various members of the family dating back decades all tucked away at Alderley Park. Edward hoped you might be able to edit them and perhaps pull them together in a suitable fashion to have them published. He believes they are quite extraordinary."

I took a sip of tea, letting the warmth coat my throat as I considered. I doubted the family letters were as interesting as my cousin believed. Most people's family history was a yawn. Editing letters would be quite a step away from fiction. However, doing so could earn me some money, which my cousin could afford to pay. Those few clambering for another Nancy Mitford novel could wait, I supposed.

"Oh, Muv, why would Naunce want to spend her days editing a bunch of old letters? Sounds incredibly drab." Jessica rolled her eyes, and Deborah nodded in agreement.

"Oh, I don't know about that, Decca." I waved my hand. "Maybe a hundred years from now, someone will want to read *our* letters. I think the project sounds *fascinating.*" I was half jesting, but half curious to get a look at what my cousin found so interesting—not to mention the nice bank draft.

"Oh, I'd read those letters." Aunt Vi winked. "Think of the gossip. Maybe even the scandal."

Muv looked a little less keen about the project than she had a moment ago, but I grinned, and offered everyone a scone. "I'll write to Cousin Edward and tell him I am willing to have a look."

Muv nodded approvingly. I could hardly remember the last time I'd earned that particular nod.

Aunt Vi picked up a biscuit and dipped it into her tea. "I heard a vicious rumor this morning. Some nonsense about King Edward considering abdicating the throne in order to marry the American Wanda Simpson? Or was it Wendy? Absolutely absurd."

"Wallis, I believe." I recalled the masculine nature of the name when my editor asked me to write a piece about Mrs. Simpson for *The Lady.* "Indeed, very ridiculous."

Absurd felt like an understatement to think of the king giving up his throne in order to marry an American socialite divorcée. It was unheard-of, and quite delightful in at least one respect. This scandal would drive any discussion of my Nazi-leaning sisters from the minds of London's gossips.

"Naunce, have you and Peter replied to your invitation from Ambassador von Ribbentrop for the soiree at the German embassy?" Muv caught me off guard with the change in subject. No doubt the approval she'd granted me was about to be surrendered. "Anyone who is anyone will be there."

"Oh, do say you'll go." Jessica had a desperate look in her eye. Obviously Muv and Farve were dragging her along.

"I'm terribly sorry to say we have a previous engagement."

In a rare show of humor, Prod wrote our response, declining the German ambassador's invitation in Yiddish, and afterward we'd celebrated this bit of cleverness with a champagne dinner at the Ritz.

There were some days when I could still see the brilliant, handsome and hilarious young charmer I'd fallen for peeking out from underneath the man Prod had become. Quite unfortunate that moments like those often ended with me watching him walk away arm in arm with the Sewer.

"Anyone care for more cucumber sandwiches?" I held up the tray, trying to distract myself from the downturn of my thoughts.

February 21, 1937

Dear Lady,

Decca has run away with our cousin Esmond Romilly. I suppose Muv and Farve ought to have paid more attention to her socking away money in her running-away account. Though I admit I myself did not think she was so serious . . .

Much love,
Debo

The letter was delivered to me from Rutland Gate, setting my head spinning with confusion. Jessica was supposed to be touring Dieppe, France, with the Paget twins. How could she have run away with Esmond Romilly? As far as I knew, they weren't particularly well acquainted. Esmond was our second cousin on Farve's side and the nephew by marriage of Winston Churchill. Though, truth be told, we all speculated that Churchill fathered Esmond, given his affair with Esmond's mother.

This was not the state of things I'd hoped to return to, only recently back from a trip to Rome with Aunt Vi in which I'd sought distance from my misery-inducing husband. When I'd left in January, I informed him I might not be back, and he had a choice to make between me and Mary Sewer. At first, Prod thought I was joking. However, after a few weeks he must have sobered up, because I received a letter from him, begging me to come back and claiming he'd broken things off with Mary.

Since I'd arrived home, Peter was attentive in a way I didn't recognize. In a way I'd wanted for so very long. Now he walked into the room and noticed me, took in my drawn brows and pale cheeks.

"What has happened?" Prod drew closer.

"Decca's run away." I held out the letter.

"To where?" he asked without glancing at the page.

"I don't know."

"Any word from your parents?"

I shook my head, wondering what I'd missed. I'd been so occupied with my own problems, and with the drama surrounding Unity and Diana. During the frenzy of Pam's wedding a few months ago I'd not thought to pay attention to Jessica. Had she been acting differently? Plotting? If I'd noticed, would she have confided in me?

"I'll call for a driver."

Crossing the threshold at Rutland Gate, I immediately sensed disruption and sorrow. Ordinarily the gramophone played softly, but it was oppressively quiet, save for the tick of the grandfather clock.

The housekeeper whispered a greeting as she took our coats, and we hurried to the drawing room, where Muv sat with Deborah and Pam on either side of her.

"Farve's in his study with Tom." Muv's voice was monotone. "Diana is on her way. We've sent a telegram to Unity."

I left Prod in the drawing room and headed toward the study. My father sat in the high-backed leather chair at his wide oak desk, with a full snifter of brandy, eyes on the telephone and a few opened letters before him. Tom nodded at me, his face grim, and then he quietly exited.

A fire crackled in the hearth on two measly logs, and the window curtains were drawn halfway, giving the study a darkened, somber ambience.

Farve glanced up at me, but the usual brightness in his eyes was dulled.

"She's eloped," he said. "I didn't know she was so unhappy. What a grand scheme of a lie those two developed."

Farve gestured toward the letter on his desk from Nellie

Romilly, Esmond's mother. Apparently, on February seventh, when Farve and Muv thought they'd dropped Jessica off at Victoria Station to embark on her trip with friends, she'd instead met Esmond and they'd headed to Spain, which was in the midst of a civil war.

What a young fool. I hoped she'd not truly married Esmond yet. If not, there was still time for us to control the social damage.

The destination showed there'd been advanced planning, because the couple would have needed visas for Spain. Yet the letters she and I exchanged during my sojourn in Rome contained no hints of plans to run away, nor any trace that she'd fallen in love.

Quite impressive, actually. How does one hide infatuation sufficient enough to induce elopement? What a romantic whirlwind it must have been: hearts beating full of desire along with the fear of being caught. Jessica had not wanted to be left out of so many things growing up, and it appeared the spotlight was one of them. Well, she'd have that now. If it wasn't quickly contained, this elopement would be a major scandal by marrying underage to a Communist.

I returned the letter to the stack.

"Is it impossible for a single Mitford girl to lead a quiet life?" Farve asked, taking in a long sip of his brandy.

"Pam," I said with a rueful smile, bending to kiss him on the cheek.

"Jessica is too young to wed, and to that impulsive rascal, it will be the death of me."

"We'll get her back, Farve. I'll go to Spain and get her."

"You can't possibly go alone, dear."

"I can, and I'll drag her back here for a good dressing-down. Maybe Nanny Blor should come with me, now that I think of it."

"Why not Prod?" Farve asked.

I was taken aback by the suggestion. We'd not been abroad since the disastrous summer trip, which I tried not to recall. Generally, Farve thought my husband a perfectly *filthy rat*, which he'd written in pencil in his copy of *Wigs on the Green*—right beside my dedication to Prod.

"He is your husband," Farve said as if he was passing sentence.

"He is." I straightened.

A knock sounded at the door, and Peter slid into the room. "Pardon the interruption, but I think I may have a way for us to force Jessica's return."

We waited in silence, permission for Prod to go on.

"Sir, you can have her declared a ward in chancery. Legally extradite her home under court supervision." Prod looked completely assured.

I'm sure I looked completely surprised. After all, when was the last time Prod had come up with an effective or useful idea of any kind?

Yet his notion of making Jessica a ward of the court could work. A silly part of me pictured him as Mr. Darcy, determined to win my affection by saving my sister as the hero had in *Pride and Prejudice*. That part of me was a fool.

"She is not of legal age," Peter continued, "therefore her marriage is not legal."

Farve nodded. "That might work."

When we left Rutland Gate, I sat close to Prod in the taxicab, my fingers entwining with his. "Thank you," I said.

Peter's gaze fell to mine, and he smiled. The smile was genuine, I hoped. My skeptical mind warred with my heart, after so many instances when I'd fallen for his false charm. "I meant what I wrote in the letter I sent to Italy, Nancy."

"What, precisely?" I wanted to hear him say aloud he wanted our marriage to work. I think my running off to Rome had put a fear in him that I wouldn't always be there. Maybe he'd failed to consider that point when he'd sashayed out of our marriage with Mary and any number of his other mistresses.

"I want us to be happy again," he said.

Looking at him in the half-light of the moon through the taxi-cab window, I had a startling thought: I still believed in love.

But should I believe in love with *this* man?

There was only so much pain a heart could take.

A few minutes later, the night stars tinkling overhead, music blaring from one of the houses down the road, we were walking hand in hand up the stairs to our front door. My foolish heart pounded. The moment the door closed, Peter slipped his fingers under the collar of my fur, sliding it over my shoulders and down my arms, kissing my neck as he did it with intent.

"You're so beautiful," he murmured. "So delicate." He lifted my hand to his mouth, blue eyes searching mine.

I swallowed hard. Wanting to sink against him, but at the same time, worried he might push me away.

Peter tugged me closer until my body was flush against his. Sensations I'd nearly forgotten churned, melting the ice of so many months of disappointment. My skin tingled, and my heart raced as if trying to leap from my chest.

When he leaned in to kiss me, I welcomed it. When he led me upstairs to our bedroom, I followed, steps still hesitant. But when he undressed me, told me how much he'd missed me, kissed every inch of my skin, I melted.

The outside noise of the world disappeared. We made love twice that night. Each of us giving away pieces of ourselves, until I experienced the same girlish wonder of our wedding night. I drifted to sleep allowing myself to dream of happiness, long deferred and forgotten.

Several days later, we received an urgent telephone call from Farve. Reporters swarmed Rutland Gate. Deborah was in a frenzy because the *Daily Express* named her as the runaway instead of Jessica in their article titled *Peer's Daughter Elopes to Spain*. Tom threatened to sue anyone with a camera, and at the same time tugged Farve, who promised them all bodily harm, back in the house.

The mistaken article about Deborah added to a growing avalanche of terrible gossip—joining headlines like *Another Mitford Anarchist* and *Consul Chases Peer's Daughter*.

Worse still, Esmond Romilly refused to surrender my sister, defying the order to send Jessica home. Thankfully, with the help of Esmond's uncle Churchill, arrangements were made with the foreign secretary to secure the two runaways on the HMS *Echo*, along with nearly two hundred Spanish refugees. At first the waywards, as I now referred to them, tried to refuse, but the ambassador informed them if they did not board, the refugees would not be saved, and it would be their fault.

Prod and I were to meet the rebellious couple in Saint-Jean-de-Luz, France, when the HMS *Echo* docked. We hoped we would be able to make some sense out of things before bringing Jessica home safely, and Esmond too, though I really didn't care a fig about Esmond.

Standing dockside as their ship arrived, we waited for the young couple to disembark, doing our best to ignore the dozen reporters and press photographers who stood not far off, peppering us with questions.

When the waywards came down the gangplank, I waved a glove in their direction, shocked to see how bright and beautiful Jessica looked. In fact, I'd never seen her so vibrant. Her arm was slung through Esmond's, who walked down the plank like a cocky prizefighter who'd won the round.

Bubbly and laughing, Jessica approached us at a half run, and flung herself into my arms, as though she'd just returned from her honeymoon—which it had clearly been despite the lack of legal wedding.

The press screamed questions, and cameras flashed.

"Darling," I said. "You look positively divine."

"Love will do that," Jessica simpered, gaze sliding toward Esmond, who smiled back at her as though he were a hound who'd caught a kitten.

The semblance of a grin I managed likely looked more like someone being boiled alive than enjoying a reunion. The wayward chit almost destroyed our parents with her lies. Jessica knew the scandal her elopement brought, knew it would gut our parents to have her run away. Not to mention the political upheaval that had been necessary to bring her back. Despite how I felt about her actions, this was a public moment, and I'd hurt my family further if we didn't paint the right picture for those bloody cameras.

"Romilly." Prod stuck out his hand toward him in a manner meant to intimidate. For once I didn't mind his tough posturing. Esmond needed to be put into his place.

The nineteen-year-old lad stared down at Prod's hand long enough to make the group uncomfortable, but finally took it for a shake that escalated on both sides until it was rougher than necessary.

"I've taken rooms for us all at a hotel down the street. Taxi's waiting," Peter said. "Let's get you settled in before these nags eat us alive."

We rushed away from the press, taking refuge in the taxicab.

But Jessica and Esmond were not pleased to learn we'd gotten them separate rooms. Jessica would be housed in a two-bedroom suite with Prod and me, while Esmond had a room of his own.

"You're not married, dear," I reminded her as Peter unlocked the suite's door.

"When did you turn into a pinch-faced old dower?" Jessica crossed her arms over her chest, her tone nasty and defiant, which caught me off guard. Then I remembered she'd also surprised me by eloping. "I thought you'd be on my side through thick and thin."

"I've not changed. I am on your side, believe it or not. The entire reason I'm here is because you attempted to elope."

"I didn't *attempt* anything." Jessica's stomping foot reminded me of her youth. "I was quite successful."

I pressed my lips together, determined not to fling cruel words back. The nitwit didn't know the half of it. She was too young and naïve to understand, reminding me much of myself when I'd dreamed of a life with Hamish. The thought softened my ire somewhat, making it easier for me to keep my temper. "Well, in any case, you'll be staying with Peter and me, and we shall discuss the next steps over dinner."

I tried to slide my arm through hers and draw her across the room's threshold, but Jessica backed up a step.

"I don't think you understand, Nancy."

Her retreat from using my nickname was doubtless purposeful, and I experienced a sharp shot of pain as her barb found its mark.

"I would love for you to explain it inside the suite." I side-eyed a chambermaid moving past us, wondering if she was clever reporter in disguise, hoping to get details for whatever rag she wrote for. Oh, what juicy morsels she got as she set down her little cleaning basket and tied her shoe.

"I have no intention of going into your suite." Jessica squared her shoulders, grabbing hold of Esmond's hand. "As far as I'm concerned, Esmond is my husband, and nothing you say can change that."

"I need not say anything," I replied, "for no matter how often you proclaim he is, you are not, in fact, legally married, and you shan't be until we return to England."

"Now, see here," Esmond started, but Prod's hand clamped on his shoulder stilled his tongue.

"I think it would behoove the two of you to consider there have been and will be more serious consequences to your behavior." Peter's face took on a pinched look that reminded me of Farve delivering a childhood reprimand. I rather enjoyed seeing the paternal side of him. "Of immediate concern," he continued, "as you observed at the dock, there are prying eyes lurking. Unless you want to have your picture flashed all over every paper in Europe and England with unflattering headlines suggesting you abducted and soiled the reputation of a young lady, this needs to be handled with discretion."

Esmond and Jessica clamped their mouths closed, but the fiery glower in their eyes spoke volumes. Gone was the friendly, joyful mood in which Jessica had come down that gangway. In the place of my smiling sister was a staunchly stubborn young woman, staring at me as if I was a traitorous enemy to be reviled.

I had a very bad feeling we were not going to win this fight.

Jessica and Esmond refused to return with us to England. No amount of prodding, nor the promise of Farve giving them a yearly stipend, convinced them.

So Prod and I returned to England alone, having failed in our mission.

For the next two months, every family gathering, phone call or note devolved into a discussion of the waywards, as bitter debates roiled the family. Farve categorically declared he would not see Jessica until she'd come to her senses. Mother took a different approach. So on the eighteenth of May, just under a week after King George VI and his wife, Queen Elizabeth, held their coronation, Muv and Nellie Romilly traveled to Bayonne, France, with a silk dress for Jessica from Harrods in their luggage, prepared to witness an exchange of vows between Jessica and Esmond.

Not a moment too soon either, for by summer my scrappy sister was already with child. Jealousy overwhelmed me when I first heard. How was it fair that two children, poor as mice, who'd run away, worrying so many and inconveniencing the British military, had been given this gift? How unfair that despite the many times Peter and I tried since reviving our marriage, my womb remained stubbornly empty. The sting of this injustice was particularly hard to bear because Peter was again losing interest in me and our marriage.

On top of perhaps losing my husband again, I was not willing to lose a sister, even a wayward one. I feared Jessica would always see me as the enemy who sided with the "adults" in her time of need. So I wrote her playful letters, trying to regain her affection. Every word I inked was painful, but I hoped they would bear fruit.

With the family drama once more out to tide, leaving the shores of my sanity dry for a moment, other forms of writing were retaking my time and attention. I was able to concentrate more on my *Ladies of Alderley* project, taking a trip out to Alderley Park in Cheshire for a few days to study the aging family letters my cousin had been so keen for me to edit and assemble. Most of the massive manor house on the three hundred acres had been destroyed in a fire in 1931, and my cousin had moved into the farmhouse. Lucky for him, the letters were not destroyed. Now he planned to sell off the estate piecemeal, so I supposed he needed a way to consolidate everything. And perhaps to make a few coins with the publication.

There were thousands of letters between the ladies of Alderley, and at first, I was skeptical—how was one to decide which should go into a volume? Would I ever be able to read them all? Almost as soon as I dove in, I was engrossed. My mind started to tick. The writings of my distant relatives came alive. Characters peeled themselves from the caverns of my brain, like walnuts coming loose of their shell.

The experience gave me an epiphany of sorts. I wrote immediately to my sisters, all of them—hoping Unity and Diana would not burn my missive on receipt—suggesting we each save our own letters. What fun it might be for us to live on in their pages, and what entertainment for some future readers to encounter the Mitfords, rising up from a massive ship of crumpled paper.

Fairly early in my sojourn, I agreed wholeheartedly to the commission my cousin offered. The letters were fascinating. For once

I didn't struggle with finding the right idea and words needed to formulate an enticing narrative. It was wonderful to lose myself within the art of writing. Additionally, it was a relief to know what I edited and presented was history, and would not bring a rift in my family as *Wigs* had.

As I worked, my thoughts occasionally strayed to Peter, whose communications waned with each day. Though he professed to miss me, I sensed an air of dismissal both of me and my new work. It dawned on me he'd enjoyed me hopeless—having given up on writing—and now felt betrayed I'd renewed my passion for the pen once more. Was he jealous? Had he resumed his own extramarital passions in answer to those feelings? I tried to distract myself from wandering too far down a path of paranoia, images of him lying drunk in Mary Sewell's lap, spending my evenings in Cheshire listening to the radio and drinking cordials with my cousins.

On one such evening, an announcement came across the wireless that Neville Chamberlain had replaced Stanley Baldwin as prime minister. Oh, how I disliked Chamberlain, as did so many. He was a timid, milquetoast sort of man with no talent for leadership. I suppose the silver lining as such was railing against Chamberlain would give my fellow Brits something political to rage about that had nothing to do with any member of my family. A welcome relief at this point, because there seemed to be an innate need amongst us many Mitfords to become the talk of London, and indeed much of Europe. Was there anyone in Germany, France, England and now Spain who didn't know our name?

Chapter Ten
Lucy

"I GOT THE FAIRY tales!" Lucy burst into Heywood Hill book-shop after the Sotheby's auction.

Oliver grinned from behind the register, pumping his fist in the air. "I bet you're chuffed."

"Beyond chuffed," she replied, the very British lingo rolling off her tongue as if she'd been in London for longer than a week. Now if only she could be as successful with her Iris quest, she'd really celebrate.

A handsome man stood beside Oliver. He was about her age, give or take a couple of years, and his startling blue eyes un-abashedly took her in, causing heat to creep up her neck toward her cheeks. He leaned an elbow casually on the counter, the sleeves of his blue-and-white-striped oxford shirt rolled halfway up his forearms. One ankle of his chino-clad legs crossed over the other, revealing shined brogues.

"I'm sorry." She laughed, glancing back and forth between Oliver and the newcomer. "I didn't realize you had a customer."

"Oh, Gavin isn't a customer. He's a book curator, used to work for us but he's gone off on his own, cheeky bloke."

Gavin stepped forward and held out his hand. "Gavin Thacker. Pleasure to meet a fellow bibliophile."

Lucy was surprised by his pleasant Scottish accent. "Lucy St. Clair." She put her hand in his, warmth in his sure grip.

"Exactly what fairy tales did you get?" Gavin nodded toward the slip of paper in her other hand.

"First editions in pristine condition, leather-bound. They'll be delivered later today. I'll show you if you're still around."

"I may have to come back to see them." A lock of his dark hair fell across his forehead.

Oliver cleared his throat. "Gavin, here, is working on a library for a bird lover. I was just telling him about the bird book at Chatsworth."

"It was gorgeous." Lucy turned toward Gavin. "Worth a look if you have the time."

"Sounds as if I need to make the time," Gavin said.

"Have you considered Ackerman's *The Genius of Birds* for your client's collection?" Lucy offered.

Gavin's smile returned. "Aye, I've only just finished reading it. One of my new favorites, along with Stryker's *The Thing with Feathers*. And a definite 'must buy' for my client's library."

Lucy smiled back. "My mother was a fan of birds."

"And you?" Gavin asked, a brow raised.

Lucy gave an exaggerated shudder. "The poor creatures were ruined for me after reading Daphne du Maurier's *The Birds*."

Gavin chuckled, the sound a low scrape against his throat that she found oddly calming. "And here I thought we could be friends."

The shop phone trilled, and Oliver picked up. Lucy found herself hoping that didn't mean Gavin would head out the door. She didn't want their conversation to end.

"So, your client is looking for older bird books?" Lucy hoped to keep the Scotsman talking and therefore in the shop.

"Yes. We're creating a library-menagerie combination."

"Fascinating. How will you do that?"

"I am going to incorporate various birdcages into the shelving, and I also plan to make the rails along the stairs and balcony into extended tree limbs."

"Ingenious. I'd love to see the finished product."

"It will be one of a kind. If you're still in London perhaps Oliver can bring you out for the unveiling. Of course, it will also be in *Vogue*."

"Impressive." Lucy rocked back and forth on her heels. "That's the kind of coverage that will yield more clients."

Gavin nodded. "I am a lucky bugger this go-round. What does your project entail?"

"A private library in Midtown Manhattan. Aiming for five hundred volumes to start, with a focus on classics and first editions, including a Mitford collection. But my client is quite eclectic, and so I'll be assembling a mix of nonfiction and coffee table books, as well as bestsellers from over the years." Lucy leaned her hip against the register desk. "And you'll appreciate this: in a nod to Chatsworth, I'm creating a secret door with bogus titles."

"Enchanting."

"Here's hoping. And maybe I'll be lucky to get some nice coverage as well." For a moment they just stared at each other. Then Lucy flicked her gaze deliberately away, trying not to blush. Gavin was handsome, charming, intelligent. She carefully folded the auction paper and tucked it into the folder she had under her arm so she could put it with the other records.

"What's the prize?" Gavin asked. "I mean in the collection," he clarified, clearly realizing that she might have missed his meaning.

Lucy felt a blush creep over her cheeks. "Right now, I'd say the volumes I snagged today, but a signed copy of *Dracula* will give them a run for the money."

Gavin blew out a low whistle. "Impressive. If you ever find yourself in Scotland, the ruins of Slains Castle are rumored to have inspired Stoker."

"I had no idea. I would love to visit Scotland."

Gavin grinned. "Perhaps on your next project."

"If I am lucky . . ."

"Sometimes we have to make our own luck." He winked, not in a flirty way but more conspiratorial.

Lucy laughed. "You and me both."

"Well." He straightened up where he stood, and waved at Oliver, who was now taking notes on whatever the person on the other end of the phone line was saying. "It was nice to meet you, Ms. St. Clair."

"Lucy, please. And it was lovely to meet you as well."

Gavin ambled toward the door.

Lucy bit her lip, watching him and wishing she had an excuse to call him back, although even once he was gone, she'd be surrounded by fellow professionals with whom she could discuss books and library designs.

Just as he reached the door, she called, "Gavin, wait."

He turned slowly, curiosity knitting his brows.

"Do you want to get a cup of tea? I have a list of books I've been having trouble locating. I mean, I know we're competition, but maybe you'd have some leads."

"I'd love to. There's a great place around the corner."

Lucy shoved her notebook back into her purse. "Excellent."

Less than five minutes later, they were sitting, mugs in hand, at a table by the window in a cozy tea shop.

"You know we're not really competition, right?" Gavin eyed her with interest.

"Maybe not on this side of the Atlantic, because you have more connections than I do." She smiled and did a mock eye roll.

He shook his head, laughter crinkling his eyes. He dipped his spoon into his tea, stirring in a drizzle of honey. "No, not at all. Because rare-book experts have to stick together. Help each other. We're in the business of spreading book love, right? And when we do it well, everybody wins."

What a breath of fresh air. His sentiment mirrored her own views on other curators and rare-book experts as colleagues not competition, a unique find himself considering the environment she'd left behind at Emerald Books. He was a respectful fellow professional. Not to mention he was friendly in an endearing sort of way.

Remember, this is about business. After all, she needed to finishing procuring the list of books remaining for this project. Gavin could be a useful contact for future curation projects as well.

They pored over her list, with Gavin graciously offering leads on several items.

"So," Lucy hedged, taking a sip of her remaining tea. "I am here on business, but I am also trying to solve a bit of a family mystery."

"Do tell." He leaned in, eyes full of genuine interest. Was there anything more appealing in a man?

"Years ago, my mother bought a book at Heywood Hill—one of Nancy Mitford's novels. There's an intriguing inscription in it that reads: 'My dearest Iris, Without you, my path might have followed a less elegant trajectory than Anna Karenina. I will be forever grateful not only for your lack of pity, but for your friendship. For pulling me back from the tracks and setting me on a path that pushed me to pursue love, happiness. To leave the darkness behind and really live. No truer friend could have ever been found. With much love, Nancy.'"

Gavin's cocked his head, seeming interested. "Wow. That's powerful."

"Isn't it? My mother and I always wondered who Iris was, and whether she saved Nancy's life, literally or figuratively. And why did she never collect the book from the shop? Or was she even aware that it was there? Anyway, I've not been having very much luck answering any of those questions, even now that I'm here in London." Lucy shook her head with a sad sigh. "I know it's a long shot, but have you heard anything about it?"

"I can't say as I have. But I am sure you know Nancy worked in the shop during World War II."

"Yes."

"Did you know she was an active contributor to the war effort?"

"I've heard that." Lucy paused, trying to tie together the strings of information in her mind. "I think I read that she joined the Air Raid Precautions unit."

"That's right, and you're in luck: there's a temporary women's ARP exhibit at the Imperial War Museum right now, highlighting lesser-known female volunteers. Might be a chance something on this Iris lass could turn up."

"Fantastic." Lucy set her cup down and offered him a grateful smile. She was reminded of Gavin's earlier comment about making her own luck.

"We could . . . go together," he suggested. There was a hesitancy in his tone that suggested he was unsure she'd agree.

"I'd love the company. Besides, two heads are always better than one."

"Tomorrow, lunch?"

"Yes, that sounds good. What time do you eat lunch?"

Gavin chuckled. "Whatever time you do."

As the sun set that evening, Lucy poured a glass of wine and settled down to read another letter from the package. The envelope was unmarked by the post, having never been sent. Splotches of something spilled marred the name and address of who it was meant for. Lucy slipped out the single folded page and carefully opened it, a gasp on her lips.

Darling Iris,

I ordered several charming music boxes for the bookshop. The dancing girls remind me of Adele Astaire. They aren't ballerinas, but flapper girls, down to the red of their lipstick. The music is a jazz piece that you and I danced to at the canteen just before the blitz.

Everything was so surreal then. All of us preparing for what felt like nothing, only to find our heads nearly blown off. I think maybe it feels a bit like that now. I'm sitting in the shop. The sun is shining outside, a few customers are meandering past. There's no whining alarm. No horns blaring. No wardens rushing past. And yet at any moment, I know the tranquility of what I see can be destroyed.

I've got to go over the numbers so I can let Heywood know how the shop's doing. How he can even want to know such things while he's facing the enemy in the trenches is beyond me. I'll write again.

But the letter stopped there. Why didn't Nancy finish it? Why didn't she send it?

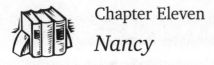

Chapter Eleven
Nancy

December 1937

~~Dearest Peter,~~

THE MONTH OF DECEMBER found me ensconced in the attic of my cousin's farmhouse at Alderley, buried beneath piles of dust and crumbling letters, completely immersed in the Victorian era and my great-great-grandmother's life. I adored the details of the Victorian upper class. Every day seemed so much easier back then. A story of leisure and riches. Their lifestyle laid out on the pages like a golden age compared to 1937 Britain. How I wished to sink back in time, even if it required wearing a bustle. To take a walk on the grand park, or gossip over tea.

The ladies of Alderley reminded me so much of my own sisters, with their passion for quarreling, their differences in opinion and one thing we Mitfords seem to excel at no matter the generation—finding the weak points in one another's armor. *We have improved upon their eyebrows, however*, I thought, gazing at the women depicted in pictures with brows thick and dark, much in need of a tweeze.

The lamp beside me flickered, then fuzzed out, making a sentient hiss that sent chills racing along my arms. The attic was entirely black.

When had the sun set?

I'd been up here since after breakfast, wiling away the hours in another world, absorbed by the history, the fascinating life.

Standing up, I tried to get my bearings in the dark, lest I fall attempting to remember where the stairs were, what stacks of letters and artifacts I'd left out, what trunks I'd left open. Arms out, I moved forward, tripping not once or twice but three times on my way. Next time I'd need to remember an electric torch.

At last I found the railing, breathing a sigh of relief that I hadn't tumbled down the stairwell, cracking my head open. Though I supposed in such a case one of the staff would eventually find me before I bled out, or at least I hoped. They'd ring the newly minted 999 emergency number, and the doctors would rush out, only to phone my family telling them I'd lost too much blood and died on the way to hospital.

Muv and Farve would mourn me, of course. My sisters too. Deborah most of all.

Prod, however, was a conundrum. Half of him would probably rejoice at finally being free of me; the other half would miss my wit, and my purse. Things between the two of us had fallen ever more steadily into a grave we each held a shovel for, one of us digging and the other putting the dirt back in. Never in sync, never reaching the completion of our goal—perhaps never sharing the same goal. I had a duty to salvage my marriage, didn't I? I couldn't quit, not like Diana. But, oh, how I wanted to at last put down that shovel.

Back in my room, I found a cold dinner on the small round

table by the window. Thoughtful of the staff to leave it for me. This wasn't the first night I'd missed the evening meal, and cousin Edward assured me he took no offense.

I sipped the glass of wine left beside my plate and glanced at the clock. Nearly ten. Collapsing into the chair, I picked at the cold chicken.

Our housekeeper at Blomfield Road often fed me such dinners on nights Prod was out gallivanting, or on holiday somewhere. I never dined alone at my own table, finding it too depressing a prospect.

I took another sip, letting the aroma roll around my tongue. Alone like this, with only the sound of the ticking clock, I could think more on the one word evading me and thus ruling my entire existence: *happiness.*

A dangling carrot. *Keep chasing after it, keep shedding bits and pieces of yourself. One day you might be able to grab hold and tug it close enough to feel a spark of joy.*

My eyes lit on the telephone on the side table in my room. I lifted the receiver, asking the operator to dial Blomfield. I waited long enough that I thought he wouldn't answer when I finally heard Peter.

"Nancy? Is everything all right?"

"Yes, just fine. I only wanted to hear your voice."

"Why?" Prod sounded confused. "Are you certain you're all right?"

"Yes, and my project is going well."

"When will you be home?" He sidestepped my comment on my work, as usual. So much for my attempt to start a meaningful conversation.

He'd been so discouraging of late, and his moods irked me.

At one minute he was encouraging, the next, dismissive, thinking my commission made me less serious than other writers, the pay abysmal.

"Soon." The single word felt like giving up in a way. Like the letters I'd penned to him about the project while here and subsequently burned without sending. Although he did want me home.

"Good. Well, I'm going to go back to bed."

"Sorry for waking you."

"I thought you were having an emergency."

At least he was worried, which had to imply some level of care. "No, I'm fine, honestly. Just missing you." The admission was difficult. With the concern in his words, perhaps he missed me too. "Maybe you could come here? Get away for a day or two and we can travel home together?"

Prod huffed on the other end of the line. "I've got a lot going on, Naunce. I don't have time to gallivant in the countryside."

"Is that what you think I'm doing? Gallivanting?" How I wished I'd not given him the satisfaction of saying I missed him.

Another drawn-out, exaggerated sigh. "I think your time would be better served elsewhere. Doing something you can respect yourself for."

"Good night," I managed to say around my strangled tongue, anger and disappointment a bitter pill to swallow. My self-respect wasn't the problem.

Every time I opened up my heart, he cut a piece off, chewed it up and spat it back out again. I was reliving my mistake with Hamish all over again—so desperate for a man's love I put up with the indefensible.

I believed part of his dismissiveness, his lack of respect, was that we'd been unable to conceive. The doctor had performed a rather painful curettage on me the year before, scraping away at my insides. He'd declared me fit to conceive, but still my womb sat empty, a hollowness eating away at the parts of my soul Prod hadn't already devoured.

I wanted a baby. A child to stare up at me and smile with wholesome, unconditional love. Someone to love me, even if my husband did not. I wanted very much to feel a love so strong I'd die for it.

I set down the receiver and went back to my wine, staring into the half-empty cup.

Jessica was due to give birth any day now. Though Esmond tried to forbid her to see me, I'd managed to navigate my way to their tiny flat in the East End of London. She was big as a house now. *House . . .* I shuddered to think of the squalor of their tiny, dirty one-room habitation. My future niece or nephew might contract some illness if it survived being birthed there.

My heart skipped a beat. Surely Muv wouldn't let anything happen to a grandchild. She'd spoiled Diana's two Guinness boys. East End notwithstanding, any child born to Jessica and Esmond would be her grandchild and therefore well cared for.

The jealous demons I tried to keep locked away swirled in my wine-drenched gut.

Jessica, who'd defied everyone in running away, and Diana, who'd shoved her husband aside and stuck up her nose at societal conventions to become a man's mistress, both had babies. *Where is mine?*

"Do be sorry for me," I whispered to no one.

January 1938

Dearest Evelyn,

Please find enclosed, my introduction to the volume of family letters I'm editing. As always, your impeccable advice is most welcome.

Much love,
Nancy

Ice and misery slicked over the London streets, kept me inside, deeply enthralled in the *Ladies of Alderley*. I was so close to the end. Ready to hand it over to Edward to be published.

It'd been two weeks since I'd rung up Jessica proposing a visit with her and her new baby. I feared her wastrel husband continued to feed the lie that I was not to be trusted.

Putting aside my edits, I hopped on the tube, braving a mugging rather than riding in a taxicab that would slither about the frozen streets to 41 Rotherhithe Street in the East End.

The four-story, half-dilapidated building looked as joyless and wretched as on my first visit. The windows were scummy, with one on the bottom broken. A man sat on the ground outside, drinking from a dented flask and looking as though he'd been there for at least a decade. Ignoring him, I looked up, half expecting to see a cradle hanging out the window as Deborah told me it was on her visit, the baby girl happily swinging in the wintry breeze, but there was none.

Jessica answered the door after half a knock as though she'd been waiting in the entry for me. Her hair was a bit in disarray, her clothes wrinkled and stained, but there was color in her cheeks, and her eyes shone with happiness.

"Esmond's gone to work, so we have a little bit of time to visit." With a nervous smile, she reached for my arm and tugged me inside.

"Good." I took off my overcoat, shivering in the cold. The flat's heater must have been broken.

I placed a small cake Sigrid had baked onto the table, shuffling papers aside to make room. Then I gathered my sister in my arms. She smelled of sweat and sour milk. I wanted to pluck her from the shabbiness in which she insisted on living and take her home for a soak in the tub. "Where is Julia?"

Jessica nodded toward a bassinet. "Sleeping."

I was relieved not to see the baby yet, knowing how much it would hurt to hold her in my arms. "Let's have tea."

Jessica put on the kettle, then settled at the table, opening the cake tin and breathing in the sugary confection. "Smells heavenly."

I rummaged in a drawer, finding a crusty knife, which I wiped off on a towel and brought over with two forks and plates. As I cut our slices, Julia's cry pierced the frigid air.

"Oh, she'll be hungry." Jessica alighted from her chair and lifted the tiny, punching bundle from the bassinet in the corner. "Do you mind if I feed her?"

"No, not at all." My heart ached. Seeing the infant snuggled against my sister was going to be painful. I poured the tea while Jessica lifted her shirt and quieted her hungry baby against her breast.

"How are you doing?" I hoped Jessica would be honest with me.

"Tired and exhilarated all at once." She peeked at Julia, smiling with pride. "She's such a little beauty. I can already tell she's got a bit of Mitford cheekiness in her."

"I'd expect nothing less." I almost added *of a baby born while her parents were on the run*, but stopped myself. "How is Esmond?"

"Just fine." Jessica did not expound. But I was doubtful, glancing around the tiny, dirty, overburdened flat.

"I could send Sigrid for an afternoon, if you like, to help out a little while you are busy with Julia. Treat for the new mother."

"If Esmond came home to find her here, he'd be displeased. Muv offered Nanny Blor, but Esmond says that's a complete contradiction to what we believe in."

I wondered what *that* was exactly and if those beliefs were shared by my sister or imposed upon her. I wondered how much their lifestyle affected him given Esmond was off working, and not trapped all day in squalor.

"While he's at work, then." I winked. "What he doesn't know won't hurt him, and it might help you."

Jessica laughed, scooping a bit of cake onto her fork. "If he came home and everything was tidy, he would definitely know. Besides, I like the idea of tending house."

Vaguely disappointed she would not allow me to help, I let the matter drop.

"Have you heard about the children's transport?" Jessica changed the subject. "Resistance fighters in Germany are sending Jewish children here, trying to get them away from Unity's murderous boyfriend." She shook her head in disgust at our sister's infatuation, and then pushed a newspaper across the table toward me.

Though she hated Hitler as much as, if not more than, anyone,

Jessica still retained a soft spot for Unity, despite our sister's horrifying attachment to the monster.

I took a sip of tea, reading the first paragraph of the headline story. The first of the refugee children would arrive in Britain today.

I was proud of our country's show of compassion, but it was a chilling development nonetheless. For parents to surrender their children to strangers, to be shipped who knew where—how dreadful things must be across the channel. Once the children arrived in England, where would they go? Would anyone I knew with a country house take in the ravaged children? Our family had not been asked. Nor had Muv volunteered—she would have mentioned it.

"I can't imagine being separated from Julia. It must be devastating." Jessica tucked baby Julia against her shoulder and patted her back until she was rewarded with a loud belch. Such a sound seemed impossible for so tiny a body.

My sister lifted Julia into the air and passed her to me without warning. The baby was nearly weightless. Tiny toes poked out from the bottom of her gown, and tiny fingers plucked at the collar of my shirt before I settled her in my arms. The warmth of her was terrifying and comforting all at once. So small, so frail, her head wobbling on a delicate neck—with the slightest movement I might break her. Her wide blue eyes stared into mine. Innocent and trusting. The back of my throat grew itchy along with my eyes. I blinked and smiled until the tears dissipated.

"I heard a rumor today." Jessica stirred cream in her tea. "You won't believe it."

"Try me."

"Diana is pregnant with the Ogre's baby."

I felt as though I'd been punched in the gut. Years ago, before she'd been divorced from Bryan, but already the lover of Mosley, Diana had had a secret abortion. Nobody but I knew of it, so I didn't mention it now.

"How did you hear?" I asked.

"Muv let it slip on her last visit Diana hadn't been feeling well because of her condition. I asked what condition. Muv paled, ruffled like the feathers of her hens, and blamed the stress from travel back and forth to Germany and the Ogre's position in government."

Julia grabbed at my shirt, and I stared down into her pretty eyes. What an angel. Then came a rumbling in her undercarriage, and I quickly passed her back.

"Oh, come now, don't you want to learn to change nappies?" Jessica teased.

"Next visit, I'm bringing Sigrid as my companion."

Jessica laughed and changed the baby, then she looked about nervously. "Esmond will be back soon."

My cue to leave. I cleaned up the table, turning on the tiny sink to rinse the dishes. No water came out. "What's happened?"

"The super turned it off. We're a bit behind." Jessica shrugged as if it was completely normal.

Perhaps it was. I'd come to know the bailiffs at Rose Cottage on a first-name basis, they were around so often. Sliding into my overcoat, I opened my purse, pulling out five pounds. It wasn't much, but for Jessica it would be enough to help. Besides, it was better for Jessica to have it than for Prod to take it from my purse later for a night of booze at his club.

"I can't take that." Jessica tried to shove the money back into my purse.

"You can, and you will."

"You and Prod are nearly as poor as we are."

I laughed. "On some days, yes, but not today. Besides, consider this a payback with interest."

"For what?"

"I stole a pound from your running-away account ages ago. Needed it for taxi fare."

"No, you didn't."

"I did." *I didn't.* But it was the only way Jessica would take anything I offered.

"All right, if it's true."

"It is." I kissed her and the baby, then wandered out onto the crowded, stinking East End streets. On the bumpy tube ride home, I couldn't get far from the memory of Julia in my arms. Despite her poor situation, Jessica oozed happiness. Practically glowing with vitality and love. Was it better to be poor and happy, than wealthy and disappointed?

I was neither.

But perhaps I'd been looking for all the wrong things.

March 12, 1938

Dearest Mark,

The headlines on the Daily Express *this morning were most terrifying—*

Germans March into Austria: Britain Makes Protest "In Strongest Terms"

Hitler is intent on his expansionism, and the Treaty of Versailles is not going to hold him back. How dare he eschew the sacred agreement between Germany and Britain and her allies? Are we to live through the Great War all over again?

But I tell you, what I fear for most is all of Europe, but second is Unity. Though we are estranged, I hope one day she comes to her senses and returns home. If not for her own sake, then for the sake of Farve's heart.

Oh, do let's have lunch soon. I miss your good cheer.

Love from,
Nancy

"Ah, so you've seen." Prod came up behind me at the breakfast table, resting his hand on my shoulder. He set another paper down beside the one I held. The *Daily Herald*'s headline was more dire: *Germany Invades Austria: Hitler Sends Ultimatum, Schuschnigg Defies Him.*

"There will be another war." I worried my lower lip. "How can there not be? How far will he take his Nazis?"

All the way to England . . . I could hear Unity's voice in my head telling me how fond her Führer was of England, how he admired the country and wanted to visit but feared the British government would turn him away.

Prod moved to sit down heavily opposite me, plucking up a piece of toast and slathering it with butter. I was proud not to have burned all the pieces this morning, and from the look on his face, Prod was pleased.

"An invasion is certainly not good news." Prod bit into his toast and mused as he chewed. "Hitler's sent one hundred thousand troops. France is worried. I know the British Cabinet plans to hold an emergency session this morning. So much for their warning to Germany not to use force against an independent state. Hitler doesn't give a damn."

Perhaps it was a surprise he'd not chosen to do so sooner considering in 1936 he'd invaded the Rhineland. It was only a matter of time before the German army moved on to another sovereign state. Now Nazi flags flew in Austria. *Where will they be next?*

By teatime, news on the wireless stated Germany had rejected the demands of Britain and France and would not pull out of Austria.

"Does this mean war?" My fingers shook, sloshing the tea in my cup. I set it down. The bit of scone I'd eaten sat like a ball of lead in my belly.

"Chamberlain says we'll not declare war for now. He prefers sanctions." Prod shook his head.

I nodded, hating the world of politics, the confusion of it all. But at least there was the chance we'd not go to war.

What I wouldn't give to return to Alderley, and the piles of letters that kept me shut out of reality.

And yet a part of me still yearned for the next great idea. One that would propel me from obscure novelist, a lady playing at being a writer, to a well-respected literary talent. A dream that rested just out of reach, and I'd not the energy quite yet to rise to the challenge.

May 28, 1938

~~Darling Evelyn,~~

~~Some things are too heartbreaking to write on paper . . .~~

My curse was late. Never regular, I've often gone a month without. But something felt different this time. I clutched my breasts, which were heavier, achy. Could it be I fostered a fetus? Pregnant, *at last*?

The latest curettage my doctor had done months ago might have actually worked. Oh . . . what I wouldn't give if Prod and I were finally blessed with a child. Everything would change.

Sitting at my dressing table, preparing to make a trip to Heywood Hill bookshop for a literary society meeting, I stared into the looking glass at my belly, imagining it swelling with the growth of a child. A hot flush crept over my chest.

Me, a mother?

Prod, a father . . .

If it were true, I hoped it was a little girl, because two Prods in one house would be too much. Oh, how I could have shrieked with laughter at that, and instead picked up my lipstick, spreading a vibrant red along my smiling lips.

My silent pleasure was pierced by the ringing of the telephone. I hurried from my bedroom, down the stairs, to answer.

"You need to come to Rutland Gate." Farve's voice on the other end of the line was very serious. "Muv needs you."

My mind raced as to what this could be about. Unity? Muv's health? "What's happened?"

Farve let out a long, tortured sigh. "It's Julia." There was a lengthy pause as I imagined Farve pinching the bridge of his nose and trying to find the words. His voice was thick when he finally managed, "She's died."

I lost my balance, clutching the table tightly. The antique brass-and-crystal lamp on top wobbled then fell. But I didn't care. Jessica's baby had *died*? I couldn't have heard correctly.

Both Jessica and Julia had been sick for weeks with the measles epidemic, which had struck her East End neighborhood hard, but Jessica had been on the mend . . . and I thought Julia too. *Oh, Julia.* Tears ran down my face, and I gave a hitching sob. My greatest fears and premonitions upon seeing their sad, cold and dirty flat had come true. All of our family's concerns about the squalor in which my sister and niece lived . . . Guilty thoughts riddled me. If only I'd somehow been able to get through to her before.

A clinic had refused to inoculate Julia when my sister asked at the beginning of the outbreak, simply telling my sister to breast-feed Julia and that would give her immunity—even though Jessica had never had the measles herself. How could she hope to transmit immunity?

It had been a disaster, which Muv and Farve had railed about for days. They offered to send help, but Esmond refused. If only Esmond hadn't been so damned proud . . . Julia would be alive and well, tucked in the nursery at Rutland Gate with Nanny Blor to fawn over.

The nurses Esmond managed to hire (too late) to care for my

sister and niece had not been enough. This was Esmond's fault. Not mine. Not anyone in my family's. But Esmond. If only he'd heeded my warnings at the dock. If only he'd listened to reason the countless times anyone had spoken.

I gasped in a wretched breath. Sweet baby Julia, who I'd held in my arms only months ago, warm and wiggly. I squeezed my eyes shut to the world, frozen in place, trying to force out the image of my darling niece lying cold in her bassinet.

Farve cleared his throat. I'd forgotten I still held the receiver.

"I'll be there soon." My voice cracked. I hung up the receiver, and sank into the chair beside the table, staring at the floor, the mosaic of the woven carpet blurring as I cried. I tried to call Jessica, but no one answered. Rising, I grabbed a jacket and headed for the door.

I walked the two miles to Rutland Gate, hoping the fresh air would help sweep away my tears and clear my mind.

The house was somber. Curtains drawn. No music. Much as it had been when Jessica had first run away little more than a year before. What sadness had been wrought on our family since the day she'd run off with Esmond Romilly.

Muv squeezed me tight, her body trembling. "I wanted to drive straight to the East End, but when your father spoke to him on the telephone, Esmond refused us."

Farve cursed under his breath. "Bloody damn fool."

"He knows we blame him," Muv said. "We asked them to stay at Rutland Gate at the start of the outbreak. I offered the services of Nanny Blor." She sank down on the settee, wiping her tears with a handkerchief. "We all feared this. Now it's come to pass. I suspect he'll never forgive us for being right."

"Esmond's own mother also offered," Farve growled. "Think the fool will blame her too?"

"I'm not sure he'll ever recognize that his juvenile stubbornness cost his daughter her life." I couldn't wrap my head around the idea that while a pandemic ran rampant through the streets of their dilapidated neighborhood, Esmond refused all help.

I regarded Farve, looking defeated and slumped in a chair. He felt he'd failed Jessica, and in turn failed Julia. Guilt pinched the creases of his face. How much he'd aged when Jessica ran away. Now this.

My anger rose, despite my efforts, and turned toward Jessica. She'd been so selfish. Jessica wanted to torment our parents for whatever perceived injustices she'd suffered growing up in her privileged life. From the moment Jessica could walk, she'd tried to run. Tried to outdo her sisters in all things, including the tabloids. As a family, what more could we have done?

Tucked in a corner on her favorite reading chair, Deborah sniffled, face in her hands. Muv sobbed openly into her handkerchief, and Farve paced angrily. I couldn't bear to be in the room a minute longer.

"I'll see about tea," I said firmly, glad for an excuse to disappear downstairs to the kitchen.

But I only made it as far as the stairwell, then, pressing my hand to my womb, I sucked in a sob. The cool veneer I'd been able to maintain cracked. Sadness for my sister mingled with a sharp and sudden fear for my own child's survival. I slid down to sit on the stairs, crying until I had nothing left inside me.

August 1938

Dear Evelyn,

I've accepted an invitation to visit West Wycombe. I do hope you'll come for a visit while I'm there. Your company does more to cheer than all the sunny days in summer.

> *Best love,*
> *Nancy*

With Jessica gone for two months now to Corsica with Esmond to heal from the loss of their child, the fetus and I were swept to the Palladian Dashwood residence in the country—West Wycombe Park—home of my good friend Helen.

Prod had gone off with a friend—*male*—to France on a holiday. I was supposed to be with him, but in my current state of misery I'd chosen to remain home. Likely for the best. I had no patience for his antics, and he none for mine.

Pregnancy was not for the faint of heart, or the hearty, I decided. Anyone who thought it easy was either lying to themselves or not altogether human.

The oppressive heat in London without the slightest breeze from the Thames made it all the worse. The stench of summer in the city made me want to gag. Familiar and ordinarily pleasant odors, such as the onions Sigrid cooked, did too. The baby demanded foods I wouldn't dare touch before it was inside me, and then made me toss them back up, the little tease.

The very slightest bit of annoyance had me ready to hurl whatever was nearest me in whatever direction the displeasure was coming from. Often this was Prod and whatever book I was reading.

My moods shifted as often as the contents of my stomach. I could be dancing with Prod, as if we were the two happiest people in the world. Then he'd say the wrong thing . . . God, Prod always said the wrong thing.

Of course, that wasn't exactly true. *Poor Prod.* He probably had no idea how tedious he was. When I advised him of his tiresomeness, rather than take my counsel, he called me a cruel, bitter woman. I was not too proud to admit my pregnancy wasn't a happy time for us. Little wonder when he skipped off to France.

A soft knock sounded at my borrowed bedroom door before Muv poked her head inside. I gathered up the Alderley letters I'd begun taking with me everywhere, having convinced my cousin a second volume was in order. Muv approved, hoping I'd given up my aspirations of being the female version of Evelyn Waugh. She couldn't see that abandoning my literary dreams tore me apart.

"My plans are arranged for Germany," she said, still halfway in the room and halfway in the corridor. "You'll be all right?"

Unity was sick with pneumonia, currently in the care of Hitler's favorite doctor in a German hospital with Farve by her side. Muv was going to Bayreuth to take her turn. The very idea of my parents being in such close proximity to the Nazis, and beholden to Hitler, was nauseating.

"I'll be fine. Do make sure to wish her a speedy recovery." It sounded as though she'd been at death's door. After the loss of Julia and the near loss of Jessica, Muv and Farve were taking no chances in losing another.

"We'll leave in the morning for the cottage," Muv said, speaking of the home in Swinbrook she and Farve had bought after having to let our larger childhood manor home go due to expense.

"I'll be ready." I went to my dressing table, picked up the ornate brush from Prod and ran it through my hair, watching the dark curls sheared into a short length bounce back.

"You're certain you'll be able to take care there?" Muv asked.

"Muv, Debo is nearly a grown woman now. How hard can it be?"

Muv stared at me a moment, lips pursed, head cocked to the side. "Do you recall nothing of when you were her age?"

"Are you trying to point out that I'm thirty-four?"

Muv scoffed. "Don't remind me. It is only a reflection of my own age. To know I've still a girl at home is positively overwhelming."

There was a little flutter in my belly. The baby? Or nerves?

"Debo and I will be fine. Your youngest scrappage will be fine with your oldest."

Muv didn't crack a smile. "Be sure to take care of yourself, Naunce. You must rest as the doctor said, else risk losing your child."

"I am very good at resting," I said. A complete lie. I was *restless*.

"I'm glad you'll have a nurse to look after you."

I turned away to rub a little color on my lips so Muv wouldn't see my irritation. The care everyone took made me feel infirm. As though I were a precious porcelain doll that could crack at the slightest touch. "If it makes you feel better about leaving, Muv," I said, poking at her a little.

She shook her head and turned to go, then swiveled back. "I almost forgot, Helen has requested you join her in the drawing room for one last tête-à-tête before we depart."

"Will you be joining us?"

"I'll join you for dinner."

I rose, fashionably dressed, belt cinched tight just above the bump in my belly. Pregnancy was no excuse to be frumpy.

Muv's eyes swept over me. "You really ought to loosen that belt; you'll suffocate the poor thing."

"The fetus is fine."

Muv's gaze snapped back up to mine. "Don't call it that."

I shrugged. "That's what it is."

Muv's brows drew together, in a look of never-ending scrutiny and judgment I was all too familiar with. "I do hope for your sake you'll have a son who dotes on you the way my Tom does on me, rather than a daughter who, well, never mind." She cut her passive insult short.

"If I thought for one moment it was a boy, I'd take my bicycle all the way back to London."

Muv gasped at my threat to cause myself a miscarriage. I felt instantly contrite, because it wasn't exactly true. I'd wanted a child for so long the sex didn't matter.

"Nancy." Muv's voice was strangled.

"I'm not myself," I said. "It's all too much, positively stifling. I feel sick all the time. I don't know how you managed being pregnant so many times without going mad. After this I should be done."

A foreign look of maternal concern momentarily softened Muv's features. "Oh, Naunce, its only because I didn't know any better. When you're young, not much can bother you. Your body is supple, made for childbearing. But at your age, well, every ache and pain is surely worse and more lasting."

She turned and went, leaving me stunned. There was no

doubt where I got my waspish tongue from. *Oh, Muv, how you wound me.*

Arriving at my parents' cottage the next day, I settled in, making sure to take care of myself as instructed. Lying about as best I could at the cottage, keeping any walks short. However, even with Debo for company, after two weeks bored out of our minds we headed back to London and Rutland Gate, in need of the distractions of the city.

Farve arrived back from Germany by early September, relieving me of my nanny duties to Deborah and sending me back to Blomfield Road. I arrived to find Peter lounging in the sitting room, a whisky in hand.

He leapt up, gaze sweeping over my changed form. We'd not set eyes on each other in months. I was keenly aware of the differing shape of my body, uncomfortable at the roundness, the swells. The bags beneath my eyes from lack of sleep. I'd opted for a slightly more comfortable and airy dress in a color that would hide the sickly pallor of my face. Good thing too, because I could tell Prod scrutinized every inch. Prod did not like women who were not thin. As a gentleman, he ought to keep in mind that however I looked, he'd made me this way.

I should have embraced him, but I hung back, self-conscious. Holding my breath. Whatever he said next would make or break me.

"I'm fat now, dear," I said, lips pursed, hoping to defuse my growing discomfort with a jest.

"Hardly." Peter came forward to embrace me, whisky on his breath. "You look stunning." His hands, at my waist, skimmed to the front, and I cringed, waiting for him to say something awful.

But he didn't. He leaned in, kissed me again, then led me to the sofa, pushing an ottoman into place and propping my feet.

"I've been instructed to treat you like glass."

I groaned, letting my head fall back on the sofa.

"It's a good thing I'm out of work," he continued, bringing my attention sharply back, "so I can make sure you're taken care of."

I stiffened with shock, my stomach plummeting. Didn't he realize the words coming out of his mouth were a study in contradiction? How could he take care of me, of our child, without income? He'd spent the last two years, surprisingly, steadily employed, and I'd grown used to the stability. We both had.

"Peter," I said, a warning edge in my tone.

"Oh, Naunce." He gave an exaggerated sigh. "Don't start in on me."

I bristled, sitting bolt upright again.

"Calm yourself. Think of the baby." He sat beside me, awkwardly stroked my hair. I wanted to grab his hand, tear it off and throw it out the window. "I've got an interview in two weeks with the BBC. I'll get the job, I promise."

My muscles relaxed a little, until I remembered his promises generally meant nothing. "Why so long?"

"The manager I'm to meet with is on holiday. So, for the next two weeks, my sole job is to be your doting husband."

That might actually be nice. We'd not seen each other in so long, and now we'd have a chance to rekindle our relationship before he started with his new job.

For the next two days, Peter did spoil me. He woke me with breakfast in bed, carried me down to the sitting room. Brought me my books, papers and pens. When Dollie, Lottie and Millie needed walks, he either came with me, offering an arm, or took them himself. He let me wax on, listening with an attentive air, as I told him all about the Alderleys and how incredibly clever they were.

Our housekeeper kept the house clean from the many things he discarded, thankfully. Feeling better, and the allotted "rest time" prescribed by my doctor having been lifted, I dismissed the nurse Muv had arranged.

Despite his regaling of tollgating-type things, Prod also made me laugh, so much so he worried it put undue stress on my body. We talked of politics, including how Unity had been offered an apartment by Hitler and considered taking him up on it. Did that make my sister the devil's mistress?

Jessica and her despicable husband were back in London living near the Marble Arch, having abandoned the home where they'd lost their daughter. I didn't blame them. Esmond continued to dictate the terms for seeing my sister—my whole family in disfavor. Even more so now with rumors swirling in London that Muv had returned to Germany not to look after Unity, but to participate in Hitler's Parteitag.

The tranquility of my first week home was shattered with a simple telephone call. News that Prod's brother had intervened with the BBC job opportunity. Apparently, Francis had told the television corporation that employing Prod was inadvisable as he was nothing but an irresponsible employee. The heartless bastard—not that he lied; my husband *was* irresponsible—but I still resented the fact he'd ruined us from astride his high horse atop a pile of money.

"How could he do this to me?" Prod shouted, pounding his feet into the floor as he paced.

I was at a loss for words. Sibling rivalry was something I dealt with myself, but never to the extent of ruining a life, of loss of income. Francis didn't care he threatened the financial security of an unborn child. Neither did their mother, for Lady Rennell had barely sent her congratulations.

I searched for words of comfort, but found nothing sufficient. This was not the news Prod needed, that *we* needed. For the first time in months I felt like vomiting.

I marched over to my desk, snatched up a piece of paper and angrily wrote the name *Francis* on it. I waved the paper triumphantly toward Prod, grinning almost maniacally.

"What are you doing?" Prod asked incredulously.

"What my father does." I wiggled my brows conspiratorially. "We'll stick your brother in a drawer and pray for revenge."

"Oh, that's nonsense." Prod waved away the notion, heading instead for the cellaret to pour himself a drink.

I shrugged. "Maybe it is. Maybe it isn't. Farve does it all the time." I opened a drawer and shoved the note inside, closing it tight. I hoped Francis would get his due. Or at the very least, that Prod would somehow find a job. I didn't know what we would do if he didn't.

Mid-September 1938

~~Dearest~~

Pain ripped through my abdomen, shocking me awake.

I sat bolt upright in bed, my hand coming to the small bump that housed a future Rodd.

Another wave hit me, and I gasped, this time prompting Prod to scram up in bed too.

"What is it? What's happened?" He rubbed his eyes, staring at me in surprise before leaping up to look out the window as if he'd expected us to be the victims of some disaster.

Which we were, but not the kind he foresaw.

Wet, hot stickiness seeped from between my legs. I was too afraid, too weak, to pull back the covers to see what horror awaited me. Another stab of pain had me gagging. By now Prod realized I'd not been awoken by some unseen force, but my body.

"Naunce." Panic filled his voice as he rushed forward and pressed the back of his hand to my forehead. "What's the matter?"

I leaned over the side of the bed, gagging, retching and terrifying him. Then he peeled back the covers, and there was nothing I did that could frighten him more than what he saw. His eyes were wide with horror. I didn't need to look to know what the dreadful wetness was soaking through the mattress. *Our baby . . .*

I opened my mouth to scream, but no sound came. My voice caught somewhere in the back of my throat.

A guttural moan escaped Prod as he stumbled back.

"Call . . ." I sucked in a breath, feeling light-headed, my vision blurring. "Call the doctor."

As I laid my head back against the pillows, heart pounding, my body expelling our baby, I sobbed until consciousness left me. I woke to Prod shaking me, face looming over mine with worry.

"The doctor is on the way. Stay awake. He said you need to stay awake."

No. I wanted to sink into blackness. To slip wet and sticky from the world the same way my baby was. What more did I have to live for? A failed marriage, a career that struggled to breathe, impending poverty and now, worst of all, the baby I'd so longed for, ripped from my womb.

I laughed bitterly, the sound rasping. My eyes slid closed but not before I witnessed Prod's look of shock.

"Why are you laughing?"

I told him this life, this deplorable life, was one great joke. That I'd come screaming into the world, and I wasn't going to leave it without laughing first. I wasn't going to simply fall away without one last show of obstinance.

"Nancy." Prod shook me again, and my eyes popped open. "Stay awake. Did you ride a bicycle? Jump? Run?"

I narrowed my eyes, the bitter laughter souring in the back of my throat. "You think I *did* this?" My lips peeled away from my teeth. "This is not me. This is a sign from God that he does not trust us to have a child. You cannot provide for a child. We are not *meant* to have a family. We were not meant to be . . ." It was on the tip of my tongue to say *happy*. But that would be giving away too much. Already I was giving away pieces of myself until there was nothing left.

Prod did whatever he pleased, when he pleased, and I was left alone.

"You don't mean that. You're . . ." He swallowed. "You're not well."

"I mean every damn word," I hissed.

Prod backed away. "I'll go wait for the doctor downstairs," he mumbled.

I was too weak to say anything. Lying in the pool of blood, seeping and seeping, afraid to move.

Maybe it wasn't over yet. Maybe the doctor could save our baby. As I thought it, I knew it was a lie, but a feeble lie was all I had left.

📖

November 1938

FROM THE MOMENT SHE was born, Diana had everything. Like a person who never wanted for anything, she found it easy to discard things that mattered to others, and to flaunt the things they coveted.

She had a wealthy, handsome husband who loved her—she divorced him.

A baby grew in her womb—she aborted it.

And now those same two things were within her reach again—albeit both were secret for the time being—a husband, a baby.

I thought enough time had passed that I would not feel the pain of loss, the longing for what Diana had. Yet here, standing amongst a group of Mitfords, some of whom pretended to be stunned, in Diana's bedroom in the English countryside she shared with the Ogre, staring at the sleeping bundle in her arms, my heart wailed, and my gut ached nearly as badly as it had the day my own baby bled away. Propped against silky pillows in an angelic white dressing gown, her face made up with the right amount of pink on her cheeks and lips, Diana looked sweet, innocent. Her golden hair was fashioned in sleek finger waves as though a stylist had come in before our visit. Perhaps one had.

Though not all had been privy to Diana's secret pregnancy, several of us had guessed. But we'd not known she'd married the vile man now standing proudly beside her, paw possessively on her shoulder. The papers had been screaming for days about how Diana had clandestinely married Oswald Mosley in Germany two years prior. I shuddered to think that Hitler had stood as witness. *Hitler.* She might as well have slapped us all in the face.

Diana was a traitor to her country. Yet no one spoke it aloud. Not even Farve, who appeared content to simmer and bite back his anger. Did visiting her make *us* traitors too?

Looking at the wrinkled face of Diana's infant son, so reminiscent of his father's, I had no desire to cradle him close.

Unity, back from Germany for the blessed event, looked smug, her lip curled in satisfaction. *Another Fascist for the cause.*

Muv appeared pleased. Deborah gushed over the baby and how beautiful Diana looked for having just given birth two days prior.

Tom looked complacent, and it was hard to tell if he'd known all along or he didn't care.

Missing from the family reunion was Jessica, who'd long since metaphorically abandoned ship. I understood her finding this moment unbearable. As unbearable as it was for me. I'd never held my baby in my arms, never fed or burped it, never rocked it to sleep singing songs Nanny Blor had crooned to calm us.

Rumor had it Jessica and Esmond were fleeing farther from us still, planning to escape to America. But could one ever believe rumors?

Prod had refused to come, distancing himself from me and our loss.

Standing amidst the smiles and joyful fuss, I wished I'd done the same. It was hard to breathe. All the emotion I'd held back for months readied to burst, hemorrhaging in front of them all.

I forced myself to stay, every smile I gave feeling as false as I was sure it looked. As I turned to leave, Diana called me back.

The rest of the family filed out, the Ogre too, leaving me alone with my sister and her third son.

"I never got a chance to say how sorry I was about your unfortunate incident," Diana said. "I truly was devastated for you."

I pursed my lips, trying to hold in the retort threatening to tumble out. Trying to ignore that she'd called the loss of my baby an unfortunate incident.

"I know how much you and Peter wanted a child." She glanced down at her own baby, a satisfied smile on her face.

But it was so much more than a smile. A smile might have been easier to bear, but this look was content, full of confidence. As if she'd conquered the world and reigned victor. Well, she had, hadn't she? Three sons, and the only child she'd ever lost, she'd lost by choice.

I'd had no choice.

All the things Diana worked for were now in her grasp. Oswald Mosley, whom she'd chased after as relentlessly as my dog Dottie chased the squirrels on Blomfield Road, was finally hers for keeps.

"Why did you keep it all a secret—your marriage, the baby?" I asked.

Diana looked up sharply. "It was only a secret to those who didn't know."

I bristled at her reinforcing the knowledge that I'd been one of those left in the dark, enlightened only by the rumor Jessica shared.

"I didn't want to upset you," she said evenly, as if it were the most obvious thing in the world.

"What about Jessica?"

"Jessica only worries about herself; why should I worry about her?" Diana asked coolly. Her chin rose a little, and she stared at me with her ice-blue eyes. "Cruel things happen to us all, Naunce. I cannot be blamed if God saw fit to take your baby and Jessica's but not this one. I too have made sacrifices."

Heartless, superior, smug. To bring God into it—as if God somehow looked after Fascists with special care. Fury flamed red behind my eyes. "What sacrifices have you made? Oh, wait, I know: your morals, your honesty, your loyalty to your country and your family. You have abandoned your soul for Fascism."

Diana let out a short, bitter laugh, waking her baby, who stretched and screwed up his face as if he'd cry, but then didn't.

"You're jealous, Nancy. You always have been," Diana continued, voice calm, as if she were exchanging pleasantries with a stranger. "Jealous of my looks, of my intelligence. Jealous because I had the courage to walk away from a marriage that made me unhappy. Jealous of the babies I've borne. Jealous of my being with a man who gives me joy. Why can't you be happy for me?"

Diana's words cut me to the core, all cruelty and selfishness. *She wants to hurt me.* I realized in that moment, my sister would never change. She deserved not a single moment more of my time, not a second more of my pain.

Unable to summon a farewell, I turned away from her, from the pain, from myself, and fled.

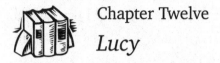 Chapter Twelve
Lucy

LUCY SPENT THE MORNING poring over book lists and making contacts for the Masters' library project. Now there were only thirty minutes until she headed to the café to meet Gavin for lunch before they went to the Air Raid Precautions exhibit. The perfect amount of time to read through more of the Mitford letters.

Iris was out there; she just had to find her.

Today's letter was all about family politics. Lucy discovered just how deep into Hitler's camp Unity Mitford fell. Beyond rallies and lunches, Unity was given an apartment by Hitler. The diary of Eva Braun, Hitler's mistress-turned-wife, included a jealous passage about Unity. Then there was Diana, whose marriage to the British Fascist leader Oswald Mosley had taken place in Germany with Hitler as a witness. Apparently, their mother was also a Fascist, even found Hitler charming. Her leaning contributed to the downfall of her marriage, as their father was not in agreement.

So much conflict. Holiday gatherings must have been grim and tense.

Along with the masses of family drama Lucy unearthed, she also came across the same Irises she and her mother had found over the years. None of which were the one she sought.

Lucy climbed the stairs buttoning her light fall jacket, and flung her purple-and-blue scarf around her neck, breathing in the light scent of jasmine left over from her favorite perfume.

Curzon Street was bustling, and for a split second Lucy viewed it not in present day, but imagined it as it looked in pictures from the 1940s. As she walked down the street toward Park Lane, looking for the café, she wondered if this was the route Nancy had taken on her way home from the bookshop. Did she stop at any of the boutiques or restaurants to meet her mysterious friend Iris?

Nancy wrote about lunching with so many people, but conveniently left out the one person Lucy sought.

Lucy ducked into the sandwich shop. Gavin hadn't arrived yet. She ordered them each a water, then mused over the Irises she'd come across in the letters.

Aunt Iris Mitford, sister of Nancy's father.

Iris Mountbatten, a debutante, and great-granddaughter of Queen Victoria.

Iris Hayter, who was mentioned briefly in a letter in the 1950s.

Iris Grey, whom Nancy didn't meet until the 1960s.

Four Irises, and none of them the one Lucy had been combing for. In her gut, she just knew they weren't right. The Iris she was looking for, Lucy was fairly certain, didn't belong to the Bright Young Things or the aristocracy. For someone who often pulled her life to pieces of their books she authored, the letters she wrote, Nancy appeared to have kept this one fragment of herself a secret. The only link being an inscription in a book—one that never found its way to Iris.

Lucy's personal journey was starting to feel a lot like finding an Iris needle in a haystack—*impossible.*

"Seems intense."

Lucy startled, then laughed at the sudden intrusion into her thoughts. "Incredibly."

Gavin took his seat. "I hope you haven't been waiting long. I got stuck in traffic."

She offered him a warm smile. "Not long at all."

Gavin shrugged out of his jacket, placing it over the back of a chair, and settled his helmet on top. "Rode my motorbike over. Gorgeous day. Soon it'll be too cold."

"I used to ride a dirt bike at my grandparents' when I was younger, but I've not been on the back of a motorcycle."

Gavin rubbed his hands together. "Then you're in luck, because that's our ride to the museum, unless you'd prefer a taxi?"

"Fun." Lucy was looking forward to riding to the museum behind Gavin. Even if the weather was in no way reminiscent of those long-ago afternoons of summer sunshine on the eastern shore of Maryland.

They chattered comfortably while they ate. Lucy thanked him for the contacts he'd provided. "Several have already resulted in acquisitions."

"Great, let me know if you run into any other snags," he offered.

"I will, thank you." She speared a red pepper out of her salad. "How long have you been riding?"

Gavin smiled and wiped his mouth with a napkin. "Since I could walk, maybe before that."

"A baby on a motorbike, now that's something," Lucy teased.

Gavin chuckled. "My da was a racer, so we grew up around them. I feel more in control on a bike than I do in a car."

"That must have been thrilling to watch him compete."

"It really was. So, what about you?"

"Last time I was on a bike I think I was fourteen." Lucy took a sip of her water, then set it back down. "I got a tire caught in a foxhole and flipped off."

Gavin leaned back in his chair. "That must have scared you. Are you sure you're all right to ride today?"

The man was giving her an out, but Lucy wasn't in London to avoid facing her fears. She was there to take leaps, both professionally and, it seemed, personally. Getting on that bike was a fear she needed to vanquish. A necessary step toward figuring out who she was and what she wanted out of life.

"I'll be fine. I'm looking forward to feeling the wind in my hair again. Plus, I can tell my sister later. She was sad to have lost a partner."

They paid their bill and headed outside, where Gavin's motorbike was chained up. He handed her a sleek black helmet, and she slipped it on and adjusted the buckle.

Gavin climbed on then motioned her onto the back. Climbing on was easy; realizing she'd have to put her arms around his waist was harder. His body was warm, taut and appealing. *Colleague*, she cautioned herself.

"Ready?" he called.

"Yes." Excitement bubbled through her.

Gavin gunned the engine, pulling them out onto the busy street. The wind was crisp and cool against her face, and Lucy relished the feel. A grin plastered on her face, she watched the buildings fly past. Little butterflies danced in her belly, but they weren't indicative of nerves so much as pure exhilaration.

She was disappointed when they pulled up outside of the museum so quickly.

"That was amazing." Lucy climbed off the bike, her body vibrating.

"I'm glad." Gavin tucked their helmets into a compartment on the back of the bike and locked it. "Now let's see if we can find any evidence of your Iris."

The museum wasn't crowded, and they made a beeline for the ARP women's exhibit.

Massive photographs, the size of walls, showed uniformed women in action on the ground in wartime London: shuffling people along streets; pulling bomb victims from rubble; pointing at queues for underground railway shelters; standing beside emergency vehicles; and putting out fires.

In one room, a massive white wall bore the black-printed names of every woman who served the Air Raid Precautions. It was easy to find Nancy knowing her surname; however, Iris was another matter. Lucy used a notes app on her phone as she scanned the long list, taking down every Iris she came upon—and there were dozens. Beyond the commemorative wall were posed pictures of the female volunteers, unit after unit, each woman uniformed, smiling with pride.

"Amazing, isn't it?" Gavin asked.

"Truly. We hear so much about women at the front, driving ambulances, working as nurses or spies. It's good to see the women serving at home given their due."

They continued through the exhibit, arriving before a row of female mannequins dressed in an assortment of dark wool-skirted uniforms, belts cinched, performing duties. Felt uniform hats sat at an angle as they held bandages or medical bags, tending victims of a bombing. There was an original ARP van, with a volunteer leaning out one window. In a morgue scene, a woman holding an indelible pencil bent over a body covered in a sheet. The final mannequin display showcased a trio of women fighting a fire. One sprayed the flames with a water pump, another tossed sand on the fictional flames, and a third rang a bell, one hand cupped to her mouth as if she was calling out for help.

Something on the woman manning the pump caught Lucy's eye—a pin fastened on the burlap bag slung over her shoulders.

It was an iris.

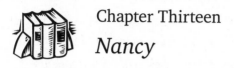

Chapter Thirteen

Nancy

May 1939

Darling Evelyn,

All the miseries I've ever borne in my life seem paltry compared to what the people around me are enduring. This afternoon I drove Spanish refugees from their camp in Perpignan, France, to Sette. Prod was back at the camp, surrounded by yet more misery.

You would be humbled by the dignity of the refugees despite their desolate circumstances. They have made me rethink every bad day I've ever had.

Perpignan's surroundings are enchanting with long-limbed, wild trees draping over a gently lolling blue-green river, and rose-colored brick streets, lined with buildings cut neatly from a fairy tale. A place where I might go on holiday. Shop and lunch and drink wine until dusk with friends like you. How out of place, and how much drearier the camp looks with such a spot as its backdrop. It seems surreal, I tell you.

Today I doled out soup to women whose faces were hollowed out with hunger, and whose children, pressed close to their mothers' sides, stared up at me with ravenous eyes.

As poor as I feel in my own social circle—a discussion we've had many times—I am rich compared to these souls who have lost everything. And still they sing, smile, grip their families in their arms with pride, joy and relief. However much of their lives have been taken, they still find small moments to claim.

I'm happy to give them all of my moments, rewarded in the split seconds when the misery vanishes from their faces. I am humbled, Evelyn.

The only writing I'm doing these days is on the pages of letters and some articles I've sent to the papers, detailing the horrors and drudgery of a refugee's life, begging the assistance from those who can afford it—which is why I have written you this lengthy dispatch. Please, whatever you can do, they need your help and that of our friends.

Love from,
Nancy

THE SPANISH CIVIL WAR had ended—with General Franco and his brutal army, aided by Hitler, claiming victory. For months now, families left to suffer at the hands of the triumphant Fascist parties scrambled over the Pyrenees mountains in the bitter cold, desperate to escape, their only belongings carried on their backs, quickly reduced in the grueling trek to only what was essential to survival—warm overcoats and blankets.

They'd trudged through snow and ice, their clothes threadbare, their boots soon riddled with holes. Men, women, children. Women heavy with child, and some who carried infants clutched at their breasts. Hundreds died while crossing. More succumbed when they finally reached their destination. They sought relief from violence, murder. They'd been accepted into France, only to be shoved behind the barbed-wire fences of an internment camp for "their" safety. Nearly two hundred thousand souls were at Perpignan. The conditions there claimed four hundred lives a day. People who survived the treacherous journey only to die of typhoid, cholera, starvation and exhaustion.

Those who helped were mostly British with a sparing grasp of Spanish iterations, and vice versa with the refugees' English. Added to the confusion was that most of the refugees also knew no French, but we managed.

Seeing the plight of the Spanish refugees as his calling, Prod marched off to care for the less fortunate. He viewed his service as a way to make up for not signing on to fight in the civil war itself as Romilly and so many others had.

Of course, at the time, Prod thought Romilly foolish. But Prod had for so long been looking for a way to fit in. A place where he could shine. So now, he was the unofficial prime minister of Perpignan. Running the refugee camp from a slapdash office, a large shed on Avenue de la Gare. One gust of wind and the hut was bound to collapse. The camp brought out the best of his talents for organizing, ordering and extolling knowledge. No one was better at telling everyone else what they ought to do and how to do it than Peter Rodd.

The letters he'd sent before I arrived were inspiring, with details of his work, the people and, beneath his bragging, a desperation to finally do something with his life.

I was proud of him—which I rarely experienced. A swelling in my chest that brought tears, and a hearty tease that the old Tollgater had finally found his perfect post. At the heart of it, I truly was impressed. The sentiment was so profound that I realized it for the truth it was, and every other moment I'd been proud paled to nonexistent.

I wanted to join him on the journey. To help people. Do my part to fight against Fascism. For all the outward noise of my sister Jessica's rantings against Fascism, she wasn't truly doing anything to fight against tyranny. When she'd run away to Spain with Romilly, what had she done, besides cause an uproar?

Here I was in the thick of it, joining other women relief workers, several months after Prod had left me in London. Most of the women volunteers spent their time helping mothers change nappies and feed their children. I only did so on occasion, typically working in the office with Prod's two assistants. But today they needed extra help, and so rather than returning to camp, I remained at the embarkation site.

They were overwhelmed. As was I. I'd not slept in thirty-six hours. I was fairly certain Prod had not passed an hour of sleep in the last forty-eight.

"*Madame*, please," a mother pleaded, pushing her baby toward me, accent thick, belly swollen with yet another pregnancy.

I reached for her child, awkwardly bouncing the whimpering infant while its mother scooped up a toddler, clutching her legs. Goodness, but she was fecund. Unlike my animosity toward Diana's ever-growing womb, I felt only pity for this woman.

"*Gracias, señora.*" She sighed with relief, collapsing onto the ground, toddler on her lap.

"*De nada, señora.*" It was all I'd learned to say—*you're welcome, madame*—and like everything else, it seemed not enough.

I held the squalling infant to my chest, staring down into its wet, brown eyes and feeling a jolt of guilt for ever considering myself burdened or deprived. I'd wanted a baby so badly, and yes, I'd been denied that. Now I saw that loss in perspective. Perhaps it was fate, for if I'd had an infant of my own in London, I wouldn't be here.

As I rocked the baby, I watched the mother take the nappy off her wiggling toddler, only to have him leap up and run off, bare-bottomed, with a laugh. The mother's shoulders slumped, but she managed to pick herself up and hurry after him.

The babe in my arms wailed as his mother disappeared. I started to sing a nursery rhyme Nanny had crooned to us, but that only seemed to make the baby cry louder. "Where is your mother, little bug?" I asked in a sweet voice.

He stopped crying for an instant, staring at me with wide-eyed horror before he renewed his screams in earnest.

What I wouldn't give at this moment to return to my regular duties at the camp. I longed for the office on the edge of camp with Prod's partners, Donald Darling and Humphrey Hare. When I'd first met them, I was the only one who found it humorous that their first and surnames began with the same letter. When I'd joked to Prod that I wondered if their middle names were given accordingly, he only stared.

I wished to climb into the decrepit van I drove, delivering supplies and messages, driving refugees to their embarkation sites at Vendre or Sette, so they could set sail for Mexico, Morocco, wherever they'd call home next. Just for fun, and to Prod's mild irritation, I wore a straw hat and shouted "All aboard," whenever I pressed my foot to the gas to take the refugees to the dock. All of these were duties I could handle far better than the irate tiny human in my arms.

"He's hungry." One of the Red Cross volunteers plunked a

bottle in the baby's mouth and gave me a look that said, *Don't you know anything?* Perhaps I imagined her judgment. The baby quieted, greedily sucking at the bottle.

Thunder cracked overhead, and clouds darkened the horizon. I peered around the maze of bodies, looking for a woman dragging a naughty toddler, but found none. A gust of wind whipped the water at the quayside, and the ships in the harbor started to sway. The women waiting to board would have to wait longer with a storm coming.

"Huracán." The foreign word, shouted by one of the displaced, sounded an awful lot like *hurricane.*

A rush of other refugees took up the cry. *"Huracán! Huracán!"*

I whirled to find the other relief workers looking just as alarmed as I felt.

Rain pelted down, drenching us. The baby stopped eating to cry in pure misery. I was wet, chilled, exhausted. Since arriving, I'd felt nothing but gratitude for my life back in London. As I stood in the downpour, the crying child in my arms, my thoughts were on Blomfield Road, dinner on the table, wine poured. But I didn't regret my decision to follow Peter. Rather than breaking down from exhaustion and the surrounding despair, I felt a renewed sense of purpose. I was helping those whom Fascism sought to destroy.

At last the mother returned, carrying her chastised toddler, hair plastered to their faces. As she set the boy down, I thrust the baby into her outstretched arms. She tucked his face against her breast to shield him from the storm.

I wished for the storm to ease quickly, granting relief to us sodden souls. Then those soaked and miserable could board the ships to freedom. To places where, hopefully, politics never lead to murder. Where they wouldn't be forced to climb icy, wintry mountains, but instead be welcomed with open arms to start anew.

Not for the first time, my thoughts were consumed by their plight, the downright loss of dignity—it was overwhelming. Filled me with anger toward not only Fascism, but my sisters Diana and Unity, who had seized tyranny like an infant's security blanket. Couldn't they see the philosophies and vile rhetoric they clung to was stitched together with the skins and souls of the oppressed?

This camp was evidence of the pain and suffering of victims of Fascism.

That night, bleary-eyed, by the dim light of a lamp, my belly growling in solidarity with the hungry, I wrote to my mother, who had fallen for Hitler's charm. I knew she'd brush off my words, but I needed to write it all the same.

If you could have a look, as I have, at some of the less agreeable results of Fascism . . . you would be less anxious for the swastika to become a flag on which the sun never sets.

I put out my lamp as Prod came to bed reeking of spirits—a pattern he repeated most nights, collapsing beside me drunk, then gone by morning. Even upon my arrival, he merely brushed a kiss on my forehead and rushed off.

It felt selfish to be disappointed in the lack of time spent together. After all, I was here to help, to be a part of something greater than myself. I rolled over, waiting for sleep. At least for once, it was not a woman taking the time my husband had to give.

Shortly after dawn, I crawled from bed, splashed water on my face in the small bowl and brushed my teeth. There was no luxury in relief work, but I still had it better at this tiny hotel than did those sleeping in bunkers.

With spring come, the refugees didn't have to deal with frigid temperatures and toes that turned black from frostbite.

I nodded good morning to the man at the front desk.

"*Bonne chance aujourd'hui, madame.*" He wished me luck as he did every day.

"*Merci, monsieur.*"

Outside, Darling waited for me on the curb, a stack of folders in his hands.

"We've received word, our next ship may depart as early as next week. So we have a lot of work to do."

"I am at your command," I teased, looking up at the perfectly blue sky. No one would have guessed we'd been in the thick of a vicious storm the day before.

"Oh, no, Mrs. Rodd, it is the other way around."

I grinned at him congenially. "How many times have I asked you to call me Nancy, Darling?" I drew out his name as an endearment, a jest I never grew tired of. "Formalities have long gone out the window considering we work elbow to elbow, me in shirts perpetually soiled with sticky baby vomit, or spilled oil from the Ford, and you looking dapper as ever."

Darling chuckled and opened the door for me to get into the van. "I take no blame for the fact folks seem to prefer being sick on you rather than myself," he said in reference to a man who'd once vomited up his entire dinner on me.

"That was my favorite jacket," I grumbled. "I'll drive." I waved him into the passenger seat.

Although I made light of the unlucky event, the jacket was of the least concern. The ill man had a flu we feared would wipe out the camp. The Red Cross set up a quarantine area, and those who showed even the mildest symptoms were whisked away.

For a short but terrifying moment, Prod thought he'd succumb. Embarrassingly, and to our relief, it had been a result of his copious drinking. A habit he'd not been able to quit while here, but I couldn't fault him. He spent his days in one frustrating situation followed by another. After dealing with French authorities and corresponding abroad on behalf of the refugees, the atrocities of camp life, how could he not imbibe?

I myself looked forward to an evening glass of wine, or a snifter of cognac. Sometimes even over lunch, when I remembered to eat. But most of the time I forgot my midday meal until someone shoved soup or a sandwich under my nose.

"Croissant?" Darling lifted a greasy paper bag from the floor of the van.

"No, thank you." It was hard to eat when my eyes were crossed with exhaustion.

I turned the van onto the brick road, tires rumbling, and pulled up to our makeshift office. A line of women and children were already assembled, waiting for the provisions we provided, and those we couldn't since our funds were low.

"Good morning," I said cheerfully.

"*Buenos días*," came a chorus of voices. Despite everything, they still put on a good shop front.

When I'd been in England, I'd helped lobby for their cause. Even now I sent letters to London begging influential people to provide assistance.

I doled out packets, blankets and nappies, my stomach growling, and I wished I'd taken Darling up on the croissant. I didn't know when the last time I'd eaten had been, and I was in desperate need of a cup of tea.

As if someone read my mind, when I reached my desk a lukewarm cup waited. I looked around, wondering who might have left it, but everyone was either hunched over their work, or rushing around to deal with some other crisis.

I greedily drained the cup. When I finished, I heard Prod's voice outside.

He opened the door and swept inside. Dark circles hung beneath his eyes, and his cheeks were hollower than a week ago. But when he gazed at me, he offered a smile.

"Naunce." He drew closer, rested his hand on my shoulder and stooped to brush his lips across my forehead. "No straw hat today?"

I hooked my thumb behind me. "Hanging over there. I never leave without it."

Prod chuckled, then turned to Darling. "How goes the ship's manifesto for the upcoming departure?"

"Nearly complete."

"Excellent." Peter nodded. "We are awaiting the next ship, and we can wish more refugees a happy future."

Turning to me with a satisfied smile, Prod said, "This weekend we'll go to Collioure. A bit of sun will do us some good."

The idea of a weekend away at a sweet coastal town in Southern France brought a rush of elation that overtook my exhaustion. On Friday afternoon, we closed, leaving the care of the refugees in the hands of others, and took the train to the coast. The tranquility of the sea-salt air was an instant balm. The town was postcard perfect, with the Mediterranean lapping at the foot of a castle, sailboats taking wind off the beach and a melodic dinging of an old church bell.

After checking into a charming hotel, we made haste over winding cobbled streets to a café for sandwiches and chilled wine, then to the pebbled beach for a picnic.

This was the first time we'd been to a beach together since that terrible trip we made to Brittany, when the Sewer greeted us in the lobby. I forced the memory away. Prod and his mistress had parted ways.

After we ate, I kicked off my shoes and hose, and lifted the hem of my skirt as I rushed to the cool water, letting the waves lap at my ankles. I breathed in deep, eyes closed, turned my head toward the sun's warmth, letting it all sink in.

"Wait for me."

I opened my eyes at Prod's approach, his pants rolled up, the pale skin of his feet exposed. Playfully, I kicked water at him, and he splashed back with a laugh.

I took off at a run down the beach, my inhibitions set free by the wine. Prod chased me, wrapping his arms around my waist. He whirled me in a dizzying circle, the both of us laughing so hard, I barely recognized who we were. Worlds away from the dreary refugee camp and the countless disappointing moments of our failing marriage. I wanted to bottle this moment and keep it forever in a place I could revisit.

My husband set me back on my feet, and we stared at each other for a long passion-filled moment. If not for the crowded beach, I think we'd have fallen into the sand right then and there, making love beneath the sun. I slipped my hand in his, and we walked in affable silence back to the remains of our picnic. We lounged, and Prod prattled on about his plans for righting the wrongs in the refugee system, while I tossed pigeons the remnants of our sandwiches. If Prod needed to explain, to preach—and he always had—at least now his passion was for something meaningful.

We'd left our sea-bathing clothes back at the hotel, so we set out to fetch them. As we meandered back, a typewritten sign beside a bottle in a chemist shop caught my eye. I stopped walking, and started laughing heartily.

"Prod, look at this. *'Si la sangsue monte dans la bouteille, il fera beau temps. Si la sangsue descend—l'orage.'*" I wiped tears from laughter from the corners of my eyes. "If the leech rises in the bottle, it will be fine weather. If the leech descends—the storm."

Prod gave a robust guffaw as we leaned closer to examine the bottle behind the glass display.

"That leech is confused," he said. Currently the poor thing was mired at the bottom of the bottle, and the sky was a beautiful pale blue.

But as we exited the hotel, our sea-bathing suits secured beneath our outing garments, clouds moved in overhead. A scant block from our hotel, thunder rumbled.

"What do you know? The leech is a psychic," I teased as the first few droplets landed on my cheeks.

We held our hands above our heads and rushed into the closest shop—a bookstore. I breathed in the familiar, comforting scent of leather, paper and glue, and gazed with pleasure at shelf after delightful shelf stacked with books. I missed the familiar atmosphere of Heywood Hill's bookshop.

"Bonsoir, madame et monsieur," a bespectacled young woman greeted us from behind the register, a stack of volumes before her.

"*Bonsoir*," I answered, starting to browse.

"These are all in French," Prod remarked with a frown.

"Well, we are in France." I slid a volume off the shelf and flipped through the pages before putting it back.

"Why read a book in French when you can read it in English?"

I ignored his question, walking along until I found another title that piqued my interest and tugged it from the shelf. It'd been weeks since I'd been inside Heywood Hill's bookshop. I missed the comradery of my fellow literati, a circle to which my husband definitely did not belong. As soon as we returned to London, I would host a literary salon. Maybe even at the bookshop, if Heywood would allow. The idea captivated me. I'd invite my favorite writing and reading friends, and we'd talk books for hours.

I looked back down at the volume I held, *Vol de Nuit—Night Flight*—by Antoine de Saint-Exupéry.

"There's a charming café across the way. Shall we get a glass of wine while we wait out the storm?" Prod asked.

The shopkeeper approached just then. "I see *madame* is holding *Vol de Nuit*. It's a gripping tale of brave men piloting night mail planes in South America. The author himself was an aviator."

"Fascinating." I nodded, absorbed by the first page already. "I'll take it."

Prod started to roll his eyes, I could tell from the expression I'd seen a hundred times, but then he paused and smiled. "If it would make you happy."

"It would," I said, genuinely pleased at his change in reaction.

Prod took the book from me and carried it to the register, where he flirted in broken French with the shopkeeper. When we left, he handed me the parcel.

"My gift to you, to remember this momentous trip."

"Thank you." I was determined to appreciate the gesture, even though I'd planned to purchase the book myself. Prod had no imagination when it came to presents, or the delivery of them.

Inside the café we found a small marble table by the window where we could watch people walk by and sank down into a pair of wicker chairs. Prod ordered us wine and charcuterie. Soft music played, violins and accordions, very French.

As the rain continued to fall, we talked about the plight of the refugees. Prod bragged how he had the British representative in Perpignan under his thumb. "The man will do whatever I say."

"He is grateful for your enthusiasm, I'm sure." No one at the camp seemed to thrive as much as Prod on the chaos.

"It is the least I can do." Prod puffed up a bit. "Germany is out of control. I fear they'll breach the border soon."

"Into France?"

"Why not? They did in the Great War." His gaze shifted to me. I caught a faint flicker of worry there.

A chill caught me. The elation I'd felt slipped away as I imagined thousands of Nazis marching into France. Bomber planes flying overhead, perhaps even on their way to England. Would Unity, who was probably lunching in a similar café in Munich with Adolf Hitler, be sorry for her steadfast loyalty when bombs dropped on England? Would she and Diana regret becoming traitors to their own country?

"War is inevitable," Prod mused, frowning down at his glass as he twirled it. "And I fear it will be here before we know it."

"When the refugees ship out, perhaps I'll return to London," I hedged, not sure how I felt about the idea even as I said it.

Prod glanced at me, paused, then nodded. "That is a good

idea. I want you safe. You've done a remarkable job here, darling. But we both know you've not really got the stomach for it." He smiled to take the sting out of his words, but it didn't help.

I'd been here for weeks toiling endlessly to aid the displaced, taking breaks only to sleep, and when the office closed for a much-needed breather. I could have been in London, in the comfort of my house, cuddling my dogs, who were staying with Pam. Or lunching at the Savoy with friends. How dare he say I didn't have the stomach for the work?

I believed I'd done a fine job, reassuring frightened wives that they'd soon be reunited with their husbands. Soothing babies who messed on my clothes, driving a wheezing hunk of metal to and fro, safely delivering refugees to their ships. But in Prod's mind, it was still not good enough. *I* was not good enough.

I started to wonder if I ever would be.

"Perhaps I can send Unity back in my place?" I said dryly. "I'm certain she's got the stomach for it."

Prod looked horrified. "Naunce, that's not what I meant, and you know it."

"Isn't it?" I sipped my wine, staring at him over the rim.

"I only meant that you would thrive better in London."

Did he truly believe what he said, or was it that I was doing *too* good a job here? Maybe I was taking away his thunder. After all, those I worked with frequently extolled my virtues. Did my selfish husband believe I upstaged him while he tried to play king?

"You're right," I said, a hint of bitterness in my tone that I wished to rub away. "I am a 'peer's daughter,' after all, and certainly better appreciated in London."

Prod's face shuttered. How impossible it seemed now that our day had started out blissfully, with that moment on the beach.

Why did I keep allowing myself to fall for those brief happy moments? I needed to be honest with myself. There was just too much between us that was never said. Too much pain, anguish and disappointment. Too many losses. Too many regrets. Too many betrayals.

I doubted sincerely Prod would ever see me for more than what he believed me to be—a frivolous, silly sausage with an *Honorable* attached to my name. My writing wasn't significant enough for him. Whether I wrote for magazines, or published fictional tales he found ridiculous. Not even the two books of letters I'd edited.

The time had come for me to stop trying, at least for now. I plastered a simple smile on my face and changed the subject back to what he planned to do after the first ship left. Prod's expression cleared just as I'd expected. There was the thing Prod liked to talk about most—*himself.*

All the while, I thought about my disappointment. If I could go back and change one thing in the course of my life, it would be agreeing to share a life with Peter Rodd.

At least I could take away from this experience in Perpignan fodder for another novel, one that I wasn't going to let Prod, my sisters or Muv tell me was rubbish.

Dearest Mark,

How much London has changed. It seems the horrors of war have tagged along with me from France—or at least the cer-

*tainty that war looms nigh. How long before refugees camp
on our shores, or we are forced to flee? Perhaps I'm being
melodramatic, but my eyes were opened, my friend, and they
can never be shut again.*

*Before my departure to Perpignan, none of us took the gas
masks the government issued to the public seriously. At least
not so many in our circle. Now I see women carrying their
masks in fashionable purses as though they were an ordinary
accessory . . . In fact, I've just bought one at Harrods in a fashionable shade of blue. It feels absurd.*

*With love,
Nancy*

In July, leaflets were distributed to help us prepare for a
blackout—instructing us to cover our windows so as not to emit
light at night, turning our homes and neighborhoods into potential targets. Even automobiles and lorries were to turn off their
headlights once the sun set and drive about in the dark, or not
at all.

In August, our prime minister ordered a blackout trial in London with all the rules to be followed save for allowing automobiles to leave on their weak sidelights to illuminate the road. By
the first of September, the blackout was in full effect. And when
the sun fell, so too did all the light of London.

I obtained blackout fabric to cover our windows. If a house
was found to be without their blackouts, or one forgot to close
them by accident, allowing even a sliver of golden light to pierce
the night, a disgruntled ARP warden or policeman would knock,
demanding the situation be rectified, and likely issuing a fine.

If Luftwaffe ever came this far, and all indications pointed in that direction, no one wanted to be the cause of German aircraft flying over London seeing a beaming light as a target.

I donated the fabric left over from covering my windows to Heywood Hill, glad to help protect the bookshop, which had become like a second home. Wandering the streets at night had never bothered me before when streetlamps shone and the sidewalks bustled until the wee hours. But now, in the dense, unbroken darkness, nothing was familiar. At any moment someone could bump into you, sending you sprawling on the pavement with your teeth through your lip.

By day, workmen lined the streets, painting white squares every twelve inches on the pavement until it resembled a checkerboard, to help pedestrians and drivers at night. Similarly, white stripes were put onto traffic lights. Even on trees, which was brilliant considering how many seemed eager to wrap their vehicles around the trunks.

Some silly sausages were even putting white stripes on their dogs and cats, which led me to tease that the cows in the Cotswolds would soon be branded in black and white as well.

Many were digging up their backyards to put in Anderson shelters—semicircular steel havens buried in the ground for protection against bombing. Fortunately, Farve had seen to that the year before at Rutland Gate and helped me at Blomfield.

By mid-August, needing a break from the city—and Prod, who'd returned home from Perpignan—I joined Muv, Farve and Deborah in Inch Kenneth. The Scottish air was fresh, and when it was dark it was because there wasn't another soul around for miles. Walks on the moors and throwing sticks to the dogs on the shore were the order of the day. I enjoyed Muv's bread with the stews she experimented with. Deborah delighted us with reading letters from her friends in London.

Getting mail on this gloomy island was nearly impossible. I was surprised they had a wireless. There was no telephone, and the only way to get any news out was to take the small boat to the hamlet of Gribun and search for civilization, although Muv had arranged a series of medieval smoke signals with the postmaster there, involving a black disc hung on the shed and a pair of binoculars with which to see it.

The morning of September third was different. News came, and it wasn't good. At eleven a.m., on the Scottish isle, the four of us waited with bated breath beside the wireless in the great room as it crackled to life and words we'd all been dreading from the prime minister came through loud and clear.

"I am speaking to you from the Cabinet room at Ten Downing Street. This morning the British ambassador in Berlin handed the German government a final note stating that unless we heard from them by eleven o'clock that they were prepared at once to withdraw their troops from Poland, a state of war would exist between us. I have to tell you now that no such undertaking has been received, and that consequently this country is at war with Germany."

The rest was drowned out by my racing thoughts. A chill swept down my spine, gripping me tight. For so long now, we'd been warned of the prospect of war, but perhaps not believed it was true. All the preparations we'd made with the blackout, gas masks, had seemed meaningless when nothing came to a head.

Yet the prime minister's words were clear, popping the bubble of the phony war with one line: *This country is at war with Germany.*

I had to get back to London, to Prod. He'd enlisted after his return from France, and now that we were at war, he was certain to be called up. Would he be shipped abroad? A chilling numbness tingled my limbs, and I curled my feet tightly under me, trying to hide from my family the sudden fear I had at such a prospect. With his only wartime experience thus far aiding refugees, how would he get on with a gun in his hand staring into the eyes of the enemy? How would any of the men, for that matter? The last generation to fight had been during the Great War.

"Since they are closing all the places of entertainment, I shall just stay here," Deborah said to Muv and Farve.

I drew in a breath and quickly replied, "That is for the best," knowing that Deborah would be safer on the island than in London.

"This is simply terrible news." Muv shook her head. "We must pray for Hitler."

My throat went dry from silently screaming.

We were only at war because the bastard had crossed into yet another country, choosing to occupy more people. What heinous crimes Hitler and his jackboots had already committed were too unspeakable . . . And Unity, perfectly happy with it all, with Muv standing behind her, patting her back.

The instructions continued on the wireless, but I no longer listened. I stood abruptly. "I'm going to pack. I need to return to London."

"Do inquire about Unity," Muv begged.

I nodded, my thoughts swirling to Unity in Germany. Muv and Farve had asked her to return home, but she'd refused. Then they'd allowed her to return to Munich with a full automobile of furniture for the apartment Hitler had commandeered for her.

I'd never understand. She'd callously declared that the charming flat had once belonged to a young Jewish couple who'd supposedly "gone abroad." One would have to possess a wooden block for a brain to believe the couple had actually gone on holiday. Likely told to leave, or forced into one of the terrible work camps we'd all heard rumors of.

Unity was so enamored with her Führer, she'd threatened suicide more than once if our two countries should go to war, declaring she would shoot herself in the head if such came to pass. She just couldn't bear the thought of the man she loved being at odds with her beloved country. Was she going to shoot herself now?

She might have been loathsome, but she was still my sister. I didn't want her to die. Unity had been warned by the British consulate she needed to leave Germany or risk being put into a work camp for enemies of Germany. Yet we'd gotten no message about her return.

"Farve, will you have our boatman prepare the *Puffin*?"

Brow wrinkled with concern, Farve nodded absently.

"I'll go with you," Muv said, "and then I can drive you across Mull to the ferry."

Oh, how I would much rather have had Farve on that journey. Muv waxed on with concern for Hitler on the long winding roads, completely shredding my thin veil of patience. With each word, she metaphorically rubbed thistles into my open wounds.

"Well, you might as well wish Britain to be occupied," I snapped. "You cannot wish for peace with a demagogue and despot. You have put your stock behind a madman who will be the ruin of us all, and possibly the death of your daughter."

Muv swerved the car to a stop on the side of the road, her

features pinched. Anger radiated from her in such waves as I'd never seen before. "You can get out of this car and walk the rest of the way if you truly believe that."

I stared down the road, reaching for the handle, very much considering it. But we'd miles to go, and I'd never make it in time, not with my bags leastwise.

I let out a long sigh. "Unity . . ." But I cut myself off. "She's not a quitter, Muv, and she's made enough friends in high places not to get herself tossed into a camp."

That seemed to be enough to appease her, for she turned back onto the road. After several minutes in silence, Muv said, "I hope we shall lose the war."

I bit my tongue on the words that came immediately to mind, and instead said, "I should hope not, for it would mean the loss of Tom, not to mention many of our friends and cousins, and our freedoms. Peter has joined up, and I'd like him to return."

"I expect he'll get shot soon."

Muv's crisp words could have been her fist for all they slammed me back against the car seat. Clearly, she had gone off her head. No doubt Peter had been a torment to me for years, and my parents did not respect him, but to wish him dead?

We were silent the rest of the way. When we reached the quay, Muv barely said goodbye to me as the porter took my bags from the trunk and hauled them to the ferry.

"I'll write as soon as I know anything about Unity," I offered, though it pained me to suggest I'd remain in contact at all.

Muv nodded, that same tense look on her face, though this time some of the anger was replaced by true fear. I found it hard to believe Unity would actually shoot herself. I knew her convictions to be more that of a fanatic, but to murder herself seemed a touch too far, even for her. Besides, what good would that do? Wouldn't she much rather come back to London and tout her love affair with the Führer, all while clutching her signed portrait of him, than rot useless in a grave? Ridiculous. When she returned, she'd be lucky not to be tossed into Holloway as a prisoner of war.

The several-hours-long ferry ride melted into an overnight train from Oban, Scotland, to Paddington Station in London. The windows on the train were blacked out, and every time I reached to peel away a corner of the paper, I received a glare from a cantankerous old wretch sitting opposite me. The train was packed with people, more than half of them in uniform. Nothing like my train ride to Scotland a month ago. At one point, near the border, the train was so packed, people stood in the corridor.

By the time I hauled my aching body off at Paddington, I could barely stand straight. I half expected to see Prod waiting for me on the platform, but then I realized I'd forgotten to wire him, and so he didn't know I was returning.

On the platform, huddled together was a group of children with labels hanging around their necks, presumably with their names and addresses. They carried satchels of their belongings. Most of them were crying. Eyes wide, fear written in the pinched creases of their brows. They looked so much like the refugee children in France. Worn-out and worry-ridden. Were these refugee children from Germany? Poland?

"Mrs. Rodd." A porter touched his cap in front of me and indicated my luggage, which he'd tucked into a neat pile on the damp platform.

I thanked him and sat down on my suitcase, exhausted. I just needed to take a moment to breathe before I tried hauling it all to a taxi line. I was running seriously low on funds. Enough that I'd need every shilling for the taxicab driver, and none for a porter to drag my things for me.

A woman stopped in front of me, her dark hair done fashionably, red lipstick slicked over her lips and a touch of rouge on her cheeks. Her dress, in red and white polka dots, was the latest style, but her jacket was threadbare at the cuffs. A polished burgundy iris brooch on its lapel caught my eye. She smiled down at me, and then her gaze shifted to something behind me, her lips moving as she read.

I followed her line of vision. Plastered on the wall above me was a large advertisement poster. The image in black and white pictured a woman with short hair and a finger wave, behind the wheel of a utility vehicle with Air Raid Precautions (ARP) and Auxiliary Fire Service (AFS) logos painted on its side. Topping the broadsheet and in bold print were the words:

WOMEN REQUIRED
FOR MOTOR DRIVING
& TELEPHONIST DUTIES
APPLY ANY FIRE STATION

A glimpse of a new fictional character marched across my vision, her story tickling the edge of my brain. A combination of this stranger, the poster and the battle within me to be useful, to atone for the wrongs of the Fascists in my family. This new heroine was a woman involved with the War Office, perhaps within the Special Operations Executive (SOE). A woman of strength and character. Fashionable, pretty and intelligent. Deceptively witty. With red lipstick.

"Are you going to sign up?" the woman asked me, nodding at the poster. "I don't know how well I'll do with driving, but I'm quite adept with the telephone."

Prod's words came back to haunt me. *We both know you've not really got the stomach for it.* I glanced down at my gloved hands, folded in my lap, the handle of my suitcase digging uncomfortably into my rear.

Well, wasn't I pathetic here, sitting on my pile of luggage when this woman before me was full of excitement? I looked up to find her studying me, truly taking me in, and I imagined her thoughts—that I was too snobbish to bother with war work. She regretted asking me, shifted nervously as though contemplating her retreat.

I straightened my spine where I sat. Being of a certain class did not mean that I couldn't help. I'd driven a truck with supplies and refugees at Perpignan. I'd learned—and I'd prove again—that I had the stomach for hard work, no matter what Prod said. Even if it made me bone-weary. Even if I'd rather be writing or reading or listening to music or dancing, anything that didn't take place in a war zone. What I'd come to learn was that I wasn't satisfied sitting at home.

I stood and met the stranger's eyes. "Grand idea. We must all do what we can. And I happen to be an excellent driver."

She cocked her head at me questioningly.

"My husband has enlisted," I offered. "And so has my brother." I kept mum about my sisters. "Why should I not?"

A slow smile spread on her face. "My brother too. I was thinking of joining the Women's Voluntary Services, but this looks more up my alley."

"Same." I turned in a slow circle, looking for the nearest fire station. Why not now? "And would you look, just over there?" I pointed. "Serendipity."

"Shall we go together?" Polka Dot grinned widely, and I grinned back.

"Yes. I'm Nancy Rodd." I left off the *Honorable* on purpose.

Thankfully, she didn't recognize the name Rodd. If I'd used Mitford, then I might never have learned her name in response.

"Sophie Gordon." She stuck out a gloved hand, and I shook it.

"Delighted." Wasn't her name the perfect one for the heroine I had just imagined? As wholesome as pigeon pie. "Let me just leave my bags with the porter."

Splurging on the porter had been less than a split-second decision. This time around, Prod would have to give me the few shillings from his pocket for the taxicab when I returned home. I'd certainly done it for him enough times.

Moments later, Sophie and I walked arm in arm across the street to the fire station, and signed up to serve our country.

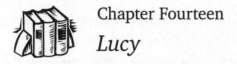 Chapter Fourteen
Lucy

LUCY TUGGED HER PHONE from her purse and opened the notes app with the list of names she'd made at the women's ARP exhibit. She'd not been able to look at it for the last two days while she'd been immersed in her library curation. The women depicted at work in the various displays—including the one wearing the enameled iris pin that had fired Lucy's curiosity—weren't specifically named. There had been a plaque, however, listing names of volunteers who had done various jobs inspiring the figures, which Lucy had snapped a picture of.

None of them had been named Iris. But at this point, Lucy was starting to wonder if Iris was a given name or just another one of Nancy's pet names she was often doling out.

Was it a coincidence that the woman putting out fires had been wearing an iris pin on her satchel? Lucy didn't want to even think about that. Not when she'd been chasing an Iris all this time without any luck, not to mention none of the other figures had been wearing one. This had to be a gift from fate.

There had been only three women depicted in that scene.

Nellie Gibbs
Sophie Gordon
Marjorie Brook

A quick internet search returned a substantial number of hits, but at first glance, very little in substance in terms of WWII volunteers. After all, these were fairly common names, even etched onto a plaque. They were likely ordinary women—working girls, mothers, housewives—who'd gone to bat for their country and then returned to obscurity. Nancy Mitford and her sisters were talked about because of their family, their celebrity in political and social circles and because several of them were published writers.

But, Nellie, Sophie, Marjorie, they were ambiguous. It was probably going to take substantial digging to come up with any relevant information that led to uncovering Iris's identity. Fortunately, Lucy had a sister who was a librarian.

Lucy fired off an email to Maya listing the details she'd acquired and asked for help. Her sister's reply was almost instantaneous: *Absolutely! On the case!*

Smiling at her computer, Lucy barely noticed the sound of footsteps until Gavin's delightful Scottish brogue voice said, "Something's made you happy. What did you find?"

"Just a message from my sister." Lucy turned her smile on Gavin. "She's going to look into the women we found at the museum."

"Brilliant."

"Are you picking up a book?"

He spread his hands, eyes on her. "As a matter of fact, I'm not."

"Oh." Lucy pursed her lips. "Maybe I can help you find what you're looking for?"

"I think you can." He leaned in.

Lucy stood, pushing her chair under the desk and coming

around. "I do owe you. Tell me what it is. I've made a few contacts of my own in the week I've been here. I just might be able to impress you."

Gavin chuckled. "You already have. At present, I am looking for *you*."

Lucy playfully tapped her chest. "Me?"

"I'm hoping you'll be free to walk around London a bit on your midday break. I know a great place for fish and chips."

She was glad that he'd sought her out, and flattered. "I would love to. What did you have in mind?"

"Depends on how much time you have. If you're up for it, I thought I'd take you on a bit of a circle. But no pressure." Gavin held his hands up.

Lucy looked at the clock. "If you throw in a changing of the guards, I'm in. I've barely had time to do any sightseeing since I've been here."

She shrugged into her jacket, tied on her scarf and followed Gavin out of the bookshop. They made their way to Buckingham Palace first, squeezing their way to the wrought-iron gate, lucky it was midweek and the crush of tourists wasn't too bad. The Queen's Guard marched in their black-and-red livery, their dark bearskin hats ruffling in the fall wind as they performed the ancient ritual of changing the guard.

From there they made their way to the Serpentine Bar and Kitchen in Hyde Park, and enjoyed fish and chips while chatting and watching people canoe around the lake.

When they finished, they walked past the Serpentine waterfall and the Holocaust Memorial, then followed the tree-lined path toward the Diana fountain. Several people were dipping their hands and feet into the oval-shaped ring. The gate was open, and they crossed the path before dipping their own fingers into the cool water.

"During World War II, there were antiaircraft guns set up in the park," Gavin said when they continued on, taking in various other sculptures. "Can you imagine it?"

"That's wild." Lucy shook her head, glancing at the collection of people lounging, relaxing, riding bikes, running. It hardly seemed like the same place she'd seen in pictures from the 1940s.

"It was definitely another world." Gavin kicked an acorn from the footpath into the grass.

Their route came to an end at a busy intersection.

"And that is the famous Marble Arch." Gavin swept his arm wide toward the large, carved marble structure they were about to pass under.

"This is the path that Nancy Mitford would have taken on her way back to the bookshop from her home on Blomfield Road," Lucy said.

"Want to go look at where she lived? It's only a mile or so down the road," Gavin offered.

Lucy glanced down at her watch, disappointed. "I wish I could, but I really need to get back. I've only got another week to finish my project, and I hate to get behind."

Gavin smiled at her, a hint of sadness in his eyes. Her own sentiments were reflected there. She couldn't believe that in a week she'd be back in her freezing office rather than adventuring in London.

"That's too bad." Gavin's fingers brushed hers. "We'll have to make another go of it before you head back."

"I'd love to."

"Ice cream?" Gavin nodded toward a cart. "We can eat that on the way back."

"Yes. I'll have chocolate."

Ice creams in hand, they continued down the street.

"Did you always want to be a book curator?" Gavin asked, wrapping a napkin around his mint chip cone.

"I knew I wanted to do something in the book industry. Runs in the blood: my sister is a librarian."

"Brilliant. What other ideas did you have?"

Lucy licked a drop of chocolate from her thumb. "I thought about being a writer, or maybe an editor at a publishing house. But in the end, I realized my passion is all about reading and enjoying books as opposed to writing or fixing them. What about you?"

"Much the same, not surprisingly." He chuckled.

She grinned. "We were meant for it."

"Aye." Gavin stopped outside Heywood Hill bookshop.

"This was a wonderful break in my day. Thank you." She stopped herself from asking if he wanted to do it again tomorrow.

Gavin pulled out his cell. Thinking he was getting a call, Lucy waved at him and mouthed *bye* then started for the door.

"Wait, Lucy," he called. "I was going to get your mobile number, if you don't mind giving it to me."

"Oh." Lucy turned around, pleasantly surprised. She pulled out her phone, and handed it to him. "Enter yours in mine, and I'll enter mine in yours."

"Deal."

Inside the flat, Lucy sighed as she settled into the chair that looked out over Curzon Street and opened the next letter from Nancy.

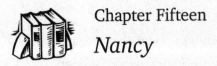

Chapter Fifteen
Nancy

September 1939

Darling Evelyn,

I've found a new calling beyond writing. I can hear you now telling me not to quit. I promise I won't. I can think of nothing worse than a manuscript so painstakingly crafted being lost. So I promise one day soon you shall have the pages. In the meantime, I find I can only read old, dried-up essays these days—isn't it funny? Have you read Carlyle's The Life of John Sterling?

> *Love from,*
> *Nancy*

THE HEAVY HELMET, EMBLAZONED with an *A*, crushed against my skull and neck. I climbed into the ARP van at dusk, wincing at the setting sun and my new duty of navigating through London's overwhelmingly dark streets without the use of headlights.

My experience with the decrepit Ford in Perpignan, France, used to ferry refugees and supplies, seemed nothing in comparison to driving the ARP van.

Sophie climbed into the passenger side and slid me a conspiratorial smile. "Are you certain about this?" She straightened her helmet.

I grinned confidently. *How hard can it be?* "I've ridden these roads my entire life. I suspect I could with my eyes closed."

"It'll be about the same," she quipped.

My bold assuredness, however, did not last. I bumped over several curbs, knocked into sandbags. Nearly took out a man hurrying across the street. Then when I made a turn from a roundabout, I crashed into something hard, bringing our vehicle to a screeching halt, bodies jerking forward.

I groaned as my forehead bounced against the steering wheel, Sophie's cry echoing in my pounding head. I touched the aching spot, checking for blood and finding none.

"Are you all right?" I asked Sophie.

"Yes. You?"

"Yes." I put the van in park and jumped down from my seat to inspect the damage on the road.

My shoes hit the ground, and I swayed a little in the dark. No flames leapt from the vehicle, which was a relief. Though I couldn't see two feet in front of me, there was a flurry of swearing.

"Is anyone injured?" I called.

In the dark I made out the silhouette of a smaller car in front of the van. A man climbed from it and shook his fist.

"You imbecile! Couldn't you see I was stopped?" he snarled.

"In the pitch black? No," I replied rather tartly. "However, you are in luck, as I'm driving an ambulance. Are you hurt?"

"You shouldn't be driving anything!" he screeched.

I had a fair idea that if the streetlamps were lit I'd see his face was purple.

"The government may agree with you now, sir," I teased. "Please, do accept my apology. It's my first night, and I really could not make you out in the dark."

"I want your name and the name of your superior." Goodness, but the man was a dog after a meaty bone.

Sophie appeared at his side, her hand on his elbow. "Oh my, sir, are you quite well?" Her tone was slightly patronizing.

"What?" he sputtered.

"We must be certain you did not hit your head. I think I hear a slur in your voice. Do you hear a slur, Nancy?"

"I hear something," I murmured.

"It's absolutely true," Sophie said.

"A slur? That's preposterous?" As he blubbered, Sophie led him off the street to sit on the darkened sidewalk atop sandbags piled in front of the shops to protect them from potential bombings. Once settled, he said, "I am feeling a little nauseous."

"Why was your vehicle stopped here?" I asked.

He cleared his throat and waited a few breaths before saying quietly, "There was a kitten in the road."

"Ah, so you stopped to avoid hitting the poor creature," Sophie purred.

The man had to be lying. How could he have seen a kitten if we could barely make out the road?

"Yes, yes, it's the decent thing to do." He waved his hands in the air, dark shadows blurring. "He ran off, perfectly fine."

"Well, that's good. So if there'd been no kitten, there'd have been no stop on your part, thus no *accident* on ours." Sophie's emphasis on *accident* was strong.

I couldn't believe it. Sophie was convincing the man the accident was his own fault. *Brilliant.* And also *true*, because stopping a vehicle in the middle of a blacked-out roundabout was quite dangerous.

An area warden approached briskly. "Accident?" He stopped beside me, lifting his lantern a moment to shine it on the scene. "Everyone all right?"

"Yes," I said.

"I'm Warden Ekpenyon, but people call me Uncle Sam." His Nigerian accent was thick but his English perfect. He stuck out his russet-brown hand to mine, and I shook it.

"Nancy Rodd, ARP driver."

"Have you called it in?" he asked.

"Not yet."

"I'll do it." Using his two-way radio, he made the alert about the accident. As it crackled off, he asked, "Can the vehicles be operated?"

"I think so."

"Think you can maneuver the ambulance back to your station?" he asked.

I nodded, though the very idea made me slightly trembly.

"Sir, can you drive home?" the warden asked our patient.

The man stood on legs that seemed stronger when his eyes were on Sophie. "Yes."

"Good. Move along, then," the warden urged.

The man looked ready to argue, wanting compensation perhaps, but Sophie interrupted. "We will not make a complaint of your automobile blocking the street and barring passage to a government vehicle. Drive safely, sir, and mind the kittens." Her voice was practically singsong.

As we climbed back into the van, Sophie let out a long-drawn-out sigh. "That was time-consuming."

I smiled, liking Sophie even more. "You were brilliant."

She shrugged. "I have older brothers—they taught me a lot."

"Alas, I'm the eldest, and had to rely on my own tricks." My favorite being the time I'd dressed up in disguise as an old, scarred-up tramp and frightened the wits out of Pam. She'd not realized it was me. I sometimes still teased her by showing off the lurching gait and asking in the same crooked tone if she might spare some tea.

Sophie laughed. "I merely convinced him of the truth."

"You could be a spy."

"That's next on my list." She winked.

When we got back to the station, our supervisor demanded my keys, with a clipped "We'll find you another post. Hope you like driving, Sophie."

"What will you do now?" Sophie frowned at the keys now dangling from her manicured fingers.

"Bandage a few banged heads?" Though the idea of dealing with anyone who was sick or injured sounded absolutely dreadful.

"Something tells me that will not be as exciting for you."

I nodded, mulling over the idea. "Perhaps less excitement is what I really need."

Sophie regarded me with appraising eyes. "I've only known you a short time, but pardon my saying so, you strike me as someone who cannot survive in a state of boredom."

"You are not wrong, Sophie. But alas, excitement always seems to get me into trouble."

"NAUNCE."

Prod's voice startled me as I hurried toward the front door, already late to my first aid post in Paddington. Normally he was gone hours before me as his shift at the post in Chelsea started at dawn.

I backtracked to the sitting room to find him at my writing desk, dressed in his khaki uniform, one leg crossed over the other.

"What are you still doing here?" I prepared for him to say he'd been fired from his volunteer position. Everyone in London was stepping up to do their bit, including us.

"I'm setting off on Friday for training in the Cotswolds." He tapped a paper on the desk. "My commission in the Welsh Guards."

Today was Monday, which meant by week's end, he'd be gone. We still didn't know where he'd be stationed. I prayed it wasn't at the front, opposite Hitler's line.

"Oh," I said breathlessly, the announcement taking the wind from me. "But they said it would be months."

Everything was changing so fast, like trying to catch a bird in a forest that flew just out of reach, me tripping on tree roots as I tried to keep up.

He shrugged. For once he didn't have an overly long explanation, which was almost as startling as the pang in my chest at his leaving. He might have been a disappointing husband, but he was familiar. I hated anything familiar disappearing. Friends and family trekking off for the unknown. Everything disrupted.

The safety of London in question. I didn't want Prod to be shot either.

"We'll have a proper send-off for you on Thursday."

Prod gave a subtle shake of his head. "That won't be necessary."

"Yes, it is. It's what we do when someone is expected to ship off." I finished tugging on my gloves. "I'll have Sigrid write up the invitations. We'll have dinner and toast your success against Hitler and his brainless foot soldiers."

He nodded slowly, toying with his cuff links. "I am certainly open to toasting the death and defeat of the vile Germans."

"I suspect some of the Germans hate Hitler too." They had to, I was sure of it. Just as with the Spanish civil war, Germans were fleeing their country seeking refuge.

"Then I shall spare those when the time comes to shoot."

Our banter was easy, a familiarity between us that came from those who'd struggled and survived. We'd been wrestling with our own demons for nearly a decade. No longer young, or in love, but we'd a bond of sorts. Strange to think of the fleeting passage of time. I kept it from my mind most days, allowing a glimpse only in the quiet of night, when moments of pain and sadness flashed back.

I was no longer in love with the idea of being in love.

I tried in those times to remember good things, good times. Such as the moment on the beach in Collioure, or how he'd put his arm protectively around me on the docks in Saint-Jean-de-Luz as we'd waited for the waywards to debark, the playful look he sometimes got in his eye.

But for every good moment, there were a dozen bad. Not enough to keep us together, and yet I knew he'd never let me go.

"Don't become a German favorite," I teased, trying to make light. "I'll expect you home when Hitler is put down."

A half smile turned his lips. "Piece of cake."

A silence stretched between us for several moments, interrupted by the yaps of Dollie and her new brood of puppies.

"We'd best be off." Prod left the letter on the desk. "See you at dinner?"

I nodded quietly. We walked out onto the street together, headed toward Paddington Station, where he'd catch the train to Chelsea. Our walk was mostly silent, a few idle quips on the weather. As we reached Paddington, Prod gave a tip of his hat before he trudged off in the opposite direction. Watching him go, I wondered, would the divide between us lengthen? I prayed he didn't get shot.

Whatever happened with this war, I was certain of one thing: Prod and I were never going to be the same.

At the first aid post, I joined several women knitting and chatting around a radio. We all awaited orders to act, or for an ambulance to bring someone in—but nothing yet, as we'd not seen bombers on our shores.

Sophie was not a part of this unit, still successfully driving. We caught glimpses of each other in passing between shifts. I longed for her jovial chatter amongst the dull and awkward silences of the women here. Fortunately, their shifts started before mine, leaving me in dogged silence for the remainder of my time.

I longed to hear the sirens. Boredom seemed almost a worse thing than fresh bodies coming in. My fingers grew numb from rolling bandages, and I considered using the indelible blue pencil in hand—supposedly to mark the foreheads of the dead with their private information—to plot out the newest story percolating in my mind ever since that day on the train platform when I'd first met Sophie Gordon.

By Thursday, we'd not heard one siren, nor seen one body. I clocked out at exactly seven in the evening, hurrying home to prepare for Prod's going-away party.

The house smelled delicious from Sigrid's cooking. Though I'd asked her to keep it simple for the sake of our dwindling funds, she'd made Muv's Scotch collops, a savory minced beef dish, accompanied by roasted potatoes and spinach with sorrel. For dessert we'd have an apple compote with cream. My stomach growled in anticipation.

I found Prod in our bedroom staring out the window, outfitted impeccably in black tails, a crisp white shirt and perfectly knotted bow tie.

He turned, a snifter in hand. "Best get dressed; our guests will be here soon."

"I'll be ready."

He closed the distance between us, kissing my cheek. The liquor on his breath was strong. I shut my eyes, worried he would drink himself into oblivion and not wake in time to arrive with the rest of his unit. But I said nothing, simply nodded, waiting.

"I'll see you downstairs," he said.

I offered a soft smile, a light hand squeeze. In less than twelve hours he'd be off to train for war. Watching him leave, I had the chilling thought that tomorrow when he crossed the threshold it might possibly be for the last time.

Desperate not to let my melancholy take hold, I toed off my sensible first aid shoes, and stripped out of my uniform. I scrubbed my face and slipped into a Madeleine Vionnet gown, a few seasons old and gifted to me from a friend's closet. The black silk crepe fabric felt sinful as the bias-cut skirt draped down my legs. Cinched at the waist, the dress was pleated over the chest, and gathered in the center of my breastbone with a metal bar. Two swaths of fabric extended from the metal bar over my shoulders, leaving my arms bare and plunging down the sides of my exposed spine.

With my hair touched up, cheeks pinched, the bruised sleepy smudges under my eyes powdered and a slash of red lipstick in a shade that reminded me of my new friend Sophie, I made my way downstairs. Two dozen guests were already gathered, chatting and clinking glasses.

Their voices quieted at my entrance, and I could make out the sound of jazz softly playing on the gramophone.

"My lovely wife," Prod exclaimed, raising a glass. He walked toward me on legs that were less than steady.

I held his elbow and we made our way around the room, a glass of champagne pushed into my grasp. I smiled until my head started to pound. The blinds were drawn tight, of course, but with the way the main entry door opened and closed as people came and went or stepped out for a bit of cool night air, we might as well have been sending Morse code signals to the Nazis. The thought of being bombed put quite a damper on the cheer Prod's send-off was supposed to ignite.

What were we doing hosting a party? It seemed ridiculous now that it was happening. Stupid and frivolous.

Sigrid announced dinner was ready, and everyone filed toward tables set up for the occasion, looking for their place cards.

Of my family, only dear Tom had come to our party. Since he was quartered nearby, he and his friends were often companions at our table. Jessica was in America, and Diana and I still weren't on speaking terms. Muv, Farve and Deborah remained on Inch Kenneth. Farve had publicly condemned Hitler, leaving Muv in a state, and Debo in the middle of a domestic battleground. The poor thing wished she was here. I supposed it was good under the circumstances that only Tom graced us tonight. I smiled at my brother as he took the seat to my left.

As we ate, I ached to laugh with everyone, to join them in stories of Prod's leadership at Perpignan, but the muscles in my face protested along with the slow throb at my temples. I barely tasted the meal Sigrid had prepared.

To my right, Prod laughed heartily. I heard the echoing haunts of laughter in the back of my head, like ghosts that occupied corners of my mind. I wanted to drift out of the house. To breathe in the crisp autumn air as I marched down a quiet, black road into nothingness. Of course, if I were to do that, then I'd be tackled to the ground by a rugby player–esque bag snatcher who'd taken up residence in Paddington. And really, that would ruin not only my mood but his, as my purse would be found quite empty.

When the last of our guests left well after midnight, I wandered out into the yard with our pups, rubbing my hands up and down my gooseflesh-covered arms. I stared up into the black sky, some of the stars blotted out by the large silver barrage balloons. These flying elephants in the sky were somehow supposed to keep the Germans from bombing us. A marble toss in the sky, hoping to keep the other player from advancing. They reminded me of the scarecrows Muv used to put in her garden that only seemed to collect crows rather than shoo them away.

In the starlight, the lumps in my garden from where I'd planted shone. All the skills I'd learned from Muv were necessary now that Farve cut my monthly allotment, and Peter's family threatened to do the same. Not to mention his army pay was barely enough to cover his uniform expenses and whatever mess hall bills he accumulated.

There were rumors of rationing to come. How likely was that? Despite the announcement of war, all of the preparations held a phony ring.

Millie, and my new French bulldog, Abbey, snuffled around the mounds of my victory garden with tiny green shoots. When they started to dig, I snapped my fingers and called them away. Of course, the other pups now wanted to know just what they'd found, and trotted over to paw at the earth.

"Don't you ruin my vegetables. If there's a ration, there'll be no more treats for you."

I chased them over the cabbage and onions, finally stopping two of them near the carrots.

The house was quiet as I reentered. Prod must have turned in already, or passed out more like, from his imbibing. Tomorrow he'd wake up, still smelling of booze, and trudge to the train station. The house would be strangely quieter.

I tiptoed into our bedroom, noiseless as I undressed in the dark and slipped into bed without even removing my makeup. In the morning, Sigrid would frown at the stains on my pillowcase, but right then I didn't have the energy to stand, let alone scrub.

I stared at Prod's profile beside me, snoring lightly. A sudden chill took hold of me. There was every possibility that this would be the last time I saw him sleep. The last time we shared a bedroom. While the rumors flying had a phony ring to them, the very realness of war, of my husband being sent to the Continent, was not fake at all.

The scared part of me wanted to curl up closer to him, seeking comfort in the familiar. But there was too much emotional distance between us. I remained frozen, watching him sleep, dreading the moment the sun rose.

When Prod landed in Germany, there was every possibility that my sister's lover would order him shot.

I rolled over with a deep sigh, staring up at the ceiling, hating how the war had divided my family, revealing the terribly unforgiving flaws in some of us. Sleep would be hard to come by.

I woke with a start a couple of hours later to Prod dressed in his uniform. He looked sharp and handsome, but his eyes were dull as he watched me push myself up.

"I'm off," he said flatly.

"How about some breakfast before you leave. I'll make eggs and toast."

"I'm not hungry." He fingered his collar, glanced at himself in the looking glass above my dressing table.

I flipped the covers back, the chill of the room as much a shock as his downtrodden demeanor.

"A little tea or coffee, then?"

"Nothing, Naunce."

I walked to him, the distance between us palpable. A good wife would put her arms around him. Wish him well. And I was a good wife, even if I'd long ago abandoned the notion of marital happiness. So I reached for him, and he let me pull him close, leaching the warmth of sleep from me, as I whispered, "Godspeed, Peter."

Darling Evelyn,

I am tucking the pages of my latest work in a box in the back of a closet, and for good reason. An idea has sparked, and like a high-spirited pup in wont of play, I cannot ignore it any longer. This work in progress is something new, a bit different for me. My heroine, she is a woman of our time, steeped in war and adventure. Bolder than my past heroines, perhaps even someone we all—dare I say me?—wish to become.

More to come soon . . . I promise.

Love from,
Nancy

The next several days at the aid post were quiet. This time I'd prepared for the boredom, having brought paper and pencil to write. While the other ladies knitted and chattered, the wireless on in the background, I sank inside myself to create a new character, a new novel.

At the top of the paper I scrawled: *The Secret Weapon.* And then I started to write . . .

Sophia Garfield had a clear mental picture of what the outbreak of war was going to be like. There would be a loud bang, succeeded by inky darkness and a cold wind . . .

I grinned down at the words, remembering just how I'd feared during my journey from Scotland that a bomb would fall, twisting train tracks, shattering cars and sending bodies flying as smoke blackened the sky.

That voyage had been quite uneventful. Arriving in London, I'd expected to see troops marching in lines, their chants of *One, two, three, four* echoing against the buildings. My imagination had been running wild. Wasn't war supposed to be that way? For months we'd waited, and nothing.

I was tired of waiting for war, at the same time fearing it. My muse came alive in the little oxygen-deprived underground at Paddington Station where I volunteered. I no longer waited for bodies, but piled them up on the pages. When the ladies inquired about my scribbling, I waved them away, completely ensnared in Sophia's story.

I wrote Aunt Vi, describing my burgeoning novel. She loved to hear my plots and teases. No one in my family understood the need for creation in the midst of war.

I wrote too, to my dearest friend Mark, painting a picture of my gutsy, patriotic Sophia, and received an amused reply that my latest would have him singing propaganda songs.

My imagination ran wild, enjoying the escape from reality. I toiled away my days in the impermeable, electric-lighted cellar of the aid post. Keeping my brain from rotting like the inside of a bad walnut. Sophia's adventures gave me purpose and joy.

I tentatively told Peter that I was writing again, hoping at least he'd support me because it would bring us income, but in his return reply, not a peep was mentioned about *The Secret Weapon*. In fact, he only complained about the lack of flavor in his meals, comparing them to my oft-burnt toast and dry eggs.

As a result of his dismissal, I burned his letter, and in my manuscript, I let Sophia do what I'd imagined many times being married to a man who no longer piqued my interest—I let her be in love with someone else.

October 5, 1939

~~Dear Unity,~~

When I was a child, books had always been my salvation. The promise of an escape. And when I wrote, it was much the same. Going on adventures, retelling tales. Escapism in its greatest form. I let myself be dragged into *The Secret Weapon*, avoiding the ache real life provided. Tried adding a touch of humor even when I felt like I was drowning.

Several weeks later, as I sat in the same spot writing at the Paddington Station first aid post, I received a frantic visit from Deborah. She barged her way inside, standing over my desk in the bluish-gray light, and thrust several newspapers at me.

"Nancy, look at this!"

For a panicked moment, I kept my eyes on my sister, too afraid of reading whatever it was that had caused her to burst through the depot door. Deborah nodded and pointed at the rumpled papers. My gaze cast down toward the headlines printed in bold black ink.

Unity Freeman-Mitford—Quarrel with Hitler Reported: Overdose of Veronal

Overdose . . . Was that why she'd been in the hospital? She'd not shot herself, but instead she'd taken a heavy sedative? Dear God . . . And survived.

I flipped to the next paper.

The Girl Who Loved Hitler: Unity Mitford Dead

I nearly choked on that one, so swiftly did my breath leave

my body. "No, it can't be true." But my voice held no power. I quickly shuffled to the next paper.

Hitler Quarrels with Miss Mitford

And the next . . .

Himmler Orders Death of Hitler's British Lover

All of the newspapers reported conflicting details, but one thing was consistent: that Unity had died.

I couldn't feel my fingers. They shook so violently, the papers fell to my desk. My face went cold as all the blood drained away, and the energy left my body.

"You must come with me to Rutland," Deborah insisted.

I nodded, and arm in arm, my sister and I rushed from Praed Street. Muv was in her own frantic state over the news, already having seen the headlines.

The phone rang constantly. Mostly reporters wanting information. I slammed down the receiver, only to pick it up a dozen more times with the same result. Reporters hounded us for information we didn't possess.

And then finally, Muv answered the phone, swaying as she clutched the receiver. "She's alive," Muv said through her tears to Farve, who looked relieved. "In hospital in Munich."

However, Unity had tried to kill herself. *Twice.*

My sister had shot herself in the head. When that had failed, and she'd regained consciousness in a hospital bed, she'd tried again by swallowing her swastika badge, which had been left on her bedside table.

Both attempts caused her to endure countless hours of surgery. Despite the diligence of the doctors, the bullet could not be removed from her brain, because they feared removing it would cause further damage.

How had none of this information made it into the German papers, where it would surely had been picked up by the British press? Somehow Hitler and his minions had managed to keep her attempts and condition from being reported. The doctors, Muv's friend had confided in hushed tones over the phone, had been sworn to secrecy, which only allowed rumors to fly.

The rabid reporters were not satisfied only with calling Rutland Gate; they phoned me on Blomfield Road too. I wanted to ignore the piercing rings but feared I'd miss news from Farve or Muv. Endless days passed without any news of my sister's current state, all of us in an unceasing cycle of worry over whether Unity was still alive.

Until Christmas Eve.

Finally, Muv and Farve, and the rest of us, were put out of our misery when word arrived. Evidently, Hitler arranged for Unity to be moved from the hospital in Munich to Bern, Switzerland. Switzerland was neutral ground, and both Unity's Nazi friends and British friends had access to her there. And so, we discovered, did we.

Though Hitler had moved my sister to a place her family could safely retrieve her—*a courtesy*, as Muv worded it—I still hated the very ground he trod upon.

I recognized his action for what it was, even if Muv didn't, or couldn't. No courtesy on his part. No special gift. The dictator simply wanted to be rid of a problem—and that problem was Unity. My sister was once the light of his eye, and now she was weak, ruined, a stained blot on his reputation.

Shuffling her off to Bern, wiping his slate clean, was the least he could do.

After all, he'd been the one to gift her with the gun.

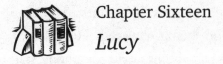

Chapter Sixteen
Lucy

Dear Sophie,

I've waited several days to catch you at the station, but alas our paths have not crossed. Are you free for tea after your shift this Tuesday?

Best love,
Nancy

LUCY PUT AWAY THE letter she'd been puzzling over that morning, and headed downstairs from her flat to Heywood Hill. Nothing more than a slip of a note, but the addressee was a Sophie. Was Sophie another friend in the long string of acquaintances that Nancy Mitford had, or was she *the Sophie* that Lucy had on her list of possible Irises?

The bookstore was busier than usual when Lucy arrived that morning. A loud hammering sounded from the back room, drawing her there before she headed down to the offices in the basement.

A repairman was chiseling half of one of the center shelves on the far left away from the wall, which looked to have collapsed onto the one below. There were a few holes in the wall behind it where it appeared the broken shelf had ripped out the anchoring nails, and also torn down some old wallpaper in the process.

"What's going on?" Lucy asked, concerned for the more-rare books kept back there that might have been damaged in the process.

"One of the shelves broke loose overnight." Oliver frowned, then his eyes widened as he lurched forward to stare at the wall.

Lucy followed his line of vision as the repairman stepped out of the way to discard the broken shelf, fully revealing the spot. Her heart lodged in her throat.

There on the wall, hidden behind a fold of displaced wallpaper, was a cluster of signatures. Lucy's hand came to her mouth as she gasped. They weren't faded at all. Preserved in time by the wallpaper and the subsequent shelving that had been screwed into the wall over top of it.

"I can't believe it," Oliver mused. He reached for the paper and gingerly tugged to reveal the names. "Just like you said."

Nancy Mitford.
Evelyn Waugh.
Heywood Hill.
Cecil Beaton.
Anne Hill.
Mark Ogilvie-Grant.

"Serendipity." Lucy read the names again, imagining the six Bright Young Things sipping champagne and signing their names over a few laughs. "You can't put that shelf back up. You've got to frame the wall."

Oliver nodded vigorously. "Absolutely. Nancy Mitford and her dazzling literary chums. Incredible."

"I've read about some of them," Lucy said. "What I wouldn't give to go back in time and rub elbows with Evelyn Waugh and Nancy Mitford."

The shop was in an uproar most of the end of the day, between everyone working there taking breaks to admire the wall and anyone who came into the bookshop being ushered to the back to take a peek. Instead of replacing the shelf, Oliver did indeed commission the repairman to put a glass frame over the spot, and then to secure the rest of the shelving to prevent further damage.

Later in the afternoon, as Lucy again found herself staring at the spot, which now had a small label beneath it, Oliver approached.

"I don't think I'll be able to go a day without looking," Lucy said with a laugh.

"Me either." He shook his head. "I have to admit I thought you were mad the first time you mentioned it."

"I thought she might have been teasing." Lucy sighed. "I only wish there were one more name here."

"Iris?" He raised a brow.

"Yes." How she wished.

"How is your search progressing?" he asked.

"My sister is looking into some of the names from the ARP exhibit for me, but I'm afraid I've hit a dead end."

"Well, if she comes up empty, let me know. I have some contacts at the British National Archives who might be able to help you."

"Oh, that would be excellent. Thank you, Oliver." Lucy was really going to miss the team spirit at Heywood Hill. It wasn't that she hadn't made similar connections at Emerald Books, but more that some of the competitive natures of her coworkers had put a damper on her enthusiasm.

Lucy returned to her desk to finish out her day. Her inbox was full of messages from booksellers, auctioneers and private libraries, responding to requests for volumes and allowing her to tick off more on her special project. Additionally, there was an email from Mr. Sloan with an updated and signed addendum on the secret staircase addition to the Masters' library project.

As she finished checking off the last of her to-do list, Lucy's inbox pinged a new email notification. It was her sister.

Hey Luc—

If you've got time to chat tonight, it would be easier to talk through what I've found than to type. I did get a quite a few hits on each woman's name on various ancestry and genealogy lists, but it's hard to say if any of them are truly your girl. After all, these names are fairly common. Of the women I found, there was no mention of Nancy Mitford. Two of the women I located are buried at sites in the US, so those may be out.

Chat soon,
Maya

Lucy was disappointed but not particularly surprised. This was not what she'd been hoping for—an obvious Mitford connection. But that had been a long shot. If only the museum had paired the iris-pinned mannequin with a specific name, she'd be able to move in one direction. But for now, her Iris needle in a haystack had morphed into an Iris-Nellie-Sophie-Marjorie sand pit.

When her phone buzzed a minute later with Gavin asking if she had dinner plans, Lucy thought, *Why not?* A date with Gavin would keep her awake until it was time to talk to Maya. Plus, she knew he'd love to see the signatures on the wall, along with the newly framed publishing offer for Nancy Mitford that Oliver had hung beside them.

Chapter Seventeen
Nancy

January 1940

Dear Nancy,

We thank you for the opportunity to read your manuscript The Secret Weapon. *It is with delight we that we wish to offer you a publication contract with Hamish Hamilton. This book is just the read people will be looking for, and so we plan to move quickly to press if you accept our offer. We do, however, have one caveat: we would like to change the title to* Pigeon Pie. *We hope that the lighter title will make clear the moments of levity laced through your work.*

We look forward to working with you again.

Sincerely,
Jamie Hamilton

I'D BEEN AWAITING HAMILTON'S review of *The Secret Weapon* as eagerly as a child waits for their beloved nanny to open a gift they've made.

Soon after sending the piles of ink-stained manuscript papers, I received the offer letter. While I was elated at the offer, I couldn't help wondering if their desire to change the title meant they thought my tale lacked substance. After all, I had written a character who was quite adamant that she'd rather not go out spying after having her bath.

However, I didn't dwell on my doubts, because the letter also came with a much-needed advance. As Prod and I were now quite broke, I was grateful.

Some problems seemed to come round again like the spinning of a wheel, and being low on funds wasn't the only one. I also suspected Prod was indulging in another affair that had begun before he'd left. I became suspicious of the assignation while he was at training.

This time, the object of his fancy was my cousin on the Stanley side, Adelaide Lubbock, a woman whose son had been a page boy attendant at our wedding. She was in charge of the ARP post in Chelsea—Prod's assignment. In the middle of a war, he'd decided to humiliate me with someone in my own family. Like all of his past lovers, Adelaide had children—an extra twist of the knife. Just another way to subtly point out I wasn't good enough because I couldn't be a mother.

I ran into Adelaide as she stood in line waiting for her rations of bacon and butter, a packet of sugar already clutched in her basket, and she offered me a wave.

"How you must miss Peter." She spoke in a rather odd way, and blinked too many times. The rapid blinking was a tell. Prod did the same thing when he lied. "I hear his rations are positively medieval compared to ours. Oh, dear me." Her face colored as she revealed this fact about Prod that even I had not known. It was obvious they'd been exchanging letters, which would have been odd since I'd not known them to be close.

Adelaide scrambled to recover. "Our house seems utterly ghostly with my husband in his regiment, and my son at school in Canada. Must be the same for you. Are you feeling . . . lonely? Or are you getting plenty of letters from your dear Peter?"

The nerve of such a question. I could read between her blinks, and she was digging to find out if Prod was writing to me as he was to her. I could have scratched her eyes out, but instead I quipped back a hasty half-truth: "Not too many. But fortunately, I've my friend Robert staying on as guest to keep me company, so I'm not bouncing around my house alone as you are." I'd started letting out rooms to friends, and my brother, Tom, on occasion, to make some money and keep me company.

Adelaide raised an eyebrow, and for just a split second, she stopped blinking. "Really?"

"Yes." I didn't care what she read into my statement. Given she was an adulteress, maybe she wanted to paint me in the same light. Though the idea was preposterous, given the fact that neither I, nor any other female, was Robert's type. Maybe she'd even tell Prod she thought I was having an affair. It would serve him right to wonder even for a fleeting moment. "Well, I must be off."

As I wandered away, I heard her whispering rather loudly to the person in front of her, "That was Unity Mitford's sister. Have you heard that traitor was received at Folkestone by a military cavalcade? Outrageous."

I fled at a near run, determined to get my rations another day. I didn't want to think about Unity, or how her return home was filmed by the press and made into a newsreel played at the cinemas. How my father was questioned in Parliament about the use of a military guard to escort her when he'd merely asked the local police to help make sure his injured daughter was not harassed and questioned by the press.

The journey from Switzerland had been ghastly. Unity was in constant pain from the bullet still lodged in her head. The slightest movement caused her to moan or even shout in agony. Muv was beside herself throughout the entire trip, according to Deborah, who'd gone with her for support. I'd not volunteered to be part of Unity's retrieval. I didn't believe she deserved to return to the country she'd sided against, and would have been content had she remained in Munich, or better still, been sent back to one of the work camps we'd initially thought she'd been put in.

As if Unity's arrival back on English soil weren't challenging and humiliating enough, the cars meant to drive my family back to West Wycombe wouldn't run. They suspected tampering. While the vehicles were being repaired, they were trapped an extra night in Kent. All the while, the press never let up. Muv was even offered £5,000 to give an exclusive interview—she declined.

Perhaps I should have gone; for that amount of money I'd have been willing to be interviewed by just about anybody. I immediately regretted the thought. Not because I pitied my sister, but because, even broke, I loathed the idea of sinking to that level.

Without an interview from our family, the press was content to make up a story on their own. Muv made certain Unity looked well put together when she arrived by stretcher—sitting up in her bed, hair coiffed, a blanket held fetchingly to her cheek. But reporters claimed she was no invalid, given her looks. Instead, they painted her as a traitor seeking to avoid punishment.

I knew, however, that Unity was not playacting. Deborah

wrote, entreating me to believe Unity was changed from that of a stubborn woman to a mere child in temper and manner by the bullet she'd administered to her own head. But when I'd gone to visit, looked into Unity's eyes, I still saw that some of that same obstinate girl remained.

By the time I reached home from the market, the fire in my cheeks from my encounter with Adelaide had died, but my lungs burned from the cold. Gladys met me in the kitchen and took the empty basket. Sigrid had fled back to Russia some time ago. England had become wary of anything having to do with Bolsheviks. Most didn't draw a line between Communist and non-Communist Russians. Thankfully, Gladys had returned to London, though she could only work for a few hours a day, which meant I did my own shopping most of the time.

"Were they out already?" Gladys frowned into the barren wicker basket, then studied me with her keen brown eyes.

"Yes," I lied, feeling a twinge of guilt. "I'll be fine with toast and eggs for dinner."

Gladys clucked her tongue as Nanny Blor had when I was a child ruining the floor with muddied feet. "Won't be long until bread and eggs are rationed too, Mrs. Rodd."

"I'll get a few hens." I waved my hand dismissively. "My mother taught me quite a lot about raising hens when I was growing up. I know all about the droppings board and nest box, and bran mash. Those are things you don't forget."

Gladys looked impressed, which hadn't been my objective, but I took it all the same.

"I'll go tomorrow," she said. "Perhaps I should buy a few extra things. What do you think? Tea? Flour?"

"That's a good idea."

"I'm sure you've heard how hard things were to come by in the Great War." Gladys placed a pan on the stove, then filled the kettle with water.

Indeed, I had. I remembered Muv complaining about things that seemed trivial to the child I was back then, like olive oil and shoes.

I stopped in the back hall for a quick snuggle with my dog, then headed upstairs to change into my uniform. As I changed, my thoughts strayed to Adelaide and how I had inserted a character very much like her into *Pigeon Pie*. Perhaps I'd wondered about her far longer than I'd admitted to myself.

My thoughts were jarringly interrupted by an air-raid siren. I hurried down the stairs in my sensible shoes to gather up the dogs and Gladys, and make our way to the Anderson shelter in the yard. But I found myself rather blasé about the warning. They teased us with the noise, keeping us on our toes, when it would only come to naught.

"You hang tight," I said to Gladys on the threshold, passing her the dogs' leads. "I've got to get to my post."

"You aren't going to take cover?"

I looked up at the hazy sky, silver balloons waving in and out of the clouds. "It's just a test. I don't want to be late, especially if they need me."

"Then I'm not going to stay in here." Gladys pushed her way out of the tin can half buried in the ground. She stood with hands on her hips, dark curls having escaped her bun and now flying with the wind. She narrowed her brown eyes, giving me a challenging look. "I've laundry to do still."

"Very well. But if my dogs get bombed by a German, I'll haunt you."

"I'll haunt myself."

I gave my sweet cherubs one last kiss, cautioned Gladys again to seek shelter, then headed off.

Sirens continued blaring in that keening low-to-high pitch pattern. I ran down the street, making twists and turns through people hurrying for cover. I arrived at Paddington, my heart racing, and plunged down into the cellar. A collection of other ARP ladies, including Sophie, were already huddled around the radio, listening to crackling static.

Some of the others were on edge, arguing that despite the cloud coverage, every alarm had to be considered a true warning, until we heard otherwise. But the sirens quickly quieted without any of the rumble we'd been training for, and the radio announcer confirmed it had only been a test, as I'd suspected.

"How are you?" Sophie asked. We'd not seen each other in nearly a week.

"Smashing, as you can see." I grinned.

She laughed at my sarcasm. "We should take in a picture, the two of us in our uniforms." She gave a salute then laughed again.

My mind flashed to Unity's face on a cinema screen. I'd not yet told Sophie exactly who I was, but people talked; surely she'd figured it out by now. At least I hoped, because that meant she'd not changed her opinion of me based on my family. Still, I found myself swallowing hard before saying, "Maybe we should."

"Or we could go dancing?"

I nodded. I'd only danced at places like Café de Paris, the Ritz and the Savoy. It would be my guess those weren't exactly Sophie's scene. That seemed better, safer somehow. "I'd love that." I missed the carefree days of my youth.

"Well, I'm off. This face won't beautify itself." Sophie touched up her red lipstick, straightened her iris brooch, then waved goodbye.

When she'd gone, I found myself touching my own pale lips, feeling suddenly very old, and very tired.

I SLID ON my overcoat at the end of my shift, exiting the unbreathable chamber to find my brother standing outside the door.

"Good evening," he said, winking and offering me his arm.

"To what do I owe this honor?" I slipped my arm through Tom's with comfortable ease.

"I happened to be passing by, and thought I'd escort you through the dark rather than imagining you running for your life."

"Aren't you a darling old boy?"

Tom was staying with me—not Robert, as I'd told Adelaide. What I hadn't mentioned was that he was a paying guest waiting to be shipped out. Between him and several friends' frequent visits I was hardly alone, and even better, had a few extra pounds in my pocket with which to pay the mounting bills.

The sun had already set, but the sidewalks were not yet empty as people hurried, huddled in their overcoats, hats and gloves, from their posts or places of employment to the train stations or to home. Six months had passed since the declaration of war, and we'd yet to see much of anything on our own shores.

The ice of winter was slowly melting into spring, and in my garden, the hens proudly pecked their way through the sprouts and heads of vegetables that were miraculously robust against the frost. I seemed to have a knack for it. And thank goodness, because the majority of our meals were clever concoctions with a base of vegetables given the meat ration.

On Fridays we had fish. And I dared not part with my dear hens in favor of a chicken dinner, for eggs were another way I was able to gain pence. The ladies at the first aid post were happy to add my eggs to their baskets, and I was pleased to share the news with my sisters of having employed our childhood money-making scheme with Muv to good use now.

With the additional pence from the sale of eggs, I bought extra provisions. Given my connections with those in Parliament, I was offered fair warning that coming next would be tea and margarine.

Tom guided me around a trio of young children running down the street.

"You should be home," he called after them, shaking his head. "No one is taking the war seriously."

"Are you surprised?" I asked. "The only thing we know about it is what we hear on the wireless or see in the papers. I fear people have begun to wonder if Hitler is even a real threat to our country."

"But surely some of their brothers, fathers and sons have shipped out. I suspect I will be soon too."

"Don't say that, Tom. I can't bear the thought of you leaving." Would all the men eventually be conscripted? Oh, when would the terror end?

"All right, I won't say it. When it is time for me to go, I will depart in the night, leaving a note upon your doorstep. And then you shall know I have gone."

I laughed. "You're too much."

"Better than not enough."

"Touché."

My little Victoriana was dark, no lights peeping out from behind the drawn blackout curtains. I double-checked that we'd arrived at the right house as we started to open the gate, as more than once I'd accidentally gone through my neighbor's yard. But the key fit in the lock.

The house smelled of pea soup, entangled with the aroma of freshly baked bread. My mouth watered, and my stomach grumbled. I'd barely eaten my toast that morning, and had subsisted on one cup of tea after another, my subconscious already preparing for the impending ration that might cut my habit down to a tenth of what it was now.

"Ah, Gladys, I would marry her," Tom said. "If she weren't already taken with that fire-watching fellow."

"She is so very dear to me. I'll be sad when they wed, if she decides to tend her own house."

Besides the scents of our dinner, we were greeted by the yips of the dogs as they rounded the corner and barreled toward us, sliding on the wood. Abbey splatted against my legs and fell backward. I bent down, crooning as Tom scratched the fur behind their ears.

These were my babies, my beautiful, loving, loyal children.

"There's nothing better than being greeted so enthusiastically upon returning," Tom commented.

"The joy of their welcome never wanes."

"I'll dole out the bowls for us," he said.

"You are my paying guest; allow me."

"And also your brother."

"I insist." I slipped out of my overcoat, hung up my purse and mask bag, then trotted into the kitchen to scoop out the delicious soup had Gladys left to simmer in a pot.

With the bread sliced and the rather unsavory lump of margarine spooned into a bowl, I served our dinner.

There was such a peacefulness about this moment, but the agreeable companionship wouldn't last. Just as I knew Hitler seemed to be bulldozing his way across Europe, with a new Russian buddy at his side, soon our phony war would turn into a reality, and my brother would be pulled way. But for now, I was determined to be grateful.

April 9, 1940

Dearest Mark,

Reading this evening's headlines, my thoughts immediately flew to you, Tom, Peter and all the other lads fighting Fascism. While Prime Minister Chamberlain continues to insist we're doing well, one must suspect otherwise based on the papers. Headlines like these hardly foster confidence in Britain's success:

Hitler Invades Norway and Denmark: Allies to Take Action Forthwith (*The Evening News*)

Allies to Fight the Nazis in Norway (*The Star*)

Germans March into Copenhagen (*The Evening News*)

Diana is about to burst with her fourth. Probably another

boy, as if she needed another. Do you think they'll give her an extra ration of meat? Even if they did, she'd probably give it to Mosley, just as she's given everything else to him, including her very soul.

I've gotten quite used to my duties at the first aid post, raveling and unraveling unused bandages. Not a single forehead yet to write upon.

Who do you find scarier, the Bolsheviks or the Nazis? I should think pairing Russians with Germans would be the scariest of combinations.

With the Germans taking Oslo, rumor has it our British troops will have to parachute in to fight. Peter's unit may be deployed on that mission. What a terrifying idea. The Norwegian government in exile has arrived in London of all places. I think I'll have to brush up on my Norwegian so I can understand what they say while we take tea. Perhaps the French will soon join us here as well; I do so prefer their company, though under the circumstances I fervently hope they remain in France.

Tomorrow I'm headed to Weston Hall with Debo and her beau, Andrew Cavendish. My youngest sister certainly doesn't lack for ambition. Quite high aim, actually. Marrying a duke's son would be an old-style feat, though he's a second, so she isn't likely to be a duchess. Northamptonshire will be a bore chaperoning the two of them. If only Andrew's aunt by marriage—Adele Astaire—would join us.

I hope you are well. I miss you dearly.

Very best love,
Nancy

*P.S. You probably won't get this, nor half my letter if the cen-
sors have anything to do with it, but I have included a piece of
delicious chocolate my dear friend Iris shared with me. And
as always, dearest Mark, burn after reading.*

May 6, 1940

TODAY SHOULD HAVE BEEN a day of elation. So many years
have passed since the release of my last book that I ought to
feel accomplished, elated even. Yet I was near tears as I sat at
Heywood Hill bookshop, pen poised to sign copies that no one
seemed interested in buying. Indeed, the ink in my pen has likely
dried up, just as shriveled and useless as I feel on the inside.

Pigeon Pie appears destined to be an early, and if I'm being
honest, extremely unimportant, casualty of war. It was single-
minded, selfish even, of me to be offended that all the months of
hard work put into the book would result in so little reward. Not
that the failure is entirely the fault of my efforts. My publisher
hadn't kept the original publishing schedule, and instead pushed
it back months, until all the humor I'd woven into the novel's
pages had grown as stale as the air in the cellar of Paddington
Station.

Readers will never understand how hard it was to thrust levity
onto the pages when I sat in a gloomy, smelly room waiting for
bombs to drop on my head. They will not realize the escapism I've
created, that *Pigeon Pie* is in fact a perfect cajoling masterpiece.

Anne Hill approached cautiously where I sat behind a pile of
artfully displayed copies, a forced smile on her lips.

"Do not pity me." I pursed my own lips and waved away the
emptiness I felt inside at yet another failed literary attempt.

"For what it's worth, I found *Pigeon Pie* charming." Anne ran her finger over the paper cover.

"I'm glad." I smiled, grateful for muscle memory. "And someday perhaps when the war is over, others will too."

"You have a singular humor, Nancy"—Anne tapped her finger against the book—"that only the most discerning readers will appreciate."

"Thank you." At least there was one person who understood me.

I stood up to stretch, walking toward the window, where the blackout curtains had been pulled back to let in the sun. The streets were busy, even if the shop was empty. The bell on the door rang as a customer walked in.

A woman in a spring jacket, cheeks flushed from walking, asked, "Do you have *Sad Cypress*, the latest Agatha Christie?"

"We are fresh out, but I have another book that might interest you. *Pigeon Pie* by Nancy Mitford." Anne glanced at me over the woman's shoulder, nodding subtly for me to go toward the table, but the customer's words stopped me in my tracks.

"Oh, no." She waved both of her hands. "I'm not a fan of Ms. Mitford's books. Had quite enough with *Wigs on the Green*."

Anne averted her gaze from me, offering the woman an understanding smile. "I too had a spot of trouble with that one. But I've read *Pigeon Pie*, and I believe Mitford has redeemed herself."

I ducked into the pages of a Charles Dickens, pretending to read as I listened. I'd much rather have sunk into the floorboards and live out the rest of my life in the cellar.

"Well . . ." the customer hedged.

"I believe so strongly that you'll like this one," Anne continued, "that I'll sell it to you at a discount. Once you've finished, I bet you'll send your friends in to buy copies."

Oh, dear God, so it's come to this . . . Before I could hear the woman's reply, I fled the bookstore, brushing past them both.

📖

May 24, 1940

MY SHIFT DIDN'T BEGIN for hours, but here I was, at barely seven a.m., waiting for Sophie. There was something calming about her. I felt I could share anything, and she wouldn't judge me. I didn't have to keep up pretenses or worry she'd find me lacking. We'd met on neutral ground, and that ground had remained steady beneath us.

Despite it being the end of her night shift, Sophie bustled in from parking her van, looking fresh as spring, her blue hat sporting an iris. Driving through the night never seemed to diminish her.

"Nancy, have you decided to take the wheel again? I could use your help with the old boys."

I tried to smile, but my face was too brittle. It cracked.

"What is it?" she asked, coming forward.

I glanced from side to side, not really wanting to share so publicly what was on my mind. I needed to confide in Sophie, to speak to her the way I might have been able to speak to my other dear friends, Mark and Evelyn, had they not been with their regiments, leaving me to lament on paper musings. "Tea?"

"Always."

Across the street, just opposite of Paddington, was a small café, blessedly slow for the hour. We took a seat outside and ordered.

"You look as though you've seen a ghost." Sophie peeled off her driving gloves and tucked them into her purse.

By now, she knew exactly who I was and to whom I was related. But nothing had changed between us, and I was so grateful for that. I drew in a deep breath, leaned forward and forced myself to whisper, "Oswald Mosley was arrested yesterday. He's in Holloway prison."

Sophie sat back and let out the breath it seemed we both held. "He's been jugged? My God . . . Have you spoken to Diana?"

I shook my head, feeling lighter already. "I doubt she'd welcome my call. And she'd not phone me herself unless it was to blame me somehow."

"And . . . are you . . . to blame?" Sophie asked carefully.

I let out a surprised laugh. "Not this go-round. Though I'd not be sorry if I were. I wish I could have had him jailed years ago when I first realized what a dangerous person he was. He tried to change this nation, and succeeded with my sister. He took her soul." I paused, shook my head. "No, I have to admit she gave it to him willingly. She would do anything for him, *has* done anything for him."

Sophie wrinkled her brow in thought. "She's not been run in?"

I fiddled with my napkin. "No. They probably think she's just a woman. You know, wife, mother, socialite. Incapable of being dangerous."

Sophie nodded, knowing all too well how men often underestimated women.

"If they only knew how treacherous," I continued. "She spent more time in Germany with Hitler than Mosley." *Though not as much as Unity.* I sighed. However disloyal it was to speak of my family's actions, I had to get it off my chest. "What's the point in arresting the Leader when his handmaiden is still doing his bidding?"

Between Diana's machinations and Unity practically licking Hitler's boots, I shuddered to think about the numerous conversations exchanged between Diana and Herr Hitler. What sort of promises did she make? Did she share the secrets of the good British men she'd dined with? Give Hitler a set of keys to Buckingham Palace? Of course, the latter was an exaggeration, but if she'd had access, it wouldn't surprise me to learn they now dangled from Hitler's belt.

"How much trouble can she cause now, though? She's just had a baby," Sophie said. "I've never had a baby, obviously, but my friends seem really tied down."

Unless you're Diana. "The last three didn't stop her."

Our tea was served, and we drank in silence, watching the London streets slowly come alive. Norwegians, Belgians and other national dignitaries seeking asylum in London doubtless mingled in the morning crowd. We'd become a refuge for foreign powers, despite being separated only by a thin channel from Hitler and his goons.

Our new prime minister, Winston Churchill, of all people Esmond Romilly's uncle by marriage, reported Germany's conquests nightly by wireless. He didn't placate us by holding back. The Germans were winning the war, despite counterattacks. Belgium, France, Luxembourg and the Netherlands were now under Nazi rule.

My mind traveled the short distance from the café where we sat to the Home Office and the few connections I had there.

Should I attempt to talk to someone about Diana? What kind of a sister would that make me? *Not a good one.*

What was more important: the safety and security of our great nation or the feelings of a sister who'd already proved herself a traitor? Framed that way, I had little choice. If I'd told the Home Office earlier of her actions, would anything be different?

It was a chilling thought, and one I needed to remove from my mind.

"Can I ask you a personal question?" I hedged, changing the subject.

Sophie smiled. "I won't stop you."

I stared at her ringless finger, where a clear indentation showed signs a ring once resided there. "Why don't you wear your wedding band?"

Sophie's gaze followed mine. "My husband died in a training accident."

"I'm so sorry." My voice tightened with emotion.

Sophie smiled wanly, staring outside as if her husband might be waiting across the street. "It's all right. Geoffrey was a gem, and I'm grateful for the time we had."

"Was he in the army?"

She nodded stoically, running her tongue over her teeth. "We weren't married long, but I loved him very much." She flashed a sad smile. "Perhaps one day I will find someone half as decent as he was and love again."

"I hope you do. A woman as charming as yourself deserves what she wants."

Sophie cocked her head to the side, laughing a little. "So do you, my friend."

I shrugged. "Prod is still alive, but I don't love him. And I'm not sure I ever did."

Was love always the measure? Diana loved the Ogre, but I wouldn't wish their love on anyone. Was love enough, in my sister's case, to excuse the inexcusable? *Is love enough for me?* I'm not sure I've ever found that elusive beat of the heart to begin with.

Two days later, the news crackling from the wireless was grim and terrifying. At Dunkirk, in France, our troops were facing massive bombardment from the Germans. Calais was lost; Belgium was lost.

And Peter . . . He was there in the midst of it all, leading his men in the charge. I prayed he was alive and not bleeding on a beach. Prayed the wide-scale evacuation by sea—orchestrated with every sort of volunteer, including fishing boats—would be successful in saving our men. Prayed for the battle to end.

Days passed. We sat glued to the wireless as Paris was bombed, and Churchill shouted into every parlor, kitchen, café and hospital basement that *we will never surrender.* Like the thousands of wives and mothers, I lay curled up on the sofa, clutching my puppies to my chest, wondering if I would ever see my husband, my brother, my male friends again.

The Germans weren't going to relent in their plot to gain access to Great Britain. We were Hitler's ultimate conquest. With their attack of our troops on French soil, the Nazis surged forward, nearly completing their invasion of France. Hitler's army sank our ships, and captured our soldiers in Saint-Valéry-en-Caux.

I agonized over having not gone yet to the Home Office about my sister. Could anything I knew have contributed to the Nazis' crushing our men?

Ten days after the first signs of trouble in Dunkirk, as I was thinking all was lost, Peter trudged through the door looking tired and broken.

Springing up, I tossed myself into his slimmer arms. He trembled as he embraced me back, relief flooding between us. I led him upstairs and drew him a bath. We didn't speak as I poured in soaking salts. There was no need for words as he disrobed and sank into the tub. I couldn't imagine the horrors he'd seen. The torment of trying to save his men from injury and death, from pure evil, must have been crushing.

I washed his back, running my soapy fingers over the knotted muscles beneath his bruised flesh. And he fell asleep more than once. When he was clean, I tried to tuck him into bed, but Peter pulled me down with him. We made love in the quiet dark, and when we were through, I was pretty certain it was Peter's tears that wet my shoulder.

Several days later, we listened to Charles de Gaulle over the wireless, imploring his Free French forces to fight the Nazis.

"France is not alone! She is not alone! She has a great empire behind her! Together with the British Empire, she can form a bloc that controls the seas and continue the struggle. . . ."

De Gaulle crisply assured his people of British support, and Peter told me he was returning to his regiment, though this time they'd be billeted on our own shores.

"When do you leave?" I asked.

"Tomorrow morning. First light."

De Gaulle continued, "She may, like England, draw upon the limitless industrial resources of the United States. . . ."

I swallowed back my fear and nodded. We'd still not spoken about what happened on the beaches at Dunkirk, nor how close he'd come to his limits, even death. But I respected him for the calm way he told me he was about to return to war.

We hadn't spoken about Adelaide either, or about what he did when I was at my first aid post. Nor had we made love again. With war and death looming, it didn't feel like the right time to have those discussions. Besides, if the past taught me anything, it was that any discussion of the sort was not likely to change my marriage.

When he was gone the next morning, I felt a bit melancholy. But it was a different sort of emotion overwhelming me as I— and even the wooden bones of the little house around me— breathed a sigh of relief.

📖

June 20, 1940

Dearest Mark,

Inquiring minds want to know your stance on forgiveness. Does one beg for it no matter the transgression? Or is there some leeway between intentional harm and unintentional harm? Do reply, for the curious want to know.

And I almost forgot, I will be delighted to join you for the literary salon at Heywood Hill bookshop Saturday next.

Love from,
Nancy

"Mr. Jebb will see you now."

I rose from the firm leather chair, jittery and unnerved. It was not every day I was called to the Home Office to presumably report on my sister—and it was a duty long overdue. Muv would shove me headlong into the first grave she saw if she knew.

The door to Gladwyn Jebb's office opened, a yawning cavern that was about to swallow me whole. But I was here for a reason. A good one. I had to do my duty to my country.

I tried to summon some of the positive pluckiness of Sophia Garfield, but despite the red lipstick, I felt sick inside.

"Mrs. Rodd." Gladwyn stuck out his hand, squeezing my fingers gently. Though the decades had aged him, giving him some gray at his temples, he looked as handsome as he had in our youth. "So lovely to see you again."

It felt odd for him to call me Mrs. Rodd. Painfully formal when we used to run around the London streets dressed up as caricatures, chasing clues. "And you as well."

"Have a seat."

I perched on the edge of yet another uncomfortable leather chair.

"I'm glad you telephoned," Gladwyn started.

I'm not certain, as he looked in my eyes, that I was glad I'd made that call. But then I brought to mind images of my friends, my husband, my brother abroad, facing off with Hitler's men, and managed to straighten my spine and find my resolve.

"I have some questions about your sisters." Gladwyn stood suddenly. "Care for tea?"

My stomach was too tied up in knots. I shook my head, folding my gloved hands in my lap. "No, thank you."

He walked to a sideboard and poured himself a drink. "We've known each other a long time, haven't we?"

"We have."

"And we can be honest with each other, can't we?"

"I should hope so."

He smiled, settling back into his chair, drink in hand. "There's no need to be nervous, Nancy." His voice was low and reassuring.

"I'm not." I smiled confidently, waving away his very accurate assumption. "I've come for the good of Britain. For our men fighting overseas."

"Tell me about Diana."

"She is dangerous. If you've any doubt about how dangerous, examine her passport. She's been to Germany many, many times."

He nodded but said nothing.

"As a personal guest of Hitler." I mentioned how the Führer had been at Diana and the Ogre's wedding, how she considered him charming and handsome and never found fault with any of his political views. That she and her husband were at the forefront of British Fascism. "And make no mistake," I continued. "Diana may be a woman, but she is every bit as involved as Oswald when it comes to spreading Fascist propaganda. She's an extremely dangerous person. Perhaps more so even than her husband, because fewer people see her for what she is."

"And what of your other sisters?"

"Unity is innocuous now, though she walked side by side with Diana until the bullet lodged in her brain robbed her of that capacity. Deborah is an innocent. And Jessica, if she weren't in the United States, would be sitting here beside me." *In fact, Jessica would have beat me here.*

"And Pamela?"

Oh, sweet Pam, as loyal and simple as a hound—but her loyalty currently wasn't one hundred percent with Britain. "She and her husband have been to a few BUF rallies, and attended Nazi rallies in Nuremberg but are not in league with Diana and Oswald."

"Isn't her husband a pilot in the RAF?"

I nodded, chewing the inside of my cheek. "Yes." *Perhaps he is hiding behind a mask of fidelity to country.* But I didn't say that aloud. I was no expert, and so left that judgment to Gladwyn. I was already damning my family enough. "I believe Pam is harmless."

"What about your brother, Tom, and your parents?"

"I'm certain you've heard my father's speeches in the house. He is not a fan of Hitler. As for my mother, she is not a threat. And Tom, he is fighting for the British right now."

Gladwyn leaned forward, elbows on his wide oak desk. "Why tell me all this?"

That was a question I was certain to have to answer for the rest of my life, but not one for which I struggled to find the words. "Because it is the right thing to do. So many of our men died at Dunkirk. So many more will die before this war is over. If my husband, my brother, some of the friends you and I share, don't come out of this war, I would never forgive myself for not trying to do more to stop Fascism on the British front. Make no mistake, if Diana could sneak Hitler into this country and undermine the government, she would. She believes in it that strongly."

"But she is merely a woman."

A laugh itched to release. "Which is exactly why you should not underestimate her. Others will. For years she's hidden behind her angelic visage, and her fairer sex. Beneath that mask there is a conniving Fascist who will do anything to save her husband, and herself. I cannot in good conscience allow her to continue."

Gladwyn nodded. "Nancy, I assure you, we will take your warnings into serious consideration."

I swallowed, feeling hollow inside, despite the victory of having done my duty. I wouldn't change telephoning Gladwyn. But that didn't make the knowledge of having condemned my sister any less sour.

📖

July 6, 1940

~~Dear Muv,~~

~~I beg your~~

Sophie leaned against a wall outside the first aid post, a lit cigarette between her gloveless fingers. She wore her ever-present iris brooch on the lapel of her ARP uniform. After she'd first told me about Geoffrey, he'd become a regular feature in conversation. I'd learned she'd received the brooch as a gift from him before he'd shipped out.

"I thought you could use a drink. My shift doesn't start for a couple of hours." Sophie dropped her cigarette and ground it out with the heel of her shoe.

"What makes you think I need a drink?"

"The rather green pallor of your skin, and the headlines."

I sighed. "I've been trying to avoid the papers." *And the aftermath.* Diana had been arrested, and our entire family was once more hurled into the limelight. We walked in step together toward the little café that had become our own. "In fact, I'm planning on heading out of town."

"Anywhere special? I presume the South of France is not a contender."

"Indeed not." I gave an exaggerated sigh. "Though I long for the days when I could walk along the Seine without the black cloud of a Nazi flag flying overhead. I am going to Highcliffe Castle, south of here along the shore. Peter's aunt owns it. She's always insisted I'm like a daughter to her. I've volunteered to assist her with the evacuees being processed there."

We sat down at a little round table and ordered deviled eggs and glasses of wine, when what I really could have used was a whisky soda.

"Sounds divine." Sophie sipped her wine between dainty bites.

"Come with me," I suggested on a whim.

"Leave my post?"

"They can do without you for a few days." The egg in my mouth tasted off. "Do these taste all right to you?"

Sophie shrugged. "They taste like eggs."

I set mine down, rinsing my mouth with wine, and then waved over our waiter to bring me a glass of water. The last time I'd had an aversion to eggs, I'd been pregnant.

"Are you all right?" Sophie asked.

I shook my head, feeling a little faint. "Just nerves. My sister deserves to be in Holloway prison—but I can't help feeling guilt. She was forced to give up her children."

Sophie sniffed my uneaten egg, then popped it into her mouth. "Since we've yet to see a bomb drop on London, I suppose the ARP can do without me for a spell."

Several Frenchmen tugged at the café tables beside us, forming a longer one for their party. They ordered drinks and conversed loudly in French. With seven thousand Free French forces in London, it was a wonder the entire café was not full of them.

"Do you speak French?" Sophie asked me.

"I do."

She grinned conspiratorially and leaned closer. "Tell me what they're saying. They must not want Brits to hear since they aren't saying it in English."

"Perhaps. Though, if we were in France, we would likely speak English."

"Oh, Nancy, no, we would only speak French because it is *très chic*."

I laughed and cocked my head to the side, toying with the stem of my wineglass. "They are saying that for Frenchmen like them, a government still exists in France, and is supported by a Parliament that has been created in a territory not occupied by you know who . . ." There was a pause in the men's conversation, and I worried they had overhead me. My mind whirled a mile a minute, because if I was hearing correctly . . . they were *not* Free French.

"And . . . ?" Sophie encouraged.

"Because that branch still exists it cannot be considered extinct. He is saying that establishing the government elsewhere—here in London—is a clear sign of rebellion, and that de Gaulle will need to take care because of it." My eyes widened, and I took a gulp of wine, then gave a shriek of laughter as though Sophie had said something quite hilarious. "I believe these men are . . ." I bit my lip, unable to say aloud that these men were Vichy supporters and therefore Nazi collaborators.

Sophie mouthed the word *Vichy*, and I nodded.

I had inadvertently stumbled across a traitorous conversation. "Laugh at me," I said quietly, and Sophie did. Perhaps too well, as she drew the attention of the men.

"We'd best be on our way," she said.

I nodded. As I stood to leave, I surreptitiously glanced in the direction of the men at the table, trying to memorize their clothes, the angles of their faces. Perhaps one last meeting with Gladwyn Jebb was in order before I left for Highcliffe.

July 8, 1940

Dearest Mark,

I am being punished—

Curled in the tub at Highcliffe Castle, knees tucked up to my chest, pain was gouging me from the inside out—the same pain as when I'd lost my first child. It was happening again. I'd not even had a chance to rejoice at the life growing inside me.

I'd sat here for hours, missing breakfast, unable to move. Calling out with a broken voice, "I'm not feeling well," when anybody knocked.

There was a razor I'd found in the cupboard. Probably one a past male guest had used to shave his face.

I'd set it on the edge of the tub. The silver of it glinted in the yellow light of the bathroom, winking at me, beckoning me to put myself out of my misery forever. I'd picked it up, put it to my wrist, but each time I went to press hard, there was a knock at the door. I was reminded, as I'd been that time I put my head in the oven, that there were people who would be sorely put out if I were to take my life.

Yet I couldn't summon the gumption to pull myself from the tub, nor to dispose of the razor, and so we both sat here, staring at each other as I suffered the loss of another child.

As morning drew into afternoon, the pounding on the door did not cease, and then I heard a pair of sensible shoes clicking over the wooden floors before Sophie's floral scent swept into the bathroom. How had she gotten in?

"I picked your lock. Are you not feeling . . ." She stopped, taking in the sight of me, and the pink-tinged water around me. Eyes wide, her gaze slid toward the razor. "Oh! Did you . . ." Sophie's hands came to her mouth.

"I didn't. I've lost a baby," I managed to say around chattering teeth, and holding up my arms to reveal my unmarred wrists. "Do not pity me. This was God's doing. And what I deserve." I pressed a hand to my still-cramping belly.

Sophie clucked her tongue, pocketed the razor and then grabbed a large towel. "Out of the tub. And, Nancy, no one deserves this. Least of all you."

After she heaved me from the tub with a strength I never would have guessed she possessed, I stood on shaky legs, leaving traces of the baby I'd not even realized Peter and I had created behind. My body as bruised as my heart.

Sophie dried me off and helped me to dress, even fashioning the necessary sanitary items.

"If we could," I hedged, "keep this between us. All of it."

"I won't say a word, except to you." Sophie gripped both my shoulders. "This isn't your fault. You know that, right?"

I shook my head, my throat tight. It was perfectly indecent of me to even be standing here, for Sophie to have ever seen me in this state. Yet for some reason, around her, I could let down whatever indomitable guard kept proper Englishwomen from reacting in anything other than placid, polite tones.

"It's because of my sister," I whispered. "She's been taken from her children. If only I'd not agreed to meet with the Home Office."

"No." Sophie's voice was clipped as she moved behind me to brush out the tangles in my hair.

"If I'd just left well enough alone—"

"Then Hitler would be on our shores. You did the right thing, Nancy, and I won't hear you say another word about it. You did nothing to cause the loss of your child." She tried on a half smile. "Unless you spent the morning jumping off the kitchen table."

"I did not. Nor did I ride a bicycle."

"Are you a wallower?" Sophie stood before me, pinching my cheeks and dabbing on a bit of lipstick from my dressing table.

"For most of my life," I teased.

Sophie chuckled. "You told me not to pity you, and I'm going to take you at your word. Besides, it will do you no good to cry into your pillow for the short time we are here. You can do that when you get home."

"I'd rather do neither."

"That's the spirit." Sophie unpinned the iris from her cardigan, transferring it to my lapel. "This will bolster you for the day. It has certainly brought me strength. But I expect it back."

My hand, feeling as though it weighed a hundred pounds, touched the delicate petals. "I wouldn't dream of keeping it. Are you certain you'll be all right without it?"

Sophie nodded, checking her hair in the looking glass and then dabbing on a fresh bit of lipstick. "You need it more than I do."

I swallowed around the lump in my throat. I wanted to tell her what her friendship meant to me, but the words lodged.

Sophie squeezed my hand, telling me without words that she knew.

"You need to get some rest. I'll have something sent up for you to eat. And should I send for the doctor?"

I shook my head. Lying in bed alone sounded like the very last thing I needed. "I don't think I need a doctor. It was very early on, and I don't want to rest."

"Are you feeling well enough now to help me and Aunt Vi with the evacuee children from London? They're making an awful mess downstairs, and rounding them all up to feed is proving to be rather like trying to herd frightened sheep from a pasture. They keep running in different directions."

Aunt Vi's castle had become a processing center for children evacuating from London and Southampton. They stayed with her for a few days before being distributed to local families. A few were even going so far as Canada.

"I'll help. What could be more fun than rounding up children?" I gave her my best sarcastic look. Just doing so made me feel more like myself.

"Promise me, then, if you start to feel weak or faint you will rest and allow me to summon a doctor."

"I promise."

Down in the dining room, the good tablecloths had been replaced with great sheets, which were easier to launder. Children whined about the vegetable soup as we served them, one even going so far as to ask if we hadn't a tin of salmon he could have instead. But like any hungry person, they were ultimately unable to resist, and soon the children slurped up the savory broth they'd been complaining about minutes before.

When we finished, we took them outside to the courtyard to play, my dogs chasing them in circles. I sat on the edge of the dolphin-and-boy fountain with Sophie, and Aunt Vi joined us.

"I will be distraught when the two of you leave," she said, dabbing at her glistening brow with a handkerchief before tucking it back in her sleeve. "Not a butler or footman to be found in miles."

"If you'll have us back, we'd be glad to help again," I said.

"You are always welcome." Aunt Vi patted my hand.

A few days later, what we'd feared had finally come to pass—the Germans were bombing our beloved country. The Luftwaffe attacked Wales, Scotland and Northern Ireland. Sophie and I scrambled to pack our bags and race back to London. Our break was over. I had a sinking feeling it would be a long time before we had another. It would surely be only a matter of time before the bombers tried to sink London. And we had to be there for her.

August 24, 1940

~~Dear Peter,~~

The sounds of the sirens wailing jolted me from a deep sleep. I fumbled for the lamp on my side table, managing to switch it on before knocking it over. The clock read three a.m.

Millie went wild barking, causing the other dogs to go mad.

"Hush, hush," I said, but my words were drowned out by the keen of the warning bells, and the shouts from an ARP warden on the street.

This isn't a drill.

I pushed back my covers, tugged on a robe, thrust my feet into slippers and rushed through the house. I whistled to the dogs as I went, trying to draw them out to the Anderson shelter. Despite it being summer, the night air was chilly, and the cramped, dark shelter beneath the ground even more so. I shivered, seeking warmth from my dogs, wishing I'd followed the official shelter instructions completely and put a set of quilts and pillows down on the narrow metal bench.

Outside, the sirens continued in echoing tempo, and my breathing matched it—low and shallow, high and fast. From a distance came a new sound. A great terrible rumbling . . .

Bombs hitting a mark.

I shuddered violently, curling deeper against the metal bench, my dogs trembling in my arms. The roaring crash was followed by the cracking answer of the antiaircraft guns. Over and over.

The dogs whined, frightened by the staccato noise. Fear

permeated my soul. I shivered against a cold that was bone-deep and rubbed at my arms. Why hadn't I sought out another live-in companion? Or asked Gladys to stay the nights—she wasn't yet married, as her beau had gone off in Peter's regiment. Millie jumped down and paced at my feet, panting and whimpering. Though I couldn't see her, I knew that when there was a pause in her antics, she was staring up at me, wondering why I wasn't doing anything about the noise. What could I do? What could anyone?

"We'll be fine, sweet pup, we'll be fine." I said it as much for myself as for her. I lifted her onto my lap, pressing my face to her neck. I closed my eyes against the bombs and the antiaircraft guns, even though I couldn't see them from within the shelter.

I prayed that we would be all right. I'd never been one to get down on my knees and plead, except as a child hoping for a new pet. But I knelt now, my knees pressing into the hard, cold earth.

The bombs seemed to come for an interminable amount of time in a pattern I started to recognize. A whistling, then a rage-filled crash that shook the earth and made me feel as though the bomb that fell was right on top of me. How close were they?

I touched the side of the shelter, expecting to feel the heat of the flames, but the metal was as cold as ice.

And then as swiftly as it had gone, lost in the sounds of war, silence returned.

From a distance, I thought I heard someone shouting my name. The shouting grew closer. I shoved at the shelter door with shaking hands and it opened. I was face-to-face in the dawn light with Sophie.

"Thank God," she said, tugging me against her. The sharpness of her iris brooch pressed against the thin layers of my robe and nightgown, but I didn't care, embracing her tight. "You're shaking."

In the distance, smoke rose up into the morning sky, but thankfully there appeared to be no flames in my immediate vicinity.

Sophie's gaze followed mine. "Oxford Street."

I nodded, relieved and terrified all at once. Oxford Street was about two miles to the east. Could have been a world away, and yet it was a few minutes' drive.

"Any casualties?"

Sophie nodded. "A few. But the boys were taking care of that, and as soon as I could, I drove here to make certain you were safe."

"I have to help."

"I'll drive you back to the station. But you should change first."

I nodded. "Cup of tea while you wait?"

Sophie bent down to reassure a yipping Millie. "I'll make it for us both while you get dressed."

"Come on, duckies." I snapped my fingers at the dogs. "And you too, Iris."

Sophie grinned at my nickname for her, and straightened. "Do you happen to have any sugar? I haven't had any in ages."

"Yes." I didn't have much, but there was enough for a few generous helpings. I'd give it all to Sophie if she wanted. Did she have any idea how dear she'd become to me? We'd not known each other even a year, but already she knew so many of my secrets, and she'd pulled me from the darkest corner just the month before.

So yes, I'd give her all my sugar, all anything, if she asked.

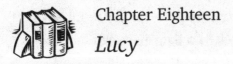 Chapter Eighteen
Lucy

LUCY LOGGED OUT OF her computer at the bookshop after speaking with her assistant back in DC then headed to her flat to get ready for her dinner with Gavin. Butterflies danced in her belly as she waited for the door buzzer to ring. Lunch with a colleague and exploring different parts of the city with a friend felt different than dinner out. They *were* different.

She hadn't come to London for romance, and in less than a week she'd be walking down the busy Washington, DC, streets toward her office at Emerald Books. There was something about Gavin that had her wishing there weren't an ocean between their two cities.

When the buzzer finally sounded and she headed downstairs, a rush of air caught her as she opened the door, blowing her scarf over her face and giving her a mouthful of wool.

Gavin laughed, making his brogue a little thicker as he spoke. "Welcome to London's charming autumn weather." He held up his hands toward the sky.

Lucy unwrapped the scarf from around her face and smiled. Gavin leaned in, kissing her on the cheek. "I hope you're hungry," he said.

"Starved."

"Good." His smile widened, bringing out a dimple. "I'm taking you to one of my favorite spots, the Mews of Mayfair."

"That sounds a little like we're traveling back in time."

Gavin chuckled. "And yet I promise to remain in the present."

His words, spoken so casually, could have been taken two ways. Physically in the present, but also mentally, and she liked that. He was always just so casually kind.

"I'll admit, though"—he cocked his head toward hers and offered an elbow—"I thought you might like it as much as I do because of its background. It started life as two eighteenth-century stable houses connected by a courtyard."

"Oh yes, that is right up my alley. People who like old books tend to like history too, don't they?"

"I certainly do."

They started to walk, her hand in the crook of his arm. "No motorbike tonight?"

"It's not too far. And parking is hell."

"And it's gorgeous out," Lucy added.

In a few short, pleasant blocks they were at the Mews.

"We're a little ahead of time." Gavin glanced at his watch. "Fancy a drink?" He gestured to the courtyard bar.

"Yes." Lucy smiled as he led her to a small round table. "I want to thank you again for being such a great guide. Helping me with my search for Iris. Between the ARP exhibit and our little tour the other day, you've made such a difference in my London stay, and I really do appreciate it."

"My pleasure, lass, truly."

Lass . . . She liked the way that rolled so easily off his tongue.

She glanced down at the menu. "These cocktails are hilarious," Lucy said with a giggle, pointing at the menu. "I'm trying to decide between the Illegal Marriage or the Public Scandal."

"They are clever, aren't they? I myself was thinking of either the Marriage Act or Titti, but might just stick to my regular mule."

Lucy leaned against the table, unable to quit her smile as she watched Gavin read through the menu. In that precise moment, there was nowhere else she'd rather be.

"How goes the research?" he asked as their drinks arrived, along with a hummus board to share.

"It's not really going much of anywhere at the moment. But I hope that will turn around when I get back tonight and call my sister. She's been doing some digging. Today, I found a fifth Iris, but it was a small child Nancy Mitford once cared for. So I'm fairly certain that isn't her. I can't help thinking, or maybe hoping, we're really onto something with Nellie, Sophie and Marjorie." She told him about the brief letter she'd found in the stack her mother had left behind addressed to Sophie.

"So many bread crumbs and yet no loaf. I wish I could help."

Lucy glanced over and smiled at his generosity. "You've already helped me so much."

"Anytime. So, I know you're a Mitford fan, but what I don't know about you is what your favorite childhood tale was," Gavin said, taking a piece of pita and dipping it in the hummus.

Lucy sipped her cocktail—the Public Scandal, which seemed fitting given what she'd been uncovering about the Mitfords— as she considered the question, enjoying the bubbles from the champagne and the sweet tang of strawberry and kombucha. "This might seem strange, but Ken Follett's *Pillars of the Earth.* I got hold of a copy when I was about thirteen, and I've read it half a dozen times."

"That's a heavy book—literally: a thousand pages."

Lucy laughed. "What can I say? I've always been a sucker for history. Most people find the cathedral building scenes boring, but I read every word. What about you?"

Gavin chuckled, splaying his hands on the table, and she took note of a few scars along his fingertips. "*The Call of the Wild*, hands down."

"Did you get these scars adventuring in the Yukon with sled dogs?" Lucy teased, reaching out to run her index finger over the white jagged lines on his hands.

"I wish, though I did have a dog named Buck growing up. These are from rugby. Just because I like books doesn't mean I'm not a badarse."

Lucy's head fell back as she laughed.

"You have a lovely laugh." Gavin chuckled right along beside her.

They chattered about his rugby and other youthful antics until it was time to head over to the brasserie. Over a bowl of gnocchi for her and a Yorkshire hot pot for Gavin, along with glasses of wine, their conversation turned back to their true passions—books and authors.

"If you could invite any author to dinner right now, who would it be?" Lucy asked.

"That's not a fair question. I cannot be forced to choose."

Lucy giggled and touched his arm, feeling the heat beneath her fingertips. "Come on, just one! Jack London? Oscar Wilde?"

Gavin rubbed his chin, deep in thought. "Probably Sir Arthur Conan Doyle. I'm a huge fan of Sherlock Holmes, plus he's Scottish."

"Hmm . . . that's a good one," Lucy said. "I think I may have to crash your dinner."

"Anytime. But then I get to crash yours. Let me guess, you'd pick Nancy Mitford so you could ask her who Iris was."

"That's not entirely why." Lucy laughed. "I'd pick Nancy even if I already knew Iris's identity, just to have one evening where I too was a Bright Young Thing."

Gavin smiled at her, as if he thought she already was, and Lucy's heart thudded a little harder.

After dinner they meandered through Mayfair, stopping in an antique shop that had an intoxicating display of old books in the window. After sifting through the titles, they drifted in separate directions, browsing the items on display, looking for any hidden treasures.

And that's when Lucy saw it. Her breath caught. She blinked disbelieving at what glittered from beneath the glass. *An iris pin.*

"Is that . . . ?" Gavin joined her, his breath as shallow as her own at the sight of it.

"Looks nearly the same, doesn't it?" She glanced up at him, hopeful he'd agree.

Gavin waved the attendant over to unlock the case. He handed Lucy the pin. The metal was cool to the touch, and the lights caught the burgundy petals, making them sparkle. Was it too much to think it was fate that once more teased her with a clue to Nancy's past? This pin looked exactly like the one she'd seen at the ARP exhibit. *A sign.* Had to be. She was on the road to discovery. At least, she hoped.

"I need to get this," Lucy said.

"If nothing else, you've come this far, and it's a great keepsake," Gavin agreed.

She purchased the pin, and waited for Gavin to pay for a few books. They headed back out toward Curzon Street, packages in hand.

Nearly there, her phone buzzed with a text from Maya. She wasn't going to be able to make their call. Some sort of computer crisis at work.

"Darn." Lucy showed Gavin the text.

"So the mystery continues," Gavin drawled.

"If you hadn't told me you were a fan of Sherlock Holmes, I should have guessed."

He chuckled.

Outside of the bookshop and her flat, the only light was that of the streetlamps, and a few visible stars in the sky. She glanced up at Gavin, taking in the shadows of his features, the soft look of his hair.

"Thank you again for an amazing night," she said.

"My pleasure. I'm glad I met you, Lucy. I've never known a lass who loved books *and* having fun as much as you." He brushed a lock of hair from her cheek.

Lucy's breath caught. She wanted to lean into the touch, which was gone too soon. "Well, you're the first rugby bibliophile I've ever come across." She purposefully kept her tone light.

The same couldn't be said for Gavin, whose gaze met hers, all serious now. "And in a few days, you're leaving."

She nodded, feeling as though she'd met a kindred spirit. If they'd had the time to pursue it, where would the road have led? She wanted to say, *Let's make the fun last. Stay with me tonight.* But instead she said, "Meet me for lunch tomorrow?"

Gavin smiled, a little hint of melancholy in the creases around his eyes. "Aye."

And then he leaned in, brushing his warm lips across her cheek. She closed her eyes, breathing in his scent, wishing she had the nerve to turn her face just a little, so that his mouth would meet hers.

But then he turned his, and she didn't need to wish a real kiss into being as his warm lips slid over hers.

Chapter Nineteen
Nancy

Dearest Evelyn,

I miss you dearly, my friend, and I do hope you are taking care. Perhaps by the time this letter reaches the shores of West Africa, your regiment will have already been sent home. In the meantime, please enjoy this short little tale I wrote just for you. It's based on a true story, and I daresay the cabbie rivals your driving.

Love from,
Nancy

WE WERE NOT GIFTED with silence for a long time.

Sirens wailed, and the rumbling of bombs echoed dully in the cellar of the Paddington Station first aid depot along with the groans and screams of those in pain, those dying. The blood . . . so much of it, mingled with the soot of ashes.

I did what I could to tend the injured, cleaning and wrapping bloody scrapes, and sending those who needed stitches or bones set on to the nurses and doctors.

Then I took up my blue indelible pencil for a task I dreaded most. A task that I dearly wanted to become numb to. After having done it so many times, there should have been a normalcy to it. But there wasn't. Every dead body shook me to the core.

Lined on the floor were a few of the departed, brought in so far on Sophie's ambulance, likely more to come. My hand shook as I bent and wrote, "Name Unknown," along with the street name belonging to the first victim.

The pencil slipped in the moisture on his forehead, and I cringed as my palm slid over his cheek.

"I'm sorry," I muttered, choking up when it struck me he wouldn't hear my apology.

Though there'd not been many yet, every *unknown* was a tragedy. Sometimes we found papers in their pockets identifying them, or family members who'd clutched them, cried out their names.

Even in my sleep, I could hear those echoing wails. They woke me with a start, even when the bombs ceased.

Though they didn't cease for long.

Day and night, the air-raid sirens wailed as false warnings, and other times bombs plunged down on London. If I was home, I rushed to the Andy in the yard, and if I was at the first aid post, I stayed put in the gray cellar, awaiting the bodies.

Starting on the seventh of September, the Germans launched an attack that seemed never-ending, and unreal. I trembled in the time that passed during the bombings, sometimes ten or twelve hours of nonstop eruptions. The screaming bombs made my flesh creep with their awful din. They attacked us at all hours, but their favorite time was the middle of the night.

Even in the moments of actual quiet, our minds were left buzzing with the phantom sounds of the sirens, the waves of aeroplanes diving in to drop their loads and the ambulances constantly tearing up and down the street. Sleep was a thing of the past—and not just because many a night saw me curled up in the uncomfortable shelter buried in the backyard as if it were a grave and we'd already been obliterated. For even when I closed my eyes under the eiderdown on my bed, I imagined those unholy great fires that seemed to be everywhere.

I started to hate the shrill ring of the telephone, for it always brought news of this friend or that acquaintance with their house blown apart. So many had been displaced that one of my friends opened up her manse in West Wycombe to those amongst our set who found themselves suddenly homeless.

At such a dire time, the country would've suited my nerves better, but I'd made a commitment to do my bit with the ARP. And at last my indelible pencil was put to use, labeling foreheads of the dead. Though there were not yet many, I cried every time.

On my way to the first aid post, I scurried through rubble, past roped-off homes and businesses, still blazing or smoking, in ruins. Roofs were blown away, windows shattered, the fragments littering the pavement. When I stepped in the street to avoid the debris, I ended up leaping out of the way of lorries whizzing by full of rubble—the pieces of people's lives, thrown away like garbage. Or ambulances. So many ambulances.

I was proud of the women I'd once internally mocked for their knitting and gossip. Embraced their determination as they sweated, working to soothe and bandage the wounded. How different they were from the spoiled French who'd come to London along with our soldiers when Dunkirk was evacuated. I'd volunteered at their canteen in White City, and they'd groused about the hard English beds disrupting their sleep. One had even gone so far as to whine about not having gone to the theater yet, to which I'd replied, "*Je trouve ça un peu ridicule.*" How ridiculous they were being. I'd reminded them I could be doing the cooking, which would cause them worse suffering. The Frogs had not enjoyed being told they were ridiculous, and had also seemed to believe I'd threatened to poison them. In any case, I was determined not to go back.

On the tenth of September, I awoke from a deep sleep to a different kind of wailing—a child. In my groggy state, I first thought I'd been visited by the ghosts of my own dearly departed. As my mind cleared, I realized the sound was very much a part of this world and coming from somewhere in the house.

There was a great clomping of boots, and Peter pushed into the room as I sat up dazed. His uniform was wrinkled like he'd worn it for several days, and his hair was mussed as though he'd been in the direct line of attack.

Have we been invaded by the Germans?

"Sorry to wake you." He seemed flustered, tugging at his shirt collar. "We have . . . guests."

"What sort of guests?" I climbed from bed, pulling on sensible wool pants under my nightdress, then wrapping on my robe, shoving my feet into loafers.

"Children." He looked very sad and boyish for a moment. "One of my soldiers . . . His house in Brixton blew up a few hours ago. His wife is having a miscarriage, and he had nowhere to send them . . ." He ran a shaky hand through his hair. "So I thought . . ."

I'd also lost a child—two—so the pain and terror of the unknown woman miscarrying, God knew where, twisted my heart and gut. "I'll help. Of course I will."

I followed Peter to the kitchen, lit with the yellow of a dim lamp. Gladys wiped soot from the children's tiny faces. They appeared about three and six. A boy and girl.

"Hello, duckies." I dampened another dish towel in the sink to wipe off the girl while Gladys shifted her focus to the boy. "My name is Nancy." Telling them to call me Mrs. Rodd felt cold given the circumstances and their fright.

"N . . . Nancy," the little girl said, as I gently administered the warm cloth to her skin. "I'm Iris."

"My friend's name is Iris too," I said.

The little girl's eyes widened.

"I'm Sam." The lad pushed his face close to his sister's, not wanting to be left out.

"Well, Iris and Sam, would you like some warm milk?" I hadn't much, but when they nodded, Gladys was quick to light the stove. They sat at the table, wrapped in their overcoats, each holding a stuffed teddy with tinges of soot on the fur.

After several sips, the children fell asleep at the table. Rather than risk waking them, we merely covered them where they were. Peter collapsed on the sofa in the parlor. I urged Gladys back to bed, then took a place at the table beside the children, laying my head on the cool wood, and closed my eyes.

We woke to sirens. Iris and Sam startled, fearful and wailing. The sun was high as we rushed into the yard, suggesting midday. I ushered the children hastily into the Andy. Gladys followed with the dogs and some scones from the day before, snatched up in a tea towel, for the children to snack on.

"I have to help where I can." Peter paused outside the shelter, looking up at the sky. "Keep safe, Naunce."

Before I closed the Andy, the whistle and thunk of an incendiary hauled me up short. The house next door burst into flames.

Peter ran across our small yard, hopping the short fence, then he turned around, pointing at me. "Shut the door, Nancy!"

I hesitated for a moment, wondering if this was the last time I'd see him. Then another whistling thunk, too close, unfroze me, and I slammed the Andy shut.

I tried to keep the children occupied, making Millie do tricks, and playing word games. Attempted to keep their minds—and mine—from the dreadful thuds outside that meant another destroyed road, house, someone's dreams, their life.

When at last it was quiet, an eerie silence that followed the attacks, we cautiously opened the door and climbed from the shelter. Peter sat, covered in sweat and soot, on the stoop of our unscathed house.

"I should take the children to Nanny's house," I said. "It feels as though the Germans are gunning for Paddington, doesn't it? They'll be safer a little farther off."

Peter nodded, his features drawn. "Good idea."

I bundled Sam and Iris in quilts and took a taxi to Nanny's house, where she welcomed them with open arms. The sweetlings were so stunned they'd barely spoken, let alone done any of the naughty things myself and my siblings had at their age.

Too tired to walk, I took a taxi, but a block from Nanny's the sirens howled again.

"Hold on to your 'at, miss." The driver swerved around screaming lorries and ambulances as the aerial bombardment pounded. He turned hard to the right onto Fitzjohn's Avenue, with me clutching the seat in front me. And then the building directly before us exploded, gone in a shower of debris, engulfed in flames and black smoke that violently shook the taxi.

I grabbed the door handle, intent on getting out, but he

stopped me. "I'll get you 'ome, miss, never mind that. Just a little bomb."

I'd never heard anyone say, *Just a little bomb.* This was what war did to a person when they were on the street day after day . . . It became normal. Changed you. But I wasn't hardened, not yet. I feared at any moment I might start screaming.

The cabbie whizzed around the Home Guard, rushing toward the fire. A member of the guard shouted for us to stop, and when the driver didn't listen, I swear they shot at us. By the time the taxi shuddered to a halt on Blomfield Road, I was so shaken it took a full minute before I realized three houses had vanished. In their places were great, yawning pits of smoke.

With a trembling hand I swung the taxi door open, setting my unsteady feet on a street I thought would certainly scorch. I hurried up the front stairs, tired and shaken, and pushed into the house, calling for Peter and Gladys.

Gladys rushed toward me from the kitchen, holding Millie in her arms. "Oh, thank God you're safe, Mrs. Rodd. Mr. Rodd has gone back to his regiment, and I didn't know what I'd do if you didn't return."

I was disappointed I'd not been back in time to say goodbye. Was the last image I had of him going to be sitting on the stoop? I forced myself to breathe. I'd nearly been blown away in a taxi, after all. But we were alive. I pushed my hair from my face, where it seemed to want to crowd, as if providing its own shelter for me.

"We're leaving," I said to Gladys. "It's no longer safe here. Get the good linens, and your things. I'll gather up my own and we'll head to Nanny's too."

Lord knew if we'd be any safer there.

A few days later, Buckingham Palace was bombed by the

Luftwaffe, leaving the residence slightly crumbled. Fortunately, the king and queen, and the rest of the royal family, were safe.

Day and night, the bombs kept coming. I wondered how in the world the Germans could be making them fast enough to keep up with the pace they set for dropping them. Hitler ordered the assault to continue relentlessly into October.

But they had not broken us. Londoners climbed out of the rubble each morning to start anew. Despite the whacking the Germans seemed fit to give us, there was rarely a hint of down-heartedness in the city.

Even when they bombed St. Paul's Cathedral. The church withstood the bomb, the outer shell standing stoic and strong. But inside was a different story. The explosive mined its way through the floor into the crypt, leaving a gaping chasm that smoked with ruin. *So much like my marriage.* All appeared well from someone standing on the outside, but inside, we were destroyed.

What better evidence of this than the letter I received from Peter as his regiment headed out of the city. He didn't know for how long, or exactly where. The note included not a single word of reassurance or love. No emotion whatsoever. Awful letter in front of me, I sat down with my pen, scribbling on the first bit of paper I could find—my appointment diary. Every thought that came to mind flowed through my pen, as if I were trying to tell my past self what I knew now.

Love is a punchy physical affair . . . Marriage is the most im-
portant thing in life & must be kept going at almost any . . .
Women, as well as men, ought to have a great many love af-
fairs before they marry, as the most critical moment in a mar-

riage is the falling off of physical love, which is bound to occur sooner or later & only an experienced woman can know how to cope with this . . .

But did *I* know how to cope? It was hard to be honest with myself in the answer. My marriage was well and truly over, and yet I was stuck.

📖

To my darling Iris,

I understand the house you've been assigned is closer to Paddington, but do know that you are always welcome here on Blomfield, with Gladys and me. And never mind Peter, you are not imposing in the slightest. Do let me know if you've changed your mind, as your company has always only been a treat.

Best love,
Nancy

Two months to Christmas without an end in sight. What was once a merry time turned bleak, and for some deadly. Several friends had lost their houses and fled to the country, or been forced to billet together. Gladys and I returned to Blomfield, my house still standing.

Despite my relative good fortune, rare was a moment when I didn't feel ill. There were no more days off with the ARP. Too much to do, and not enough people to do it. I could barely eat, and even though I felt ready to collapse, sleep taunted me like all the lovers of Peter's past.

I stared into the looking glass on my dressing table, taking measure of the lines etched around my eyes. Dark smudges bruised beneath. Deep hollows in my cheeks. My hair gone gray as ash, as though an incendiary had buried itself there, slowly burning through the length. I felt older than Muv. Defeated. What was the purpose of this life? Why keep on living?

From the distant downstairs, a knock sounded. A moment later, Farve's booming voice filled my house. What was he doing here? He never came to visit. Worried, I forgot my wrinkles and sprang from my dressing table, down the stairs.

"I need your help, Naunce." He stood looking awkwardly in my vestibule, never quite fitting in my little house. His personality was so much larger, and his head nearly touched the top of the doorways as he passed through.

"What's happened?" My heart skipped a beat. I could see no reason that would warrant Farve coming to see me rather than making a telephone call from his comfortable study, unless it was to relay bad news.

"Nothing so dire as what's crossing your mind. The government has requestioned Rutland Gate for the housing of Jewish refugees. Given Herr Hitler and the Luftwaffe's propensity for targeting Paddington, I rather hoped you'd lend a hand with this refugee business. I cannot possibly sort it, and Muv, well, she's horrified at the prospect of such people in her home, as I'm sure you can guess."

I will never understand how my mother, who had always

seemed more forward-thinking than my father, had come to admire Hitler, and Farve to loathe him.

"Do you think the first aid post could spare you? I'd have you move into the mews cottage behind the house. You can bring your maid."

I was torn. We'd been busier than ever at Paddington. I'd even started sleeping in the hospital cellar with the other ARP ladies some nights. When my shift was over, I often joined Sophie in her ARP van. I'd become quite adept at putting out fires. I was needed there. And now needed by Farve.

Caring for refugees would be a different sort of work, but still progress in the fight against Fascism. Who else would do it? Diana was still in prison—and if not, she would probably burn the house to the ground rather than have it filled with Jews. Deborah was busy flitting from one party to the next as though the country weren't on fire. Tom was abroad with his regiment. Pam was busy on her farm. Jessica was still in the United States. Even if Muv hadn't been an anti-Semite—which she was—her hands were full with Unity, now a bed-wetting, babbling shell of her former self. Given Unity was a Nazi, some might say that was an improvement.

I sighed. Like always, the duty of upholding the family fell to me.

"I'll just pack up a few things." I looked about the house, barren of anything precious. I'd shipped our valuables to Inch Kenneth for safekeeping in case the Germans finally hit their mark.

"Is Muv at Rutland Gate?" I asked, returning to the foyer, bag in hand.

"She's at Swinbrook cottage with Unity. Best she remain there.

I appreciate your willingness to keep the house in order." Farve took my bag. "I'm headed to Inch Kenneth."

Not Swinbrook with Muv and Unity?

My parents spent much time apart, and when they were together, Deborah reported fierce arguments. My marriage had been broken long before the bombs fell, but it would seem this war was destroying my parents' union.

I glanced at the emptiness of my house, the very sadness of it. *I should be glad to be gone from here*, I thought. *Much easier to forget life's rejections.*

Rutland Gate was full to the brim. Unlike the days of endless parties and gaiety, I met the somber faces of nearly seventy Polish Jewish refugees from the East End of London, who'd been bombed out of their shelter. With Muv having removed most of the furniture, they slept on straw palliasses on the floor. Each family had a room for themselves, and at night, they camped out in the safety of the cellar.

We got right to work, Gladys and I. At first, I tried to maintain my post at Paddington, but aiding refugees took much of my time. Reluctantly I requested a leave of absence, which was granted.

Thank goodness for Gladys and our charges, who kept their spaces clean, for I was a terrible housekeeper. When Muv stopped by on a trip into London, the finger she ran along the mantels came back clean. Not that this fact kept her from complaining.

While Gladys minded the house, I managed the rations, assisted in meal preparation, secured medical appointments, helped children at their lessons and even mended clothing. I was grateful for both the time I'd spent in Perpignan with the Spanish refugees, and at Highcliffe with Aunt Vi. Each had taught me different skills needed. I found my life rewarding, even if exhausting.

We were all in need of good cheer, so I organized a dance near the end of the year, and researched the Feast of Esther, purchasing small gifts for the refugees to celebrate with money from Farve. We formed a tight bond, especially on the nights we huddled in the cellar while German aeroplanes dive-bombed the city. And then one morning, a younger woman cornered me in the pantry.

"Mrs. Rodd . . ." Zivah pressed her hand to the stomach of her beige dress and looked at me with such fright.

"Have you need of feminine products?" I worried she'd just started her menses.

Face pale, she bit her lip, on the verge of tears. "No . . ." Her eyes flitted sideways.

"Are you . . ." I hesitated, hoping she'd fill in the words, but she didn't. "Pregnant?"

Zivah nodded, dark eyes swimming.

"What do you want to do, darling? Do you know who the father is?" I hated to even ask such a thing, as it implied something I didn't want to say.

She nodded, wiping her face the cuffs of her sleeves. "The same age as me, sixteen. We can't be parents."

I stared at her flat belly, a stab of jealousy in my veins at how easy it was for two children to be gifted with what I longed for. What was the difference between me, these children, Diana? Love? Desire? Naïveté? I swallowed the bitter thoughts.

"Please." Tears spilled down her cheeks, and my heart clenched. "I need to be . . . rid of it."

My hand came to my throat, and I forced it down, to rest on

her weary, shaking shoulder. What made her think I knew of such things?

"Help me," she pleaded.

Help her how? Of course, I'd heard of ways one could dispose of an unwanted pregnancy, but were they really things I should share with a child? Guilt riddled me.

"What about a nice stay in the country?" I offered. "You can return when you've had the baby and it's been adopted."

Zivah shook her head vehemently, dark ringlets hitting her cheeks and getting stuck in the tears. "My mother would kill me before I made it to the train station."

"I highly doubt that, darling."

"I don't."

She looked so serious, and I understood then that if I didn't help her, it would be someone else. Someone less concerned with her well-being. There was a fierceness about her, a determination to see her desire through. With or without me.

So instead, I recollected my research on Lady Stanley when I'd been editing the family letters for my cousin—something that seemed now ages ago—and I said rather hoarsely, "Then I suggest you take a tremendous walk, until your feet can no longer hold you up, and then take a great dose of salts and have a hot bath."

"That will really work?" she asked, incredulous.

I sighed, resigned. "I haven't the faintest idea, but it seems to have been the remedy for ladies in distress a hundred years ago."

The girl wiped her eyes, with a handkerchief I offered. "I also suggest you don't do *that* with a boy again, until you're ready for the responsibility of raising a child."

Zivah nodded vigorously. "Yes, Mrs. Rodd, I won't."

That night, when the sirens wailed, we retreated to the cellar.

"Where is Zivah?" her mother asked.

I grimaced, imagining her still on her long walk, a German bomber sighting her in his target, her death my fault.

"I'll find her," I said.

I rushed up the stairs, pushing through doors, and peering in bedrooms, bathrooms, until I found her, weak and near unconsciousness in a pink-filled tub.

"Dear God," I said, lifting her from the tub, laying her on the cool tile floor and shaking her shoulders. "Wake up!"

Zivah opened her eyes weakly, then rolled to the side and threw up.

"I don't . . . I don't feel so good," she murmured, skin puckered from having sat in the tub for hours bleeding.

I grabbed a cloth, wetting it in the sink to wipe her face. "We need to get you dressed and to the cellar. The Germans are having a fete." As if to prove that point, the din grew nearer and the house shook.

Zivah's eyes were panic-stricken, her movements slow as she drew on her clothing. I drained and rinsed the tub, cleaned up her vomit and fashioned her a sanitary napkin just as Sophie had done for me.

"I'm sorry," the girl said through her tears, and I stopped moving for a moment.

I gripped her shoulders softly, the way Iris had taken mine at Highcliffe. I looked into the eyes of a frightened child. "Do not apologize, darling. As far as I know, you were having a bath and didn't hear the sirens. If you feel sick, it's nerves. Understand?"

Zivah nodded, gratitude breaking through the clouds of her fear.

I nodded perfunctorily, as if nothing were amiss. With an arm around her waist for support, I guided her down to the basement, and safety.

November 14, 1940

Dearest Mark,

Do you remember when we'd wake early at Swinbrook, usually hungover from imbibing too much the night before, and Farve would stomp around telling us all we had no idea what it was like to live on rations, that we were all a bunch of gluttonous imps? After having to procure the rations now myself, I daresay I will use his line if I'm ever given the chance when this war is over. Queue lines are absolutely dreadful, and I'm lucky to get bread that is edible, let alone enough to feed everyone it's intended for.

Love from,
Nancy

I rose before sunlight and crept out of Rutland Gate with ration coupons and a collection of wicker baskets. With sleep elusive, it didn't hurt to start my day early at the baker's, when the bread would be freshest and, hopefully, the lines shortest.

Sixth in the queue, I huddled in my overcoat, blowing air into my gloved hands.

"Mrs. Rodd."

I raised my head to see Gladwyn Jebb standing next to me, hat pulled low, a paisley scarf thick around his neck and chin.

"Mr.—"

He cut me off before I could say his name, leaning in to whisper, "I need to see you. I'll pick you up tonight."

I swallowed. "All right."

And then he walked away, calling, "Good day to you!" over his shoulder like the old friend he was, as if we'd just had a pleasant interaction, instead of such an odd one.

Bread in hand, I hurried to the newspaper stand, lifting the day's paper. The headlines read as usual about the devastation caused by the Luftwaffe attacks. Nothing that struck me as out of ordinary—or explained my summons to the Home Office.

All day, my mind was on Gladwyn Jebb and what he could want. Why a secret meeting at night, when traversing the city was all the more dangerous?

When I stepped out of Rutland Gate after dinner, I spotted a black motorcar parked in the street. Moonlight illuminated a man who stood in front of it, hat low.

I'd barely taken steps to the sidewalk when Gladwyn called softly to me, "Nancy," and beckoned me to the car.

I hastened forward, climbing inside and sliding across the cool leather of the seat. Gladwyn sat beside me and told his chauffeur to drive. I folded my gloved fingers in my lap, mostly needing to still the jittery feeling in my limbs.

Gladwyn settled his hat on his lap. "My driver is quite adept with no light, even with the bombs dropping."

I nodded, reminded of the taxi driver who'd maneuvered me through the bombing months ago, unfazed even when we were fired upon by the Home Guard.

"Nancy." Gladwyn's voice beckoned me back to the conversation. "Your sister, Mrs. Mosley, has been petitioning Churchill to allow her early release."

"Diana? Early release?" The blood drained from my face, and even my fingers felt numb with cold at the prospect.

"Several members of Parliament back her. They feel she isn't a danger."

I swallowed my surprise, and then checked myself. Diana had bewitched men from the time she'd learned to bat her eyes. Prison wouldn't have ended her ability to charm. Not to mention, men of our class more often than not believed a woman incapable of serious political thought, let alone being a threat.

"They couldn't be more wrong." I glanced toward the driver.

Gladwyn noted my line of vision. "You can say what you need to. Nothing leaves this motorcar."

"Diana is and remains a dangerous Fascist. She might be petitioning Churchill, but her allegiance is to her husband, and by extension, to Hitler." My fingers wound tight around one another. "She must remain imprisoned. Think about the reach she's had in her petition with limited access to pen and writing paper, and no telephone. Out of prison, she can use her connections to collect information for the Third Reich. She could help the Nazis win this war."

"My thoughts precisely. You have confirmed my suspicions."

My mind went to the refugees at Rutland Gate. Some of them had fled their homeland in terror. Diana would hate them without knowing them, simply for their heritage. If that hatred found its way to British shores . . . the thought was too terrifying to contemplate.

I suppressed a shudder. "Gladwyn, for the sake of the country and our need to win this war, you must see that Diana remains imprisoned."

"What about Pamela and her husband, Derek?"

I let out a sigh. There was a chance I'd underestimated my country-living sister and her husband. All one had to do was observe war-ravaged London to know it wasn't worth taking a chance. "Keeping them under observation is probably safest given their antidemocratic and often anti-Semitic views. I fear, like my mother, they are eager for this war to end, but they do not necessarily agree about who should be the victor."

Gladwyn frowned. "So you think your mother should also be under observation?"

I shook my head, let out a little laugh. "A bit vitriolic, yes, but otherwise, she's harmless. And given my father's opposing views and position in Parliament"—I didn't mention that they were currently living apart, as it seemed irrelevant and embarrassing—"I do not believe my mother is one to bother over."

"You've been very helpful, Nancy."

"I believe in doing my duty for country. I hope God will forgive me for informing on my family."

Gladwyn's voice softened. "I think you will find Him merciful in this situation."

"Yes, but will my family be?" Somehow I doubted it. We were anything but forgiving.

"I promise no one will ever know of our conversations, least of all your family."

"Thank you."

"I appreciate the information you provided on the French officers you overheard at the café some months ago. It was not wasted."

The car rolled to a stop outside Rutland Gate. I nodded, hoping my information on Diana wouldn't be either.

"I'll be in touch."

I didn't know whether to say I looked forward to it or not. A weariness tightened my chest. My conversations with Gladwyn Jebb were a torment to the soul even when they unburdened my conscience. This was my chance to do something about those who would happily invite Hitler to our shores.

So I climbed from the car with a simple "Good evening to you," and hurried up the darkened stairs hoping that the blacked-out street had kept me hidden.

Had kept my secrets safe.

January 1941

Dear Evelyn,

The Christmas holiday haunts me. Diana sent money with which to buy myself a gift. Money from a Nazi . . . Rather than spend the money on myself, I used her gift on the refugees in my charge. Seemed fitting that way.

I was able to visit with her two youngest sons—Mosley's children; Bryan Guinness keeps his two boys tucked in the country—when Muv and Pam stopped by Rutland Gate. Al-

exander is a darling duck, the spitting image of Diana with the same memorable blue eyes. But where she lacks warmth, the toddler is full of it. The infant, Max, was drooling in the way they do. Muv and Pam chatted about Jessica's baby, due any day, lamenting that with the mess of the world it may be years before we met the child. Isn't that the way of things now? I will be so glad when Britain—with hope—wins this war.

Do let's see each other before your unit is shipped out again. I am fire watching and back to living at Blomfield again now that my refugees have been evacuated to the country after Rutland Gate sustained damage from a bomb, one of the dreariest wartime occupations you might ever imagine. I am in for an uneventful night, I think. It's nearly two a.m. and not a fire in sight.

Love from,
Nancy

I bustled toward an ARP meeting in the basement of one of the first aid posts, not missing the days I'd spent in the dim light.

Entering the crowded underground space, I searched for Sophie through the chattering numbers, the grayish-green light giving everyone a sallow complexion. When my gaze settled on her, Sophie vigorously beckoned me to sit.

"I'm glad you could make it." She passed me a small piece of precious chocolate as I pulled some paper and a pencil from my handbag. "You look as though you've not eaten in a week."

"Who has, darling? There's a war on."

The director clapped twice to gain our attention. "Welcome. We've called this meeting in hopes of gaining more volunteers for the Fire Watcher Service. With the Luftwaffe attacking London, we need to expand the service. Fire watchers will be on duty in shifts all day and night. They will coordinate and work closely with rescue personnel. While awaiting the arrival of the fire brigade and rescue personnel, watchers will be equipped with buckets of sand and water in order to douse smaller fires."

He paused to wipe beads of sweat gathering on his forehead due to the cramped conditions. "Additionally, we need a volunteer to give a series of fire-watching lectures broadcasted on the BBC."

Before I could stop her, Sophie gripped my elbow and raised my hand into the air.

"Ah, I see we already have an eager volunteer."

I flashed Sophie a look, gave the director a little shake of my head as I settled my hand back in my lap.

But no other hands popped up.

"Iris," I hissed through gritted teeth.

Sophie raised her brows, then whispered, "You'll thank me later. You need this."

"*Madame*," the director said. "If you will see me at the end of the meeting, on behalf of the entire ARP we thank you for your service, as will the residents of London, who benefit from the broadcasts."

And so I undertook a new duty for the war effort, rushing to appointments at the BBC Broadcasting House in Portland Place near Oxford Street. I was surprisingly adept at learning the ropes of radio broadcasting. I was proud of my work, providing useful information to the citizens of London on fighting the Nazi-triggered fires.

To my sorrow, within a month, the broadcasts were discontinued. When I inquired as to why, I was told, politely and delicately, there'd been a series of complaints about my voice being too high-pitched and aristocratic and therefore off-putting. One displeased listener even said they wished to throw *me* onto the fire.

However polite my dismissal, the ungratefulness of Londoners stung. When no one else had volunteered, I'd dutifully taken up the task. As I walked briskly home, I hoped none of them came running to me if they needed to put out their garden fire.

I suppose it was all worth it in the end, because a couple months later, I received word from Gladwyn, who thought I was just the thing the Home Office needed.

He installed me in an office where my task was to help arrange holidays for members of the Air Raid Precautions unit who were in need of a breather after endless hours with little sleep. But that was to be just a cover for a secret assignment.

How marvelous a spin our worlds can take when what we've dreamed in fiction comes to life.

If when I sat in that dull gray fluorescent hospital basement someone had told me I'd be conscripted into service for the government in a secret mission, I'd have laughed and asked if they were reading my latest novel.

Never would I guess I'd be plotting how I could infiltrate the Free French officers' club to find the mole within their midst who was feeding information back to the Vichy government in France. An Allied operation had already been leaked, and Charles de Gaulle, the leader of the Free French resistance, who sought shelter in the United Kingdom, was sentenced to death in absentia by the Vichy faction.

According to Gladwyn, it was only a matter of time before the mole was ordered to assassinate de Gaulle. If they succeeded, hope for France's freedom from the Nazi regime would be dashed.

April 1941

~~Dear Peter,~~

Dearest Mark,

Our beloved Café de Paris is the latest casualty by German bombers. Bombs fell down the ventilation shaft into the basement ballroom killing many, including the performer, and injuring even more. Debo had been there earlier in the evening with friends. Thank God she left . . .

With love,
Nancy

I was the perfect candidate.

Charles de Gaulle's life is in your hands, I reminded myself. Thus far, I'd been stymied in my mission to make contact with the Free French. Even volunteering at the canteen in White City, a favorite drinking spot for the French soldiers who'd escaped from their Nazi-overrun countries, got me nowhere.

Then chance intervened. I happened to see Baba, Cecil Beaton's sister, in a queue line outside the butcher shop. While chatting, she told me of Cecil's commission to take a photo of Charles de Gaulle.

"Charles de Gaulle," I enthused. "I am dying to meet him. He's so brave." Then offered a laugh as I added, half joking but hoping she'd take the bait, "Baba, you and I should volunteer as Cecil's assistants for the shoot." I crossed my fingers and kissed her on the cheek before hurrying on my way.

And it worked! The following day, Baba rang to let me know she'd arranged the entire thing.

We headed to Carlton Gardens, where the Free French were headquartered. I felt younger than I had in years. My hair free of the gray, dyed back to a lustrous obsidian. I wore a chic black wool skirt, matching velvet jacket, a pair of nylon stockings with seams up the back of my calves, and a pair of dark pumps.

Perhaps it was more than my wardrobe that made me feel a decade younger. My veins thrummed with the exhilaration of what I was really doing. The secret that no one knew I was listening, that no one expected me to be a spy.

The photo shoot itself was typical and lackluster. De Gaulle was charming and jovial, but said nothing useful to my mission. I despaired of yet another failed attempt when the general surprised Baba and me with an invitation for cocktails at the Frogs' officers' club to the rear of the headquarters.

The invitation by de Gaulle would not be daily, and I hoped to be asked back. To not look so obvious when I ventured into the club or the various other places my subjects frequented. To find out where those places were, and to make friends amongst the men so they spoke freely. That was how one gleaned information, after all.

The club was crowded; French soldiers, sailors and government officials lounged in chairs around crowded tables and leaned against the bar. Clouds of smoke puffed from their cigarettes hung in the air. Over the din of their chatter jazz music played, glasses clinked and forks scraped on plates. The club was a kaleidoscope of scents: spirits, fried fish, potatoes, cologne and body odor.

De Gaulle led us through a crowd as we made our way toward a table perpetually reserved for him. As we took our seats, he ordered bottles of wine for the table and a glass of Armagnac for himself.

An officer took the empty seat beside me, offering a charming smile. He had hair nearly as dark as my own. He was tall and fit, the jacket of his uniform snug against his broad shoulders and covered in pins and badges.

"*Mademoiselle*," he said.

"I am a *madame*, but do appreciate your flattery."

He grinned, a dimple appearing in his cheek that gave a softness to his strong masculine features. "Andre Roy."

"Is that your real name, Monsieur Roy?" I teased.

"I am Capitaine Roy."

"Charmed to meet you, Capitaine."

He took my hand in his and brought it to his lips. The moment the warmth of his mouth brushed against my knuckles, I nearly fell from my chair. *How very unexpected.*

"And I am Nancy Rodd, Capitaine Roy."

"Nancy, needn't be so formal with me."

"We've only just met."

"Ah, but you see, I feel as if I've known you for years."

I laughed. "Shouldn't you at least buy me a drink first?" I

wanted him to know I could see how thick he was laying on the charm.

"I would buy you anything you desired, *madame.*" And the way he said *desired* had my toes curling in my leather pumps in spite of myself.

Frenchmen and their scandalous way of flirting . . . The twinkle in his gray eyes was almost teasing and had me wondering if his toes were curled in his shoes as well.

Andre poured me a glass of wine, which I'd already decided I would sip lightly so as not to forget my true purpose for being here. He captivated me in a conversation that could have gone all night. My resolve faltered slightly. The man did not talk *at* me as Peter did, seeing through me in order to hear his own voice.

Instead, Capitaine Roy looked at me, *saw* me, eyes locked on mine. He took in my words, responding in kind and with questions. I didn't feel the need to hold back on my wit, my intelligence, none of the things that the Englishmen in my life seemed to find distasteful—a woman with her own mind.

I should have talked to the other officers who'd joined us. After all, I was here to gather information about a potential mole, not to be seduced.

Yet I was spellbound by this charming Frenchman. As he teased me, and shared delightful personal anecdotes, he touched my hand and commented on how delicate my fingers were, long and slim, the perfect opposite of his own.

His aim was clear—he wanted to take me to bed.

I felt like the younger, desirable version of myself. I saw *her* reflected in his eyes.

"*T'as de beaux yeux, tu sais?*"

I blinked at his compliment. In our family, Diana's eyes were considered the beautiful ones. My green ones were more often than not called off-putting for how I didn't shy away, but rather looked at people directly.

"*Merci, Capitaine.*"

"Your French is very good."

"*J'ai étudié le français toute ma vie.*" I was glad to have studied French all my life. My proficiency was one of the reasons that Gladwyn had given me this assignment. I could understand the language without straining.

Andre continued our conversation in French. "What is your favorite part of my beloved country?"

"Paris. I love the architecture, the beauty, the museums." I gave a sad sigh, wondering what damage the Nazi occupation had done to the city. "Then, of course, there is the fashion, the food. I guess you could say I'm enamored." With this I found my eyelids dropping as I gazed at him. I think I was enamored with him too.

This was madness. But I let it happen, because it was also my job to get close to the Free French. Naturally the best way to get close to a man was to flirt.

"May I take you to dinner tomorrow?"

I swallowed hard, flicking my gaze across the table to where Cecil and Baba sat deep in conversation with other French officers.

"I . . ." I wanted to say yes.

Andre's gaze flicked to the simple gold wedding band on my hand, which picked up the light from the sconces on the wall.

"Where is your husband?"

"I do not know." What made me be so honest?

"Abroad?"

I twisted the ring, loose on my thin finger, and shrugged. Sometimes Peter came home on leave without telling me. He stayed with his lover.

Andre dipped his head closer, the warmth of his breath on my face. "Is he with another woman?"

My mouth went dry. How dare he ask me such a thing? I should have been astounded, offended. Dumped my wine on his head and stormed out at the indignity of which he'd so casually asked something so innately personal. Again, he tugged the honest words from my mouth. "Very possibly."

"The man is a fool. You, *mon chérie*, are *très belle*. Very special."

I couldn't help myself, I laughed. "You are very, *very* good, Capitaine."

He grinned. "So you agree?"

"Yes. I'll have dinner with you."

Our dinner the following evening was delightful. The melancholy I'd felt for so long started to lift. When we finished our meal, both of us were giddy from champagne. Andre's charming compliments made me dizzy, and my flesh tingled from his light caresses on my hand. Did his heart race like mine?

As we exited the restaurant, he tugged me into an alleyway, leaning me against a wall. His hand rested casually against the brick by my shoulder, his thumb brushing lightly. If I wasn't mistaken, he too slightly trembled. My heart lodged in my throat, and I felt . . . out of body. Who was this woman going to dinner with a man who wasn't her husband, flirting with him, ducking into an alleyway? I wanted him to kiss me.

"*J'ai envie de t'embrasser,*" he said, reading my thoughts.

I hesitated a moment, fearing the scandal an affair would

cause. The guilt of betraying my vows, even if Peter hadn't been so restrained. I realized in that moment, I didn't care. I wanted the excitement thrumming through my veins. I wanted to feel young and carefree and desired.

I pressed my hand to his lapel, fingers curling into the wool fabric of his uniform and giving a little tug of permission.

When he pressed his lips to mine, every inch of my skin cried out in pleasure. His kiss consumed me, and took with it the last vestiges of reluctance. Andre's spicy cologne—bergamot and cedar—filled my senses, while the heat of his mouth robbed me of breath.

As soon as his lips left mine, I ducked under his arm and sprinted away, afraid of what would happen if I didn't put some distance between us. It was one thing to have dinner, to kiss him. It was another to answer the call of desire that would put us in bed together. I raised a hand, waving goodbye as I hopped into a taxi.

After a restless night, I sent a message to Andre at the Connaught hotel. His reply came swiftly. I was giddy, with a twinge of guilt, as I met him for lunch at the Savoy, which was surprisingly filled with many other Free French officers.

"I'm glad you permitted me to see you again, *madame*." Andre bent over my hand, lips brushing lightly on the knuckles before we followed the maître d' to a table right in the center of the dining room.

I glanced around the Grill, worried that I might see someone I knew, or worse, I'd spot Peter dining with Adelaide. But the room was a sea of strangers beneath chandeliers that sparkled in the sun coming through the windows. Light music played in the background. Waiters in their white tails rushed about, delivering meals, pouring wine, serving tea. Then my eyes returned to my companion, and I smiled.

"I don't know what I'm doing," I said.

"With me? Or in general?" Andre tilted his head in question.

"Both." I gave a soft, nervous laugh.

"We are two friends, enjoying a meal. And I insist you let me pay."

I was utterly charmed. When had I been wined and dined before? Never . . . not really. Hamish had always relied on my pin money, and, well, Peter just stole everything I had right out of my purse.

"Thank you, Capitaine."

"The pleasure is mine."

The way he said *pleasure* . . . I suppressed a shiver as his knee momentarily pressed to mine under the table.

We eschewed the newly created Le Woolton Pie for mussels in a white wine garlic sauce, and Paris artichokes. I'd not eaten so well in ages. With the war, and rest of London surviving on rations, our meal felt extremely indulgent, since restaurants were little impacted by the ration thus far.

As we dined and flirted, miraculously my guilt ebbed. Through the years married to Peter, I'd never felt the desire to even the score. This was not about punishing him. This was about something entirely different. This was about me.

I tried to listen in on various conversations between Free French officers, picking up little bits and pieces mostly about families, and the entertainments in London. I excused myself to the ladies' room, brightening up my red lipstick, spoiled by the sumptuous meal. Two women whispering caught my attention. A meeting was being planned between senior Vichy military officers and a member of the Free French—the two ladies were meant to take part as hostesses.

I smiled and made polite conversation about the music, managed to get both of their names and filed it away to share with Gladwyn in my report.

When I returned, Andre swept behind me, pulling out my chair to settle me in. As he did so, the backs of his fingers brushed my neck. Teasing me the way his smile did as he returned to his seat. On the table were a dish of fresh fruit and lemon tarts.

"I took the liberty of ordering dessert." His broad smile was more tempting than anything the waiter had brought.

I pushed the thought aside. As much as I could daydream of Andre's kiss, I needed to complete my mission. After all, spying was the reason we'd met in the first place, even if it slid into more personal territory. "I overheard something in the ladies'." I paused, not sharing the exact details, but hedging. "They said not all Free Frenchmen were loyal to the general. That some may be secretly Vichy." I bit my lip coyly. "It's not the first time I've heard such talk. What a terrible thing if true. Are you worried?"

"Oh, *ma chérie*, you needn't worry about such things." He lifted his espresso.

"I worry for Britain. I worry for France's people, and now . . ." I touched his hand briefly before withdrawing. "I worry for you."

He leaned closer. "Is that so?"

I cocked my shoulder coquettishly. "I know we've only just met, but . . . I'd hate to see you called back to France so soon, to war."

Andre put down his espresso, his fingers inching toward mine across the table. "You fascinate me, *madame*. So much so I plan only to go back to my hotel."

There was an invitation in his words, confirmed by the raising of his brow, the sensual curl of his lips. I glanced out the nearest window, which was wide to take advantage of the sun before blackout required it to be shuttered. How perfectly scandalous to be propositioned in broad daylight.

When I didn't answer, he leaned closer and whispered, "*J'ai envie de toi.*"

He *wanted me.*

I opened my mouth to answer, but my throat was dry, tongue heavy. A tingling ache of desire had settled within me from our kiss the day before.

"What do you say, *ma chérie*? Will you join me?"

I hesitated. Was I ready to take this step? Kissing him in an alleyway and dining with him were one thing; sex was quite another. But for so long I'd been starved of happiness, and with Andre I felt . . . *alive.* "Yes," I said, breathless.

At the Connaught, we snuck up the marble stairs, our shoes muted by the woven runner, like two adolescents trying to get past their iron-willed nanny. Once in his room, Andre kissed me until my knees buckled. Such passion . . . such freedom. We drew away for a breath, and he poured me a glass of wine. I looked out the window over the London streets, praying that the air-raid sirens wouldn't go off now, nor in a few minutes when I was certain to be indecent. What would Prod think if my lifeless body was found entwined with that of a Frog?

Andre approached from behind, smoothing my hair away from my neck and kissing me in the place he'd laid bare. When he started unbuttoning my dress, I didn't stop him. I watched in fascination as he unrolled my stockings, every move sensual, as though he were made for pleasure.

We made love for what felt like hours, languid, exploring each other and our own sensations. As I lay engulfed in pleasure, I wondered, was this what the French women in literature referred to as *le petit mort*? Because if this was dying, I felt exalted.

We lounged in bed the rest of the afternoon. Andre told me how he'd come to London the previous October as a liaison officer. He divulged his real name was Roy Andre Desplats-Pilter. I was surprised, though I ought not to have been. Most of the French military and government officials went by noms de guerre to remain anonymous. His mother was English, his father French. And he was very, *very* rich.

I told him about my family, not leaving out the Fascist connections, which he was certain to find out about either from me or the papers. Laying myself naked in mind and body, and with only a twinge of guilt, I admitted how making love had never before been a fraction as good as this afternoon.

He asked me where I'd heard talk about the moles in the Free French before this afternoon at the Savoy. I explained to him that the previous summer I'd been at a café and overheard a conversation.

"Would you be able to recognize these men if you saw them again?"

I thought about it, trying to concentrate as he trailed his fingers over my naked ribs and dipped to kiss my breast. "Yes," I murmured.

"Then perhaps we should meet again tomorrow."

Heat enveloped me once more as he trailed his lips over my belly. "Oh yes. Tomorrow." *And every day thereafter . . .*

April 30, 1941

Dearest Mark,

I hope this letter finds you well on your mission, wherever it is they've sent you. So secretive.

Well, I'm in need of sharing some Mitford news you may find entertaining. The youngest of the Mitford seven has tied the knot. Little Debo is now Lady Andrew Cavendish. So posh. Her mother-in-law is a duchess. I wonder if she's allowed to take off her shoes and read on the sofa?

Peter leaves soon for Africa, following in your footsteps, though not to Cairo. I suspect cousin Adelaide will be much sadder than I when he goes. Neither Prod nor I even make a pretense of liking each other anymore.

I keep myself quite busy each day volunteering with the ARP. And who would have thought, I've become quite clever at reimagining recipes using only what we have on hand.

Several friends from our set, perhaps the most vocal being Evelyn Waugh, as well as my dear Iris, have tried to convince me to just leave him, but the big D *word is not in my vocabulary. I can't fathom why . . . Oh, now I remember: Peter told me he'd never grant it. So what would be the point of suing for it?*

Besides, at the moment, I find myself quite enamored with all things French. Veux-tu savoir un secret?

Very best love,
Nancy

BETWEEN LOVEMAKING AT the Connaught and dining at the Savoy and the officers' club, my affair with Andre was an intoxicating whirlwind. I was a new woman—more confident in myself and my femininity than ever before.

Despite the thrill, I didn't forget my work. Over the next few months, I identified several men with Vichy sympathies. Andre was as eager as I to know what the French traitors were up to, and made certain we dined near them on more than one occasion.

Gladwyn was delighted with the information I presented. I was a success, it seemed. Who would have guessed the failed novelist, the failed broadcaster, could make a good spy?

I felt accomplished enough, and safe enough, or perhaps merely foolish enough, to invite Andre with me to a weekend-long house party in West Wycombe hosted by my friends the Dashwoods. All the old set was in attendance—the days of the Bright Young Things, only slightly tarnished by age—along with a host of other high-society "evacuees" who were living *chez* Dashwood.

Though we were, of course, given different bedrooms, at night I either snuck to Andre's, or he crept to mine. We made love, then lay entwined in each other's arms until just before dawn, when it was time to retreat before anyone was the wiser.

We played games, dined, strolled the grounds. It was paradise. And then it was lost when a terrible pain shot through my middle.

"Are you all right?" Andre watched me go pale as we walked in the gardens.

"I'm not feeling well, if you'll excuse me." The pain was familiar, and the closer I got to my borrowed room, the more nauseated I grew.

No, no, no! Not *again* . . . How had I let this happen?

I curled round the toilet, expunging the day's lunch, and then fell into a tiny ball of throbbing aches on the floor. With my flux so erratic, I'd not even noticed I was late. A baby . . . with Andre . . . and I hadn't even known.

I stood up, afraid of what might be coming out, but I was surprisingly dry.

Perhaps it wasn't that, but a case of appendicitis?

Either way, I needed to get to London, to a hospital. I packed swiftly, stuffing this and that into my suitcase, not even bothering with the tissue paper. While in the frantic midst, Andre knocked and then entered.

His eyes moved immediately to my suitcase, handsome brow furrowed. "Nancy, what's happened?"

"Nothing to fret over, darling. A touch of appendicitis. Best I get myself to London."

"I'll go with you."

"It's not necessary," I said airily, even though I felt faint.

"You're unwell. Let me help you."

"Well, then get your things," I said briskly, walking toward the door, suitcase in hand. "For I rather think I should leave right away."

By the time the Dashwoods' car was brought around, Andre met me in the courtyard, having explained to our hosts my urgent need to see a doctor. He worried over me as though I were fine china teetering on the edge of a table. Despite my feeling dreadfully ill, that at least felt wonderful.

A short time later, I walked into University College Hospital, collapsing in Andre's arms just as they brought a wheelchair to take me to the examination room.

"Are you her husband?" they asked Andre, who followed. He stared at me, pain in his face as he shook his head. "Wait outside, sir. We'll be in touch."

I smiled, trying to reassure him, though inside, I felt worse than ever before.

The bespectacled doctor's examination was quick, his diagnosis devastating. "I'm afraid you're not suffering from appendicitis, Mrs. Rodd, but an ectopic pregnancy. The fetus has lodged itself in your fallopian tube."

"Can you . . . save the baby?" I asked, sluggish after a shot of morphine and not entirely understanding what was happening.

"I'm afraid that's impossible, Mrs. Rodd. We need to do emergency surgery."

I swallowed, looking to the side of my bed, where a nurse, with sleep-deprived smudges darkening the light brown skin beneath her eyes, stood. I wished Andre had been there too. She took my cold hand between her two warm ones, offering comfort.

"Will I still be able to have children?" Tears prickled my eyes. "Please, *please* allow me the chance to try again."

The doctor blew out a long breath, fluffing the hair on his mustache. "We will try, but it is highly likely a hysterectomy will be unavoidable."

I fell back against the pillow, a hand covering my belly. My never-very-promising dreams of becoming a mother had come to a brutal, disappointing end.

When I woke, groggy and in pain, it was to learn the doctor had tried, and been unsuccessful, at saving my reproductive organs. My nurse, Noor, comforted me, but also cautioned in hushed tones that my life was still in danger for the next few days. That I was lucky to have come in when I had, because the pregnancy, if allowed to go on longer, would have killed me.

Would that have been so bad?

Keeping up a good shop front was not easy, and when Noor left the room to find Andre for me, I broke down, sobbing into my pillow.

How, oh, harsh world, how could you have teased me so? Flaunting the possibility of motherhood only to take it away over and over again until there was no longer a chance. The finality of it was all so *unfair.*

Diana's cruel words from her childbed haunted me, as did the wrong I'd done her by keeping her away from her own babies. I wrote to her then, confessing of my horrible experience, the depression of learning that I could no longer have children . . . Perhaps if she ever found out the truth of my treachery, she would realize I'd been punished tenfold.

Andre looked exhausted as he came into the room, wearing the same clothes he'd worn on the drive. He bent to kiss me, lingering a moment with his lips warm on mine. "Thank God, Nancy. I was . . . so worried. What happened?"

I swallowed the tears, worked to push the words past my throat. "I lost a baby. Our baby."

Andre paled, tears filling his eyes as he sank onto the bed beside me, holding my hand in his. He brought my hand to his lips and kissed it, whispering, "I'm so sorry, *ma chérie.*" Enfolded in his arms, I tucked my head beneath his chin as I sobbed. Crying out all the tears I had left to give. What we'd had, so beautiful and carefree, had culminated in my near death, and the death of my dreams of being a mother.

This was a secret the two of us would share, for I couldn't very well tell anyone else. I couldn't tell Prod, nor his family. Though they'd known I was hospitalized, they didn't bother to call, which should have vexed me, but I didn't care. I despised his mother, and she me. If she visited, she'd bring me a vase without flowers, just as her previous Christmas gift had been a bath salt jar without the salts. Her type of comfort was not welcomed.

Muv was good company when she came the next day. I of course told her it had been appendicitis. What else could I say? She brought me a book I'd requested—*Mémoires d'Outre-Tombe* by François-René, Vicomte de Chateaubriand. A collection of his works published postmortem. A vivid and fascinating account of the man's life and adventures—he lived through the French Revolution and well into the next century, extensively traveling the world. He influenced the likes of Lord Byron and Victor Hugo. Oh, to be Chateaubriand, and have my works read and admired years after my death.

"How are you, darling?" Muv appeared genuinely concerned, eyeing me in my hospital robe, which hid the massive bandage on my middle.

"The physical pain is not so bad, but naturally the idea of this immense scar marring my tum is just . . ." I shook my head, working to keep my emotions at bay.

I feel empty inside.

Muv tutted as if I were just a silly little ninny. "Oh, but, Naunce, darling, who is ever going to see it?"

I stared at Muv, unblinking, realizing in that moment that

perhaps my mother may never have made love to Farve fully disrobed. Or, worse still, she now thought I'd never make love again.

I laughed instead of crying, because what else was there to do but find the unending and ironic humor of it? I'd become one of those women quite consumed with sex. *But not just any sex, no, oh, scandal!* Sex with a Frenchman who'd quite literally swept me off my feet. "You are positively right, Muv."

She left soon thereafter, and just as I was getting into the next pages of the book, my lover made his appearance with at least three dozen white roses.

His eyes fell to the open book on my lap. "Oh, *ma chérie*, Chateaubriand? *Assommant . . .*"

I roared a laugh in earnest this time, because Andre had that effect. "Surely he is not so deathly dull?"

"Oh, he's the worst." Andre kissed me on the forehead and presented me with the roses, which smelled as delightful as his cologne.

We talked until I fell asleep. When I woke, he was gone. An emptiness filled me as I stared dully at the wall for hours. There was no room left in me for joy. For love. Our love. How could our affair continue after this? What more did I have to give?

Besides, how could I ever let him look at me again with such a mar on my flesh? A wound to signify the end of my youth, the end of my life. With his seduction and my weakness, I'd seen the very downfall of my own existence.

At last the truth was laid bare before me. I was a failure at everything I'd ever tried. Not a good daughter. A terrible sister. A philandering wife who couldn't interest her husband to begin with. A failed writer. An abysmal housewife. A bad lecturer. And now this—a womb so sour no fetus wanted to grow there, nor would ever have the chance again.

My dearest Iris,

Out of the dozens of people I call friend, you are the only one I've ever been truly honest with. And so I find that I must unburden myself to you. I have to break a man's heart, and in so doing break my own again . . .

Chapter Twenty
Lucy

"I PUT IN A request at the British Archives for more information on the three ladies you're looking into," Oliver said when Lucy arrived at the bookstore Friday morning. "Hopefully, they'll come through before it's time for you to pop home."

"Hopefully, and thank you. Coffee?" She handed him the latte she'd purchased in appreciation for the last two weeks, along with a blueberry scone.

"Thanks. We'll miss you around here." He held up the coffee in cheers.

"Only because I keep you caffeinated," Lucy teased.

"Not at all, but the coffee helps." Oliver pointed toward the door, then laughed. "Get thee back to work."

Lucy grinned and headed to her desk. After a long chat with Maya, going through the various links and nuggets she'd found, they'd come to the same conclusion. Without dates of birth, or residences, the information they'd gathered came to a dead end. A few promising leads petered out, as if Iris simply vanished.

"Have a little something for you." Ash handed Lucy a folded newspaper.

The picture headlining the article dated from a couple of decades ago. Lucy recognized the three women pictured at once. Mitford sisters dressed in finery—Jessica, Deborah and Pamela.

They were at a book launch in honor of a book of Nancy's letters. The article was a tribute to Nancy, the eldest of the Mitford children, in which her sisters shared how she had been the glue that kept them all not only together, but also in the limelight after the war. They mentioned that her novel *The Pursuit of Love*, and the subsequent books that followed, brought the family to life for millions of readers.

"No mention of Iris by name," Ash said, "but look there." She tapped the picture. "Wait, try this." She handed Lucy a magnifying glass they used to study the rarer books.

Lucy held the glass to the paper, studying the sisters. But it wasn't until she moved to a woman in the background that her mouth dropped open. There was an iris fastened to the woman's lapel as she looked over the Mitford sisters' shoulders with a vaguely forlorn expression.

"Oh my God," Lucy breathed, glancing at the matching iris pin fastened to her purse.

"You're welcome," Ash said with a wide grin.

"A face, finally," Lucy murmured. The woman in the picture looked to be in her sixties. Beautiful, with a soft smile, but completely obscure. If Lucy hadn't been looking at all the details with the magnifier, she would never have noticed. She quickly snapped a picture of the newspaper photo and texted it to her sister, hoping Maya would be able to identify Iris.

Lucy spent her lunch wrapping up her library project, then popped into an auction, snagging a few books Oliver wanted for the store before the Christmas rush. She kept an eye out for Gavin, who she'd not seen since he'd traveled to Scotland on business a couple days before, but no luck. They'd made plans to have dinner tonight. She was really looking forward to it, considering her flight was only days away. Soon she'd be stateside, an ocean between the city she'd come to love and the people she'd met.

On her way down the narrow stairs, she ran into Oliver.

"Do you have a minute?" he asked.

"Of course."

"Great." He nodded upward, and she followed him to his office, taking a seat opposite him.

Lucy was a little bit nervous about what this might mean. Something with the archives?

"We've really enjoyed having you here with us, Lucy."

"Thank you. I've enjoyed being here. I hope this won't be the last collaboration between Emerald and Heywood."

"Yes. You showed great determination and work ethic for your client, and helped add to our stock as well."

"You've made me feel at home here." Lucy smiled.

"Not difficult; you fit right in. Which is the reason I wanted to speak with you."

Lucy cocked her head.

"I'd like to offer you a job. I understand it's asking a lot give up your position at Emerald Books, and to make a transatlantic move, but we would very much like to have you as our director of curation here at Heywood."

Lucy swallowed. *A job in London . . .*

A chance to call this amazing city home. The ability to curate libraries for manor houses and old castles. If she'd only be willing to take a leap of faith in herself.

If there was one thing she'd learned about Nancy Mitford, it was that despite everything thrown her way, she'd been brave enough to rise up. Maybe that was a reason Lucy had been drawn to Nancy from the start. Maybe she too could be brave enough to start over. Brave enough to give her dream a chance.

And then there was Gavin. A move to London would allow them the opportunity at a relationship.

"Can I think about it?" Lucy asked.

Oliver gave a nod. "Absolutely."

"If I accept, I'd still have to fly back to the US on Monday. Finish out my project."

"Of course. I'd expect nothing less. I can do the visa paperwork in the meantime if you decide to accept our offer."

Lucy stood and shook Oliver's hand. "I'll get back to you promptly."

She'd done a damn good job curating the books for the library. Renovations of the space stateside were already underway. The promotion in DC was going to be hers, she was fairly certain—the culmination of all her hard work. And now this opportunity landing like the second shoe in a pair of glass slippers.

Two amazing professional opportunities to choose from. All she had to do was choose which would make her happier.

In the flat, Lucy unfolded the last Nancy letter from the dwindled stack.

Dearest Jessica,

Oh, my darling, how my heart aches. I wish I could be with you and the little one. How far away you are with an ocean between us. You must be terribly worried about Esmond. If only there was something I could do, anything. Tell me, and I will do it. I don't know how much you read, but if you want books, I could send you books?

I pray daily that he is found and returns to you unscathed.

Do come home to England, I beg you. If not for your sake, then for Farve, who has aged tremendously in his heartache for you. Though you are safer across the Atlantic, far from the Luftwaffe.

Oh, how we long for news from you.

With most love,
Naunce

Chapter Twenty-One
Nancy

March 1942

Dearest Evelyn,

You know best of anyone I abhor sitting still, wallowing in boredom. I'm predisposed to search for something, anything of distraction. The last several months have been a discipline in unproductivity and yet an enormous undertaking in doing anything I can, just to remind myself I am really doing nothing at all. Does that make sense?

I miss my refugees, and think of them often. I've had a letter from one of the young girls. She and her family are ensconced in Perth. There was such relief to know they're well.

With the RAF bombing France and Germany, I hope we defeat the Nazis soon. Do you see any end in sight? London feels so strange being filled mostly with women, children and refugees. Most of our men, unless in the Home Guard, are shipped abroad. I barely recognize the city with the people much changed and the devastation of the bombs.

While you're on leave, do say you'll visit. I long to see your face.

Best love,
Nancy

WHEN I CHECKED OUT of the hospital several months prior—following the ectopic pregnancy—I had two choices: go back to my life as usual, or escape.

Returning to normal was my first choice, and proved a rather difficult one. Everything reminded me of Andre, and our loss—my permanent loss. Despite my age, I'd still hoped for a family. I couldn't erase the way his face crumpled when I told him I could no longer see him. It was hard to admit that I was broken on the inside. That I'd allowed him in, and made myself vulnerable. That while I'd lain in that hospital bed, I'd considered stealing a scalpel and running it along my wrists. Understanding what I'd wanted, searched for—enduring love—was out of my reach, made any more connection between us seem impossible. Maybe I wasn't made for love.

Out of respect, Andre withdrew. I still had my mission for the Home Office, and made lackluster plans to visit with friends at the French officers' club, reporting back to Gladwyn anything I gleaned. When I was there, thankfully Andre was absent.

"Nancy, good to see you again." Gladwyn studied me as I entered his office, and only the brief pinch of his brow showed me he saw what I did when I looked in the mirror. "How are you?"

"Fine." My voice lacked conviction.

I took a seat opposite his desk, and he leaned forward on his elbows. "I think it best if you went to the country for a little while."

I straightened. "Are you dismissing me?"

"Only suggesting a holiday. You've been working very hard."

"I've no need to go to the country—or on holiday." Besides, the only place that calmed me was Paris, and she was under siege.

"Understood. But there's been some movement within the Free French, and I'm concerned they are trying to ferret out who is reporting back to us."

"Oh?" I thought back to last evening at the officers' club. Who had been overly eager to speak to me? Who seemed suspicious?

"It would be an easy excuse for you to put some distance between you now with the end of your relationship with Captain Roy."

I raised a brow, unaware that Gladwyn would have been privy to that, though he was in the business of spying, so perhaps I shouldn't have been. Even as I verbally fought to continue my work, a little piece of me was relieved at being forced away. Helen had invited me back to West Wycombe to recover after my hospital stint, and I'd declined, preferring to throw myself into work. But now . . .

"The country," I said.

Gladwyn nodded. "Only for a little while. The Home Office will always welcome you, Nancy."

At West Wycombe Park I could forget what plagued me. Try to erase from memory the whirlwind affair that had brought about a heartbreak. The tragedy of my broken body. My broken mind.

Fortunately for us wretches, there were houses in the country where friends still gathered. Together we worked to ignore the ills of our world—the aches carved into our bones, the deep slashes in our hearts.

"Perhaps a stay with my friends the Dashwoods."

Gladwyn nodded. "We'll be in touch."

The following day, I, along with Sophie, who'd agreed to join me, climbed into a car sent by Helen. Rain splashed on the ride over, but by the time we arrived, the sun peeked through the clouds, and Helen, along with our friends living *chez* Dashwood, rushed out to greet me. So many dear friends were all in attendance.

"Oh, darling Nancy, your presence has been sorely missed." Helen embraced me. The smiles and enthusiasm were enough to make me forget for a moment the horrors of war, the pain of loss. "And you must be Sophie."

After the introductions and greetings were complete, we joined my friends back in the drawing room, where my dogs chased Helen's corgis about the room.

"What should you like to do first?" Helen asked.

I looked out the closest window at the sky, taking in the blue with faint wisps of clouds. "Seems the rain has stopped; how about a walk about the grounds? I'm cramped from the long ride."

"I think that's the just the thing," Helen agreed.

We all donned our wellies and walked through the slick grass, stopping on the portico of the Music Temple to lounge and play a game of cards. I felt almost as if we'd traveled back in time to over a decade earlier, when we'd done the same thing after a night of lively entertainment.

The rest of my days were spent reading, playing cards, walking. There was always someone to talk to, and so I never got lonely. Rarely sank into the dark thoughts that consumed me when I was alone.

At night after a fine dinner served at Helen's grand table with twinkling lights setting her silver sparkling, we all sat around the fire knitting—even the gentlemen—and gossiping about our friends and the days of old. In the background, music played, either from the gramophone or one of the guests taking up the piano. I even enlisted the group to read about Captain Scott— who adventured to the snow-white South Pole. We discussed his journals, though some complained.

When the upstairs bathroom window jammed and snow piled on the floor around the lav, I christened it the Beardmore, after the glacier Captain Scott scaled. Helen did not particularly enjoy the jest, but everyone else did.

When it was finally time to go to bed at night, however, I lay awake staring at the ceiling. I'd wander onto the balcony outside my room, staring over the edge into the darkness, wondering if the fall would end my pain. Coming to my senses, I'd knock on Sophie's door, and we'd talk until nearly dawn. At least with my friends as a distraction, I found pockets of happiness to sustain me during the darkest times.

"I have a confession, Sophie."

"Do tell."

"It's one of the reasons I was gone. A man."

"Not your husband?" She leaned forward, undisguised surprise on her face.

"Yes. A Frenchman. He was charming, and handsome, and he loved me. When I was in hospital, I wrote you a letter about him, but I never sent it." I gave a soft, embarrassed laugh. "I suppose I needed to write out my feelings, and you're the one person I felt I could be open with."

"Where is he now?" She poured us each a small glass of sherry.

I took a sip, hoping it would help me sleep tonight. "I'm not sure. I've not seen him, and truth be told I am worried he might have returned to France."

"Do you miss him?"

I leaned back into the cushions of the settee, tucking an afghan around my legs. "I think I miss most the *idea* of him."

"The idea?"

"Yes, he was tall and handsome, rich and entirely sophisticated. He could talk the queen into going to dinner with him. But what he represented for me was . . . freedom."

"So what happened?"

I hesitated, maybe too long. "We just . . . I just couldn't."

Sophie cocked her head. "You're not telling me something. Perhaps the real reason you invited me on this short holiday."

"Let's suffice it to say what happened when you and I were at Aunt Vi's will never happen again. It is impossible. For this time the doctor's removed the possibility."

Sophie's lips parted, and she pressed her hand to her heart. "Oh, Nancy."

"You know the rules, *Iris*: do not pity me."

Sophie shook her head, as if wiping pity from her memory. "Does Peter know?"

"No one knows. But enough about that." My heart clenched, and I couldn't bear to speak on it anymore.

Sophie clearly recognized my need for a change in subject. "I simply must show you my new lipstick."

I tried on her lipstick and drank sherry, working to forget that our country was still at war, and so many people still suffering. I missed my friends in the city. I missed my work. But most of all, I missed the sensation of being cared for. Of being desired. I wouldn't say that what Andre and I had was love, but it was the closest I'd ever come to a reciprocated relationship in which I didn't feel I was the only one laboring. I *missed* Andre. And I'd been the one to push him away.

I felt lighter than I had in days, having unburdened myself to such a caring and nonjudgmental ear.

But it didn't last long. A few days later, I woke in an extreme state of melancholy now that Sophie had returned to London. I trudged to the dining hall for breakfast to find friends fixing their tea. And a shock!

To my surprise, Evelyn Waugh and Heywood and Anne Hill were sitting at the table.

"Hello!" Evelyn set down his newspaper and rose from his chair.

"Oh, Evelyn, how marvelous to see you." I surged forward to embrace him.

"Darling Nancy! Well, only for the weekend really; I've been in training. I believe I'll be leaving the country again soon, if my commander has his way."

"Where will you go this time?" I turned to Hey and Anne, giving them each an embrace as well. Then I sat down, pouring my tea, slathering a bit of jam on my toast.

"I'm not certain just yet. I've been transferred to the Royal Horse Guards. They've seen action in the Middle East and North Africa."

"I do pray this war ends soon. I've heard the most awful rumors of extermination camps," I said, recalling an article about a camp in Lublin, Poland.

"Not rumors, I'm afraid. They've been at it a lot longer than has been reported," Evelyn said. "Hitler and his murderous thugs will stop at nothing to fulfill his agenda."

The toast was suddenly dry in my mouth, the homemade jam sour, making it an effort to swallow. "Horrifying." I pushed back my toast, no longer hungry.

The dining room grew silent as we all mulled over the terrifying news, and mourned those who'd become casualties of hatred. For the thousandth time, I tried to understand how anyone could side with Fascism.

Later that evening, over a game of cards, our moods had lightened as much as they could in the middle of a war.

"Do let's have a gathering at your bookshop when I return to London," I suggested to Heywood Hill. "I long for the days where we assembled and chattered away about books."

"We would love to," Hey said.

Evelyn wagged his finger at me. "What do you expect you'll do when you return to London besides literary salons?"

"I expect I'll return to the ARP and volunteering at the canteen." I lifted my gaze from my cards.

Evelyn raised a brow. "And another book?"

I waved that away with a dismissive laugh. "I don't think I'll be writing for a long time, save for an article here and there to live by."

"And why's that?"

I cocked my head to the side and stared at him, taking note that Heywood and Anne seemed extremely interested in the conversation, which only brought the rest of our party to attention.

I let the joviality drop for a moment from my countenance. "For the simple fact, old friend, that I'm just not naturally talented."

At this admission, the other guests round the table took to shrieks of irritating laughter, near tears in their eyes as if I'd told some great jest.

"I'm perfectly serious," I mused with a narrowed brow.

"You *can't* be serious." Evelyn wiped at his eyes.

"No indeed. How would the world get on without another novel written by Nancy Mitford?" Anne Hill wrinkled her nose in question.

"Well, I daresay this table is my only cadre of fans, and I cannot sustain a living on the few of you purchasing my books." I stared at Evelyn, who alone knew I'd not earned out my advances for the last two novels. While he was quick to point out the unfortunate timing of release dates as the culprit of those flops, it didn't matter.

Heywood Hill clucked his tongue. "We've always sold out of your books."

I smiled stiffly, recalling just how Anne had sold those books by offering discounts. I glanced out the window, wishing I could run outside into the fresh air. The room seemed to be shrinking smaller and smaller around me.

"Indeed, darling." Helen Dashwood wiped at her mouth delicately with a linen napkin. "I don't know a soul who hasn't read a Nancy Mitford."

"You're putting me on." I sipped my tea if only to have something to do with my hands besides wringing them in my lap.

"You are certainly better than Captain Scott," came a grumble at the other end.

That subtle, disgruntled comment in regard to my recommended reading did pull a laugh from me. "Oh, you all are having a lot of fun with me. I do appreciate the gesture, but the truth of the matter is, my well is quite dry. To be more explicit, as desiccated as an eight-hundred-year-old potato. There's no bringing it back."

"Oh, Nancy, you are one for dramatics, which are better served on paper." Evelyn tapped the journal he carried with him. "But, perhaps in the meantime, you should spend more time with books." He glanced at Heywood and Anne. "Hey is bound to be called up again, and I'm certain Anne could use the help at the bookshop."

Anne sat forward. "Evelyn is absolutely right. I will need help. Having a friend around would be nice, especially with me worrying about poor Hey."

"Brilliant idea. You could start when you return to the city," Heywood agreed. "If you are amenable."

I set my teacup in the saucer and sat back, the rungs of the chair digging into my spine. "Work at the bookshop?"

"I'd pay you, say . . . £3.10 a week." Heywood pressed one finger to the other as if calculating the sum. "Yes, I think that should do it."

It was a rather small sum, given I'd made £5 a week writing for my grandfather's magazine, *The Lady*, a decade ago. However, between my allowance from Farve being cut in half, and Peter's allowance having been nixed altogether after his father died, his military income went to expenses, and with no books forthcoming, I could really use the funds. The articles I penned barely kept me afloat.

Though it wouldn't pay well, it was more than I had now, not to mention I'd be surrounded by books—my lifeline for all the days since I'd learned to read. Maybe I could forget myself, or at the very least sometimes forget the war.

"I'll do it." I picked up my teacup and held it in the air. "And thank you."

📖

April 1942

Darling Evelyn,

I'm writing to invite you to sign books at Heywood Hill bookshop. I'm hosting a charity event of sorts, auctioning autographed books and first editions, and would be grateful for your attendance. It is so good to have you back on British shores.

I've just finished reading Put Out More Flags. *Brilliantly done. How I should like to chat about it.*

I must tell you something fabulous about the bookshop. I proposed the shop expand from merely selling books to curating private libraries as well. After all, we've plenty of friends who have private libraries. Anne and Hey said yes!

Best love,
Nancy

I heaved open the door of Heywood Hill, my arms straining under the weight of a load of books. I settled the heavy box on the floor of the shop and stood, stretching my lower back and pulling a handkerchief from the sleeve of my black velvet coat. I blew the hair out of my face that kept coming out of its neatly tucked-in pins, then dabbed at the sweat beaded on my brow.

"Oh, Nancy, thank you, darling." Anne rushed from behind the register to peek at the contents.

The two months I'd worked at the bookshop were a welcome change. Heywood had yet to be shipped off, so he'd started to train me in the duties he would leave in my capable hands.

So many of my literary friends came by. The men stopped in when home on leave, sliding into the bookshop, settling into a chair and falling into either the silent company of a good book or some lively conversation.

Heywood teased me that I'd turned his respectable shop into a salon, which was true given it seemed filled with gossip and quips as much as serious literary discussion. He didn't complain, because the fact of the matter was, sales were increasing exponentially. Heywood Hill bookshop had become the place to see and be seen. The Mayfair shop had turned into a star place in London for all bookish types, be they reader, writer, editor, publisher. No matter, they wanted to be where the literary action was. Even better, they were willing to buy books.

As it turned out, I, Nancy Mitford, was one hell of a bookseller.

My latest project was to convince the authors who visited to sign books for charitable donations to soldiers and evacuees. This little bit of charity was also brilliant marketing, bringing distinction to Heywood's shop that it hadn't possessed before. We were not only economically motivated, but philanthropists too. Those abroad and in the trenches were grateful for a shipment of books to help them escape when they had a moment to catch their breath.

Always in the background, my friends nudged me gently, and at times more forcefully, to write another book. As of yet, nothing struck. I was currently just trying to untangle what for me was a new normal.

Immersed in my new routine, I walked to the shop in the morning, eager to work, and then to the canteen where I volunteered in the evening. Often, I returned home late at night, only to pull on my fire watcher's uniform and join Sophie. Any moment between, I dined or danced with friends, enjoyed a house party or threw one. I never wanted to be alone.

"Did you hear about Bath?" I asked. Since the beginning of the month, the Luftwaffe had retargeted other parts of England besides London, laying its destructive air-raid sights on historic cities and centers of culture. Bombing Exeter, Bath, Canterbury, York and Norwich. Who would be next?

"I heard they are targeting locales identified in a German travel guide as 'must see' for visitors. Places that we value not just for our history, but our culture. Bloody monsters." Anne shook her head.

"They're trying to dismantle our spirit one heritage site at a time," I mused. It was terrifying. "If Hitler thinks that's going to break us, that only shows how much he underestimates us Brits." Much like I'd underestimated myself.

"Let's pray that's their downfall."

I nodded. "And soon." We fell into a meaningful silence as we took out some of the books I'd brought in to make a display advertising our upcoming auction. The box was full of signed copies from Evelyn Waugh, Raymond Mortimer, Lord Berners and several others. I'd been collecting them through various luncheons and dinner parties, and at last the box was full.

"I don't know how you do it, Nancy. These are fantastic." Anne lifted one of the books signed by Evelyn.

"I'd say it was the Mitford charm, but the thing about us Mitfords is that our allure is only good when the mark is either half-drunk or completely affected," I joked, taking some of the volumes from her outstretched hand and transferring the information into the catalogue.

Anne looked startled at first and then let out a guffaw of a laugh that drew the attention of several customers perusing books.

"I tease." I winked, tucking the books away for storage until our event.

The bell over the door dinged, and Sophie walked in.

"Darling," I said. "It's been an age."

Anne looked between the two of us, confused, given most of our friends ran in the same set. She'd never met Sophie before, since my ARP friend had left West Wycombe before Anne's arrival. That had been the first time I'd introduced my Iris to people of our world, a world that seemed all too superficial when I looked at it through Sophie's eyes.

"I stopped by to see if you were free for dinner after the shop closes and to join me tonight on fire-watch duty."

"It just so happens I am."

From the corner of my eye I noticed Anne listening in as she rearranged a perfectly displayed Victorian doll set near a table of children's books. "Nancy, if you'd like to go early today, I can close up. Heywood will be by shortly, and he can help," she volunteered.

"Thank you." I was excited to spend time with Sophie and catch up. We'd not seen each other since our stint at West Wycombe.

"It's the least I could do after you procured those charity books," Anne said.

I rushed to get my purse and mackintosh from the hook behind the register, and then Sophie and I dashed.

"Where shall we go?" I asked. "How about the hostel down the way? Anne says it's a particular favorite of hers out of all the BRs." Ever since the war started, these government-subsidized restaurant chains had popped up all over London. They'd started out as Community Feeding Centres, but Winston Churchill changed the name to British Restaurants, perhaps to appeal more to the public for what they truly were—low-cost square meals.

"As long as we don't eat custard." Sophie shuddered, and I laughed.

"Goodness me, no custard. I shall have to remember that."

We hurried into the hostel. A good number of people were queued for self-serve, while others lined up to be seated for table service.

While I liked to dine at the Savoy, one didn't need to feel like a feckless glutton daily, and I much preferred the simplicity of bangers and mash. Besides, I didn't have the budget for such a luxury.

"Let's do be seated," Sophie said, and I took her lead.

Our dinners ordered, Sophie leaned in. "You'll never guess what awkward situation I've found myself in. An older gentleman—and I mean old enough to have been wounded in the Great War—has taken a fancy to me."

"Oh my." I gave a mock gasp at her disgruntled expression. "Where did you meet the fellow?"

"He's an ARP warden, showed up at a fire. Told me I was doing a fabulous job holding the stirrup pump. I'm pretty sure he meant something else."

This time my gasp was real. "You can't be serious. You're having me on."

"I'm dead serious. And while I'm not interested in the old gent, I will tell you I rather enjoyed the idea of flirting. Maybe I'm not done with that part of my life."

I scraped margarine onto the slightly stale bread we'd been served. "You're far too young to let go of that part of your life."

"You are quite right." Sophie lowered her voice as if in secret. "I've been dying to ask. How is your sister?"

"Which one?" With the din of silverware clinking against plates, chatter and laughter loud, I didn't fear anyone overhearing us.

"All of them." Sophie snorted.

"Do you have all night?" I teased, and then relayed to her that Diana was still clamoring to get out of prison. However, within the walls of Holloway, she'd been rewarded for good behavior and given quarters with Mosley, even requesting various dishes to make herself a salad.

"Salad? Does she have a kitchen or has she commandeered the prison cooks?"

"I truly have no idea." I took a sip of my ale—not my usual drink, but the best offered at the BR.

"It's madness."

"It is. I think Muv worries more about Diana than Deborah, who's still recovering from the stillbirth of her son. Terribly sad. I'm still quite heartbroken. But the doctor said she should have no problem conceiving again."

"That's awful. I'm so sorry."

"Me too. It happened just as I was leaving the hospital. I'd barely had a moment to collect my own miserable thoughts when I received the call."

"Poor Deborah, and she's the most innocent of you all."

"Quite literally."

"Is Unity still wetting the bed?"

"Every night. Screeching at Muv quite often—though I can't help but think it's just desserts for Muv, for the amount of times she's tormented me with her words."

"Still, it is a life sentence for your mother as much as it is for your sister."

"I've never thought of it that way. So sad."

"Truly. And Tom? Is he in London or overseas?"

"He's off fighting, I believe in Africa, though his letters are few and far between. He's never been good about writing. I worry so much for our boys out fighting Fascists."

"Me too. It's simply mad how the war has spread."

"It is." I sat back, the crust of bread uneaten in my hand. I didn't want to dwell on the good men falling for Britain, so I said brightly, "And how have you been? Any other admirers?"

Sophie speared a piece of sausage. "None so far as yet." She pointed her fork at me. "Don't even say it, Nancy, I can tell what you're thinking. I will not give the old gent a second more of my time. Besides, he'd likely keel over in the act, if you understand my meaning."

I laughed so hard, I nearly cried.

She grazed her fork through her mash, making a small design. "Was it worth it for you?"

I knew what she meant: giving my heart, my body to someone else. "Hmm." I cut into a sausage, watching the grease as it leaked from the confines of its casing. "I don't regret it." My voice was fuller with conviction than I thought possible. "Give yourself a chance to be happy. Don't assume it will fail because mine did."

Sophie laughed and swiped up the rest of the mash on her plate. "We will see, then. Perhaps I will—but not with the warden." She suppressed a shudder. "Well, are you ready for a night of fighting fires?"

"As always, Iris."

Hours later, armed with our stirrup pumps, we battled a fire in Berkeley Square. Smiles on our faces, happy to be defeating Hitler in our own small way.

📖

"I DARESAY, NANCY, I've not had so much fun in an age," said Evelyn Waugh. The voice of an old friend from the era of our bright youth boomed over the din of the charity auction event chatter in Heywood Hill bookshop.

"Not even when we listened to the string quartet at the National Gallery park last week?" Anne offered.

I chuckled. "It was a superb sandwich, and the music was good too, but this . . . this is paradise found." I gestured around the bookstore, where guests mingled with snifters and champagne flutes.

Evelyn nodded emphatically from where he lounged in one of the leather chairs newly placed there for the literary set that spent so many of their days here. "Who would have ever guessed my favorite spot to quote Hugo would be in a bookshop drinking brandy. I mean, darling, an evening at Heywood's these days tops the Ritz."

I clinked his glass with mine to acknowledge the elaborate compliment. "Don't forget to buy a book on your way out. This club may not have annual dues, but we do have bills all the same," I teased.

Evelyn looked at me, his face turning serious. "Have you heard about Hamish?"

Hamish St. Clair-Erskine . . . The name brought with it memories of costume parties, romance and heartbreak.

"I've not heard anything. What's happened?" I stared, throat tight.

"The old boy was captured in Tobruk."

I gasped. *Oh God, no . . .*

"Never fear," Evelyn quickly continued. "They imprisoned him in Italy, but he escaped, dressed as a woman of all things, and made it back to Allied lines."

I laughed in surprise and relief. "Thank goodness." I pressed my hand to my heart, bombarded with memories from a lifetime ago of playing dress-up with Hamish, of curling his hair.

The bell over the door dinged, and I hurried from the back of the store, where our guests gathered, to greet the newcomer.

Perusing the books on the front table was a man in uniform. But not just any man. A Free French officer I'd seen not too long ago at a dinner party. Colonel Gaston Palewski, the right hand of Charles de Gaulle. A powerful, intelligent and yet still humorous man who could hold more than decent a conversation.

I'd yet to be called back to service by Gladwyn, but that didn't matter. If a Free French officer was going to place himself in my presence, I was going to pay attention. Old habits.

"Are you here for the auction, Colonel Palewski?" I joined him beside the table where I'd arranged a vast array of my friends' works.

"Forgive me, *madame*, I do not remember your name. I'm ashamed to say I do not remember meeting you." He pressed a hand to his heart.

"Not at all, Colonel. We have not been formally introduced, but we have some of the same circles." For a moment, I cast my mind back to the cocktail party where I'd seen him delighting the entire room with his chatter. He'd be a good addition to tonight's event.

Though he was not tall, perhaps my height, there was a sturdy robustness about him that commanded attention. He had neatly combed dark hair, and save for a small mustache, his tanned face was clean-shaven. The colonel was not handsome in the way Andre was, but exuded charisma, and pierced me with his light eyes.

"I'm sorry, then, not to have made your acquaintance. What may I call you?"

"Nancy Mitford."

"The Nancy Mitford who is also Mrs. Rodd?"

I sighed. "Indeed."

With his cap tucked under his arm, he took my hand in his and kissed my knuckles as if it were another era.

"Can I get you a cocktail, Colonel?"

"*Non, madame.* I actually come bearing news of your husband, Lieutenant-Colonel Rodd."

My heart shot up my throat. "News?" I'd not heard from Peter in so long. He could have been in London with Adelaide for all I knew. Once I'd felt guilty about being unaware, but communication was a two-way street.

"*Oui, madame.* And the news is simple: there is no news," he said in a very affable tone. "He is alive and well. I had the opportunity to meet him in Addis Ababa, and he wished for me to find you and relay that."

What better way to put it that my husband was doing fine? But perhaps I shouldn't have been surprised by the colonel's turn of phrase. There was a general charm about him, a dance of gaiety in his eyes. Pure merriment, but also an intensity that was unmatched, and an innate cleverness that spilled out in his words.

"Thank you for being the bearer of good news, Colonel, when we so often hear the opposite." I offered a genuine smile, relieved at the news, but also at the colonel's genuine charisma. "We are hosting a charity auction this evening." I indicated the guests mingling around the store. "Care to join us?"

"Perhaps." He flashed me a smile, the small, dark mustache tickling his curled lips. "Pardon my saying so, *madame*, but you are not quite what I expected."

"No? Well, I suppose that's because your only description of me came from my husband." It was a daring statement, but I felt suddenly flirtatious.

He laughed. "Well, yes." He lowered his voice as if confiding. "After meeting Lieutenant-Colonel Rodd, I did imagine a woman who might be more . . . how do you say it, stuffy?"

I tried not to laugh as I answered, "*Stuffy* is the proper English term, yes."

"But you are the exact opposite."

I lifted a brow. "Why, Colonel, I should be offended."

"But you aren't." His eyes were on me, studying me.

"Surprisingly, and with no little effort on your part, I am only flattered."

"I think you make a habit of surprising people, no? You like to be surprising."

The Frenchman was very observant. "I make a habit of not having habits."

"Then the answer is yes."

I cleared my throat and indicated the table he'd been perusing. "Can I help you find a book? Or perhaps you'd like to see what we have in the back—a collection of signed books and first editions."

"*Oui*, how about one by Nancy Mitford?"

"Your reputation precedes you, Colonel, and I've no wish to become an evening conquest." I raised my brow; one side of my mouth lifted in a smile. Back in the days when I was a regular at the French clubs, I'd overheard plenty of whispering about Gaston Palewski. A ladies' man. Interested in slipping off a woman's drawers, and then discarding them with the wearer. I might be lonely, but not lonely enough to be a man's one-night plaything.

Oh, no. If I took another lover, he'd have to promise me more.

"Your directness is enchanting." The colonel chuckled. "But at least invite me to tea before discussing my amatory conquests, *madame*."

"I think tea a bit too civilized," I countered. "Will you buy a book?"

"Will you join me for drinks at the Allies Club?"

Before I could say *no, thank you*, he melted into the crowd of guests, taking a glass of champagne off a tray.

"Who was that?" I barely heard Anne's approach and whirled at the sound of her voice.

"No one. Just another disillusioned customer."

"Do we get a lot of those?"

I nodded. "In fact, one woman last week snapped her fingers at me while I was chatting with the lads and said, 'A little less darling and a little more attention, please!' The nerve."

Anne chuckled. "Will you go?"

"Where?"

"To the Allies Club?"

So she'd heard the exchange, or at least the latter part of it. "Why should I?"

"Because you love a diversion."

"Hmm . . ." This was not untrue, but was the diversion I sought one the colonel would provide? I thought not.

"Well, I'm off." Anne pulled on her mackintosh over the swell of her midpregnancy belly. "You're all right if I go?"

"Yes, perfectly." I glanced around the guests still chattering. "See you tomorrow."

When the last of our auction attendees departed, and the shop was tidied, I locked up and headed out into the night air.

Normally in the chill at dusk I hurried home, but tonight, I strolled, contemplating the changes in the city. How empty it felt, and yet how busy it remained. I missed my charges at Rutland Gate, who'd returned from the country to their East End housing now the blitz was over. Wondered how they were doing as they picked up the pieces of their lives.

I skirted people along Curzon Street to Park Lane, unable in the dark to make out the antiaircraft guns which were in Hyde Park adjacent. I traversed toward the Marble Arch, pausing to say a prayer for the souls who'd been crushed in the tube station beneath my feet when a German bomb had broken through.

Though it'd been months since the nightly bombings of the

blitz, the slightest buzz of wind still had me thinking the whirl-ing sound was the bombers diving in.

All around, where once massive buildings stood, gaping holes lay. If the buildings of the city had been teeth, they'd have been knocked out at a BUF rally. Some of the empty space was paved over, crumbling ruins of bomb sites cleared away for eventual re-building. Of the buildings left, most were empty, ghostlike, win-dows and rooftops blown off. The skeletal remnants of the solid structures remained stoically in place, preserving the memories of the streets.

The blackout was still in effect, but I knew my route by heart, and had adjusted to the light of the moon.

Once on Blomfield, rather than count the gates to mine like I used to in the pitch black, I counted the empty spaces where houses used to stand, and only the few that remained tall and proud.

From inside the house, Millie barked a greeting. I said a prayer of thanks that the Victoriana still stood. The house had repre-sented victory when it had become ours, and it still did.

📖

November 1942

Dearest Andre,

I am beyond pleased that we've remained friends, as you mean the world to me. Since you're in town, do come by Blomfield for a little soiree I'm hosting. Our old friends would love to see you, and so would I . . .

Tonight, I volunteered to host a going-away party for Heywood, whose orders finally came in. Poor Anne looked pale and miserable. Our mutual friends who weren't away fighting Nazis filled the house with laughter and an underlying murmur of witty chatter.

Unfortunately, the day before, Muv had an emergency at Swinbrook, and asked if Unity could stay with me. As much as it pained to even be in her presence, I agreed, and prayed she didn't cause a scene tonight. With the mind of a juvenile, she was often obnoxious and unruly, especially in public, often saying things that were outrageous, such as "I'll have a charcoal salad," which made no sense. The bullet had done a lot of damage to Unity's brain, forever rendering her into a childlike state. Perhaps being treated as an adult at a party would temper her mood.

I feared a disaster when she came down the stairs, wearing a moth-eaten dress and looking as if she'd been living under London Bridge all of autumn.

"Dear me." I imagined what an article in *Tatler* would say about this incident.

I happened to catch Andre's gaze from across the room. He was chatting with Cecil Beaton, whisky sour in hand. His eyes widened at the sight of my sister.

As close as we'd been, he knew all about my family. Surprisingly, being in his presence tonight was pleasant, rather than painful. I was glad we maintained a friendship. Both of us seemed healed from the hurts of our past.

"Unity, darling." I rushed to her side and took her elbow, trying to turn her back up the stairs. "I've a new dress you must wear tonight." My voice was quiet.

"A new dress?" Unity frowned, her high-pitched voice rising to suggest an imminent tantrum.

"Quite. It's so lovely. You'll look positively glamorous. Won't you try it on? Then we can have champagne."

The latter, I suspect, persuaded her, as mother wouldn't allow her to have a drop of alcohol.

As we moved up the stairs, my panic rose. None of my clothes would fit Unity. She was both taller and broader. But I was determined—and desperate—to make something work.

I grabbed the only other decent black dress I owned, whispering a word of goodbye to it. "Get undressed."

"That is very pretty." Unity touched the lace neckline, eyes glittering.

Did she remember her old gowns, the parties? How I missed the old Unity of our younger years, so original and full of life, before she'd gone to Munich and had her mind poisoned by Herr Hitler.

Unity stepped into the gown, slipping her arms into the sleeves. As I tugged it upward, I bit my lip and cringed at the subtle rending sound of the seams. The dress would need to be mended after, if it could even be salvaged.

As hard as I tried, I could not pull the fabric at the back together to attach the hooks. There was simply not enough around the middle to even get it closed two inches. I could have cried.

A light tapping sounded at the door and then Andre peeked in. "Oh," he said. Then he looked to the pile of discarded clothes on the floor. "How about your lovely black velvet jacket, Nancy? That will hide the open back." This last part he said quietly so Unity wouldn't overhear.

I stood and rifled through my clothes until I found it. The thing wouldn't button in the front, but that didn't matter, as long as it covered her exposed back, which thankfully it did.

"Now, a little lipstick," I said.

"No! No!" Unity stomped her large feet. "Farve will punish me."

"Farve isn't here," I cooed. "And you love lipstick. Especially when it leaves the little red stain on your champagne glass."

"No, Nancy. I will sleep with the chickens!"

My mind scrambled now, wondering how—short of locking her in her bedroom—I would manage if she had a complete breakdown.

Andre tutted and tapped Unity's nose. "*La belle*, Unity, let us make you glamorous, *ma chérie*. There is a grand ball downstairs, waiting for you."

He was really being so kind. To my astonishment she agreed, charmed by his ways, I assumed. I breathed a sigh of relief. What would I have done if he'd not been here to rescue me?

"We will be downstairs shortly." Andre winked at me. "Perhaps a glass of cherry soda when Lady Unity emerges?"

"Oh, I do love cherry soda," Unity gushed, champagne forgotten.

I pressed my hand to my heart, telling him without words how much his actions, his friendship, meant to me.

📖

December 1942

I RAN ALONG CURZON Street, late for opening the shop after a rather passionate breakfast discussion with Sophie about the American soldiers in London. Sophie was rather ecstatic about the addition of the Yanks, who'd joined soldiers from nearly every other country in the world here, finding their accents fascinating.

Admittedly, part of my prejudice against the Yanks was not simply from their tardiness in entering the war against Fascism, but that my sister Jessica had escaped to America, devastating Farve in the process. Now Romilly was missing in action—*poor old boy presumed dead*—for nearly a year. Jessica refused to accept it, writing to me that she believed he'd get himself out of any spot. Rather than return to her family in England for comfort, she remained behind.

There was also the incident last week when I'd taken a bus home from the bookshop. An American soldier wrapped his arms around my waist. He'd not been chastened at all when I demanded he unhand me, pointing out that I was a forty-year-old woman. In fact, the old boy got cheeky, proclaiming he preferred a mature woman. The nerve!

I'd gone home and immediately arranged another hair dyeing.

Caught up in my thoughts, I tripped over an uneven place on the pavement and went hurtling forward into a man's back. He was quick to turn round, catching me before I fell farther.

I stared into the startling eyes of Colonel Gaston Palewski.

"*Mademoiselle*," he mused. "If you wanted to speak to me, all you had to say was *bonjour*."

I laughed at his tease, righted myself and eyed the scuff on my shoe with disdain. It'd only just been polished.

"Thank you for saving me from a tumble. The last thing I need at the moment is a torn stocking, or a scraped-up nose."

"A nose so pretty should never be scraped."

I touched my nose with my gloved finger absently. "Thank you, again."

"I assume you're going to Heywood bookshop." Gaston offered an arm and steered around other pedestrians in the direction of the shop. "I missed you at the Allies Club."

"I hope you haven't been waiting there all this time."

He chuckled. "I left only to sleep."

"If I'd known, I would have come to put you out of your misery."

"Ah, but it was no misery, *mademoiselle*, to sit, dreaming of you, these past weeks."

Heat rose in my cheeks, and that strange fluttering in my chest happened again. What was it about the colonel that intrigued me? I certainly didn't know him in any meaningful way, except by his reputation, which didn't weigh in his favor. But still, the way he spoke, and looked at me with those fine eyes . . .

Outside the bookshop, several customers waited for the doors to be unlocked. With the coming holidays, we'd seen an influx of late, and if I didn't open soon, they'd march over to our competitor's shop, petulant.

"I need to open." I skirted around the charismatic Frenchman, keys dangling from my hand as I greeted customers. The colonel remained outside, watching.

Holding the door wide, I said to him, "Well, are you coming?"

"If I come inside, will you join me for dinner at the club?"

"I will think about it more seriously than I did before."

Gaston walked around the shop, eyes on me instead of the books. I had the light-headed sensation of being studied, admired. At last he bought a book, *Memoirs of le Duc de Saint-Simon.* "A gift for General de Gaulle," he said as I neatly wrapped it in brown paper.

Our fingers brushed, eliciting heat, as he handed me far too much money, and wouldn't accept the change. After he left, I couldn't stop thinking about him.

Days later, I found myself sauntering into the Allies Club with Sophie by my side. We were accompanied by a few of the other Free French officers who'd begun coming round Heywood Hill since I'd persuaded Anne to stock French books.

Onstage, a woman dressed in a sparkling gown sang the latest Kurt Weill melody about a lover. The gentlemen in our party headed to the bar to fetch drinks while Sophie and I moved swiftly toward an abandoned table by the front.

We slipped onto the chairs, expecting the lads to join us, glasses in hand. But instead, the colonel sank into the chair beside me, holding out two flutes. "Two French Seventy-Fives for two *belle mademoiselles.*"

"*Merci*, Colonel." I grinned, taking a cocktail glass and sipping the sweet-sour concoction.

"A pleasure, as always, to see you, *madame.*" He inclined his head to me, and Sophie's eyes widened. I had not yet mentioned the colonel to her. I'm not sure why, given she'd told me about the continued efforts on the part of the old warden.

"Will you introduce me to your friend?" he asked.

"*Bien sûr.* Colonel Gaston Palewski, this is Mrs. Sophie Gordon."

"Mrs. Gordon, lovely, lovely." He returned his attention back to me, one eyebrow lifted as he lit a cigarette.

"Tell me, how is the bookshop?" He offered us each a cigarette, which we both declined.

"We're overrun with holiday shoppers looking for gifts for their loved ones."

"You, *madame*, are a woman quite capable of drawing a crowd even without the Christmas season."

I knew he was flirting, but he was also right, and I was proud of that. I'd played a large role in making Heywood Hill the place to be for the literati of London. In fact, between the authors I drew and the tweaking I'd made to the shop's curation services, Heywood Hill was the most profitable bookshop in London at the moment.

"I cannot take all the credit, Colonel, but I do my bit as we all should during wartime."

"You are a natural," Sophie said. "You're so good with people, and always have a smile on your face."

"*Non*, Mrs. Gordon, it pains me to correct you after our short acquaintance, but your friend does not always smile. Often Mrs. Rodd has only a frown for me," he teased.

"I was under the impression you rather liked my disagreeableness," I quipped. "Is that not why you keep seeking me out?" I sipped casually at the French 75, barely letting the gin touch my tongue.

Beside me, Sophie shifted in her chair, looking off in the distance. "I think I see a friend over there. I'll be right back." She stood and slipped away, her ruse perfectly obvious to myself, and doubtless the colonel.

After our conversations about seeking love, was it possible

this was Sophie's way of reminding me that I was entitled to the same?

The colonel immediately leaned closer. "You intrigue me, *madame*. You have a certain *je ne sais quoi* that makes me want to unwrap you."

My eyebrows shot to my hairline. "That is impertinent, sir."

The colonel laughed. "Ah, that did not come out the way I intended." He paused. "But if we're to be honest with each other, I would like that as well."

"Do tell what you meant, then." My eyes shifted to Sophie, where she embraced an American soldier who'd been throwing darts.

"I think there is more than meets the eye with you, *madame*."

I flicked my gaze back to him. "And what meets the eye?"

"Besides a beautiful woman? From the way you dress, you've a nice sense of style, but you are, perhaps, at times without the means to truly reach your potential."

Goodness, but the man was not as smooth as I'd been led to believe. "So you are saying I'm poor and a poor dresser?"

"Not a poor dresser."

I set down the cocktail. "I'd previously heard you were charming. Excuse me, Colonel, but I see someone, anyone really, just over there that I need to speak with."

He brushed his hand on my forearm, where it rested on my lap. "Nancy. Flattery is easy; anyone may learn it. Honesty is perhaps harder, no?"

I stilled at his unexpected reply. Here I'd thought there wasn't much substance to the "ladies' man" whose reputation flourished across London. With his frankness, I was intrigued by not only his French accent, impeccable English and confident bravado, but a deeper part of him that touched something inside me. I also liked how he said my name like the city in France was pronounced, *Non-see.*

"You're right, Gaston," I replied. "But honesty needn't be brutal or insulting."

"You make me nervous," he admitted. "Not an excuse, but an explanation."

"*I* make *you* nervous?" I laughed hard enough to draw attention.

"You think it is funny, but I assure you, I am earnest."

"Continue." I picked up my glass, leaning back in my chair, offering him assurance I was willing to listen instead of fleeing.

"I admire more than your beauty, *madame.* You have tenacity, your vibrancy. You are *drôle* and serious at once. You have many sides, many Nancies, one might say. You chatter by day with brandy-drinking men who have nothing better to do than lounge about a bookshop, and you sell them overpriced books. But then you slip away to help serve meals to men at the canteen, to put out fires where needed. Unlike many of those drawn to you, you seek to be useful. To do your bit, as you say. I think many people have underestimated you for years. I think they do not know the *real* Nancy."

How had a man I barely knew, had barely spoken with except to cross flirtatious swords, figured me out so quickly? And he was right: I wasn't an open book. Most people didn't know the real me. Just pages. Layers.

"Most people are drawn to me for my social status and my family name." That was only partly true, a test mostly, because, after all, I'd once spied on the French, and there was every possibility that they were equally spying on me. I needed to make sure the colonel was not—or at least that he realized I wasn't a fool.

"Your family . . . ah, they are interesting, and at the risk of insulting you once more, in some circles infamous. But you're not one of them. And I do not want to dance with them."

"Are you asking me to dance?"

"*Oui.*" He stood.

I considered him, staring at his outstretched hand, then rose and took it. If Gaston realized I had layers, pointing out the various Nancies, as he put it, then I needed to consider he too was more than what he let everyone else see. It was no less than he deserved. I was intrigued.

Being on his arm as he led me to the floor and twirled me through a dance was both thrilling and oddly comforting. One of his hands on mine, the other at the small of my back. He wasn't the most handsome man, with his pockmarked cheeks and silly mustache. But the way he held me exuded power and captivated me.

When I looked into Gaston's light eyes, I didn't see a man who simply wanted to take me to bed, but another soul that reached out and touched mine, saw me for who I was, which he'd demonstrated in his description of me at the table. As we swayed, I began to feel that stirring of wanting, and being wanted in return. I wasn't sure if I was ready to go down that road again . . . but I wanted to find out.

So, rather than taking a taxicab with Sophie, I let Gaston walk me home, leaning into the anonymity of the dark. I hoped to use the extra time the two-mile stroll would take to sort through my feelings.

"I will not let you in my house," I warned as we set out. I

snuggled into my overcoat, my breath puffing out in tiny white clouds.

"I do not expect you to." His face was serious. "Tell me a story, Nancy."

The first thing that came to mind, was the one I'd made up about Diana, Mosley, Mark . . . "Shall I tell you the tale of 'Two Old Ladies from Eaton Square'?"

Gaston gasped. "Is it a true story? I live at Eaton Square."

I laughed. "No, it is made-up."

"*Non, non, ma chérie*," he begged. "Tell me a *real* story."

Nearly halfway to home, snow started to fall, draping the bombed-out buildings in a blanket of white.

"Shall I hail a taxicab to take us the rest of the way?" Gaston asked.

"Oh, no, I like the snow." I closed my eyes, lifting my face to the sky. A cold flake hit my cheek.

"Oh, Nancy," Gaston said. "I would kiss you."

I slowly opened my eyes. "But you can't," I said, smiling.

"I *want* to kiss you."

"But you won't. You asked me for a story." I wrapped my arm through his. "A real story." There were so many I could tell— painful accounts illuminating the darkest truths of my past. But I wasn't ready for that. So I started with something innocent. "Let me tell you about the time it was snowing when I was a girl, and our Labrador had gone missing." I regaled Gaston with one childhood story after another. I had him laughing and begging for more as we went, until finally, my house loomed before us, and it was time to say good night.

"Let me see you tomorrow." Gaston took my cold hands in his, heat from his fingers sinking through my gloves.

"I will be at the bookshop and the canteen. Might even be putting out a fire."

"Then I will find you wherever you are. And when you take a break, we can have tea. Or I can hold your stirrup pump."

"And if I say no?"

"Then I will wait until you say *oui*."

And so it went, for days and days. The colonel popping his head into the bookshop, lamenting the pricing, and then asking for a book we didn't have in stock, on purpose, I think. He would wink at me before leaving, slip me a chocolate, or leave a rose on the register desk. Always discreetly.

Sometimes I said yes and we went to the Hostel, where there was little chance we'd be recognized. On such occasions we shared stories, mostly me at first, but then he opened up as well. Told me how his father emigrated to France from Poland when he was young, living with an uncle after the death of his father. How as a boy, he'd often gone roller-skating in the square of their flat, and how his father would take Gaston and his brother hand in hand through the salons of the Louvre. That they would make their own museums in the drawing room at home, and invite all the neighborhood children over to peruse their "exhibits." At fifteen he'd been sent to Brighton College in England to study English, and had even attended Oxford in his early twenties, which explained his grasp of the language.

But perhaps the most touching of all was that he too had spent time with his brother in a large cupboard, playing games and contemplating the mysteries of life.

Then one day, as he dropped me back at the bookshop, I invited him to a Christmas gathering I was hosting for friends and family. He lowered his eyes for a moment—thoughtful eyes I'd grown used to—then he said, "Ah, but Nancy, I am Jewish, so I fear half your family would not wish me there."

"If they only knew you, that would never cross their minds." But I was dissembling, for on some level, with a few of my relations, he would be right.

"Perhaps in time." But his eyes showed he did not believe his own reassurance.

"Come have dinner with me at Blomfield after Christmas, then."

Gaston's eyes widened—a private dinner, in my residence. This was a new line we'd both be stepping over, for I'd yet to let him cross the threshold. "I would like that very much, Nancy."

"So would I." And I meant it. Something was growing between us.

I'd tried to deny it, to push away the feelings he awakened inside me. Perhaps I was healing. To ignore that would be to ignore what I'd so longed for—happiness, companionship and, dare I even dream it, *love*.

January 1943

Gladys,

For tonight's supper, please prepare one of your delicious meals for two as I'm having a guest. Enclosed are the ration cards I've been saving. Do please make yourself an extra pie

to take with you to your friends, as a thank-you from me for
allowing my dogs to stay the night with you there.

Very best,
Mrs. Rodd

Ice clung to the trees outside, making crystals out of the branches, and deadly icicles dripped from rooftops throughout London.

I worried with the weather that Gaston would reschedule dinner, but he insisted he'd not miss it even if he had to crawl. At half past seven, I pressed the pin of my gramophone in place, and soft classical music broke the echoing silence.

When his knock came, I drew in a deep breath, smoothed the skirt of my black Dior dress and headed for the door. On the threshold, Gaston stood in his uniform and overcoat, red roses in hand.

"For you." He leaned in to kiss me on each cheek in the French fashion.

I breathed in his woodsy, masculine scent—bergamot, patchouli, citrus and black pepper. Bergamot reminded me of Andre. But rather than be sad about it, I knew Andre would always be a part of the Nancy I'd become. I took in another deep breath, drawing Gaston nearer to me, wishing we could stand all night in the open doorway—crisp winter air at his back, the warmth of his body near mine.

"Come in." I walked toward the kitchen, drawing him along in my wake, and putting the flowers in a vase as he stood at my side.

"Smells decadent." Gaston had eyes only for me. Whereas most who visited studied their surroundings, Gaston didn't seem to notice he was in a new place as he followed me back to the dining table.

"I cannot take credit for the meal," I said.

"You must; you are the hostess." He took off his cap and placed it on the sideboard. Then removed his overcoat and slung it over one arm.

"I can hang that for you."

Gaston smiled warmly. "I can take care of it myself." He turned back around, heading toward the coat tree by the door.

By the time he returned, I'd placed the warmed dishes on the table.

He came around behind me as I poured him a glass of wine. "*Merci*, Nancy."

Gaston's fingers touched mine as he took the glass. I held my breath. I don't know what I thought was about to happen—a touch, a kiss?—but he only pulled out my chair and indicated for me to sit. As he pushed the chair back in, his fingers brushed my arms, and once again, I inhaled his scent.

Dinner was a slow and lovely thing. We talked for hours, mesmerized with each other. As the time passed, my mind drifted to what would come after dinner . . . and I longed for it rather than being nervous. Each gesture of his masculine hands made me wonder how it would feel to have his fingers trace their way over my naked flesh. How would it feel to be wrapped in his strong arms?

When I stood to clear the table, Gaston insisted on helping.

"Shall we retire to the salon?" I asked as we finished stacking the plates in the sink. "I can build up the fire and pour some port."

"That sounds *magnifique*, only allow me to build the fire for you."

When his fire was crackling in the hearth, we took our glasses of port and sat on the sofa, close enough that we nearly touched.

"Nancy, if you do not wish . . ." He was giving me a way out.

"But I do." I nodded, not hesitating a second. "Oh, how I do."

It was me that leaned in this time, demanding his kiss. His mouth was velvet on mine, tasting faintly of the lemon dessert, and port. The hair of his mustache tickled my lip, and I laughed.

"Do you always laugh when kissed by a lover, *ma chérie?*"

A lover . . .

"No." I ran my fingertip over his lip and the short black mustache. "But you tickle."

"I want to make you laugh again. It is a beautiful sound." He kissed me again, this time with heat and fervor, an energy that grew moment by passing moment.

I could barely breathe. When his mouth trailed to my neck, I laughed and gasped, as his tongue traced the divot at the front of my throat.

"*Je veux te fair l'amour,*" he whispered against my ear.

"Oh yes, make love to me."

Gaston swept me into his arms as if I weighed nothing at all and carried me upstairs to the bedroom I'd shared with Peter. To the bed I'd not even allowed Andre to share. Guilt tickled at the back of my mind, but I quickly pushed past it. My marriage had died long ago, and what I had with Gaston . . . It was that giddy, wild, wide-awake feeling I knew came with falling for someone.

Hours later, my heart pounding, my skin still flushed, I felt satisfied in a way I had not for months, maybe even years. Gaston had consumed me utterly, worshipped me like no other.

He came back the next night, and the night after that, and so many nights I lost count until he became a habit, woven into the threads of my life.

We dined sometimes on food Gladys prepared, sometimes on fish and chips he purchased on the way. One evening, he brought a picnic basket of sandwiches made in the style of his favorite *boulangerie* in Paris. Another time, I went a little overboard, asking Gladys to pick up a dinner I'd ordered from the Savoy.

After we ate, we walked my dogs, and sometimes he even petted the chickens. As our life together expanded, we snuck into a cinema in the dark so no one recognized us while we enjoyed the films, and each other. At the end of every evening, we made love until we couldn't breathe, speak, move. Collapsing in a heap, we slept until just before dawn, when I'd wake to him kissing his way down my body, and we'd make love again.

Gaston would slip from my house, returning to his flat, where he rang me up every morning, chattering away for half an hour or more, begging me for stories. "Your life should be a book. Everyone would buy it, even at Heywood Hill prices."

I brushed his comments aside, telling him I was perfectly happy writing articles, and had just had one published in *Lilliput*, and another the following month.

Twelve Blomfield Road felt like an extension of heaven. I worked during the day, did my volunteer shift and then came home, waiting for the sound of Gaston's singing out in the street, always an indication that he'd arrived.

Throughout the rest of winter and into early spring, it seemed nothing could spoil the mood, not even the occasional reminder that I had a husband. But, this time, not even Peter could put a damper on my happiness.

📖

April 1943

THE BELL OVER THE door dinged, and I pushed the last book on the shelf, while calling out, "One moment!"

Emerging from the back of the shop I found no one there. It was dark outside, the curtains already drawn. I was quite alone, though I'd sworn I'd heard the bell.

Then I saw it on the register desk—a red rose laid there so carefully against the wood—and I smiled.

"Are you still here, darling?" I expected to see Gaston pop from his hiding place, but there was only silence. "I'm closing up the shop in a moment; you'll be locked in until morning."

Still silence greeted me. I breathed in the scent of his rose, noticing there was a piece of the paper on the desk beneath it.

Written in French, Gaston's long scrawl etched into the note.

Darling Nancy,

My love, my lady, the most enchanting woman I've ever met. I cannot wait to see you tonight.

Your Frog

Gathering up my things, I stepped outside. As I put the key in the lock, a hand brushed my waist. I glanced up to see Gaston's teasing smile.

"You are going for an air of mystery tonight," I said.

He held up another flower. I took it and pressed it to my nose.

"I was trying to be romantic," he replied.

"You are succeeding."

I looped my arm in his as we walked back to my house, where I'd spent more happy moments with Gaston than any other person. I never worried about Peter coming home, finding us there. He was away, and when he was in London, it wasn't my bed he sought.

After a dinner of Woolton pie and salad left to us by Gladys, Gaston turned on the gramophone and pulled me into his arms. We danced slowly, the scent of him surrounding me, bringing pleasant memories and hope.

He twirled me in his arms, and I smiled against his shoulder, resting my cheek there. When the song ended, he dipped me backward and pressed a kiss to my lips, then pulled me toward the sofa, where he slid off my shoes and stockings to rub my feet in long, languid strokes. Gaston had the most marvelous hands, which never tired, and seemed made for pleasure.

"I have news." By the somber tone of his voice, the loss of his smile, I guessed it was not good news.

"Oh?" I said tentatively, retrieving my feet from his lap and tucking them beneath me, feeling suddenly vulnerable.

"I have received new orders."

My voice sounded choked when I said, "Paris? Let me go with you."

"*Ma chérie* . . . how I wish that were the case. But . . . it's not Paris. Not yet. Algiers. We're going to take a stand against the Nazis and Vichy. Will you write to me when I'm away?"

I gazed into Gaston's eyes, trying not to cry. "I don't want this to end."

"*Moi, non plus.* This is not an end. Merely a change. Write to me, beautiful things. I will visit when I can. Telephone every chance I get."

"I'll write every day until I see you again." I curled into his arms, pressed my hand over his heart, feeling the steady, strong beat.

"Ah, ma chérie. Mon coeur."

He called me his heart with such conviction I felt safe sharing my deeply held secret. "I love you, so very much." I'd never used those words before. Not for Andre, Peter or even Hamish.

Gaston leaned down to kiss me, wrapping me in his strong, loving arms. I felt complete—whole—as if despite war and personal failures, there was nothing wrong in the world, and only good things to look forward to.

My thoughts drifted away, and I gave myself over to his passion. *Someday when this war ends, we will walk the streets of Paris together.*

Chapter Twenty-Two
Lucy

"OLIVER OFFERED ME A job." Lucy said the words casually as she speared a cucumber from her salad.

Gavin stopped, his burger in midair. "Are you going to take it?"

"I'm not sure." She watched the emotions play on Gavin's face. What she thought was hope flashed through his eyes before they became guarded. "There are a lot of advantages to accepting. But also, I'd have to leave behind my life in the US. My job there, family, friends."

Even as Lucy said the words, she knew she'd have less regret than she hinted at. She'd made a pros-and-cons list about the offer. The columns on her list favored London. But she still hadn't decided. What held her back was the fear of the unknown, she supposed. Was she going to let her fear keep her from what she wanted?

"What do you really want, Lucy?" Gavin asked.

Lucy set down her fork. "I want to get ahead in my career. Either way, I will. Right now, I'm sitting at a crossroads, with promotions on both sides of the Atlantic. If I stay at Emerald, I've got a measure of security. The position at Heywood is even higher up the ladder, but I'd be leaving my old world behind for a new one."

"Sounds like an adventure," Gavin said with a dimpled smile. "And, if I'm not mistaken, isn't that what you told me you craved?"

"Yes. But if I'm going to jump, I need to make sure I've considered all the consequences."

"Don't talk yourself out of what you really want."

She had a habit of doing that. She nodded. "Thank you."

After dinner, they took a long walk through Hyde Park, kissing under the stars. The warmth of his body consumed her. She could have stayed in the park all night in his arms. The spell unbroken, they made their way back to Curzon Street. At the stairs to her flat, Lucy wanted to invite Gavin up. But something gave her pause. In a few days, she might not ever see him again, and with the monumental decision still to be made, falling into bed on a whim seemed like a bad idea and a complication.

"See you tomorrow?" she asked hopefully.

"Aye." Gavin kissed her one more time.

Inside her flat, Lucy went to the window, looking down to see if he was still there, half thinking she'd change her mind about inviting him up. But he'd already gone.

The following morning, Lucy rose early, only to be frustrated by an email from her sister. Maya had been unable to find any pictures related to the woman in the newspaper article—the one with the iris pin. It appeared that once again Iris had slipped through Lucy's fingers and back into oblivion.

With a list of final things to complete for her project, Lucy went down to her office and hit her lists and spreadsheets hard. One final box of books she'd been expecting arrived—a whole slew of first editions. She checked each one over to make sure they accurately met their descriptions, and then had them repackaged and shipped. By the time she glanced at the clock, it was nearing five.

"Lucy, do you have a minute?" Oliver approached her desk.

She knew he was looking for an answer, but it had only been a day. Lucy nodded, following him up the stairs and preparing to tell him that she still needed just a bit more time. The shouts of "Surprise" from a circle of her fellow Heywood Hill staff, and Gavin too, stopped her in her tracks.

"Oh my God!" Lucy covered her cheeks with her hands.

"On behalf of all of us here at Heywood Hill, it has been a pleasure." Oliver popped a bottle of champagne, pouring out flutes and handing one to Lucy. "Bon voyage on Monday. And dare I say we hope to see you back in London soon."

Lucy's heart warmed as they raised their glasses, wishing her well on her journey. Lucy gazed from face to face, realizing that even though she'd only been in London for a couple of weeks, everyone here had become her friend.

They all wanted to see her back soon, but understood, to her relief, that she still needed some time to mull the idea over. Even Gavin wasn't pressuring her for an answer.

Champagne finished, the group walked down the street to a pub, pushing together tables in the center and filling them with good cheer. Maybe this circle of people hoisting pints was the connection she'd been searching for. The idea of returning to DC brought on a profound sadness. That sadness also brought certainty.

"Are you all right?" Gavin leaned his shoulder against hers, murmuring the words so no one else could hear.

She smiled, pushing away her half-eaten shepherd's pie. "Yes. Just realizing I don't want to leave."

Gavin's arm went around her, and he rubbed her shoulder. "You've got reason to come back."

"I do." She nodded. "Many reasons." Including this kind, book-crazy Scotsman.

Every reason led to the same conclusion: there was no place she'd rather set down roots than right here in London, where her own story could begin a new chapter—one in which she was the protagonist in control.

📖

Four days later . . .
DC, Masters' Library

LUCY WAS PUTTING THE final touches on the Mitford collection in the library. Unpacking volumes and arranging them on their designated shelves. As she lifted *Pigeon Pie* from the top of the stack of books shipped from Paris, a piece of paper slipped out.

She stooped to retrieve it off the tapestried rug. The paper was old and yellowed with age. A name was scratched on the envelope in a familiar scrawl—*Iris*. This was now the second time Nancy had left a message for Iris in a book, and Lucy the one to find it. If this wasn't a sign she was meant to know Iris, then she didn't know what was.

Slowly, Lucy peeled back the flap of the envelope and pulled the folded sheet from within. Nancy Mitford's handwriting bloomed to life on the paper, etched in black ink.

June 3, 1973
7 rue Monsieur, VII

My dearest Iris,

It's been an age since we saw each other. Feels like another world entirely now, doesn't it? When we scrambled over darkened roads in search of light, and tapped at the empty shelves of our bare cupboards in search of something to eat. I never told you that meeting you on that platform at Paddington was a turning point for me. Or that you were the inspiration behind Sophia Garfield, who lies at the heart of this very book. My own copy. And the letter left here for the day I know where to mail it. You were always a smart thing, so I suspect you noticed how similar your name, Sophie Gordon (my beloved Iris!), was to that silly character's. Though your personality was by and large much more charming than Sophia's. And you were a better friend. For the times you saved me, and you know every one of them, especially the time you gave me permission to be happy, I thank you.

I wish we could have said goodbye. I wish I knew you now. May this letter somehow find its way to you in a time when dreams come true.

Best love,
Nancy

Tears stung the backs of Lucy's eyes. She touched the pin on the scarf she wore around her neck, part fashion, partly for warmth. The iris pin, from the friend Nancy lost, and whom Lucy had been trying to find.

The definitive answer to who Nancy's friend Iris was had finally been answered: *Sophie Gordon.*

Lucy read the letter again, then tucked it carefully back into the envelope, and then into her purse. She had to find Sophie Gordon. To give her this letter, and her own copy of *The Pursuit of Love*, which had been meant for Sophie. Lucy liked to think that she and her mother had simply been holding it for safekeeping.

When dreams come true. The last line of Nancy's letter replayed in her mind.

When the last book sat on the last shelf of the magnificent library, it was time to make her own dreams come true. In fact, it was a process she could begin right now.

Without hesitating, Lucy emailed Mr. Sloan from her phone, tendering her resignation. Then she sent a short message to Oliver accepting the position at Heywood Hill.

Chapter Twenty-Three
Nancy

November 1943

12 Blomfield Road, W9

My own dearest darling, Gaston,

How I wish you were here today, and safe. I shall have to console myself with the memory of my Frog's voice. To think about what you might say to calm my nerves.

I've had bad news. A certain someone has been released from her cell along with her very ogre-ish—and still Fascist!—husband. I'm a mess of worry. What plans might they have cooked up in Hol to further harm my beloved country?

I am torn too . . . I have missed my sister, and as terrible a thing as she is, part of me wants to see her. I confess I wrote her while she was in prison, perhaps out of guilt.

As if the surprise of Diana's release isn't enough, my dear friend Mark was imprisoned in Austria and escaped, only to be recaptured and put into a camp in Germany. How is it that the good people are being caged, whether by bars or duty, while those who believe such atrocities should be committed are let free?

And the press . . . They will not leave me alone! Simply maddening! They ring up the bookshop every minute of every day, and sneak inside to try and ask me questions or see if Diana has stopped by. You can't imagine how annoying they are, little flies buzzing round. And there's always at least one asking if I've seen Unity lately, or if she's been in contact with Hitler. I've half a mind to pull a great tease and tell them the devil's been up to Inch Kenneth, but you know they'll take it as fact and then the pitchforks will come, string up my family before the sun sets.

You can imagine Muv and Unity are beside themselves with glee over Diana's coup. They are trying to plan a party, but they don't seem to realize that the two jugged lovers are being released to house confinement, not to go about the London circuit. It just seems so unnatural to hold a party and everything is glee and cheers when our proud loves are off fighting for a war that they would have gladly conceded to evil.

I miss you, darling, ever so much. The nights are so very cold . . . And whenever my telephone rings, I hope that it will be you, but, alas, I am disappointed more often than not.

I have kept my promise, writing you every day. But I am not sure you get all of my letters, and I'm certain not to have received all of yours, for they come too few and far between.

Your friend the Prince de Beauvau-Craon has been good company, though I do think he is quite in love with me. But never mind that, for the only thing I see fit to speak to him about is you, darling, ~~you~~!

###

I've only just come back to finish this story. You see, there were the warning bells and then a missile hurtling itself from the clouds, all red and orange rays reflected in the sky like fire, as if it had already exploded. Oh, dear me, I think I have got too used to bombs, for my nerves no longer rattle.

Well, this letter is growing incredibly long, and possibly too boring for you. If you've not the patience to read it, I'd never blame you.

Oh, do write to me soon. I long to hear from you. At night I imagine I can hear a tune in the street, the latest Kurt Weill, perhaps, and I sit upright trying to decipher if it's been a dream or you've returned to me.

Missing you ever so much,

With the most love,
Nancy

April 7, 1944

PINCHING THE BRIDGE OF my nose, I batted away the clouds of dust blooming up from shifting a stack of books in the storage area of the bookshop's cellar.

With Easter coming in a few days, the shop was remarkably heavily trafficked. The usual set of lads chatted in the red room, now unofficially called Club Nancy. I'd retreated temporarily to the cellar to make sense of the endless piles gathering dust around its edges, which we'd let go far too long.

Anne had left more and more the running of the shop to me and my assistants after delivering her daughter. I was glad to be in charge of the bookshop while Heywood was away and she was busy mothering. In her absence, I wanted to get the place in ship-shape before the lot of us ended up buried.

Picking up the pile that I'd culled from the mess, I hurried up the stairs. I settled the lot down on the register desk, creating yet another cloud of dust. My assistant behind the desk coughed.

"Let's get these sorted." Together we sifted through the pile, a stack of nineteenth-century classics we'd recently acquired at an auction.

The work was busy and kept my thoughts from Gaston. I missed him terribly—a grief compounded by Peter being back in town making me miserable. He'd burst into the shop, all pompous, jesting he half expected me to have French soldiers on either arm. Someone must have told him about Andre, Gaston or both.

From Addis Ababa, Peter went to Italy, arriving home tanned and in good shape. He brought an armful of gifts—oranges, ham and brandy—which I was grateful for as food was becoming scarce in London. Often what was available was inedible. Only a few days earlier, chicken I'd purchased was maggot-ridden when Gladys cut into it.

Along with gifts, my husband brought his customary rancid rancor. He made no attempt to conceal his infidelities—flaunting his mistress in a manner that suggested he thought paybacks were due. The man really was an extraordinary cad.

Still, we had a celebratory dinner at the Ritz. Keeping up appearances at least required that. I begged several of our friends to join us so I didn't have to be alone with him. Peter droned on and on, even getting snippy with me at any mention of the French, drawing several raised brows. Then, as we waited for dessert, Adelaide sauntered by on the pretext of meeting a friend, and Prod invited her to join our table. It was an obvious setup, and if I recognized it, so too did everyone else at the table.

The old Nancy would have been jealous, staged a fainting episode, feeling wholly inadequate. But now I didn't care. I had the upper hand because Prod was jealous, and I was not. So, with Adelaide sitting right there, I made sure to throw out as many of French quips as I could. Several of my friends joined me in regaling the table about the French's charming nature and delicious food. If our not-so-silent battle was immature, at least it was fun. Peter's face grew redder with every word.

At the evening's conclusion, Prod staggered from the table. I wistfully hoped now he'd be willing to grant me a divorce. I wanted out of this wretched situation.

Thank God, Sophie invited me on a short day-trip escape to Brighton. We took the train and picnicked on the beach, then lounged in the sun.

"I've not seen you so relaxed in quite a while," Sophie said, scooping a handful of sand. "Why do you suppose that is?"

"Less noise." I looked out toward where the waves lapped softly at the shore. The waves calmed the overwhelming noise that roared in my head. Both inside and outside. Even the loud, painful silence when I was in Prod's presence of late.

Sophie smiled. "I know what you mean. Do you think it better to be unattached and not so alone, or married and alone most days?"

The question took me aback, her candid summation of my marital situation absolutely leveling me. "I am not alone most days, I make sure of that. See here, I am with you."

Sophie smiled, and raised a brow. "Touché."

"Without good friends on whom to rely, Sophie, how can one survive?" *For I certainly would not have lasted a decade married to Peter, or my tumultuous family, without them.* "Time again and again, friends have been my saving grace, the people who raise me up and motivate me to go on."

"Oh, you mean your French friends, then?" she quipped with a little chuckle.

"And my British ones." I gently shoved her shoulder. "I've counted on you to get me through the fog of war and the mess that is more than occasionally my life." Sophie, my Iris, first drew me out of the dark at the train station, and had since offered me a shoulder to lean on, both physically and emotionally, many times.

"I count on you too, Nancy. You are the paste that binds so many together."

"I am bookbinding," I said with a laugh. "Holding the pages of our universe between my sleeves."

Several weeks later, with Peter off again, I woke to the sharp, incessant tone of the telephone bell. Afraid for what news could wake me so early. I rushed to answer.

"Nancy, how I've missed you, *ma chérie*." It was a voice I'd longed to hear for so long.

"My colonel," I sighed into the phone. "Come back to me."

"I'm in London assisting de Gaulle in talks with Churchill. I'm on my way now, *mon amour.*"

I rushed to prepare, and by the time he arrived, I had pearls at my neck, a sleek black skirt, a pressed silk blouse, even my best hose. My cheeks were flushed from excitement, red lipstick on. My arms, oh, how they itched to wrap around him.

"Oh, my darling." I leapt into his arms and buried my face in his neck, the scent of him so familiar, the comfort of his arms reassuring.

"My Nancy, *ma chérie, mon amour.*" Gaston's lips met mine. This was exactly the dizzying excitement of anticipation melting into passion and relief that any heroine in a book would feel when her lover returned safe from war.

Today, I was that heroine. The woman who was finally embracing happiness. Even if mine turned out to be brief—for the war was not over and men could be fickle things—I resolved to take it, wrap it in a beautiful package and tuck it in my heart.

After a lengthy embrace at the door, I drew Gaston inside, scrambling to retrieve a gift I'd hidden for when he returned—a French translation of *The Picture of Dorian Gray.*

"I have something for you." He drew something small from the pocket of his uniform, a gold circlet ring of filigreed fleurs-de-lis.

"Oh, Gaston, *c'est très belle.*"

"Like you." He pressed his lips to mine, then slid the band onto my right ring finger. He looked steadily into my eyes. "How I wish it were the left, *ma chérie.*"

I stared down at my finger, the light from the window making the gold glow. This felt so right, him standing here before me. The dreariness of waiting for his return evaporated as if it had never been.

"Come, I must give you a proper English tea." I led him to the little table where tea was set out. I poured him a cup with two lumps of sugar I'd saved from my rations. "I wrote you every day as promised. Did you get any of my letters?"

"Every one . . . and I kept all of them." From there he repeated some of the stories I'd told him, making me giggle as he added in just the right inflection.

A few days later at luncheon with some society friends, one mentioned a rumor that my colonel had been frightened during a recent raid. "No indeed," I said boldly, "for he was with me all night, and I can tell you most assuredly, he was not afraid."

She leaned in with a raised brow to confirm, *"All night?"*

I winked. "Oh, *oui*, all night." They didn't need to know that he'd come with me to help the fire watch on the rooftop. But I was done hiding Gaston.

📖

December 1944

Mon chéri, *Colonel,*

What a relief it must be to you to be back in Paris—a Paris with streets free of Nazis. I wish I was there walking with you along the Seine, dining at the Ritz, gazing at the Paris lights. I bet in Paris, we would not have to thwart society like we did in London last summer.

The Heywoods have made me a business proposition—a partnership in their bookstore. Already I am there day and night, and perhaps, if I accept, they may be interested in my opening a shop in Paris. Then my dream of living in that beautiful city will come true.

I know you pooh-pooh the idea, but I cannot fathom why. When this long war is finally completely over, how I should love living in Paris, and will not miss dreary London and the backstabbing of its social circles one bit. Of course, it is Peter I would miss the least. I'll be lucky if he ever grants me a divorce. For now, I simply stare at my right hand, and pretend it's my left.

Oh, how hard you must be working with de Gaulle!

I stopped writing, so much more on my mind, and yet so little to say. If only this war that kept us apart would end and I moved to Paris, my life would be complete.

As it was, I was expected to host a party for Prod, who'd invited Adelaide, amongst the many other dozens of guests. Peter and I weren't even pretending anymore. Which suited me fine, if only he would divorce me, but so far he'd rejected the idea.

I cast a glance in the looking glass. The woman looking back at me appeared tired. Years now of little sleep, not enough food and endless hours of work had made me extremely slim, my skin thin. Dark bruises of exhaustion smeared beneath my eyes, which seemed just a tad too wide. At least my hair dye did wonders to cover the gray.

Grooves etched around my eyes and lines around my mouth suggested I was a woman who laughed unceasingly. That was the thing about me . . . I was very good at covering up my sorrows with a laugh or smile. I'd spent years of my life pretending joy.

The irony of that was not lost upon me—because at last I saw where joy was to be found. *Paris.* If only I could get there.

I signed my letter with love and took to the stairs.

March 1945

Darling Evelyn,

I'm taking a leave of absence from the shop and my duties with the ARP to write a book at last.

There comes a time in a woman's life when she finally says she is done; she's had enough and now it is time for her. I thought I'd been down that path plenty of times, but apparently those were all practice routes. Life is precious, and can end in an instant. But I need not tell you that. On to something more gossipy for you.

After a short stint with my darling youngest sister— Deborah says hello—and her husband, Andrew, I am embarking on a journey to Faringdon House, though it won't be the same without you in residence. Lord Berners is allowing me an extra-long stay so I can at last pen the novel that has been plaguing me for five long years—along with you, darling old boy, who will not relent. I've nearly forgotten what heaven a holiday can be—but even more so, what glory it is to live in a world of one's own imagination. I cannot wait to begin!

I think I shall call this manuscript something along the lines of Chasing Joy, *or* For the Love of Happiness. *I'm not entirely sure just yet, but I know it will be an epic tale of a woman who goes after just what she wants. A grand tale of friendship too. And family. The war, and how it entreats people to go in so many different directions. A touch of old too, life in a country house, and where we all wish we could be.*

Do say you can tear yourself away. I long to see you.

Love from,
Nancy

Sitting down that first morning at Faringdon, clean paper laid out, pen before me, I realized I'd forgotten what heaven writing was. Pulse thrumming, I put pen to paper, and for three days, I scarcely stopped. Only interrupted my writing with the occasional meal and a break to wander about the house or grounds. Berners had created a place like no other, with things that had to be seen to be believed, such as his paper flower garden full of pigeons painted in bright colors, like plumes of rainbow confetti, as they flew past. Or his hounds that wore pearl necklaces—likely more expensive than my own. There were tiny jests about the house, such as a sign down near the floor in the dining room where if dogs could read they'd take note: *No dogs admitted.*

In the midst of my little slice of heaven, I was struck with dreadful news.

The first of us Mitford children had died. How unfair that it would be poor, sweet Tom. *My Tud.* My confidant, my playmate, my troublemaker. My dearest and only brother.

Seated on the leather footstool, the thick carpet at my feet scattered with pages I'd been trying to sort into a coherent scene, I felt crushed, as if a piece of myself had died in Burma with my brother.

"Nancy." Through my shock and the gathering tears, I stared at Lord Berners. He had the heavy burden of relating the cruel news. "I am so sorry." He held out a small cup of brandy, which I absently took, but couldn't seem to sip. Numbness took hold. I wasn't certain I could swallow, let alone gather the strength to bring it to my lips.

Of any of us, besides Deborah, he deserved death the least. Certainly not first.

"He was killed in action?" I asked.

"As a result of an injury sustained in action, yes. Pneumonia set in after the bullet wound was treated."

So many of our boys gone off to fight, and so many not coming home. How many more losses could we endure? How much pain?

I barely saw Lord Berners other than a haze of a man in a suit. He was a friend, but not one I could confide this deep sorrow to. The man I could share it with was in Paris. I blinked, trying to force the tears away.

Sophie's question came back to me. *Do you think it better to be unattached and not so alone, or married and alone most days?*

Here I was in limbo, both attached and not attached. Alone, yet not alone. This was what she had meant when she'd casually referred that day to infinite loneliness.

"I'll tell the others you won't be down to dinner," Lord Berners offered.

"No." I managed to speak through the thickness of my throat. "I'll be down. Tom would want that."

And he would. Tom was no wallower. In fact, he'd tease me for crying, calling me a great baby, if he were here. *But he is not, and he never will be again.*

"Are you certain?" Lord Berners looked worried. "I can have a plate sent up."

I shook my head, sipping the brandy at last. "No, no. I don't want to be alone."

That was perhaps the closest I'd gotten to actually saying the truth out loud.

I dressed slowly and came down to dinner. I smiled, I laughed. Kept myself busy with conversation so as to keep from falling apart. Imagined Tom at the table nodding in approval.

After dinner, I retired to my room, a yawning cavern of gilt, lace and silk that was cold as the grave. It taunted me, pressing me to realize what my life had become.

The only way to combat such sorrow and despair was to write. To make up a story in my head. To focus on bringing my family, *Tom*, to life on the pages. That was how I honored those I'd lost. By really, truly living. The title came to me just after midnight, when my fingers cramped and my eyes stung—*The Pursuit of Love.*

As night passed into day, and day slunk back into night, I wrote at a feverish pace. Surrounded by papers piling, ink stains on my fingers, I lived as if within a trance. Barely sleeping, barely eating. Existing only in my own world. In tales of my childhood, with laughter like ghosts from the past rising up from the pages.

I remained elusive in my room until the eighth of May. But then I was awakened—all of Europe was. The Nazis were defeated—and Hitler dead, having taken his own life, depriving us of retribution. When I heard he'd shot himself, I wondered, did he use the same gun he'd given my sister?

They said he'd poisoned himself too, perhaps not wanting to risk being failed by a bullet as Unity had been. His mistress-turned-wife also poisoned herself. One of the terrible monsters also poisoned their own dogs—which was the only thing I felt sad about. Poor animals—what had they done but belong to devils?

While the world celebrated the end of the war, I triumphed in the birth of *The Pursuit of Love*, piled in crinkling pages, scratched with ink and tears. I prayed this time, just maybe, what I created would be embraced and celebrated across all of England, if not the world.

📖

June 1945

Dearest Tom,

You'll never read this letter, and neither will anyone else, as I plan to burn it immediately upon finishing. But I find myself missing you terribly at this moment, and so I'm doing what I know best: writing to you in a letter. Writing out all the happy memories, the pain, the tears. Oh, darling Tud, why did you have to leave me? You were my ally from the time you toddled into my room and tried to steal my ribbons, until the day you died, stealing my breath . . .

London looked the same as when I'd left, but it didn't feel the same. There was a renewed lightness of spirit, released by the absence of war. People no longer feared the tinny alarms warning of an imminent attack. Or the whizzing of planes and dreadful *thunk* of dropping bombs. The city was blissful without explosions, hissing fires, endless cries and shouts. Without the unforgettable thunderous booms of buildings collapsing.

Traffic returned to ordinary, the chatter of people returned from the country and soldiers reunited from abroad filled the streets. I could finally open my curtains.

Heywood Hill bookshop was positively bustling. How glad I was to stand in the madness of it all. I leapt into work with my spirit full of joy.

The Pursuit of Love was in my publisher's hands, and they were already roaring about it being a delightful read. They gave me a larger advance: a fortune at £250. More than double what they'd paid me for my last novel.

Oh, how I hoped I could actually earn out the advance this time. For that would mean the book was as well received as they anticipated. Maybe even royalties to follow. If the book did well, I promised to buy myself new clothes. To wear something different from the old hose I'd darned a hundred times, the threadbare tweed skirts, the blouses and dresses that were growing thin at the elbows. A dream come true.

Even with big dreams of clothes and shoes and hats, I held tight to the cash, afraid of how quickly it would be gone. I feared this small fortune would disappear quicker than the enthusiasm for my last novel.

A sort of imposters' syndrome leaked its way into my brain. Spreading itself out wide like a cellar leak. I was afraid my readers would hate the book, loathe my heroine Linda. Book critics all across Britain would write deplorable reviews berating me for thinking I knew anything about anything. Compare me to my great writer friends, such as Evelyn Waugh, whose own wartime novel *Brideshead Revisited* had released earlier in the year to stunning acclaim, and find me lacking.

Gaston was still in Paris, and Peter was home, happily ignoring me as he worked to organize German prisoners by day and gallivanted off with Adelaide by night. At least he had some of his priorities right. I could respect him for his work, even if the love between us had been as delusional as Hitler's British ambitions.

With the literary worries jumbling in my head, I hurried from Blomfield to visit dear Mark, finally home after being imprisoned in Germany. I was eager to see him.

When I was ushered into the drawing room, I was taken aback by the sight of Mark standing on stick-thin legs. The sharpness of his bony arms, which wrapped me in welcome.

"Oh, my dear old boy," I crooned, taking a look at his pale, gaunt face, and grateful for the smile. "What torments you must have endured."

"The worst was the hunger." He eyed me with an acuity I'd not noticed before, his eyes haunted.

"Oh," I breathed and hugged him again, pretending for just a moment he was Tom, and everyone else we'd lost. "I'm so glad you didn't let them destroy you."

Mark squeezed me tight for a moment longer.

"I've brought you this cake." I handed him a tin holding a layer cake filled with jam, like the one my mother made, which he'd dreamed about while imprisoned.

"Oh, what heaven, Nancy." He set the cake down on the table.

"Do you remember how we used to live for that cake after a night out and too much champagne?" I took a seat on his settee.

Mark chuckled, his teeth far too large in his thin face. "Do I ever. Do you mind?" He gestured to the tin.

"Of course not. I'll ring the bell."

With plates and tea brought out, I cut him a thick slice, and gained more satisfaction watching him eat the cake than I experienced in my own slice.

"What will you do now you're back?" I asked.

"Nothing for a time, but I'll grow bored of it, I'm sure. Probably my previous pursuits. Botany. Greece." He gestured to the walls, cluttered with various botanical wonders and souvenirs of travels past. He smiled, showing a glimpse of my old friend.

"I shall be proud of you no matter what you decide." I served him another piece of cake. "And even prouder when you've got meat back on your bones."

"And you, Nancy? Have you finished the book?" He tucked into the second slice.

"Indeed, I have. I've just bought this fabulous hat to celebrate." I showed him the straw-colored hat with large purple velvet bows, the only indulgence I'd allowed myself. "It has got me plenty of looks and compliments so far."

"Very pretty." He plucked it from my head and tried it on.

"Do you think it's too much?" I scrutinized the bows.

Mark chuckled, placing it back on my head. "I think just the right amount. Like you, my dear."

After we finished with our tea and cake, Mark invited me to walk in the back garden.

"Tell me of the bookshop?" He tucked my arm into the crook of his thin one, our shoes crunching on the gravel.

I gazed in wonder at the blooms recently planted in his once-perfect and still-overflowing garden. So very different from the paper confections at Lord Berners' estate. And yet better somehow. This garden had been laid low by war but, like the man who planted it, seemed determined to bring itself back to glorious life.

"I'm a bit embarrassed to say, but just the other day, I had the greatest gaffe . . ." I stopped to smell a particularly beautiful flower.

"*Cypripedium*—the lady's slipper orchid," he informed me. "Now, go on and spill. I need a laugh."

"All right, all right. After a long night of stocking books— after our move from Seventeen Curzon Street to number Ten—I simply could not rouse myself the next morning. I decided to go into the store a little bit late. But in my haste to leave the night before, I somehow missed a crucial step. Oh, Mark, old boy, I forgot to lock the shop!"

"You forgot?" His hand flew mockingly to his cheek.

"You simply do not understand, old boy."

"Help me, dear one, help me to understand."

I gave him a little playful glower. "Well, by the grace of Providence, Heywood was in the city and stopped by the shop to find it full of customers trying to buy books from one another, and not a Nancy in sight to ring them up!"

Mark threw back his head and laughed. "I'm guessing he was not best pleased. Do you still have a job?"

"Thankfully, I do." I bit my lip. "But I have been working on my papers, Mark."

"Your papers?" He studied me from the side, brows drawn together.

"Yes. Papers so that I might go to Paris."

"For how long?"

Only Gaston and Gladys knew my intentions. I'd tried to convince my housekeeper to come with me to Paris, but she'd told me once I was ready to move, she was going to find a new position until she and her husband started a family.

It was time to give voice to my dearest wish. "I want to call Paris home, Mark. Perhaps open a bookshop. Maybe just write. But above all, I go in the pursuit of love."

"A man?"

"Myself." And yes, Gaston lived there, but this was a move I'd been long planning, even before I realized it. For every time I ran into troubles, I ran to France.

Mark let out a long breath, then he nodded. "I hope you will be very happy there. If the war taught me anything at all, it is this: time is short and not at all wasted on the pursuit of happiness."

May 1948

PARIS WAS A DREAM. And so was my little flat at 7 rue Monsieur. The last two years there had been utter bliss.

My only regret in leaving London was that I'd not been able to say goodbye to my dear friend Sophie Gordon—my Iris. She'd left ahead of me, traveling to Canada with her fiancé, intent on emigrating. She told me she'd write with a forwarding address, but alas, none ever came.

I left a copy of *The Pursuit of Love* with a special inscription for her at Heywood Hill, knowing, or at least hoping, that if she ever came back to London, she would look for me. I included my forwarding address with the book. I've heard nothing yet, but I haven't lost hope.

Ours was a friendship born on the brink of war, and fed by comradery when our country was at its worst. It seemed only natural that we parted at war's end. Or perhaps that was only what I told myself on the days I missed her most. And truly, even at such times there was no bitterness. I wished her all the happiness in the world—for the war had stolen her first love, and I was glad she'd given herself a chance to try again.

For the first time in my life, I was happy.

I had no worries. My closet was full of beautiful, fashionable clothes. I had more money than I could ever spend. Food and wine aplenty. And most important, I had love . . . oh, the love that I had. Love for life and for myself.

Then there was this glorious ivy-covered courtyard where I often took tea with a good book. I glanced down at my left ring finger, no longer bearing the thin gold band given to me by Peter on our wedding day. At last we were legally separated and with no hard feelings. Well, at least none on my side. I was certain Prod was missing the money he'd believed himself entitled to.

In the place of the wedding ring I'd gladly shed, I wore a princess-cut topaz I'd purchased. It represented a commitment I'd made to live this life for me. To devote my days to a continued pursuit of love, ambition, *joie de vivre*. To forgive. To heal.

I still spent time with Gaston. But he was a man loved by many, and I didn't desire to rein him in. That would only take away from the charm of who he was. And how I did love to tease him about his admirers—even adding one as a character in *The Pursuit of Love.*

Besides, we could be together without a contract binding us.

If I was honest, that suited me as well as it did him. I'd only recently been set free of my own ties and obligations. Not just my marriage, but all the expectations that my family and London society put on me, and by extension I put on myself. I desired to continue living as I had the last two years in Paris—uninhibited, loving, or *not* loving, whomever I wanted. Free to be myself as I finally understood who that was.

Outside on the terraced patio, my dog curled at my feet, birds chirping where they rested on a chimera jutting from the stone above me, I shifted my gaze from the topaz down to the letter from my publisher.

Dear Nancy,

We are delighted to write to you with the news of our acceptance of your latest submission . . .

My submission was a sequel to *The Pursuit of Love.* The book of my heart, written in the height of my despair for the loss of my brother, had been a wild success. Already it had been reprinted many times, with foreign translations and film rights eagerly snatched up. I tipped my head up toward the sun, letting the warmth seep into my skin.

Was there ever anything so glorious as a Paris sun? Well, perhaps there was, and it was being a successful novelist.

In London, a hazy gloom draped like a suffocating mantle

over my being. As soon as I crossed the channel, the gloom melted. And my career suddenly took wings.

What was there to miss of my old life? My friends visited, and the who's who of Paris came by my flat for cocktails and talk of literature. In fact, my soirees were so popular and well attended that fellow Brits often teased that my residence ought to be the official cultural annex of the British Embassy.

Tucking Hamilton's letter into the book I'd been reading, Evelyn's latest, *The Loved One*, I sipped the last of my tea.

"Bonjour, madame."

I blinked up at one of my new neighbors, smiling down at me with a basket of vegetables from the market slung over her arm.

"Bonjour, and how are you?" I replied in French.

"Bon, et vous?"

I smiled brightly, my French crisp and clear as I responded, "I've never been better."

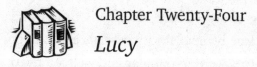 Chapter Twenty-Four
Lucy

Six Months Later . . .
London

THERE WAS SOMETHING SO magical about spring in London.
Or maybe witnessing the blooming trees, shrubs and flowers in
Hyde Park reminded Lucy so strongly of the changes in her own
life over the last six months.

Working at Heywood Hill had been wonderful. Besides curating libraries for several town houses in London and its outskirts,
she'd already worked on a collection for a historical manor home
and recently been asked about refurbishing a library in a castle
on the border of England and Scotland. She'd also organized the
tackling of curation projects for private collectors, museums and
even a few cafés and hotels.

Never once since arriving in London had Lucy looked back
with regret.

Maya and her family had visited, taking in London during
Christmas and New Year's Eve and falling in love with Gavin
just as Lucy had.

Lucy's only frustration was she'd yet to find Sophie Gordon.
Several times she'd thought she was close, getting responses
from descendants, but it would turn out that while their Sophie

had volunteered during the war it was either in the United States or for the Women's Land Army. None for the ARP in London.

But Lucy wasn't giving up. This was a mystery that would one day be solved, she was certain.

She poured herself a glass of wine and settled onto the sofa in her den to read this month's novel for a book club she'd formed at Heywood's. Moments later, the door to the flat swung open.

"Honey, I'm home," Gavin teased, as he always did when he arrived at their Curzon Street flat from work.

Lucy closed her book and leapt up to greet him. "Takeaway for dinner?"

"Italian?"

"Perfect."

"Something's come for you in the mail." Gavin handed her a square, cream-colored envelope. The return address revealed it was from Marina McTavish, a woman in Canada who Lucy had messaged nearly a month before.

"Another Iris dead end, I'm sure." But she was wrong. Her heart pounded as she skimmed the words. "Gavin, we've found her! Listen . . ."

Dear Lucy,

I was so happy to get your letter. I think my mother, Sophie Gordon, is the woman you've been searching for. She came to Canada after WWII with my father, whom she'd married. In their retirement, they returned to Northern England so Mum could be closer to her family.

I've enclosed her address and phone number so you can contact her—she is Sophie McTavish now, and expecting your call. I did not spoil the surprise by telling her about the note from Ms. Mitford. I will leave that to you, a reward for what appears to have been a very lengthy search.

Best wishes to you and yours,
Marina McTavish

"I'll get the champagne," Gavin said as Lucy whooped in excitement.

"I'll get my cell."

Lucy began dialing Sophie's number with trembling fingers. She'd been waiting so long to connect with the woman who'd dominated so much of her life. Her finger hovered over the last number.

"Are you all right?" Gavin asked.

"Yes, just nervous. I don't know what to say."

"Sure you do," Gavin urged, rubbing her shoulder. "You've probably been rehearsing it since you were eight, at the very least in the months this search has taken."

Lucy laughed. "True."

"So push the call button."

Lucy nodded and finished dialing in the number, waiting for the sound of the ringing to halt with an answer, or the disappointment of hearing voice mail click on.

At last, an older woman picked up, her croaked greeting proof of age.

"Mrs. McTavish, Lucy St. Clair calling. I just received your daughter's letter."

There was an indrawn breath on the other end of the line. "Oh, dear, I'm so very glad you called."

Lucy sighed in relief. "Thank you for being willing to speak with me."

"A friend of Nancy's is a friend of mine." Pure pleasure radiated from Sophie's voice.

"I confess, I never met her." Life had been cruel, taking Nancy from the world before Lucy was born.

"But she was alive in your heart," Sophie replied.

She knows. She understands.

"For most of my life," Lucy said. "And you were always in hers—and mine."

They chatted for nearly an hour, and Sophie only rang off after Lucy promised to take the train north for tea the following weekend. When the call ended, Lucy sat staring down at the letter nestled in her lap. Warm tears of joy streamed down her cheeks. She swiped them away.

"I wish my mother were alive to meet Sophie. Oh, how I wish she were here."

"She is here." Gavin lifted Lucy's hand from her lap and pressed it over her heart. "She is with you always. You fulfilled her quest. Solved a mystery the two of you pondered for decades."

"You're right. And maybe it was meant to be my quest because I needed it. Without the search for Iris, and all the places it took me, I might never have discovered the things about myself I needed to learn to take my dreams into my own hands." She leaned against him, pressed her lips to his chin and then her cheek on his heart. "I might have gone back to DC, never been a curator for Heywood Hill, never met an awesome Scottish bibliophile to spend the rest of my life with."

"I don't believe that, lass," Gavin said. "Your love of Nancy Mitford's work and your quest to solve the Iris mystery might have set you on the path, but neither one provided you what you accomplished—*you* did that."

Lucy smiled. Gavin was right. When the time came, Lucy had been the one to find the courage to pursue her own happiness— her own future—much like Nancy Mitford herself.

Acknowledgments

WHEN I WAS IN second grade, my teacher told my parents that I would be an author one day. The aspiration of being a novelist took many years to achieve, but I'm fortunate and grateful to wake each day with the knowledge I made that dream come true. Believing in yourself is the first step—but having the support and encouragement of others makes the journey that much more rewarding and successful. I would not be where I am without so many marvelous people cheering me on, including my amazing readers.

I want to thank my incredible agent, Kevan Lyon; my amazing editor, Lucia Macro; and her associate editor, Asanté Simons. Thank you to the hardworking people in the sales, marketing and publicity departments including: Jennifer Hart, Kaitie Leary and Holly Rice. My gratitude to all of the remarkable people of William Morrow, including the publisher, Liate Stehlik; Ploy Siripant, for the stunning artwork; Diahann Sturge, for the beautiful interior design of the book; and Janet Rosenberg, for the thorough copyedits.

Thank you to Madeline Martin, for her encouragement and support of this book. This journey wouldn't have been the same without her, and I'll be forever grateful we were able to tread the path together; to Stephanie Thornton, Sophie Perinot, Christi Barth and Heather Webb, for reading early drafts of this book t it into tip-top shape; to Denny S. Bryce, Lori ⌐renna Ash, for all of your help with plotting ⌐ne cases, pouring me wine; and to my brilliant Lyo-⌐esses, for their sisterhood.

A special thank-you to my wonderful husband, Hoff, and our three clever daughters, Ash, Dani and Lexi, who have joined me on research trips in Europe, patiently gone down documentary rabbit holes, and listened to me ramble on about things they probably didn't find as interesting as I did, but love me enough to listen. Ash, you are *wondair* for carrying on the legend of books, and for being my most enthusiastic fan. I love you all so very much.

And finally, though I can't say it in person, I thank Nancy Mitford, in spirit, for the hours of entertainment she's provided me over the years, and the true honor it was to dive into her personal journey.

About the author

About the book

Insights,
Interviews
& More...

Meet Eliza Knight

Andrea Grant Snider

ELIZA KNIGHT is an award-winning, *USA Today* bestselling author of women's historical fiction. Her love of history began as a young girl when she traipsed the halls of Versailles. She is known best for her novels *My Lady Viper, Prisoner of the Queen* and as a contributor to the collection *Ribbons of Scarlet*. She is a member of the Historical Novel Society and Novelists, Inc., and the creator of the popular historical blog *History Undressed*. Knight lives in Maryland with her husband, three daughters, two dogs and a turtle. ✿

Author's Note

Taking on the Mitfords for *The Mayfair Bookshop* was a massive enterprise due to the abundance of information available on the family, including thousands of letters, as well as the countless articles, memoirs and biographies.

I first discovered Nancy's books in high school from a history teacher who was quite fond of Mitford's *The Pursuit of Love*, published in 1945. I heard of the Mitfords again in college while acquiring my B.S. in Family Studies, when one of my professors was lecturing on the birth order of siblings and how very different we can all end up from one another. If there was ever a line that exhibited such, it was the Mitfords'.

The interesting thing about families is they come in all different sizes, with a variety of personalities. Even within my own I find that to be the case. My husband and I have three daughters, all of whom are quite distinctive in behavior despite their similar appearances. We have a dancer, a sports enthusiast and an artist. Only one of my daughters is an avid reader, only one is an competitive athlete and only one is a devoted gamer. I am one of four children myself, and the story continues there in the same fashion. My father is one of seven, and there again you find so many distinct personalities, with varying views on politics, religion, hobbies, health, social norms, etc. It's all very intriguing, hence my decision to major in Family ▶

Studies. So when given the chance to take a deep dive into the mind of a Mitford, I couldn't resist.

The infamous Mitfords were a large family, starting with their matriarch, Sydney Bowles (Muv), who married David Freeman-Mitford (Farve) in 1904. David was one of many children, and the second son to Algernon "Barty" Freeman-Mitford, 1st Baron Redesdale. Sydney's father was the founder of the magazine *The Lady*, which employed both David and eventually Nancy Mitford. In 1915, David's older brother died in the Battle of Loos, which left David as the sole heir. David didn't seem to have a good grasp of finances, as he frequently bought and sold property, more often than not, with financial disadvantages. As a result, Sydney was very frugal, even raising chickens and selling the eggs. Their seven children often complained of being poor, not well educated and having their house seamstress make their clothes rather than designers. When asked about this in a later recorded interview, Diana clarified that they were poor in comparison to their rich aristocratic friends, but that they had large houses, servants and an allowance, so not poor in the sense most of us would consider when using the term.

Nancy was the eldest of the Mitford children, born to David and Sydney on November 28, 1904. She was perhaps the instigator of all the nicknames, which I toned down for simplicity. Nancy was alternatively known as Naunce(ling), The Old French Lady, The Lady, Dame, Susan, Soo (the latter two of which she and Jessica couldn't remember the origins of). As an adult, Nancy did complain about her lack of education, as she and her sisters weren't sent away to school, but instead educated by a series of governesses and their mother (with the exception of Deborah, who did go to school and quit because she hated it). The children did, however, have free rein of a very large library, of which they took full advantage. While Nancy might have thought herself uneducated, her prose and witty commentary suggest otherwise. In addition to her writing, Nancy was heavily involved in the war effort, and I tried to highlight all of her various activities. I only found one brief reference to the car accident she had while driving the ARP van, and it was in a parking area when she was starting off her shift, so I decided to give that scene a bit of a flair by making it out on the road to highlight what it was like driving during the blackout.

Pamela, "Woman," was born on the November 25, 1907, just a few days shy of Nancy's third birthday. Nancy wasn't happy to no longer be an only child, which she teased her sister about relentlessly. (Nancy was sometimes called cruel by her siblings, who didn't always enjoy her mockery.) After she suffered from polio as a child, Pam lost some mobility in her leg, which lasted throughout her life. Where Nancy was seen more as an acerbic personality, Pamela was often calming—which is probably why on her deathbed, Nancy was happy to have her sister by her side taking care of her. Pam is the least talked about sibling in the family and tended to prefer a quiet country existence. Pamela's husband, Derek Jackson, was a renowned physicist. In fact, he was a visiting professor at the Ohio State University during the time that my grandfather attended (though he was not a student of Jackson's). In the library at OSU, there is a collection of videotapes, slides and letters that belonged to Jessica Mitford. When I discovered this during my research, we were at the height of the pandemic, so as of writing this note, I haven't been allowed to visit, but my oldest daughter (a future librarian) is a student at the university and plans to look when they return in the fall.

Thomas, "Tud," was born January 2, 1945. Unlike his sisters, who were educated mostly at home, he went to Eton, bringing home friends who would later be popular in the Bright Young Thing era and become close to his sisters, Nancy in particular. It's actually rumored that Tom had a brief affair with Hamish St. Clair-Erskine, who was Nancy's fiancé for a time before she married Peter Rodd.

Diana, "Honks," joined the Mitford family on June 17, 1910, and would become one of the most controversial of the siblings. Despite being six years younger than Nancy, Diana was well known in the Bright Young Thing crowd as well. She was quite often modeling for various photographers, including Cecil Beaton. At a young age, she married Bryan Guinness, heir to his family's fortune, but ultimately grew unhappy and shockingly chose to divorce him after the birth of their second son. In the book I mentioned that Bryan took the blame, which was standard ▶

during that time. In another unprecedented move (and much to her mother's disappointment), Diana became the mistress of Oswald Mosley, the leader of the British Union of Fascists. They spent a lot of time together with Hitler, and Diana even spent time with the dictator and Unity without Oswald. Hitler was even a witness at their secret wedding. Nancy and Diana did not ultimately agree on politics. Nancy likely felt guilty for what she told Gladwyn Jebb, and her culpability in Diana's subsequent arrest. However, more likely to have been responsible for her arrest was the letter sent by Diana's former father-in-law, as well as her association with Hitler. Nancy never told her sister about her confession, and Diana did not find out until after Nancy had passed away. Though they were at odds during the war, they became close again later in life, when Diana lived in France. I think what saved their relationship was not talking politics in the end, as they were never on the same page. Some dinner conversations are just off-limits.

Unity Valkyrie, "Bobo," was born on the August 8, 1914, in London, though she would brag later that she was conceived in Swastika, Canada, as it was the symbol of the Nazis, whom she idolized. At some point in her teen years, she became enamored with Germany, Hitler and Nazi ideals. She convinced her parents to enroll her in a language school in Munich, where she became obsessed with meeting Hitler. Which she did, even growing close enough to have lunch with him and visit his house, and was eventually secured an apartment from an evicted Jewish family by Hitler. The gun she shot herself with was also a gift from Hitler. It was rumored they were lovers, but there is nothing to necessarily substantiate that besides conjecture. Even if Eva Braun, Hitler's girlfriend turned wife, did write a jealous note in her diary in regards to Unity. Nancy struggled with Unity's choices and beliefs. Despite not agreeing on politics, Nancy did love her sister and tried to maintain a pleasant relationship with her. After Unity's attempted suicide, Nancy tried to help her mother with her sister when and where she could.

Jessica Lucy, "Decca" (yes, Lucy is named after Jessica!), was the second youngest of the Mitford siblings, born on September 11, 1917, nearly thirteen years after Nancy. She was also quite controversial, her politics swinging in the opposite direction of Diana and Unity, who were ardent Fascists. Jessica was a Communist. After moving to America and the death of her first husband, Esmond Romilly, she married Robert Treuhaft, a civil rights lawyer. While in her earlier days in the book, Nancy believes Jessica hasn't done much to fight the good fight, this becomes Jessica's mantra for the rest of her days, and she was involved in civil rights activism until she passed away. Jessica had four children—two daughters with Romilly, and two sons with Robert. Tragically, her infant with Esmond was not the only child she lost. Her firstborn son with Robert was, sadly, hit by a bus when he was a child. She was also a writer (*Hons and Rebels*), an investigative journalist (*The American Way of Death*) and a musician, recording a duet with her good friend Maya Angelou.

Deborah, "Debo," Vivien, the youngest of the brood, born March 31, 1920 (nearly sixteen years Nancy's junior), was perhaps the most traditional. Her playmates growing up were Jessica and Unity (Nancy not so nicely nicknamed them Nit, Sic and Bor, taking the middle of their names as a mean tease). Though Deborah was younger than Nancy, they were still close. In the book, when Deborah comes to Nancy with the newspaper clippings about Unity, it was actually Nanny Blor who approached Nancy. For the purposes of the story, however, I made it Deborah to give her more page time with Nancy. When Deborah married Andrew Cavendish, second son of the Duke of Devonshire, she did not expect to be a duchess. After all, her brother-in-law Billy was young and healthy. Billy married Kick Kennedy just before he was shipped abroad for war where he was killed in action. Deborah took her position as a duchess seriously, working to build the dukedom until her end.

Nancy Mitford had hundreds of friends, all mentioned in her writings. In my first draft, I included them all—quite a challenge for my early readers and editor—which required cutting. I chose two main friends for the most interaction, Mark Ogilvie-Grant and Evelyn Waugh. Of course, there is also Sophie "Iris" Gordon, but here is where I admit she is an amalgamation of my great-grandmother Iris, who I was quite close with, and Nancy's own fictional character Sophia Garfield from *Pigeon Pie*. ▶

Lucy St. Clair is also a fictional character, as is her connection to the St. Clair-Erskine family. Having been born in DC and living in the DC metro area most of my life, I chose to set Lucy's American life there. Emerald Books is a fictional company I created for Lucy's job as a book curator that would allow her to travel overseas to work at Heywood Hill just as Nancy did in the 1940s. Admittedly while writing this book, the pandemic prevented me from visiting Chatsworth. My descriptions of the rooms are as accurate as I could make them with the resources available. The key that opened the secret door was a creation of my own making.

The real G. Heywood Hill Ltd bookshop was established in 1936 by George Heywood Hill and his future wife, Anne, both of whom were among the Bright Young Things set, along with Nancy Mitford. Originally opened at 17 Curzon Street, they moved to number 10 a few years later. The bookshop is known to be the Queen's favorite, and is also famous for Nancy Mitford's employment during World War II. One of the oldest bookshops in London, Heywood Hill has established a reputation that is world renowned. They offer a special subscription service for readers—A Year in Books—where you get personalized book selections sent to you every month, and who doesn't love book mail? Additionally, they offer library creation services, which was the position Lucy chose in the end. The characters working in the shop are fictional and not the real employees of Heywood Hill; however, the owner is in fact the Duke of Devonshire.

As for the inscription written by Nancy in Lucy's copy of *The Pursuit of Love*, this was also created by me, as were the majority of the letters. There are a few instances where I used portions of real letters, due to their poignancy. One was from Unity to Nancy regarding the publishing of *Wigs on the Green*. Another was when Nancy wrote to Muv in Perpignan. Additionally, there are references to real letters and their subjects discussed throughout the book. A small passage Nancy wrote about marriage in her appointment diary is also included. For those of you who wish to read more on the copious Mitford letters, please refer to my bibliography on page 12 of this section.

The Mitfords had a distinctive dialect and idiom. I tried where

I could to put that into their dialogue for an authentic flavor. It is true Nancy received complaints about her voice when she was doing the BBC fire-watching broadcasts. During a recorded interview of Deborah Mitford, she said most people thought their way of talking was very annoying and that even she herself did sometimes. (She and Decca formed their own language called Boudledidge.) I think secret languages, phrases and ways of speaking are a lovely ingredient to any close relationship, and use them liberally within mine.

A note on a few other people in the book: Nancy's maid, Gladys Bruce, is a combination of her true maid and one I created. There were actually several servants within the Mitford employ named Gladys, and I had trouble finding information about this specific one. Additionally, within the working timeline the real Gladys left Nancy's service and Sigrid stepped in, then Gladys returned. I was unable to find out why, so it was easier for the sake of the novel to create my own backstory. Zivah (named by me), the young Jewish girl boarding at Rutland Gate, is based on a boarder who was under Nancy's care, and pregnant. The events that take place in the book are fictional based on a letter Nancy penned, mentioning "Mrs. Rodd the abortionist" and the advice she gave the girl.

Throughout the novel, where I could, I added in people who truly existed beyond Nancy's social circle. For example, Warden Ekpenyon was a real air raid warden. He published a pamphlet on his experience in 1943 that was made into a documentary. Gladwyn Jebb worked for the Home Office, and Madame Yevonde took the portrait of Nancy that appeared on the cover of *Tatler*.

I do hope you enjoy *The Mayfair Bookshop* and this little glimpse of the life of the legendary Mitfords. I'm certain to have left out something from this author's note that I altered, omitted or added to Nancy's story. The project was a massive undertaking that was years in the making, but rest assured, every decision made was done so with great consideration. In the end, this is a work of fiction, with the purpose of inviting you into this incredible world full of fascinating characters, and the hope that you take from it the importance of forging your path in the pursuit of your own happiness. ❧

For the Love of Books

I am a writer, but I am first and foremost a lover of narrative tales.

From my earliest memories, stories were a huge part of my life. My parents relay fondly that before I could speak, I would sit with books piled around me, contentedly turning the pages for hours. Apparently, I didn't have a first word, but instead a sentence: "Will you read me a book?"

As a preschooler, I eagerly ran home from the playground to watch episodes of a brand-new show *Reading Rainbow*. While my friends were having naptime, I was enthralled by my hero, LeVar Burton, who whisked me into the enchanted world of the written word.

Perhaps surprising for most is that I didn't learn to read until well into first grade, and only with the help of a reading specialist. I had trouble picking up writing and spelling too, and while other students' journals were filled with sentences from the teacher's prompts, mine were drawings of princesses, castles and other stories I was making up in my head.

By second grade, however, I made a swift turnaround and even "published" my own book titled "The Mouse Who Stole the Cheese." I was so proud of that little story, and I still have it, blue construction paper cover and all. My teacher told my parents that I was going to be an author one day, and I think they had an idea that was true. In third grade, I published a story in a charity anthology, and in fourth grade I was sending submission letters to publishers.

One of the people who supported my love of reading the most was my dad. He never said no to a trip to the bookstore, and if we passed one during a drive, we'd always pull over. I can still picture the one on the side of Ocean Highway that we passed on trips back from the beach. We'd come out with stacks, and as I got older, we'd share books too, just like I do now with my oldest daughter. My dad loves historical fiction and thrillers— my two favorite genres. He gave me *Pillars of the Earth* when I was fourteen, a book I've read every decade since just to see how the story changes as I age.

In my early teens, half of every paycheck from my first job went into my growing personal library. I made lists upon lists of everything I wanted to read—much like I do today. There's just something so magical about a store filled with shelves upon shelves of books. Adventures waiting to be leapt into. Quaint local bookshops are my favorite. They smell different and feel different inside. There's a reason movies like *Notting Hill* and *You've Got Mail* stick with us, and it isn't just the endearing characters' stories—it's the bookshops and printed tomes that make us fall in love with reading all over again.

Once those doors open, the possibilities are endless. There are the smells of paper and dreams. The hushed swish of pages being turned. The eager booksellers ready to share their top picks, or gush over amazing past reads. Within the pages of a book, you can be anything, or anyone, anywhere. In every volume, a reader lives a whole new life, and comes away from it different from when they cracked the spine to absorb those first words.

What will your next adventure be? ∽

Bibliography of Nancy Mitford's Amazing Works

FICTION

Highland Fling (1931)
Christmas Pudding (1932)
Wigs on the Green (1935)
Pigeon Pie (1940)
The Pursuit of Love (1945)
Love in a Cold Climate (1949)
The Blessing (1951)
Don't Tell Alfred (1960)

NONFICTION

The Ladies of Alderley (1938), letters edited by Nancy Mitford
The Stanleys of Alderley (1939), letters edited by Nancy Mitford
Madame de Pompadour (1954)
Voltaire in Love (1957)
The Sun King (1966)
Frederick the Great (1970)

JOURNALISM

Noblesse Oblige (1956), edited and with the essay "The English Aristocracy" by Nancy Mitford
The Water Beetle (1962)
A Talent to Annoy (1986), essays, journalism and reviews from 1929–1968, by Nancy Mitford, edited by Charlotte Mosley
Nancy also wrote numerous articles for *The Lady, Vogue, Vanity Fair, Tatler, Lilliput* magazines, the *Vanguard* (journal) and newspapers.

TRANSLATIONS

The Princess of Cleves (1950), a novel by Madame de Lafayette, translated by Nancy Mitford
The Little Hut (1951), film by André Roussin, adapted from the French by Nancy Mitford

Bibliography of Further Reading

COLLECTED LETTERS

A Bookseller's War (1987) by Heywood and Anne Hill
Love from Nancy (1993), edited by Charlotte Mosley
The Letters of Nancy Mitford and Evelyn Waugh (1996),
    edited by Charlotte Mosley
*The Bookshop at 10 Curzon Street: Letters between Nancy Mitford
    and Heywood Hill* (2004), edited by John Saumarez Smith
The Mitfords: Letters Between Six Sisters (2007),
    edited by Charlotte Mosley

BIOGRAPHIES AND MEMOIRS

Hons and Rebels (1960) by Jessica Mitford
A Life of Contrasts: The Autobiography (1977) by
    Diana (Mitford) Mosley
The House of Mitford (1984) by Jonathan Guinness
Nancy Mitford (1985) by Selina Hastings
*Diana Mosley: Mitford Beauty, British Fascist,
    Hitler's Angel* (2003) by Anne de Courcy
The Sisters: The Saga of the Mitford Family (2003) by
    Mary S. Lovell
Wait for Me!: Memoirs (2010) by Deborah (Mitford) Devonshire
The Horror of Love (2011) by Lisa Hilton
*Nancy Mitford: The Biography Edited from Nancy Mitford's
    Letters* (2012) by Harold Acton
The Six (2017) by Laura Thompson
Life in a Cold Climate (2019) by Laura Thompson

Bibliography of Works Listed in the Novel

Vile Bodies by Evelyn Waugh
The Iliad by Homer
The Wonderful Wizard of Oz by L. Frank Baum
Dracula by Bram Stoker
Rebecca by Daphne du Maurier
To the Lighthouse by Virginia Woolf
White Fang by Jack London
Frankenstein by Mary Shelley
Pride and Prejudice by Jane Austen
1984 by George Orwell
The Haunting of Hill House by Shirley Jackson
The Tell-Tale Heart and Other Stories by Edgar Allan Poe
Rosemary's Baby by Ira Levin
Coraline by Neil Gaiman
The Handmaid's Tale by Margaret Atwood
It by Stephen King
Jamaica Inn by Daphne du Maurier
Regency Buck by Georgette Heyer
A Tree Grows in Brooklyn by Betty Smith
Beloved by Toni Morrison
The Genius of Birds by Jennifer Ackerman
The Thing with Feathers by Noah Strycker
The Birds by Daphne Du Maurier
Anna Karenina by Leo Tolstoy
Vol de Nuit (Night Flight) by Antoine de Saint-Exupéry
The Life of John Sterling by Thomas Carlyle
Sad Cypress by Agatha Christie
Pillars of the Earth by Ken Follett
The Call of the Wild by Jack London
The Sherlock Holmes series by Sir Arthur Conan Doyle
The Picture of Dorian Gray by Oscar Wilde
Mémoires d'Outre-Tombe by François-René, Vicomte de Chateaubriand
Put Out More Flags by Evelyn Waugh
The Loved One by Evelyn Waugh
Memoirs of le Duc de Saint-Simon ∼

Reading Group Guide

1. Before reading *The Mayfair Bookshop* had you heard of Nancy Mitford and her works? If so, what is your favorite? If not, which one do you want to read first?

2. What do you love the most about a bookshop? What is the most memorable shop you've ever been to?

3. Every book we read has the ability to alter our lives or way of thinking, even in small ways. What is one book that changed your life?

4. The Mitford family dynamic is unique in some respects— it's not too often you have a sister who is the rumored lover of a Fascist leader, let alone two sisters—and not so unique in others (secret languages, inside jokes, etc.). In what ways did you connect with the family or see similarities with your own?

5. Nancy Mitford remained committed to Hamish St. Clair-Erskine for five years, during her prime marrying years. Why do you think she did so? And do you think she was as naïve as people say, not fully grasping that Hamish was gay, or maybe thinking that she could change him?

6. For many women, family or employment obligations, and even more often, fear of failure or loss, keep them from pursuing their dreams and prioritizing their own happiness. What is one thing you try to do on daily basis that brings you joy? What dreams have you left unfulfilled and what is one step you can take to realize them?

7. Nancy makes the difficult decision to tell Gladwyn Jebb about her sister's involvement with Hitler and the danger Diana poses to the UK. Would you be able to inform on your sibling?

8. Nancy really struggled with her sisters' relationships with Fascism and support of the Nazis. She loved her sisters but couldn't understand their politics. Despite this, she ▶

attempted to maintain cordial relationships. What would you do if a close family member supported the Nazis?

9. If you had the means to escape London during the blitz like Nancy could have, would you leave? Or would you stay behind to help like she did?

10. Lucy goes to London not only to work on a project that she hopes will gain her a promotion, but also to solve the personal mystery she and her mother had spent years trying to figure out. Ultimately, she decides to remain in London for a fresh start working at an incredible little bookshop. Would you be willing to leave your life behind to start fresh? ❧

Discover great authors, exclusive offers, and more at hc.com.